the BOOK CLUB WIDOWERS

A NOVEL

Dear Mom,

Thank you for always encouraging and supporting my writing! I would not have developed this skill without your investment in typewriters, paper, and love!

I love you,

John

JOHN MICHAEL DE MARCO

ALSO AVAILABLE FROM JOHN MICHAEL DE MARCO :

The Wine Steward's Lover

After 29-year-old Kate Hart's career implodes, the highly-structured, lifelong Nashvillian stumbles into grad school to catch her breath and gain clarity. Then, the unexpected arrives: A heroine's journey into ambiguity, new friends straddling the borders of tragedy, the potential reconciliation of her fractured family...and the disappearance of a handsome, intriguing young man just minutes after Kate falls in love with him.

Narcissus Blinked

Married, disillusioned advertising wordsmith Jacob is on the verge of an affair with his married neighbor, Julia. At the height of their verbal seduction Julia suddenly attempts suicide, plunging Jacob into a full-day's journey from self-absorption to self-awareness as the future of two families hangs in the balance. Almost any spiritually-hungry, restless suburbanite asking life's larger questions will relate to Jacob's plight in some manner.

The 4 Spheres of Intentional Living

This short book unpacks and offers best practices for thriving within—and synthesizing—the four "spheres" of physical, intellectual, emotional and spiritual health and well-being. Loaded with open-ended reflection questions and references to numerous thought leaders, *The 4 Spheres* encapsulates John's approach to executive and life coaching and is relevant reading for anyone committed to personal and professional growth.

Chased by the Wind: A Youth's Literary Search for God

In this rather unusual memoir, John dissects 15 books and hundreds of songs and journal entries he wrote during his teens. The result is a retrospective revelation of a young person's nascent search for God and the meaning of life, amid surprising footprints of grace. This short book will help readers to "connect the dots" across different episodes of their younger years, and find inspiration and clarity toward what's coming next.

Please visit www.johnmichaeldemarco.com
to buy books and download samples. Thank you.

Prologue

The Daytona Beach of 1979 was almost a decade away from the beach tolls; barricades; sea turtle protection zones; and general driving limitations that characterize its present state. Anyone could cruise the flat sands by day or night, a dynamic that helped designate the area as "The World's Most Famous Beach."

It was a beautiful spring Thursday evening. Tommy and Vinnie were in a raucous mood as they entertained their mistresses—Stephanie and Cathi, respectively—at The Ocean Deck. The reggae band Windjammer kept the crowd swaying as the salty air flowed through the open-ended beachside restaurant.

"Down the hatch, baby!" Tommy shouted as the bar maid in a tight pink t-shirt with a sand footprints design delivered a heaping plate of raw oysters.

"Are you guys ready for another one?" the waitress asked, pointing to the three-quarters empty pitcher of Coors smack in the middle of the table.

"Sure thing," Vinnie smiled.

"I'm scared to eat those," Stephanie remarked as she watched Tommy slurp down a couple of oysters and drop the shells onto the table. Tommy chased them with a swig of beer.

"Come on, hon, don't be a coward," he said. "What's the worst that could happen?"

"I could barf right here!" Stephanie retorted, and Cathi lightly smacked her arm. "Gross!"

"Hey, I'm not crazy about the raw stuff either," Vinnie said, reaching for an oyster. "But if you wash it down right away, it helps to mask the taste."

"Why don't I just get conch fritters instead, something I actually like?" Stephanie continued.

Tommy sighed and put his arm around her. "You're high maintenance tonight, baby. Do I need to take you home early?"

Stephanie pressed into him, and kissed him on the cheek. "Now, you wouldn't want to go do that and miss all the fun, would you?"

About 30 minutes later, the foursome stumbled into the Ocean Deck's tiny parking lot and left in Tommy's new cream-colored Continental Mark V. With Stephanie already rubbing his crotch, Tommy eased the luxury car down a beach ramp onto the sand. He drove north for a mile or so past the boardwalk area, looking for a quiet, poorly-lit spot. Tommy smiled as he glanced in the rearview mirror and saw Vinnie fondling Cathi's tits, and took a deep breath as Stephanie buried her face in his crotch.

"Park, silly," she whispered in a muffled voice.

Tommy picked a spot, put the Continental in park, and lowered the power windows halfway down before killing the ignition. Within minutes the front and back windshields were layered with steam. Tommy and Vinnie each glanced up occasionally, to be prepared in case any pain-in-the-ass cops felt the need to stop by and shine their flashlights into the car to make sure no one was being assaulted.

Each man leaned back against a locked car door, Tommy in the driver's seat and Vinnie right behind him, as the women went down on them.

The inside of the car grew hotter, and the sounds of sucking and moaning drowned out any potential distractions. None of the four heard the footsteps approaching along the sand, nor the figure who stood near the driver's side of the Mark V as Tommy and Vinnie tried to hold off climaxing as long as possible. The men were sitting ducks as the stranger precisely fired a silenced bullet into the back of each of their heads, their cocks lurching within their girlfriends' mouths and bodies leaping in alarm before going still, blood splattering everyone and everything within the Continental.

Before the screaming women could look around to figure out what had happened, the assassin raced off into the night, his victims as flawlessly executed as the plans drawn up weeks earlier.

Chapter One

APRIL 29, 2012

The bottles of Cabernet and Chardonnay were already empty. A few of the ladies laughed, clutching their books and eBook readers. Eight of the nine were finished reading David Wrabowski's *The Story of Edgar Sawtelle*. The exception, Lisa Grayton, said she'd kept falling asleep whenever she had a few precious minutes to herself.

"I was hoping to finish it this coming weekend on our trip," Lisa said. "But now John is going on some bullshit golfing business trip, and I have to bail on you guys."

"That really sucks," replied Delphi Adams, the meeting's hostess and owner of The Oracle, the used bookstore where they met after business hours every few weeks. "Too bad you couldn't get one of the grandmas to come and babysit."

"Are you referring to me?" Sixty-five-year-old Dara Wilson asked, and the group laughed.

"When you have four kids under six, you don't get too many offers of help from the family," Lisa said.

"Without spoiling everything for Lisa," Beth McBride began, "I'm still trying to decide whether there's a purpose to the ending of this book. I mean, what the hell was the point?"

"Maybe that's the idea," Emma O'Rourke noted. "Maybe there is no point. Maybe there's no final resolution, no final moral to teach. The world's just full of gray, and there's no such thing as ultimate good or evil."

Kari Blakely shook her head. "I don't know," she said. "I've known some pretty evil people in my time, especially that youth worker I told you guys about. And I think Uncle Claude definitely fits the description. I was telling Tom how I'm starting to think that dogs are better than people."

"Woof-woof," said Kevlin Lane, the youngest of the group and the only one who wasn't a mother.

"This is a change of subject," Beth said, "but has anyone talked to Liz in the past week? I know she's not been feeling well."

"I talked to her yesterday," Delphi said. "She's not up to going on the trip. I feel so bad for her."

"Shut the front door!" exclaimed Jackie Solomon. "So, of the nine of us, that just leaves me, Emma, and Kari who are actually heading down there?"

"Looks that way," Emma said. "Dara, are you sure you don't want to come? Foreigner's going to be there, that's an old school band you probably like."

"To SunFest? I'm too old for that kind of crowd," Dara said. "You all go to Palm Beach and have a blast."

"We need you as our designated driver," Jackie said. "Or, our designated grandma." The group shared a hearty laugh.

"*Not*. Is that how you say that?" Dara responded.

"Well, I haven't heard that one in a while," Emma said. "Very 90s, but nice touch."

"I'd love to go, ladies, but I'm not ready to close the studio at this point," Beth said. "Gotta keep building momentum with the newer clients."

"It's a hell of a work out there," Jackie said. "What's the matter with the rest of you? You need to come and sweat with us."

"I'm just purely a jogger," Kevlin said. "I don't like to suffer too much when I exercise."

"Let me know when you open a nursery," Lisa added, picking up the empty bottle of Cabernet and frowning.

"Hey, is it only a coincidence that the hardcore fitness mamas are the ones going to this beach body music festival?" Kari asked. "I mean, we're ready to show up those coeds who'll be there. Kevlin, what's your excuse again?"

"I've got a date," Kevlin said. "I don't get them very often with decent guys."

"Too bad," Jackie said. "You'd help us be dude magnets."

"Whatevs," Kevlin responded.

"What?" Dara asked.

Chapter Two:

MAY 2-3

Ben McBride was relieved to finally crawl his way past the Greater Orlando Area stretch of Interstate 4 and cruise through DeBary, Orange City, and other small towns on his way home to Daytona Beach. It had been another long district managers' meeting at the Next Generation Wireless regional office in congested Altamonte Springs, and Ben was dreaming of a quiet night of doing nothing.

Such a fantasy, of course, was out of the question. As soon as he walked through the doorway Beth would hand him two-year old Maddie, and head off to teach her back-to-back classes at the fitness studio. Maddie was a delight but anything but relaxing, especially during the evening when the rigors of bath and bedtime would be Ben's alone to execute with efficiency, patience, and love.

Ben's work to-do list had grown longer today as yet another rate plan change and promotion loomed on the proverbial short horizon. There were messages and resources to cascade down to his retail managers, phone conferences to conduct with business partners such as marketing and operations, and lots of studying required in order for Ben to wrap his mind around things. He wondered how customers kept up with the constant shifts in an industry that had kept afloat while many others were decimated during the "Great Recession" of a few years earlier.

It was just after 5 p.m. Beth's class started at 5:30. Ben proceeded onto I-95 South, just a mile or so from the Beville Road exit. He'd get a panicked cell phone call from Beth if he wasn't in the driveway by 5:10. Ben took a couple of deep breaths, and vowed not to act like an ass if she called.

Beth didn't call, and Ben zipped into the driveway and quickly exited his car, leaving his briefcase and stained coffee mug behind. The front door flew open and Beth stepped out in her fitness gear holding a smiling, chatty Maddie.

His wife started to say something about how she'd been about to call him, but Ben drowned her out with a loud, gregarious, "Daddy's girl!" and swept Maddie into his arms and smothered her with kisses. He saved a kiss for Beth's cheek as well, and she accepted it before giving Maddie a peck on the little girl's forehead and rushing to hop into her own car.

"Be back by 8 or 8:30!" Beth called out before shutting the driver's side door. Ben took Maddie's tiny right arm and helped her wave goodbye to her mother as Beth tore out of the neighborhood. He took another deep breath, gave a delighted Maddie a quick raspberry on her neck, and carried the little girl inside.

A couple of early birds were waiting outside of the studio when Beth pulled into the strip center. She greeted Paula Wilson and her husband Jason as she fumbled with her keys and unlocked the door, holding it open for her clients. Eight persons had pre-registered for the 5:30 p.m. class, and another five for the 7 p.m. class. Beth asked the Wilsons to go ahead and pick out their stationary bikes, as she hurriedly set her purse down and ensured that the various items needed for the hour-long routines were still where she'd left them the night before.

The others quickly arrived as well, including her book club friends Emma, Jackie, and Kari. Delphi usually attended also, although wasn't as dedicated as the other three.

Ray, the only other male, rushed in and was followed a minute later by 50-something Sarah England. Finally Delphi strode in, late and a little disheveled, handing Beth a few samples of the latest energy-inducing product she'd found at some health food store. Beth placed the goods into a large bin she kept in the corner, where they joined the other samples she'd meant to look through but never did.

"Are you all ready for another hour of torture?" Beth called loudly to the group as they settled onto their bikes and positioned their water bottles and towels. The extraverts—especially Jackie—responded with shouts and fist pumps.

The class launched with three intense minutes of pedaling, Beth facing the full group as she pedaled as well and coached them to try their hardest and not worry about who was the fastest or slowest. "Keep that heart rate going!" she exclaimed.

After the three minutes were up Beth instructed her clients to head to the floor, pick up some small sand bags, and begin tossing them overhead and catching them. From there, the group moved to a series of large punching bags hanging from the ceiling and kick-boxed for 60 seconds, alternating their legs with each kick. Then it was back to the bikes for another excruciating two minutes. This cycle repeated itself with some variety spliced in for the next 30 minutes, before Beth led them into a cool-down and stretching period on the mats that culminated in relieved applause and celebration.

Emma, Jackie, Kari, and Delphi lingered for a while after class. As she was straightening up Beth heard them talking about the upcoming weekend trip to SunFest.

"I'm ready to show off all this hard work in my new bikini," Kari said, flexing her biceps.

"Remember, I've left plenty of booze in the condo," Delphi told them. "Please make yourselves feel at home."

"That's really nice of you," Emma said. "Are you sure you can't join us?"

Delphi sighed. "I'd love to, but I can't get away from the store for the weekend. Or *any* weekend. Not sure why I still haven't sold that condo down there, but I'm glad somebody can use it now and then."

"We'll do it again, for sure," Jackie said. "It'll be even more fun next time."

Curtis Everett sat meditating in the large pasture that surrounded a small chapel where he'd spent much of the last 25 years. The sun felt warm on his face.

Two other men sat on folding chairs in front of the chapel, staring lazily out at the ranch property and ensuring that no one disturbed Curtis. They saw a few of their peers working in the large garden that was about a hundred yards to the west. A couple of golf carts were in motion near the ranch's multi-purpose building and cabins.

Birds chirped as they flew overhead. Curtis rose and stretched, and walked across the open field for a while. The men continued to remain on alert in case he summoned them.

At 4 p.m. on Thursday, May 3, Emma drove to Jackie's house where Kari had already arrived with her husband Tom. Tom chatted with Jackie's husband Phil in the living room. The Solomons' two young daughters, Audrey and Natalie, were at their mother's side and asking questions about the trip.

"We'll have to plan our own guys' trip sometime," Phil joked, handing Tom a beer. "But first we need to start going to Zumba together so we can get into shape."

"And read a book," Tom snickered. "Why don't we start reading *Gone with the Wind?*"

"Are y'all bonding?" Jackie asked as she entered the living room. "That's so sweet."

"We're trying to decide which nanny to hire for the weekend," Tom said.

The husbands got parting hugs from their respective wives, and Audrey and Natalie kissed their mother goodbye. Phil and Tom stood in the driveway with the two girls and watched the trio drive away in Emma's car.

Phil looked at Tom. "Stay long enough for another beer?"

Tom shrugged. "I'm always up for another beer. Connor will be okay at home for a little while longer."

"You should have brought him along."

"He's not big on meeting new people sometimes," Tom said. "He's busy with his sketchbook. Probably doesn't even remember that his mother is going out of town for three days."

After listening to Beth grouse about how jealous she was that her friends were heading south for a long weekend, Ben remarked that if anyone deserved a getaway it was her. Beth had been busting her ass running her fledgling business, and Ben often told her how impressed he was. Beth had longed to open her own studio since before she and Ben met eight years earlier. She'd held off pursuing this dream while suffering the unenviable journey of infertility and miscarriages before Maddie finally arrived.

"I just can't afford to cancel any of my classes right now and close the doors for a Saturday," Beth said, sipping a glass of Pinot Noir. Maddie had been asleep for nearly an hour. "Clients have to be ingrained in coming back week after week at their favorite times. Maybe in a year or two I can take a weekend off."

Ben nearly choked on his own wine.

"A *year* or two? And you complain about me working all the time." He smiled to let her know he wasn't trying to be nasty, but he wasn't totally kidding either.

Beth patted her husband's arm. "I should be busy enough by then that I can hire someone to help me run the classes," she said. "And besides, just think of all the quality time you're getting with Maddie on Saturdays and weekday evenings when you're in town."

Ben screwed up his face at her and Beth smiled seductively, holding up her wine glass to clink his. He gestured for her to come closer and she sat in his lap as they took advantage of the quiet privacy.

Emma, Jackie, and Kari were too tired upon arriving at Delphi's Boca Raton condo to do anything but brush their teeth, figure out who was going to sleep where, and chat a little more before drifting off to sleep. They'd have a full day tomorrow of music, sunbathing, and cocktails, and maybe even a little dancing. Jackie and Kari texted their husbands to let them know they'd arrived safely, and promised to try to call and check in tomorrow if they had a chance.

Kari got a brief second wind as she went through the numerous bikinis she'd packed, debating which one to wear first. Jackie muttered that she wished she could still pull off wearing a two-piece, and how despite getting back into shape her stretch marks made her too self-conscious.

Emma simply smiled and settled into bed with the latest edition of *The New Yorker*, which she'd subscribed to ever since reluctantly leaving the city years ago. The group hadn't selected its next book to read, as the members couldn't come to their usual consensus. They'd tabled the decision until after the trip, so Emma was happy to read whatever the hell she felt like for a change.

Chapter Three

MAY 6

W/hat time did Mommy say she was coming home?" Audrey asked, still chewing on her last bite of grilled cheese. She sat with her father Phil and younger sister Natalie at the local Panera Bread. They'd waited to eat lunch until about 1 p.m., to avoid the Sunday after-church crowd.

"I think by 4 or 5 o'clock," Phil mumbled, picking at his Greek salad and trying to resist the urge to glance at his phone for the hundredth time. *She's just having a great time, and didn't get a chance to call again,* Phil kept reasoning with himself.

They finished lunch and went home. Phil spent the afternoon encouraging the girls to finish their homework while he tidied up around the house. His cell phone didn't leave his side, but remained silent.

"Mommy decided to stay one more night," he fibbed to Natalie as he tucked her into bed. "She'll be home tomorrow while you're still at school. You can look forward to that." His youngest daughter took the news well, but Phil noticed that she hugged him extra tightly as he kissed her goodnight.

Tom Blakely stood in his kitchen and mixed an Old Fashioned, feeling both worried and angry. The weekend had been a nice break from Kari's drama, but failing to come home as planned was uncool. Connor was confused as the afternoon turned into dusk and nightfall, and the boy soothed himself as he usually did by sketching animals. Tom started packing his son's lunch for the next day, downing the Old Fashioned in a couple of large gulps.

Against his better judgment, Tom began to wonder if Kari had met someone down in Palm Beach County and decided to stay behind. Her combination of complaining about their marriage while being obsessed with her looks set the stage for a potential affair, he deduced. Or maybe all three women had stayed, and Kari had simply not bothered to call.

Emma O'Rourke was divorced, Tom recalled, and maybe she and Kari had both met some guys. Tom knew he was getting paranoid, but the stark absence of information left all potential scenarios on the table.

He made another Old Fashioned, and finished spreading peanut butter and jelly on two slices of whole wheat bread for Connor. Tom opened the fridge and pensively scanned the insides, in search of other items he thought his son might like. Kari wasn't around to go grocery shopping that weekend, and it showed.

Tom finished packing Connor's lunch, wandered into the living room with his glass of booze, and plopped next to the boy on the couch. He peered at Connor's sketchpad.

"What kind of dog is that?"

Connor shrugged. "I don't know. It's just the kind of dog who needs help. See how skinny he is?"

"Yeah. Is he a marathon runner?" Tom half-smiled at his weak joke.

"I don't know. I'm thinking maybe he's homeless. He needs a family to fatten him up."

Tom rested his hand on Connor's mop of a haircut. "That's a nice thought," he said.

They sat together on the couch for the next several hours, Tom watching television and drinking, Connor sketching until he fell asleep leaning against his father.

Pete O'Rourke laid on his bed texting three different friends every couple of minutes. iTunes was up on his laptop, shuffling through a wide variety of songs from Kings of Leon to Justin Timberlake to Florence + the Machine.

He scrolled down his texts and found his mother Emma's name. Pete's last text to her was sent three hours ago, and she still hadn't replied. Even though he was at his dad's for the week, Pete tended to hear from his mother at least daily. She'd not responded since Thursday night, and Pete felt that she was being rude.

"IDK what her problem is," he texted to one of his buddies, and then felt bad for dissing his mother behind her back. *But what was her deal?*

Pete sat up, considering asking his father Russ if he'd heard from his mother, and then decided against it. Bringing up his mom's name always seem to put his dad in a crummy mood, if he wasn't in one already.

Chapter Four

MAY 7

Mondays were "office days" for Ben McBride, filled with conference calls that would impact the general direction of the rest of the week. The cascading onslaught began at 10 a.m. with the regional call led by Ben's director, Paul Sawyer, who was always fresh off of the Area VP call. Paul's call usually went until 11:30 and sometimes noon. After that, Ben typically grabbed something quick to eat before prepping for the 1 p.m. call he led with his own team of retail store managers.

The Volusia Mall store had the highest foot traffic in the district, and naturally drew the younger crowd that was the bread and butter of Next Generation Wireless. Ben had seen many retail outlets come and go during the recent years of tough economic times, but Next Gen had hung in there. He used to office out of his house, venturing out to the stores Tuesdays through Fridays, and that quickly changed when Maddie was born.

Paul often tapped Ben as his point of contact when the director needed to travel for a meeting or take a vacation, and this helped Ben get the hands-on director experience that would be crucial when he interviewed for an open posting. His hunch was that an interview opportunity was less than 18 months away, having read between the lines that Paul was looking to make a lateral move if a VP opening didn't emerge.

As he set the phone down at the conclusion of Paul's call, Ben's stomach was already rumbling. He was sick of the mall food court, though. Beth chided him for not packing a lunch, and even offered to make it for him. Ben told his wife the last thing she needed to worry about was packing her husband's lunch.

Phil Solomon's own Monday felt far from normal. He taught his 9 a.m. *Introduction to the Humanities* course on automatic pilot, the PowerPoint slides burned into his memory long ago. The two or three questions Phil received after class were met with concise, although complete, answers. Phil's next class was at 1 p.m., and he was grateful for the break.

Instead of his usual routine of going to his office to review papers, answer emails, or do some writing, Phil rushed out to the parking lot and climbed inside his car. He turned east on International Speedway Boulevard, taking it all the way across the Halifax River to A1A, where he headed north.

Tom Blakely was the first to show up that Monday morning at the beachside Famoso's restaurant he'd owned for the past five years. His dayshift manager Brandi would arrive shortly, but Tom liked to get there before her in order to review inventory and improve the general cleanliness of the place. He also enjoyed a few minutes of peace and quiet, sitting at the bar and sipping from a glass of whiskey or rum.

Tom's thoughts were interrupted by someone knocking at the restaurant's locked front door. He wondered if Brandi had forgotten her key, but when Tom opened the door he was greeted by Phil Solomon.

"Sorry to bother you at work," Phil said, his eyes bloodshot. "But I'm wondering if you've heard from your wife."

Tom stared at Phil for a moment. "Come in and have a drink," he said.

Beth delayed the start of her 5:30 p.m. class by a few minutes, waiting to see if Emma, Jackie, and Kari would rush in and hop onto their stationary bikes. It was unusual for any of them to miss, but perhaps they were too tired from the SunFest trip. She hadn't heard from them since they left, and the class wouldn't be as fun without them.

Delphi Adams hadn't show up either. Deciding it was important to be courteous to the handful of people who were there on time, Beth got started.

About ten minutes into the intense routines of cycling, push-ups, sand bag lifting, and kick boxing, Beth noticed that a couple of familiar faces had entered the studio and were hanging out in her small lobby. The men weren't dressed to work out, and Beth wondered if they were there to solicit something. She ignored them for a while, and then glanced back over as it registered for her: *Jackie's and Kari's husbands, Phil and Tom.*

Had they come in person to let her know their wives wouldn't be attending class? That seemed silly. Beth gave her clients a water break, and then went over to say hello to the men.

Later that evening Ben stood behind Beth, rubbing her shoulders to relieve some of her soreness and soothe her anxiety. They'd talked for more than an hour about her three friends not returning home or calling. Beth left messages on all three of their cell phones. She called Delphi, but got her voice mail as well.

"The guys are really worried," Beth told Ben. "They don't know what else to do but wait. And what are they supposed to tell their kids again tonight?"

"Do you know how to get a hold of Emma's ex-husband?"

Beth shook her head. "Russ? No. None of us have ever met him. I think he works at her father's real estate company or something."

Ben rubbed his chin as he thought. "How about I call the guys tomorrow morning after their kids go to school, and go over and talk with them? They could probably use some support."

Beth reached a hand back and stroked his arm. "That would be great. Thank you, babe." She paused, and then added, "They said they were going to go ahead and call the police tonight."

'm new to this side of things," Daytona Beach Police Det. Sharon Rice said to her partner, Bob Sarosky, as he drove them into the Solomons' neighborhood, "but I would say this case bears all the signs of an unhappy ending."

Sarosky nodded, taking a final drag on his cigarette and then flicking it out the window. "Yeah, and a pain-in-the-ass media storm to go with it," he muttered.

Rice was recently promoted after five years as a beat cop, and the 28-year-old already had a reputation for fierce questioning. The dirty blonde-haired Rice stood at only 5'1" but looked like she spent two hours at the gym every day.

"Maybe they ran off with their secret boyfriends, and will come to their senses after the mid-life crises wear off," Rice said, rolling down her window to get the smoke smell out of the car. "And did anyone ever tell you that you smoke too much?"

"All the time," Sarosky replied. "Especially my parents, now that they've made the obligatory move down here from Ohio."

A few minutes later the detectives sat at Phil Solomon's dining room table. It was just after 9 a.m. They studied the tall, lanky fellow with graying black hair, who seemed calm as he processed the situation with the detectives and responded in depth to their questions. Joining them was Tom Blakely, a shorter, ruddy-faced gentleman with sandy, wavy hair who kept checking his watch.

"I was hoping you could tell us a little bit about your wives," Sarosky began. "Their personalities, their interests, plus anything difficult that was going on with them right now. Things like that."

Phil and Tom glanced at each other.

"Mr. Solomon, maybe you can go first," Rice offered. "Tell us about Jackie. What is she like?"

Phil thought for a moment. "She's the life of the party. Doesn't know a stranger."

Rice nodded. "What else?"

"She loves our daughters. She's very devoted."

"Anything she was upset about recently? Anything difficult she was going through?" Sarosky asked.

Phil shook his head. "No, everything has been fine, as far as I can tell."

Rice looked at Tom. "Mr. Blakely, what about your wife Kari?"

Tom glanced at Phil, looking a little embarrassed. "Kari's been doing okay. She's been really into fitness and the book club. A little too much, maybe. She's got some insecurities, if I can be totally honest."

Rice shrugged. "Honesty is important here."

"Any bizarre behavior?" Sarosky asked.

Tom shook his head. "No, nothing like that."

Sarosky reached into his thin briefcase and pulled out some paperwork.

"I'll need each of you to sign off on a copy of this form," he said, sliding a detailed sheet of paper in front of Phil and Tom. "This gives us permission to enter your wives' names into the NCIC. That's the National Crime Information Center, a database that can be accessed by law enforcement officials anywhere in the U.S."

The men nodded and signed the form.

"We'll also need recent pictures of both Jackie and Kari," Rice said. "You can just text those to one of our cell phones if you have them handy. Otherwise, email them to one of us." She and Sarosky handed their respective business cards to the two men.

By sheer protocol, Phil, Tom, and Emma O'Rourke's ex-husband Russ were potential suspects until the police were satisfied that their stories were genuine. There was no record of domestic violence reports and no criminal history on any of the men. So far, Sarosky's vibe on Phil and Tom was that they were innocent victims. He would get Rice's take when they were back in the car and on the way to visit Russ O'Rourke.

The doorbell rang, and Phil greeted Ben McBride. He introduced him to the detectives as Ben, tall and dark-haired and every bit the sales executive type, clapped Tom on the back.

"Mr. McBride, how well do you know the three missing women?" Sarosky asked him.

Ben glanced from Sarosky to Rice and back. "Not very well. I've met them once or twice, at book club family barbecues and things like that. I've stopped by my wife's fitness studio a couple of times and met some of them, I think."

"This is the most time the three of us guys have spent together, period," Tom said, offering a sad smile. Phil simply nodded.

~~~

"It's a laundry list of things," Sarosky said to Rice after they were back in the car. "Cell phone records. Reaching out to peers in the Boca police department, and officials within all the surrounding Palm Beach County municipalities. We'll have to speak with the neighbors down at the condominium. And we'll need fliers and a media release."

Rice nodded. "Lots of details. Do we have a punch list template?"

"Punch list template?"

"Yeah. A standard template where all of these items are already printed, and we just work through them and punch them out one at a time."

Sarosky smiled at her. "Great idea. Why don't you create one? Perfect way to learn, rookie."

"Terrific. You really known how to turn a girl on." Rice smiled when she noticed that made Sarosky shift awkwardly for a flashing moment.

"As uncomfortable as this will be, we'll need to speak to their kids," Sarosky continued. "Any nuggets they can give us might provide a potential lead. Signs of mental illness in one of the mothers, for example, could point to a potential murder-suicide. The more family members, especially children, ramble on about their loved ones, the more these kinds of clues emerge."

Rice frowned. "So we just come out and ask little Billy, 'Hey, was your mom a nut case or what?'"

"It's more subtle than that."

"Do you have kids?"

Sarosky shook his head. "No kids. No ex-wives. No ex-dogs. Just the parents."

"That's kind of sad."

"I know," he said. "And you?"

"I might want kids one day. But that might require me actually getting a second date with someone. Men are a little intimidated by female cops."

~~~

Russ O'Rourke pulled into the parking lot of Greater Daytona Development Corporation—known to everyone as GDD—with a very specific agenda on his mind.

Security was beefed up, and the gate guard was new and took his time studying Russ's driver's license and comparing it to his list. After parking and being permitted to enter the lobby, Russ was told by the front desk guards to empty his pockets and surrender his brief case for a couple of minutes. Another guard was waiting for him at the elevator, and personally escorted him to the second floor.

Russ walked down the second floor hallway, nodding to employees and wondering what else Mario Lazano was doing in response to his daughter Emma's disappearance. Mario was a careful, shrewd man concerning everything except for his philandering, leaving little to chance with a strategic mind that peeled back layers of possibility after possibility.

After greeting his administrative assistant Becky, Russ set his briefcase on his desk. He wouldn't bother diving into work until speaking with the boss.

Russ continued back down the hallway, approaching a secluded area and spotting the ever-watching eyes of the men whom other employees quietly referred to as the "Cubists." These were younger, impeccably dressed associates who performed some type of security work in a collection of cubicles that blanketed the entrance to Mario's large corner office. Few knew exactly how they contributed to the company's bottom line or how they were selected, but they were always doing data entry and their eyes constantly observed the activities around them. They didn't socialize with the other employees, and were never spotted in the break room or even in the bathroom. Russ had wondered out loud more than once, "Do these guys ever get to take a piss?" which always made Becky smile.

Adjacent to Mario's office, in full view of the Cubists, was the smaller office occupied by the company's director of security, Henry Reid. Henry was a quiet, polite man with thinning hair in his early 50s, powerfully built and clearly in charge of the Cubists. Mario was rarely seen in public without Henry at his side. There was much speculation about what Henry did, but unlike his staff Henry did interact with the other employees. No one was allowed to learn much about his private world, but Henry had a presence that made everyone in the building feel a little safer.

Russ paused in Henry's doorway, and pointed in the direction of Mario's office. Henry simply nodded, and Russ went in to see his former father-in-law.

Mario was on the phone but indicated for Russ to take a seat. Russ sat and gazed out the window at the ocean before glancing at the small assortment of family pictures that Mario kept on a table in the corner. There were individual pictures of Emma at several different ages, a couple of Pete, and even a snapshot of Russ and Emma together. Russ also noticed a picture of Mario's first wife and Emma's mother, Carmen.

Mario finished his call. "This market is flatter than the beach at low tide," he said, frowning. "We're fortunate that we never fell into all that speculation foolishness like so many others. We're not selling much or hiring much these days, but we have a lot of reserves to keep us going. We've been smart." Mario smiled at Russ. "You've been smart."

Russ was grateful that he and Mario had not skipped a beat in their own relationship. "Thanks," he said.

"You look exhausted," Mario said. "Tell me how you're holding up."

"Pete's worried about Emma," Russ replied. "He's used to not seeing her for a week at a time when he's with me, but she always checks in with him. I thought it was weird when she never called or texted him this time around, and then when he actually tried to call her she never responded."

Mario re-arranged some papers on his desk in an absent-minded fashion. "Why don't you bring him over to my house tonight? Have him spend a couple of days with me. It'll take his mind off of things. We'll go mini-golfing, or even shoot some pool."

Russ shrugged. "I don't know. I'll ask him, if I can get him to talk." He leaned in closer to Mario's desk, looking intently at the man who didn't seem as concerned as Russ might have expected. "What do you think we should do about finding her?"

A knock at the door interrupted Mario's answer. It was one of the nameless Cubists.

"Mr. Lazano, there's a Det. Sarosky and a Det. Rice here to see you."

Mario glanced at Russ, and then back at the Cubist.

"Thank you. Please show them in." Mario stood, and motioned for Russ to do the same.

Sarosky introduced himself and Rice.

"Have a seat, please," Mario said. "What can we do for you, detectives?"

"I'm sorry to interrupt your morning," Sarosky said, making eye contact with each of the men before settling on Russ. "Mr. O'Rourke, I was wondering how long it's been since you've spoken with your ex-wife Emma? We received a report early this morning that she's missing, along with two other women."

Rice studied Russ closely.

"We were just discussing that," Russ responded. "My son was concerned because he hadn't heard from her."

"My daughter is independent and headstrong, and she can take care of herself," Mario interjected. "Wherever she is and whatever she's doing, I'm sure she's fine."

Sarosky nodded. "I appreciate that. Has she done this before—gone off without letting anyone know when she was coming home?"

"No," Russ said.

"Just try to relax," Mario said to Russ. "She's going to be fine. Tell Pete he'll hear from his mother soon, that she just needed a little time away. For some women's business."

Russ was waiting for more, but Mario was finished for the moment.

"With all due respect, I don't think you're taking this seriously enough," Russ said, feeling his anger rising. Sarosky and Rice simply watched both men as they spoke to each other. "Pete hasn't heard from her. Whatever the hell is going on, it's not good."

Russ paused, waiting for Mario to say something, but the old man was impassive. He looked over at Sarosky, and then at Rice.

"Can you help us find her?"

"We'll do all that we can," Rice said. "We'll need your signature on a missing person's database form. And a recent picture of your ex-wife, if you have one."

"I've got plenty of those," Mario said.

"Gentlemen, any reason to believe that someone might have intended to harm Mrs. O'Rourke? Any strange events or suspicious characters as of late that would cause you concern?" Sarosky asked.

Russ shook his head. "No. I don't really keep tabs on what she does and who she spends time with, but nothing I'm aware of."

Mario nodded. "Likewise. Again, she's a very independent person. She can take care of herself."

The pair of detectives asked a few more questions, then thanked the men, said they'd be in touch, and left.

Russ glared at Mario, unable to mask his annoyance.

"The police aren't going to do anything besides paperwork. I need your help. *Emma* needs your help."

Mario simply smiled at him, waiting for more. Russ stood, sensing that the meeting was over.

"I don't need to know everything that goes on in your world, and I've never asked you a lot of questions," Russ said. "But if you were ever going to open the vault a little, this would be the time."

Without offering a handshake or a goodbye, Russ turned and walked briskly out of the office. As he headed up the hallway he ignored the ubiquitous stares of the Cubists.

Chapter Six:

It was just before noon when Sarosky and Rice arrived at Beth McBride's front door.

The young mother greeted them holding an adorable toddler girl with big brown eyes, wavy chestnut hair, and a bright smile. Rice played a momentary game of peekaboo with Maddie McBride, and the smile grew even brighter.

Beth's eyes were red and watery. She offered the pair of detectives some coffee, which they accepted, and they sat down at the McBride's small kitchen dinette. Maddie was glued to Rice's side from the start, bringing her favorite dolls and toys to show off and trying her best to listen to every word that was being said between the grown-ups.

"I just don't understand what could have happened," Beth said, retrieving a tissue from a nearby box and wiping her eyes.

"Any strange behavior that you noticed from any of the ladies in recent days or weeks?" Rice asked, shooting Maddie a quick smile as the little girl attempted to perform a pirouette for her.

Beth shook her head. "No, nothing that I can recall. They were excited about going on the trip."

"Any specific reason why they were the only ones out of the nine book club members who went on the trip?" Sarosky asked.

"Lots of reasons, I guess. I didn't go because Saturday is a big day for my clients. Dara, an older member of our group, wasn't into it. Kevlin had plans, Lisa couldn't get away, and Liz has been sick. She's recovering from breast cancer."

Sarosky paused to jot down some notes.

"Are you going to talk to each of them as well?" Beth asked.

"Yep," Sarosky said. "What about Delphi Adams? She owns the bookstore where you all meet and it was her condo in Boca where your friends were staying, right?"

"Right, I forgot Delphi. Sorry about that. Delphi was in the same boat as me, couldn't afford to close her book store for the weekend. She doesn't have any employees either."

"Tough to never get a day off, huh?" Rice smiled.

"I guess Sunday is my day off."

"Mrs. McBride," Rice continued, "off of the top of your head, can you think of anyone who might have possibly wanted to harm one or more of these women? Think as broadly as possible here. No idea is too 'out there.'"

Beth gave Rice the courtesy of contemplating the question for a few seconds, and then shook her head once again. "No. I can't think of anyone. These were just regular moms, enjoying the opportunity to get away for a weekend."

"Ever hear Mrs. O'Rourke complain about her ex-husband, Russ? Did she ever say anything about him having a temper, or displaying erratic behavior, anything like that?"

"She barely ever mentioned him. I've got some other divorced friends who complain way too much about their exes, but Emma isn't one of them. She's rather private, I think."

Sarosky jumped back into the line of questioning. "Did Emma ever say much about her father, Mario Lazano? Owner of Daytona Development Corporation?"

Beth thought for a moment.

"She's mentioned a couple of times that her dad is a very successful businessman. And she did say one time that the less she knew about his business, the better off she felt. I guess things were tough for her growing up. Her parents got divorced as well."

Sarosky nodded. "She ever specify why she didn't want to know much about his business?"

"No. She did say once, now that I think about it, that she didn't like it when Russ went to work for her father. They moved down here from New York so he could do that. She said it strained their marriage."

Sarosky jotted this down. He glanced at Rice, smiling as Maddie showed them both her Raggedy Ann doll.

"Here's our cards, Mrs. McBride," Sarosky said. "If you think of any additional information or insights that would be helpful to our search for your friends—anything at all—please don't hesitate to call either one of us. No time is too early or late to call."

"Sounds like you work 'round the clock, like my husband," Beth said.

A short while later the two detectives sat in Dara Wilson's kitchen, drinking yet another cup of coffee. Dara was a charming woman who loved to tell stories, although none of the content so far was very relevant to the case of her missing friends.

"I just feel so awful for those children," Dara said. "What a horrible ordeal to go through, not knowing whether you'll ever see your mother again."

"It is horrible," Rice said. "We'll put the families in touch with some grief counselors, to help both the children and the fathers cope with this."

"That would be wonderful," Dara said.

Dara pointed to Sarosky's coffee mug, but he shook his head. "I'm good, thanks."

"I'm wondering about the kind of people who go to music festivals like that," Dara said. "There's always some freaks that show up in those kinds of settings. I'm worried that the ladies might have been followed off of the festival grounds by a group of weirdos or something, and forced into a car."

"That's a plausible idea," Sarosky said. "My understanding, however, is that the evidence at the condo indicates they never made it to the festival. That they appeared to disappear from the condo itself on the first night after they arrived, sometime before morning."

"It's so strange," Dara said.

"It is, indeed," Sarosky replied.

Rice reached Lisa Grayton on her cell phone as Sarosky drove them away from Dara's house. Lisa sounded harried and said she was at the grocery store with her two preschoolers, but that she expected to be home in about 10 minutes. Rice asked if there might be a better time to visit later, to which Lisa replied, "There's never a good time when you have four kids, so you might as well come over now."

The preschoolers were a four-year-old boy, Winston, and a two-year-old girl, Mary Beth. Lisa talked them into watching a show in the living room, and the detectives once again found themselves sitting at a kitchen table.

"My husband John is freaking out," Lisa said. "He's overwhelmed at the thought that I might have gone with them. He even brought home flowers, which he hasn't done in a while."

"I can imagine how it must feel, to wonder if it could have happened to your wife as well," Sarosky said.

"Are you married, detective?" Lisa asked him, and smiled at Rice when she chuckled.

"No. I've been too busy working to ever settle down."

Lisa laughed. "Well, for me settling down has just meant a whole lot of work."

"Yep, that's why I haven't done it," Rice said with gentle sarcasm, tapping her notepad.

Sarosky was eager to shift the topic back to the case. "I have another question," he said. "This is out of left field a bit, but did any of the women ever mention an old boyfriend that had come back into their life? A person who was harassing or stalking them?"

Lisa shook her head. "The only one who ever talked about boyfriends is Kevlin," she said. "She's on Timber or Tinder or whatever it's called, and goes on a lot of dates, and sometimes we get the highlights. She's mentioned a couple of creeps, but no one that's made her feel afraid."

Lisa paused, and the detectives waited.

"You know, Emma did say something once in passing, while we were discussing *The Sun Also Rises*," she said. "She made a vague reference to 'the one who got away,' a guy she fell in love with when she was still a teenager. But she never elaborated."

"She didn't mention the guy's name or whether she'd ever heard from him again?" Rice asked.

"No, on both counts."

Kevlin Lane was the only member of the book club with a full-time corporate job. Sarosky and Rice stopped by the receptionist desk at the insurance agency where she worked, offered their credentials, and a couple of minutes later were greeted by Kevlin in the lobby.

"Come on back," said Kevlin, a freckled redhead who certainly looked like someone who would be popular on the dating scene. "It's been a crazy day here, too many claims." She sat behind her desk, the detectives settling into the chairs opposite her. "I guess most days are like this. I'm actually happy to get a break and talk about something else besides work. Although this is a very painful topic."

"I'm sure it is," Sarosky said. "We won't take a lot of your time."

"No worries."

"Have you ever been to SunFest in past years?" he asked.

"No, I haven't been to that one. I've gone to Bonnaroo up in Tennessee, and other more local festivals. I'd like to go to Coachella in California some time."

"Why didn't you go with your friends on this trip?" Rice asked.

Kevlin smiled. "I had a date this past weekend. It's a guy I've been interested in for a while, and I didn't want to cancel."

"Would you mind telling me his name and what he does for a living?" Rice asked.

This time Kevlin frowned. "Are you going to interview him, too? I don't want to scare him away already. It's hard enough keeping guys around when there's *not* a missing persons investigation going on."

Rice laughed heartily. "I know that's true, honey."

Sarosky smiled. "Hopefully we won't need to talk to him. We're just gathering as much information as possible. I don't mean to invade your privacy, I'm just trying to help find your friends."

Kevlin nodded. "I get it. His name is Randy Taylor. He's an EMT firefighter guy, one of those dudes that works 24 hours straight and then has 48 hours off. I was lucky enough to catch him on a weekend day off."

"City of Daytona or the county?"

"City of Port Orange, actually."

"Thanks for clarifying," Sarosky said. "Did you happen to tell him that you were turning down a girls' trip to go out with him?"

Kevlin laughed. "No, I didn't think to mention it."

"So you plan to see him again?" Rice asked.

"I do. Is that ok?"

Rice chuckled. "It's fine. We're always happy to see a fellow public servant manage to have a social life."

"Ironic, isn't it?" Liz Morgan asked Sarosky and Rice as they sat down in her living room.

"How so?" Rice responded.

"I missed out on being kidnapped because I got breast cancer. Seems my whole life has been about determining the lesser of two evils."

Rice smiled. "Well, we don't know that your friends were kidnapped."

Liz rolled her eyes.

"Yeah. They just decided to flee the country and make a fresh start."

"Can you say more about 'choosing the lesser of two evils?'" Sarosky asked.

Liz sighed. "Hmm. Let's see. There was chemotherapy and a double mastectomy vs. rolling the dice and seeing if I would live to old age. Then, there was getting divorced vs. staying in a marriage with a man who continued to have affairs even after I got sick."

"I'm sorry," Sarosky said. "Those are difficult choices."

"Yeah. But I've accepted them. There is an upside, you know. I'm single, and have new boobs."

Sarosky chuckled to mask his embarrassment, forcing himself not to stare at the aforementioned breasts and hoping Rice would rescue the moment. She did. "I bet you're the biggest comedian in the book club."

Liz shrugged. "It's between me and Jackie."

The Oracle bookstore was unoccupied at the moment, except for its owner. Delphi Adams introduced herself to Sarosky and Rice, leading them into a back room cluttered with books and containing a large table with folding chairs.

"This is where the club meets," she told them. "We were here just a few days ago, all of us except for Liz. I'm still in shock."

"It's got to be terribly upsetting," Sarosky acknowledged. "We won't take a lot of your time. I just need to ask you a few questions."

"I'll help out however I can," Delphi said, waiting.

"Tell me about your condo down in Boca," he said. "Any history of break-ins there? Anyone else down there have a key to your place?"

Delphi shook her head. "It's a really quiet place. The condo board runs a tight ship. Believe me, if anything weird or out of order happens, everybody knows about it right away and the police get called."

Sarosky waited for a response to his second question.

"As far as a key, there's an older woman named Joan who lives next door to me. She has a key. I've already called her to see if she heard or noticed anything unusual. She hadn't. She offered to go inside the condo and look around, but I warned her not to."

"That was smart," Sarosky said. "It's a potential crime scene."

"Do you think there's yellow tape on my front door and all of that?"

"Probably not. But my peers in the Boca police unit will likely be visiting your place later today. It would be helpful if you called your neighbor Joan and asked her if she would escort the detectives inside."

Delphi absorbed this.

"Unless you'd rather not put her in that position. You can drive down there and let them in instead, if you want."

"I'm scared to go there," she said. "I'm sure that sounds really stupid."

"Not stupid at all. We have no idea what's happened, or if a perpetrator might return to the condo."

"I'm going to sell it," Delphi said. "I should have sold it a long time ago. I'm almost never there."

"I'm wondering why you have a condo in Boca Raton in the first place," Rice said.

Delphi sighed. "Part of a divorce settlement from my ex-husband Richard. Almost seven years ago. I lived in it for a while, but really wanted to get away from all the traffic and rude people down there. I could sure use the sale proceeds right now for this place."

"How's the store doing?" Rice asked.

"Eh. You know of many thriving indie bookstores around here?"

Rice shrugged. "I'm not much of a pleasure reader."

"Another question," Sarosky said. "How many keys did you give to your three friends before they left?"

"Just one," Delphi said. "I gave it to Emma, because I knew she wouldn't lose it. She's pretty meticulous."

"And did you hear from them at all after they left Daytona Beach?"

"Kari Blakely sent me a text late Thursday night saying they were there, and that the place was awesome. That's the last I heard from them."

Delphi waited while Sarosky jotted down some notes.

"Hey, what about Emma's car? Is her car still in the condo parking lot?" Delphi asked.

"My peers are checking on that. We looked up her registration, so it'll be easy to identify. Unless someone has switched out the license plate."

Delphi looked at Sarosky, her eyes growing watery.

"Do these kind of cases ever have a happy ending?"

"Sure they do," Rice said, trying her best to sound upbeat. "At some point we're bound to get a solid lead. My highest hope is that someone simply wants some money, and once they get what they want they'll let your friends go."

"And then the kidnappers get to take off and enjoy their money? No consequences?"

"I didn't say that," Rice smiled. "That's our job."

Sarosky stood, ready to leave, and Rice followed his lead. Delphi followed them through the store.

"Hey, one more question," Sarosky said, turning to face her again. "Who else besides Joan, the book club, and the husbands knew that friends were going to be staying at your condo?"

"No one."

"Okay," Sarosky said, shaking Delphi's hand. "Thanks for your time. We'll likely be in touch again soon. And please be sure to call us right away if you learn anything that could be helpful."

"You've got it."

Delphi locked the store door after Sarosky and Rice left, watching them from the front window. She'd been trying not to cry during the interview with the detectives, but now the tears flowed and she sank down to the floor and sobbed.

After a while Delphi climbed back up and tried to distract herself by organizing books. She was startled by a knock at the locked door, and grabbed her cell phone in preparation to call 9-1-1. She cautiously peered through the window, and saw Beth McBride. Delphi exhaled a big sigh of relief, and hugged her friend tightly after unlocking and opening the door.

"How are you holding up?" Beth asked.

"I need to drive down there," Delphi said. "I need to see for myself what happened."

"Don't," Beth pleaded. "It's not safe. Let the police do their thing."

"I have a responsibility to be there. It's my place. I invited them to stay there, and now they're missing. This is my fault, Beth."

"No, Delphi. It's the fault of whoever decided to do whatever they did to our friends. I know you can't see that right now, but you will eventually."

They embraced tightly again, and stayed wrapped together for a long while.

"Maybe I'll find them relaxing in the condo or hanging out on the beach, having decided to stay longer and thinking no one would care," Delphi said, forcing a smile. "Maybe it's all a big misunderstanding. Maybe we're all overreacting."

Beth shrugged. "Maybe. And maybe I'll drop kick all three of them if that's the case, if they could've possibly been that inconsiderate. But you and I both know they wouldn't do that to their families."

"Yeah."

"Do you want to come stay at my house?" Beth asked. "Maybe it's not a good time for you to be alone. And Maddie would be a nice distraction."

Delphi shook her head. "That's sweet of you, but I don't want to impose. And I think I need to be alone."

"But you call me anytime you need to talk, okay?"

"Okay."

Chapter Seven:

MAY 9

After visiting with his Volusia Mall employees for the start of their shift, Ben drove toward the beachside. At a red light he picked up his cell phone, quickly toggled through the photo gallery, and viewed a snapshot of Emma O'Rourke that was taken during a backyard barbecue. Ben debated whether to text it to Sarosky, but decided that was really Russ's job to do so.

He was still looking at Emma's photo when the phone rang, startling him. It was Beth. A horn honk from the car behind him alerted Ben that the traffic light had turned green. Ben lurched the car forward and answered Beth using the speaker feature.

"Hi, what's up, sweetie?"

"I still think what you're doing is really stupid," Beth said, coldly. "It's a potential crime scene. And why do *you* have to go along?"

Ben sighed. "Babe, we've gone over this. It's not dangerous at this point; whatever happened has already happened. And I'm going because we're supporting our friends, just like you encouraged me to do."

Beth paced in the kitchen, taking a few deep breaths. "I think you'd be even more supportive if you talked them out of it."

Ben neared the large bridge that spanned the Halifax River along International Speedway Boulevard. "Their wives are missing. They need to go down and see for themselves. I would do the same thing if you'd gone. Thank God you didn't go."

Beth felt tears forming in her eyes. "Yeah. I guess you would have."

Boats dotted the waterway as Ben proceeded toward the bridge's terminus. "I'll check in with you. Frequently."

"Please do. I love you."

"I love you, too."

"It seems fitting that we're heading down in a minivan," Russ grumbled to Tom as they watched Phil pull up to the outside of Famoso's.

Tom chucked. "Why is that?"

"I don't know. Maybe because we might be a bunch of cuckolded husbands?"

Tom merely stared at Russ.

"I guess I'm an ex-husband," Russ added.

"You guess? You are, or you aren't?"

Russ smiled. "I am. Thank God, Almighty, I'm free at last."

Phil walked up and greeted the men. The three of them stood there awkwardly and watched as Ben parked.

"Is the book girl still joining us?" Russ asked no one in particular.

"As far as I know," Ben said. "Maybe she's just running late."

"She sounds like the kind," Russ said.

"Tom, how's business?" Phil asked, desperate for anything significant to talk about with three other men he barely knew.

Tom nodded. "Going really well. I spend too much time here, but that's typical for a restaurant owner."

"Must be nice to be your own boss," Phil added.

"Lots of pros and cons."

"I think that's her now," Ben said, as a woman drove into the parking lot.

Each of the men insisted on Delphi sitting in the passenger's seat as Phil drove. At first the van was silent, until Delphi finally suggested they turn on the radio.

"What kind of music do you guys like?" she asked, glancing at the three men sitting in the back two rows of the minivan.

"Anything," Ben said.

"Anything as well," Tom echoed.

"Anything but country," Russ replied.

Delphi smiled at Russ. "Well, then it's country for sure."

"Nice, very nice," Russ said, forcing a grin back at her.

Delphi called for a bathroom stop about 90 minutes into the trip, near the Palm Bay area. Phil eased onto an off-ramp and found a gas station. The crew headed inside its accompanying market while Phil topped off the tank.

Ben gestured for Russ to go ahead of him into the men's bathroom, which was only designed for one person at a time. He leaned against the wall and sent Beth a text. *At a gas station in Palm Bay. Good times. Love you.*

Delphi glanced about at the various food and drink offerings on the way to the ladies' restroom. She noticed an end-cap full of Twinkies and felt her stomach lurch.

Phil wandered inside the store after pumping gas, and glanced at the various soft and energy drinks. He settled on a Muscle Milk.

"You into lifting weights now?" Russ asked as he walked past him.

"Yeah, can't you tell?"

Ben heard his phone beep as he finished up in the bathroom. *Dare to dream,* Beth had texted back.

Delphi sat in the passenger seat, her head tilted as her chin rested on her right palm, staring at the unstimulating scenery. The men were mostly silent, save for Ben occasionally trying to stir up conversation around work-related items. All five of them worked in very different fields, Ben noted, adding that he "had a lot to learn from everyone."

"Delphi, how did you decide to open a bookstore?" Ben asked her.

It took Delphi a couple of seconds to shake out of her daze and realize that someone was speaking to her.

"I'm sorry, what?"

Ben laughed. "Why did you decide to start a bookstore?"

"Oh. Well, once upon a time I had a little bit of money, and I've always loved to read. I've always loved books. The touch of books, the smell of books, and sometimes even the people who buy books."

Phil glanced over and smiled at her.

"So, I wanted to live in a less-populated area than South Florida, and it wasn't nearly as expensive to get the shop going a few years ago up here. But I think that opening it was the highlight. It's been a little slow."

Ben nodded. "It's a tough economy here. Has been for quite a long time."

"I hear this area used to be booming," Russ commented. "General Electric was here, Martin Marietta. Tourism used to be a lot stronger. Emma said it used to have a much nicer quality of life."

"I still like it better than South Florida," Delphi said. "I've been thinking of unloading that condo, because I'm hardly ever there anymore. Now I worry that I won't be able to sell it."

"I wouldn't worry about that," Tom said. "There's always a buyer somewhere. And the media attention will shift elsewhere before long." He glanced at Russ and then up at Phil. "As depressing as that might sound. It's just the nature of a short attention-span society."

"Indeed," Phil mumbled as he drove.

"Tell you what, Delphi," Ben said. "I know a little about retail. I'd be happy to stop by and, if you have the interest, assess the overall system you've got in place there for attracting and then following up with customers. I know I'm in wireless, but retailing is retailing."

Delphi shrugged. "Sure. Don't see how it could hurt."

Ben laughed. "I'll try not to cause too much damage."

"I'm not worried about you," she smiled.

Delphi slid her key into the lock and slowly opened the front door. She stepped back rather than going inside.

"I'm sorry," she said to the four men. "I just can't go in there first. I'm almost on the verge of a panic attack here. Do one of you mind?"

Russ was closest to her, and charged forward without hesitation. "No problem," he said, and the others followed him inside. Ben shut the door behind them and locked it.

The men stayed near the foyer and allowed Delphi to take the lead on slowly exploring each section of the condo, beginning with the living room and its small dining area with a round glass table and four high-back chairs. The living room had a matching, pastel-colored couch and love seat, completed by a flat screen TV resting on a small stand. There were a few paintings on the walls and a small collection of photographs. Overall, the place appeared simple, tidy, and clean.

Delphi explored the kitchen.

"I'm afraid to touch anything," she said. "I don't want to wipe off any fingerprints."

"They've already done all that, remember?" Russ said. "They didn't find anything. Just the ladies' prints. So you can touch away, and make yourself at home."

"Sure doesn't feel like home," Delphi said, carefully opening the stainless steel refrigerator and noting a half-filled container of orange juice, a carton of eggs, and a few green apples. "Hope nobody is hungry."

"We'll go out to eat later," Ben said. "My treat."

"You don't have to do that," Russ said. "But eating sounds very good at the moment."

All five of them jumped at the sound of someone gently knocking at the front door. Russ charged forward again, motioning with his hand for the others to stay back as he peered through the peep hole.

"It's some old lady," he whispered to Delphi.

"That's probably Joan," she said. "Let me take a look." Russ deferred to Delphi, and after a quick glance she opened the door.

Joan, thin and bespectacled with short, curly, gray hair, immediately gave Delphi a bear hug. "I'm so glad you're all right, dearie," she said in a heavy New Jersey accent. "I've been so worried about you and your friends."

"I'm fine. It's my girlfriends that aren't, as far as we can tell," Delphi said, shutting the door behind her neighbor.

Joan glanced at the four men, looking them up and down. "And who are these gorgeous fellas? It's like looking at the Four Seasons."

Everyone chuckled, grateful for a break in the tension. Delphi introduced the men, and Joan gave her apologies to each of them.

"My wife wasn't able to go on the trip," Ben clarified. "I'm here to support my friends."

"That's good of you," Joan said. "What an unbelievable thing. The police talked to me for quite a long time. I didn't see or hear anything. It's the craziest thing."

"It really is," Tom said.

"We wanted to come down and see things for ourselves," Delphi said. "But there isn't much to see. Everything looks exactly as I left it."

"The neighbors are nervous," Joan said. "They don't know if someone's targeting people who live in the building, or if it's an isolated case."

"No one knows the truth at this point," Russ said. "All we can do is lift up every rug and see what's there."

"I want you to know that I'm praying for all of them," Joan said. "I lit a menorah the other day just for your wives."

"Thank you," Phil said. "We appreciate that."

Joan politely declined their offer to join them for dinner. About 30 minutes later they sat at a large booth at the J. Alexander's across from Florida Atlantic University, staring at the menus.

"The half-chicken dish is really good," Tom said. "I wish I could replicate it at my place."

"I love the black bean burger," Delphi said. "Always fills me up."

Tom ordered a gin and tonic. The other men asked for beers and Delphi ordered a glass of Pinot Noir.

"Do you guys think this was a waste of time?"she asked the men.

"Not at all," Ben answered. "You needed to see your place. I think we all needed to, just as part of the process here."

32

Phil nodded. "Yeah. I'm in no hurry to come back down here, but I think we needed to do this."

"You want me to drive us home?" Ben asked Phil. "You must be tired."

Phil shook his head. "I'm fine. Helps me to have something to concentrate on. Otherwise my mind goes in a million different directions."

Tom was already close to the end of his drink. He glanced around them, trying to spot their server.

"I think I'll definitely put it up for sale," Delphi said, sipping from her wine glass. "I could use the cash infusion. Especially if Ben gives me some tips for a store makeover." She smiled.

"I'll give you lots of no- or low-cost ideas," Ben laughed.

The group had less to say as the meal progressed. They were even quieter in the van on the way home as evening drew near. Russ and Tom both nodded off, followed by Delphi.

"What do you think we do next?" Phil asked Ben in a whisper.

"I guess we continue to stay in close contact with the detectives," Ben said. "What can I do to continue to support you, Phil?"

Phil reflected on this for a moment. "Just keep doing what you're doing. Calling. Dropping by. Showing that you care. It means a lot. It really does."

"You've got it, brother."

Famoso's had a light crowd inside as Phil pulled into the parking lot. They said their goodbyes and Ben walked Delphi to her car. She gave him a tight hug.

"Just drop by whenever," she said.

"I will."

Ben drove home, not finding any music or programming on the radio that captured his interest. He arrived in the driveway and sat in his car for a long time before going inside.

Chapter Eight:

Earlier that same day, Sarosky was uncomfortable as he watched the reporters assemble in the police department's large media room. Rice stood near him, looking more eager than nervous. "Hizzoner is ready for the show," Rice whispered.

Mayor Rinaldi was hounding the sound technicians to make sure the microphones were properly set up. Police Chief Higgins was at the mayor's side, along with a few of his direct reports. The mayor would take the lead in addressing the press and answering questions, with the chief jumping in as needed, and Sarosky hoped there would be no reason for him to speak.

Two over-sized poster boards flanked each side of the microphone stand. Each bore identical contents: large, color headshots of Emma, Jackie, and Kari, under a giant MISSING title and a police hotline number.

Sarosky couldn't believe the sheer amount and variety of media members assembled in the room, pressing against each other for position. He recognized all the local crime beat reporters from the newspapers and Central Florida television stations, but also saw microphones and attire branded with stations from Palm Beach County and every major news outlet found on a typical home cable lineup. There was even a crew from the BBC. The web site press release that went live late last night had apparently done its job.

Sitting at his laptop earlier that morning, Sarosky noticed that social media was contributing to the communication cause as well. Kevlin Lane had already set up a Facebook page dedicated to the search effort, populated with group photos of the book club and individual pics she was able to obtain. The page had already generated more than a hundred "likes." Random individuals were also tweeting links to the police department's media release, as well as re-tweeting the department's own Twitter pleas for help.

Sarosky had never used Facebook or Twitter, and reluctantly created accounts that morning after Rice "insisted he move into the 21st Century." If the junior detective hadn't sat next to him and helped him, he'd still be off the social media grid.

The two detectives watched Rinaldi as he prepared to speak. The mayor had argued for the two husbands and Russ to be present at the press conference, "to put a human face" on the case. Sarosky and Rice both felt the men were going through enough, and thankfully Higgins had the same view and was able to stall the mayor on his request. The three men would have their share of camera time if the case dragged on, and Sarosky imagined that once the press conference concluded the media would make a beeline for each of their homes or places of work.

Finally, Rinaldi stepped up to the microphone and cleared his throat. The room grew silent except for the sound of clicking cameras.

"Good morning," Rinaldi said. "Before we get to some of the specifics of this very unfortunate situation, I'd like to begin with an opening statement."

Sarosky watched along with Rice as the mayor reached into the breast pocket of his sports coat and unfolded a piece of paper. He adjusted his reading glasses, and began.

"I want the country to understand that Central Florida, and Daytona Beach in particular, is a safe, welcoming place for young families," Rinaldi said. "There is a fantastic quality of life here for couples who want to settle down in their first home and eventually start a family. There are numerous opportunities for young, single professionals. Sunshine abounds, and the cost of living is very competitive with the rest of the nation."

Sarosky saw several journalists exchanging glances, and a few of the local reporters grinning. Chief Higgins was impassive.

"We will not allow one isolated case to tarnish the image and reputation of Daytona Beach," the mayor continued. "I ask the members of the media—especially those of you from out of town—to be respectful with your coverage, focusing on the facts and supporting law enforcement's efforts to return these three women safely to their homes."

"Geez," Rice whispered under her breath to Sarosky. "That fat Rinaldi cares a lot more about his precious city's public relations than those missing mothers."

Sarosky shrugged. "He's just doing what he's supposed to be doing."

"Yeah, whatever," she said.

"I am now going to introduce Police Chief Higgins to give you some particulars on this case," Rinaldi said, and stepped back as he welcomed the chief up to the microphone.

"Good afternoon," Higgins said. "Here's what we know. At approximately 6:30 p.m. last Thursday evening, Emma O'Rourke, Jackie Solomon, and Kari Blakely departed from Daytona Beach in Mrs. O'Rourke's vehicle. Their destination was Boca Raton, where they planned to stay at another friend's condominium and attend the SunFest music festival in West Palm Beach.

"We've corroborated with family members that the women did arrive at the condo in Boca Raton. However, that was the last time they were heard from, and they did not arrive home as expected this past Sunday afternoon."

Higgins paused, glancing about at the reporters for a moment.

"You'll see that we have put together photographs and information on these three women. Extensive information is on our web site as well, and will be continuously updated as the case unfolds. We will have a minimum of one of these press conferences per week, perhaps more, as we pull out all stops to bring these ladies home.

"We're asking for the public's cooperation: If you think you see one of these women, please notify the authorities immediately. I'm appealing to those of you watching this broadcast both here in Central Florida, as well as residents of Palm Beach County. We will find these women and bring them home safely, but we will need your cooperation in doing so."

The chief paused. "I'll answer a few questions now," he added. The questions erupted like staccato gunfire, and Sarosky and Rice struggled to hear specifics.

"What evidence of foul play have you uncovered thus far?" the reporter from the BCC asked in a loud, British accent.

"No evidence so far," Higgins said.

"Any concerns that Mrs. O'Rourke is the daughter of Mario Lazano?" shouted out a reporter from an Orlando station.

Higgins shrugged. "I'm not sure why a particular parent of one of the victims has any relevance." Sarosky could tell the chief was eager to move on to the next question.

"Doesn't Mr. Lazano have a lot of enemies?" another reporter asked.

"I have no comment on Mr. Lazano. This case is not about Mr. Lazano. Next question, please."

"Do you think it's possible the women ran away from home, so to speak? Sort of an approaching mid-life crisis?" asked a television reporter from Palm Beach County.

"I can't speculate on something like that. We are gathering evidence as to whether there was any indication than any of these three ladies would have purposefully chosen to be out of touch with their loved ones."

36

"Chief, at this time are there any potential suspects?"

Higgins shook his head. "Not at this time."

Sarosky sighed. "I need a cigarette," he whispered to Rice as the press conference continued.

"You need a girlfriend even more," she coolly replied.

Chapter Nine:

MAY 10

M onths earlier, the nine women were seated at a round table in the back of
Delphi's Oracle bookstore, which had closed for the day. They each had their
wine glasses and a copy of Hemingway's famous novel The Sun Also Rises.

"Hemingway was bi-polar. Is that a pre-requisite for being a great writer or
artist?" Jackie asked.

"It seems like most of them are," Kari said. "You might like their stuff, but you'd
never want to hang out with them. And they always kill themselves in the end, or at
least cut off their ears."

Emma cleared her throat, loud enough that several of the women looked at her.

"I don't know if that's true," she said. "I've been friends with some really
interesting, good-hearted artists."

"They might have good hearts, but they're lost," Kari insisted. "They need God in
their lives. They're trying to fill a void with their art."

Beth listened to her friends debate the nature of artists and mental illness, and
then finally spoke. "I think we all need to be on something at some point. We're all a
little lost at times."

"Is that what the quote at the beginning of the book means?" Jackie asked.
"Right here, where Hemingway quotes this lady Gertrude Stein, saying, 'You are all a
lost generation?'"

"I don't know," Beth said, "but there's some timeless truth in the statement."

∼∼∼

The delicate step of Sarosky and Rice interviewing the children took place exactly a week after their mothers departed for Palm Beach County. The detectives made separate visits to the Solomon and Blakely homes, as well as Russ O'Rourke's condominium.

Phil sat close to his daughters Audrey and Natalie in the living room, as Sarosky and Rice gently asked the girls a few open-ended questions about their mother. When asked what each of them admired the most about Jackie Solomon, Audrey said her mother "wasn't afraid to stand up to her own family in South Carolina" about their racist attitudes. Phil smiled as Natalie added, "Yeah, Mommy is a brave person."

Connor Blakely wouldn't make eye contact with Sarosky and Rice, and when he spoke mumbled very short answers to each of their questions. Several times he simply responded with a shrug. Tom grew antsy watching the interview unfold, craving a drink.

It was Pete O'Rourke who gave the detectives the only data point that held some potential in the investigation. "Sometimes she doesn't take her medication, and that makes her a little unpredictable," the teenager said.

Sarosky and Rice responded with several follow-up questions, seeking examples, but Pete was vague. Russ was surprised at his son's statement, and after the detectives left he told Pete "that kind of stuff needs to stay inside the family only."

"Maybe it'll help them find Mom," Pete responded. "What if she's sick? She'd want people to know, so they could help her."

"Maybe," Russ said. "I think she'd be really mad if I'd said that to the police."

"Well, I said it. And I can't take it back now."

"Don't worry about it," Russ said, and wondered if he should tell Mario what his grandson had shared with the detectives.

Later that afternoon, Sarosky and Rice regrouped at the police station.

"Listen to this one they just passed along to me," Rice said, reclining in her desk chair in the office she was sharing with Sarosky. "Someone called in—wishing to remain anonymous, of course—and said they saw the three book club ladies at some Sun Fest concert 'after-party,' living it up with a bunch of musicians. The person says we should send detectives to each of the band's next gigs and see if the women are acting as groupies or roadies."

Sarosky frowned as he sipped his coffee.

"Groupies? What the hell is that?"

Rice laughed. "You've never heard of groupies? Those are the chicks that basically stalk musicians, and sometimes hook up with them."

"Oh, that's what they're called."

"And I hope you know what roadies are?"

"Yeah, I do, but thank you for checking."

"My pleasure." Rice sighed. "We're getting more and more of these crazy tips coming in. It would be nice to get an actual solid lead. Comes with the territory of the media circus. A couple of the really veteran cops here say the media presence hasn't been this intense since the 90s, when they had that prostitute serial killer and that dentist's wife who had a hit man blow away her husband right in his office."

Sarosky reflected for a moment. "We need to keep a steady eye on that Facebook page, and any others that get set up, for the comments that people make. Something could jump out at us. Same with Twitter."

Rice nodded. "Word on that. Listen to what a social media guru you've become, dropping platform names and all."

He smiled. "Do you think we totally dismiss the idea of having a couple of detectives drop in to every SunFest band's next venue, just to take a look backstage?"

"That's a pretty big lineup of bands, and a heck of a lot of different cities across the country. Do you think we could really convince cops in all those places to do that? Feels a little bit like a needle in a haystack approach, especially when you're not sure if the needle even fell out of the box."

Sarosky nodded. "I suppose you're right."

"I usually am."

"Ha," he said. "So, in the meantime, we've got some pretty decent exhaustive efforts to search all potential places where the missing persons might have actually gone. We've got police canvassing the downtown West Palm Beach area, talking to people who ran the festival itself. Of course they're also talking to all of the condo residents in Boca. And they're mobilizing volunteers down there to participate in the canvassing."

"What about all the hospitals?" Rice asked. "There's a bunch in Palm Beach County."

"Yeah, we've got that in motion too, and the morgues."

"And the jails?"

Sarosky raised an eyebrow. "I knew I was forgetting something."

Rice smiled.

"We've got a meeting in a few meetings with the FHP and the FBI," she said. "We're not going to let them wrestle this case away from us, are we?"

"It's a collaboration," Sarosky said, "not a competition. We'll still be more involved than anyone, I'm sure, especially if this drags on indefinitely. With a case this high profile and the kinds of victims involved, we can't expect the state and the feds to not insist on having a piece of the action. We've got multiple counties in which the women traveled and the nationwide database alert. Plus, those FBI guys have pretty spot-on evidentiary procedures."

Rice stood and paced. "Yeah, I know, I know. Just can't stand the smug attitude of some of those feds. They think we're Andy Griffith and Company down here. I mean, we're perfectly capable of collecting those moms' DNA off of their toothbrushes."

"Don't worry about it. Just do great work. That's all we can control."

Beth arrived at the fitness studio that afternoon and went through the motions of setting up for her 5:30 p.m. class. She hadn't been able to reach Delphi. For the first time since launching her business, Beth wished nobody would show up.

She heard the front door open, and forced a smile as she walked into the lobby. That smile faded upon seeing a young man dressed in casual business attire and carrying a notebook.

"Hi, I'm Cameron Brock with the *Orlando Sentinel*."

Beth felt her pulse race. *Fantastic.*

Before Cameron could elaborate on why he was there, Beth quipped, "Are you here to write a feature article on my business? I've sent you guys several press releases, so it's about time." She was surprised at her own sassiness, which felt like a pitiful attempt to distract a reporter who was obviously there for something else.

"Not this time, but I'll make a note of that," Cameron said. "Today, though, I wanted to ask about your missing clients, if you don't mind."

Cameron paused, and waited while Beth stared at him blankly. He continued, "I want to write about who they truly are, with all of their dimensions, and leave out the drama and sensationalism."

"That's very thoughtful," Beth said, as she opened the front door and held it open for him. *Maybe he'll just leave without incident.* "I have no comment, though. Let's let the police do their job."

Cameron moved toward the open door, while still trying to get a conversation flowing. "The police will certainly do their job," he said. "But there's a lot of public interest in this. Those TV vultures, all they want is sound bites they can spin any way they'd like. They're making your friends and their families seem like freaks, and they'll bother you to no end. Why settle for that?"

Beth gestured toward the door. "So far, the only one bothering me is you," she said. "Please respect my wishes and leave."

Cameron gave her a final, hopeful glance, then smiled and went on his way. Beth shut the door and stared out the window, worried that she'd spot an army of news vehicles proceeding into the parking lot. She stood there for several minutes, letting her guard down only when her Tuesday usuals, sans Delphi and the missing trio, showed up ready to sweat.

※

"So far, I haven't heard any media mention that the girls worked out together at your studio," Ben told Beth after she arrived home and informed him about Cameron Brock. Ben sat near Maddie's high chair as their daughter cheerfully used her tiny fingers to eat some carefully cut-up hot dogs with green peas.

"Maybe no one else has figured that out," Beth said, turning up the volume on the TV so she would hear if more news reports were broadcast. Maddie flung a tiny fistful of peas onto Ben's lap. The little girl chortled with delight, and Ben brushed the peas onto the floor and made "big eyes" at Maddie while she giggled even harder. Beth was relieved at the chance to smile; Maddie couldn't resist "big eyes."

The happy diversion didn't last. Beth started crying as she plopped down in the chair on the other side of Maddie. She stroked her daughter's hair. "They would have never met…they would have never gone on this trip…" Her voice trailed off.

"That's crazy," Ben said, a little too quickly and with more admonition in his tone than he'd intended. "You can't control what people do or don't do. That would be like me feeling responsible if some guy walked into one of our stores and had a fatal heart attack."

Beth shook her head, not looking up at him. "It's not the same at all. It was the relationships that led to this. My work with them created a *context for the relationships.* How else would they have possibly met, if not for me?"

She looked at Ben, as if daring her husband to contradict her again. Ben said nothing, and turned his attention back to Maddie before she started throwing food again.

For a few minutes no one spoke except for Maddie. "More!" she demanded, and Ben went to the fridge for another hot dog. Beth was deep in thought, and then glanced up at Ben with hopeful eyes.

"There's got to be something you can do," she said, her speech more rapid.

"With all the people you know across Florida, up and down the coast, especially. There's got to be people you know who can keep an eye out for them, who can ask around."

Ben held back from reacting too quickly, waiting to see if Beth had more to process out loud. He microwaved Maddie's hot dog for about 15 seconds, and then sat back at the table to slice it up while Maggie clapped her hands several times.

"I can give that some thought," Ben said. "Maybe see if the store managers have a spot in the back room where they can place pictures of the three of them, for their employees to see. Maybe…"

Beth cut him off. "Why just the employees? Why not put them in the front of the store, where all the customers can see? The more, the better!"

He nodded, plopping tiny bites of hot dog onto Maddie's tray, the little girl scarfing them up as fast as they landed. "Honey, I get what you're saying, but we're not a post office. We're very limited by corporate with what kinds of things we can do like that."

Beth glared at him. "The hell with corporate. We're taking about three mothers here."

Ben locked eyes with her for a good three seconds, and then simply nodded. Beth went to sit in front of the television, where she stayed for the rest of the evening until falling asleep.

Ben's request of his regional director Paul went better than expected. In fact, it was Paul who suggested the company sponsor a $25,000 reward for anyone who brought the police solid information on the missing book clubbers. Paul ran the concept up the ladder to Ivan the area vice president, who took it to corporate. Ben wasn't privy to all of the conversations happening behind the scenes, but the reward offer quickly became brand-sponsored.

"It's great exposure for the company," Paul noted, something Ben dared not pass on to Beth.

This piece of "good news," if one could call it that, was on Ben's mind as left the mall and drove toward Famoso's. There, he found Tom Blakely blending in with the happy hour crowd at the bar, enjoying a Scotch. Ben gave Tom a quick embrace, and told him about the reward offer from Next Gen.

"I really appreciate it," Tom said. "Any extra incentive out there can only be a good thing." Tom got the attention of the bartender, a handsome Hispanic man in his late 20s who came over to them with a pleasant smile.

"Julio Ramos, this is my friend Ben McBride," Tom said as Ben and Julio shook hands. "Please take good care of him whenever he comes in, on the house. Ben, what would you like?"

Ben glanced at the draught beer area and settled on a simple Coors Lite. He saw Tom drain the rest of his Scotch, and Julio quickly give his boss a refill without Tom needing to ask.

"Shit, I gotta get home soon to Connor," Tom said, glancing at his watch. "I have a neighbor checking on him, but the kid doesn't need to be on his own for too long."

"Hey, bring him over this weekend if you need some time to yourself," Ben offered, hoping Beth wouldn't mind. "Maddie would love a new face to play with."

Tom chuckled. "You'd have your hands full." He reconsidered. "Connor's a great kid. He could do anything, with just a little extra help and the right context." The latest glass of Scotch was already empty, Ben observed.

Julio was nearby, and Tom pulled him back into the conversation.

"This guy's the best bartender in Daytona," Tom said, patting Julio on the hand. "Probably all of Central Florida. He's a real steal. Younger than a lot of his peers around here, but has a great knack for the business and a passion for learning."

Julio shrugged, a little embarrassed. Tom's voice was growing louder, and Julio saw a couple of women smiling at him.

"It's my profession," he said. "Everybody should have one."

"He's damned right," Tom said. "That's the problem with this town: too many transients and not enough professionals. Not enough pride in what people do." Ben saw Julio hesitate before re-filling Tom's glass, and made eye contact with the bartender. The guy was in a tough spot; *how do you tell the owner of the restaurant that he's had enough already?*

"I gotta get home," Tom said, checking his watch and clumsily pulling out his cell phone. He sighed. "Nothing from Kari still. I keep this damned thing on 24-7 now, at the highest volume. Every time it makes a sound, I jump." Tom pointed to the Next Gen branding on the phone. "See, I'm a loyal customer. Even more loyal now. I drop a call now and then, but that happens to everyone."

Ben leaned close to Tom and whispered. "Let me give you a ride home to Connor, and I'll hang out with you guys for a while. I'll bring you back here tomorrow and you can pick up your car."

Tom shook his head, half-embracing Ben again. "You've done enough for me, buddy. Get home to that pretty wife and gorgeous little daughter of yours. I'll be fine." He downed the rest of the latest glass of Scotch.

Ben saw that Julio was busy interacting with customers several barstools away. The overall restaurant was filling up and the din of conversation was escalating.

"It's no problem at all," Ben said, subtly sliding Tom's glass away from him. "Let me drive you. I want to see Connor anyway."

Tom looked at him, and Ben could tell Tom had been half-listening. Tom glanced at his empty glass, and Ben leaned in close again.

"Tom, you don't want to embarrass yourself in front of your employees and customers."

That got Tom's full attention, and their eyes locked for a moment. Ben wondered if Tom was going to tell him to go to hell, but Tom simply nodded.

"I'll be right back," he said, and Ben watched as Tom went and spoke with the Friday evening shift manager.

Julio returned, and Ben leaned close and asked him whether Tom's excessive drinking was the norm. Julio hesitated, and then said, "Only recently. The guy's had a hell of a week."

Ben stood before Tom had a chance to ask for another Scotch, and was touched as Tom gave a warm goodnight to each employee they passed on their way out the door.

A few minutes later, Julio greeted a young man who ordered a glass of Cabernet while flipping through a notebook.

It had been a frustrating week for the journalist Cameron Brock. After getting nowhere talking with Beth McBride, Delphi Adams immediately asked him to leave her bookstore as well. He made a couple of visits to the University of Central Florida's Daytona Beach campus, but there was no sign of Phil Solomon. And the guards at Daytona Development Corp. simply shook their heads without bothering to waste words telling him to get lost.

Newspaper work was a thankless job most of the time, the largest slice of satisfaction resting in one's personal pride. Like many of his peers Cameron wanted to be a published author and dictate his own schedule. He spent too much time at the whim of city editors, and found his mind wasn't challenged enough by his beats as much as when he wrote a larger feature or human interest article. Cameron also longed to be at the main hub in Orlando rather than the Volusia County bureau, which felt like an outpost.

Most of all, Cameron hungered to travel and write about whatever the hell he fancied at any given time. He was captivated by early influences such as *On the Road, The Rum Diary,* and *A Moveable Feast,* along with countless other novels that romanticized the life of the itinerant scribe. Any corporate-esque gig would never fully absolve Cameron of his bohemian disposition.

The crime beat was particularly unsatisfying: all of its sifting through everyone's dirty laundry and interacting with the dregs of society. There were no truly "good people," Cameron was sadly starting to realize; perhaps his parents and his older brother, Josh, were the exceptions. The criminals and their "victims" were equally guilty in one fashion or another, and the cops and lawyers were certainly scumbags. Everyone was playing the same game from different angles, looking for an edge on someone else, and no one possessed any real soul.

Nelson, his romantic partner, might have been one of the few decent human beings as well. A hair stylist in trendy Winter Park, Nelson complained about Cameron being gone for work at night but was sometimes fickle about own his commitment to their relationship. Nelson was uncertain of what he wanted from a partner, a career, or life in general. This didn't make him a bad person, but someone difficult to trust.

The most disturbing aspect of his life was that Cameron questioned his own integrity, his own decency. How did he sleep at night as an interloper into people's messy, private affairs, encroaching upon the privacy of a family's time of mourning or an individual's self-afflicted shame?

Cameron was considering a transfer to the arts and entertainment beat or even sports. Josh Brock wanted his younger brother to be a sportswriter so he could "positively influence all the boneheads" that tried to write about sports without ever being serious athletes themselves. Josh was a high school football star nicknamed "Brock the Jock," and Cameron had written articles about his brother for the school newspaper. His older brother thought Cameron brought sorely needed depth to his description of athletes, and a natural empathy for their psychology and even a nod to mythological nuances. Josh was now a high school English teacher and on staff with the school's football team, living in the disparate worlds of both literature and sports, and was just as popular as ever with everyone around him.

Josh never made fun of Cameron's sexuality, and was his most ardent protector when anyone, male or female, said anything derogatory. The few bullies foolish enough to shove Cameron around paid dearly for it. If Josh had one character flaw it was his temper, but even that was grounded in love and a voracious need to address injustice when he saw it occurring. Josh punched white guys in bars who made snide remarks to his black friends. He beat the crap out of a guy who made fun of a young man with obvious mental challenges. Getting married, having a son of his own, and working in a school mellowed Josh and helped him keep his temper in check. But what had not changed was how much people admired Josh's unfaltering loyalty to family, friends, colleagues, and students.

Cameron wanted to be known for something wholeheartedly good, like Josh, to be viewed as a vital force for positive change. He couldn't see the path yet, nor could he fully come to grips with *why* he carried such a burden of expectations. Nelson was constantly urging him to lighten up and not "overthink" things.

Sitting at the Famoso's bar, Cameron was growing intrigued by Julio—not so much the bartender's looks, which were admirable—but the graceful skill with which Julio moved about. Julio performed a service that people appreciated and wanted, and men and women opened up to him with ease. Once people knew that Cameron was a reporter, most of them put up a wall. A few were fascinated and inquired about things he'd seen and people he'd interviewed, but most got nervous or hostile.

Cameron weighed how to broach the missing women topic with Julio. Bartenders could be incredible sources, given their knack for observing the dynamics around them with a savvy grasp on human nature. They'd "heard it all and seen it all," and while the best never claimed to *know* it all they were quick studies on a patron's intentions and needs.

It was probably best, Cameron pondered, to not get into journalist mode with Julio quite yet. He had to build trust, and Julio needed to like Cameron for simply being *Cameron* before offering any insights about Tom Blakely. Cameron wasn't looking for sensational quotes, but the opportunity to tactfully delve into the psychology of a husband suddenly missing his spouse and mother of his child.

"Ready for a re-fill?" Julio asked. "Haven't seen you here before. How's your week been?"

Cameron hesitated, wanting to sound interesting and internally chastising himself for such narcissism.

"I'm trying to figure out whether I changed the world or not," he responded, grinning. "It still looks about the same to me."

Julio chuckled, wiping down the bar with a cloth. "When you figure out how to do that, let me know," he said. "Sometimes I forget there's even a bigger world out there."

"You get the world brought to you every night," Cameron said. "A little slice of it from everyone."

"That's a good way to put it," Julio said. "Some slices I could do without."

"I'm sure."

"Still," Julio pondered, glancing about. "I think some people are just lost, buried under too much of life's rubble."

Cameron nodded. "That's pretty deep, barkeep."

"I have my moments."

Cameron was grateful for each passing second that Julio didn't inquire about what he did for a living. The best bartenders didn't pry too much about someone's personal or professional life, waiting for what was offered by their customers. Cameron left a short while later, deciding that patience was his best strategy.

〜

Ben was exhausted and troubled as he pulled out of Tom's driveway, having safely delivered his inebriated friend back to his home. Connor was reserved around Ben, polite enough to say hello but nothing beyond that.

He struggled to not judge Tom. What the hell would he do without Beth, and what kind of a single father would he be to Maddie? How would he take care of his work? Ben wondered how Phil was doing tonight, and made a mental note to check on him first thing tomorrow.

Ben began to plan his Thursday morning as he drove. He needed to pick up Tom and take him back to the restaurant to get his car, once Tom had slept off the booze. After that, perhaps Ben would stop by the Solomon house to check on Phil and the girls. There was also a struggling store manager whom Ben really needed to observe for a little, but that might have to wait a day.

He finally pulled into his own driveway, feeling guilty for arriving home so late. Beth didn't seem upset when he called her from the road; in fact, the complete lack of emotion in her voice unnerved him. The last day or two Beth had evolved from almost manic behavior about her missing clients, to a resigned state of withdrawal.

It was past Maddie's bedtime, and Ben opened the front door as quietly as possible. The lights were dim throughout the house. He walked toward Maddie's bedroom, saw the door was slightly cracked open, and peered inside. It took him a few seconds to adjust his eyes to the dark. Beth sat in the rocking chair, holding a sleeping Maddie and trying to stifle tears to avoid waking her up.

Ben started to approach his wife, and then hesitated. Instead he tiptoed away to the master bedroom and changed into casual clothes. He washed his hands and face, staring into the mirror at his reddened eyes. There were a few more gray hairs that had popped up during the past week. Ben flossed and brushed his teeth, and settled into bed with the television on low volume while waiting for Beth. He channel surfed, flipping past news broadcasts, infomercials, and a wide variety of movies. Nothing caught Ben's interest, and he left the television on one of the local news channels.

After a while, Ben got up to peer through Maddie's doorway once again. Beth was now asleep as well, the rocking chair still. He watched them for a moment, and then went back to bed and fell asleep.

Chapter Eleven:

JUNE 1

Vanessa Porter was referred to Phil by one of his professor peers, as a family therapist known to connect well with both parents and their children. Phil procrastinated making the appointment, but now that a month had passed since Jackie's disappearance he was desperate for any help in coping with the situation.

When Vanessa introduced herself, Phil was surprised by her relative youth. She was a dark-haired, petite woman whose smile and lack of pretense immediately helped increase Phil's confidence that he'd made the right decision. Phil had feared that therapy would involve some kind of lecture from a stern authority figure; he'd had enough of those from his Jewish grandmothers.

Vanessa asked about Phil's daughters and he gave her a general description of Audrey, who was almost 14, and Natalie, who had recently turned 11. They'd both been surprisingly calm since their mom left, Phil noted, perhaps too calm. Were they suppressing a powerful cocktail of grief, fear, and anger that might suddenly spill out on a moment's notice? Vanessa asked if Phil would be willing to bring the children to a subsequent session, and he agreed.

Phil told Vanessa about Jackie: how they'd met; how long they'd been married; her professional background; her special touch as a mother; her sense of humor; and her rediscovered passion for reading and fitness. Phil found it much easier to talk about Jackie and the girls than about himself, and was naively hoping Vanessa would save questions about him until the next session. But after jotting down lots of specifics on the three most important people in Phil's life, Vanessa asked, "Tell me more about what you're feeling these days."

"I feel a constant sense that I should be doing something," Phil said, staring at Vanessa's glass coffee table before him. "Even when the kitchen is cleaned and the girls have what they need for school the next day, it's impossible to relax. When I go to pick up a book or magazine for simple pleasure reading, I feel guilty; same with watching a movie. It's like the idea of enriching my life is on hold, and that God has pushed a giant pause button until I can find Jackie and bring her home."

Vanessa jotted down a few notes and waited to see if Phil had more to say.

"Has anyone else said or done something that helps you to feel that way?" she asked.

Phil reflected on recent interactions with Audrey, Natalie, and his parents. "No. No one else is telling me I shouldn't read a book or watch a movie." Phil smiled sheepishly, and Vanessa laughed.

He continued, "Perhaps, subconsciously, I don't see the *point*. Why take my mind or heart to new places that I can't share with Jackie? What's the point in learning or laughing? It just feels like I'm going through the motions."

"And maybe that's okay right now."

"Maybe."

Vanessa allowed for silence, and then inquired, "What would be some of the benefits of doing some reading, or going out and doing an activity that you've enjoyed in the past?"

Phil considered this. "A healthy distraction, perhaps," he said. "Maybe some kind of new insight I'm not expecting. Something that might help things to not feel so hopeless."

"I want to encourage you," Vanessa began, "to start making some simple plans. You'll know best what the plans are. But write some things down. Jot down some things you want to do proactively, to help you feel like you're not just reacting to what life has given you."

It made sense. Where was it mandated that a person had to completely give up on anything but the core duties of life when tragedy—even open-ended tragedy—made an unexpected calling?

But as Phil drove home, he'd no idea what to "jot down" first.

Chapter Twelve

JUNE 2

For Russ O'Rourke, life had become a giant pain in the ass since his ex-wife Emma took off for Palm Beach County and never returned.

He loved his son Pete, but the 14-year-old was a complete slob and his behavior was pushing Russ to the brink. A bachelor for a few years at this point, Russ was used to living in simple neatness and could manage Pete for a week at a time. But what had been a normal week had now turned into a month, with no end in sight.

Russ stood in the middle of his kitchen and stared at the mess, feeling his anger rising as he observed dirty dishes and cups just strewn about the counter and sink. There was a small puddle of milk on the floor near the refrigerator. Inside the fridge itself, there were half-drunk cans of soda and leftovers in Tupperware with the lids halfway off.

Pete's bathroom was even worse, with toothpaste remnants covering the sink and big streaks of gross on the mirror, and Russ was scared to look inside the toilet. He'd avoided Pete's bedroom altogether for nearly two weeks, dreading that it was an epicenter of hopeless sloth.

Russ poured a cup of coffee, trying to get out the door to work. It was Saturday, but he needed to go into the office for a few hours and follow up on some things. Since it was only 9 a.m. on a non-school day, Russ was surprised when Pete stumbled into the kitchen, barely acknowledging his father as he opened the refrigerator. Pete took a big swig from a carton of milk, and made a half-hearted attempt to screw the cap back on before returning it to the shelf. Unable to avert his eyes, Russ saw a couple more milk droplets hit the floor and waited for Pete to do something about it.

Pete simply turned to head back to his room, and Russ slammed down his coffee cup. Pete jumped.

"Pete, what's the name of our maid? I can't seem to recall; it's Rosie or Rosalina or Veronica or something like that, right?" Russ was trying to smile, but his teeth were clenched. Pete looked blankly at him.

"What?" the kid asked.

"The name of our maid. Do you remember her name?"

"Dad, whatever. We don't have a maid."

"Exactly. Which means I have to clean up every goddamned drop of milk that you leave behind, and everything else. You catch my drift?"

Pete stared at the kitchen floor. "Oh," he said, "I'll clean that stuff up. I've just been kind of busy."

Russ folded his arms. "Busy, huh? Must be tough to balance going to school, working a job you don't have, and taking care of all the dogs and cats we don't have. All while finding time to bodysurf."

"Dude, chillax!" Pete said. "All you do is get on my case these days!"

It was the wrong thing to say, and Russ got in his son's face. The kid was still a couple of inches shorter than Russ and remained on the skinny side; Russ retained the upper hand, for now.

"Listen to me, Pete," he said in as controlled a voice as possible, trying to ignore the stink of his son's morning breath. "You're not a little child anymore. I need you to pick up around here at least as much as I do. We can make this work, but you've got to do your part. If I'm on your case, it's cause you're not pitching in. Understood?" Russ glared down at him, waiting.

Pete stared at him defiantly for the longest time, and then finally mumbled, "Understood." He walked briskly to the door that led to the garage, and disappeared for a minute. Russ watched with a mixture of amusement and annoyance as Pete returned with a mop and a bucket and began clumsily filling the bucket with water. Pete grabbed the liquid hand soap and squirted some into the bucket, and used his hand to swirl the mixture around. He then slammed the faucet shut, set the bucket on the floor, and plunged the mop inside of it.

"You might want to step out of the kitchen for a minute, Dad," Pete said to Russ with mock politeness. "I'm gonna do the whole floor, and I don't want you to slip."

Russ headed into the living room to grab his briefcase, and left without saying goodbye. If Russ came home to a bucket of dirty mop water, young Pete O'Rourke might need to find himself a foster family before the weekend was over.

He climbed inside of his car and caught a view of himself in the rearview mirror.

"You're an ass, Russ," he whispered.

Chapter Thirteen:

JUNE 4

Mario sighed as he gently rolled off of Delphi and pulled her close next to him.

"Darling, can I get you a glass of water or something?" he asked her.

Delphi stared into the darkness of Mario's bedroom as she pressed the right side of her face onto his chest hair. "I'm fine," she said.

"You seem more quiet than usual."

Delphi waited a few seconds, and then slid onto her back and rested her head against the pillow.

"I'm worried that you blame me."

Mario glanced over at her, softly caressing her cheek until she glanced at him and then quickly looked away again.

"For Emma?"

"Yes."

"Why would you think that?"

"She was at my place when it happened. I befriended her, and invited her to the book club. I put her in the position to be victimized by whoever did this."

Mario sighed. "Don't you remember that I encouraged you to befriend her, that she needed to start having a life again and make some new friends?"

Delphi shrugged. "I guess so."

"If anyone around here is to blame for anything, it's me," he said. "But there's no one truly to blame except for whoever caused my daughter and her lovely friends to disappear."

He leaned over and kissed her on the forehead.

"Can you accept that?"

Delphi took a deep breath, and smiled at him. "I'll work on it."

"Good," he said, and rolled onto his side so he could press against her. "Now I think we should get some sleep. I'm an old man, remember?"

"Hah," Delphi said, rubbing his arm. "You sure don't act like one while we're in bed."

Chapter Fourteen:

JUNE 5

Around 7 a.m., Ben drove into the Daytona Beach Police Department parking lot. He spotted Sarosky's parked car, and pulled into a visitor's spot.

The receptionist looked at him in surprise as Ben strolled up to the glass-plated window.

"I just got here," she said, grumpily. "You must really need some help."

Ben smiled. "My name is Ben McBride. I was hoping to see Det. Sarosky."

"I'll let him know," she said, and Ben wandered over to the reception area to wait.

A couple of minutes later Sarosky came out, a cup of coffee in one hand.

"You're up bright and early, Mr. McBride," Sarosky said. "How did you know I was even here?"

"I recognized your car."

"That's a little creepy," Sarosky said. "Good thing you're not a creepy guy in general. Come on back."

"I have an idea that could help the investigation," Ben said as they ambled back to Sarosky's office. Rice wasn't in yet, and Ben noticed that her desk was cluttered with framed photos of at least three different cats. "I wanted to run it by you and see what you thought."

"Great," Sarosky said. "Care for some coffee?"

"I'm good, thank you."

"Okay. What's your idea?"

"Well, you already know about the $25,000 reward my company's sponsored," Ben began.

Sarosky nodded. "I do."

"I have additional thoughts," Ben continued. "I have a huge network of store employees up and down the east coast of Florida: corporate employees, and employees who work for our dealer stores that sell our products exclusively. We've already got missing persons' fliers in all of those stores, but I'm thinking we can give every employee a handful of fliers to give to businesses they frequent. As this multiples we could have thousands of people at hundreds of establishments keeping an eye out for these three women."

Sarosky nodded, thinking through the proposal. "It sounds good," he said. "And your supervisors would be okay with this?"

"It's just an extension of what we're already doing," Ben said. "My company always wants to be of service to the community. And I'll do anything I can to help my wife's friends get back home safely."

"They're lucky to have you."

Ben shrugged. "We'll see."

"So what do you need from me to aid in this effort?"

"I'd like to get the fliers delivered as quickly as possible, but it's a lot of stores for me to cover. I was hoping we could mobilize a volunteer in each neighborhood across the state to be responsible for bringing the flyers to the employees."

"Sounds ambitious."

Ben smiled. "Too ambitious?"

Sarosky shrugged. "Nah. And I have the feeling that even if I said no, you'd find a way to talk me into it." The detective paused. "You're just that good."

Beth took a few deep breaths before getting out of her car and unlocking the fitness studio. She was irritated; Ben was giving her a hard time about how often she was online checking for updates on her missing friends, and how much she communicated with Delphi. When her husband had the audacity to suggest that the two of them "were simply amplifying each other's anxiety," Beth uncharacteristically shot him the middle finger right in front of Maddie. "ONE!" the little girl responded with innocent joy.

As Beth set up for her first class, Dephi herself arrived surprisingly early and they hugged. *She looks like she's gained at least 10 pounds,* Beth thought, and then felt ashamed for doing so.

"How's the store doing?" Beth asked as she helped Delphi get set up on a bike.

"A little too good right now," Delphi said. "People are exercising their morbid curiosity. The press has finally figured out that I'm not going to talk about my friends or the case or anything besides books and book sales. I have a lot of creeps coming by, and people have even posed for pictures in the back room where we used to meet."

"Seriously? Why?"

"You know, some voyeuristic way of feeling connected to the missing mothers and the scene of the crime."

Beth's nostrils flared. "It's not a crime scene!"

"Yeah, but people see it as some kind of shrine to the missing. The hallowed space where we all sat and talked about books and drank wine. Shit, I should start selling admission tickets to that part of the store."

Beth rubbed Delphi's shoulder. "It'll pass, all this craziness. In a way, it's sad that it will pass. People will move on. The press will move on."

"But none of us can move on, until they come home."

"Yeah."

Delphi took a sip from her water bottle. "Well, I'm eager to work out and burn off some of this stress. And well as burn off some of my spreading ass." They laughed.

The studio front door opened, and Beth turned to see which customer had arrived. She screamed before she could stop herself. *It was Emma.*

"Beth, what on Earth!" Delphi responded.

The next moment, Beth realized it wasn't Emma at all as she stared at the perplexed woman before them. Although there was some resemblance to their missing friend, the woman's face was a bit gentler than Emma's and her hair lighter.

"I'm so sorry," Beth said as she approached the woman. "You look like someone I know."

The woman smiled. "No worries. Are you Beth?"

"Yes. Welcome."

"Thanks. I'm Naomi. Am I too early for the class?"

Beth shook her head. "Not at all. Come on in, I'll help you get set up."

The rest of the class trickled in and Beth got started. She noticed that Naomi grasped the routine fairly easily while Delphi was struggling to keep up, seeming devoid of drive and energy. Beth caught herself glancing toward the front door several times during class, an annoying habit she couldn't seem to kick.

Chapter Fifteen:

JUNE 16

Sarosky had finally fallen asleep when his cell phone rang. He groaned and reached over to his nightstand to see who the hell was calling just before midnight. Maybe it was Rice, having had a brainstorm that couldn't wait until morning.

Ben McBride.

"This is Sarosky."

"Detective, it's Ben McBride. I'm sorry to call so late, but I just thought of something."

Sarosky paused, waiting, and then finally responded. "And what is that, Ben?"

"Do you think it would be all right if I stopped by to talk to you about it in person?"

Sarosky sat up, caught off guard by the question.

"I don't think that's a good idea, Ben. We can meet at the station or for coffee tomorrow, or you can just tell me what's on your mind."

Ben paused. "Are you sure?"

"Yeah. I'm a very private person when it comes to my home life, Ben. Most cops are. I'm sure you understand that."

"Yes, I do. I apologize," Ben said. "Okay, let me try to put my thoughts together."

"Okay, take your time." Sarosky rubbed his eyes and waited. He needed to take a piss now that he was suddenly awake.

"I think this is a potential lead that no one is considering," Ben began. "It's a longshot, but in my opinion everything is on the table right now."

"Go on," Sarosky replied.

"What if they never actually made it to that condo in Boca? What if they were intercepted along the way, by someone who knew where they were going? Who even went so far as to put their stuff into the condo, and find a way to spread their fingerprints throughout the place?"

Sarosky reflected upon this. Spread the fingerprints? He really had to piss.

"Can you give me a minute to take a leak?"

"Uh, sure."

"Thanks."

Ben waited, holding his cell phone against his ear, relaxing on the living room couch. Beth and Maddie were sound asleep.

"I'm back," Sarosky said. "Sorry about that."

"All good," Ben said. "So what are your thoughts?"

"It's not totally implausible. Whoever 'intercepted' them would have had to know about the condo address, somehow. Perhaps it was on a piece of paper, or in a GPS, or in one of the ladies' cell phones. Then, there's the matter of how Mrs. Solomon and Mrs. Blakely texted home that first night. But I suppose anyone could have sent those texts, pretending to be the women."

"Exactly," Ben said, feeling relieved that Sarosky was taking him seriously.

"The challenge," Sarosky continued, "is finding any evidence that they were stopped along the way. The texts sent later that night are consistent with a reasonable time frame of someone driving from Daytona Beach to that particular location in Boca; as opposed to hours later. So, if they were intercepted and abducted, the abduction didn't take very long."

"And your peers have checked hospitals, morgues, and all those places along the way from here to South Florida?"

"Yes sir," Sarosky said. "This is a very high profile case. Every law enforcement agency that can smell blood is involved."

Sarosky paused. "Sorry, that was in poor taste."

Ben was too busy brainstorming additional theories to even absorb the remark. "Do you think, perhaps, that they never even left town? That they could be holed up somewhere around here, and someone else drove Emma's car down there with all of their stuff?"

"Who would want to keep them hostage here?"

"Who would want to keep them hostage anywhere, Detective?"

Sarosky chuckled. "That's the $25,000 reward question, courtesy of your philanthropic employer. I gotta get some sleep now, Ben. See you soon, I assume?"

Ben yawned. "You sure will."

〜〜

Julio Ramos loved his job, his co-workers, and the customers he served. The situation was almost perfect, with one glaring intangible: Tom Blakely, and whether he could continue to run a busy restaurant.

Now 28, Julio had left South Florida two years earlier to get a fresh start. He'd made the mistake of sticking around Deerfield Beach after finishing a history degree at Florida Atlantic University, and no one was hiring history majors into well-paying jobs. His mother Esmeralda was thrilled that he'd finished college, the first of anyone in the family to do so; but the rush of walking across that stage quickly wore off as Julio needed sustainable income.

One friend after another let Julio down, pulling him into doomed business ventures, until Julio took ownership and moved to Daytona to temporarily live with his grandmother Celia. He held two jobs at different restaurants, learning bartending on the fly, and soon saved enough for an apartment deposit. A new environment helped Julio tap into the strong work ethic that was instilled by Esmeralda, who had raised Julio and his sister Juanita with little help after the children's father died when Julio was just eight.

One of those restaurants was Famoso's. Tom had quickly noticed something he liked in the young man, and gave him additional responsibilities behind the bar. Julio parlayed his college skill at memorizing big chunks of historical knowledge into memorizing and applying the professional bartender's famous "little black book."

Tom paid to send Julio to a couple of bartending courses, made sure he got the necessary licenses and certifications, and invited him to the Blakely house for dinner a couple of times. During slow periods at the restaurant, the two would talk casually about Tom's entrepreneurial journey and what it took to acquire and successfully operate a business. In his mind, Julio began sketching the early foundations of a future business plan.

Then tragedy struck Tom a little more than a month ago, and Julio began to see his boss's social drinking in a new light.

"I don't really want Kari to come back," Tom mumbled to Julio one night. "And I feel like shit about that."

Kari seemed nice enough during Julio's visits to the Blakely home. She was talkative, but Julio was used to people going on and on about nothing particularly interesting. Kari especially liked to tell whomever would listen about how much she was working out and how much weight she'd lost. It also seemed like Mrs. Blakely was shopping more frequently for tighter fitting, shoulder-baring, and neckline-exposing clothing. Julio liked their son Connor a lot, and enjoyed the times when the kid would come to work with his father and sit at the bar and sketch. Connor had an unquenchable thirst for Mountain Dew, and Julio kept his glass full.

Julio looked over now at a nearby booth where Tom sat with the journalist Cameron Brock, whom Julio had befriended in recent weeks. Until now, Cameron hadn't secured an interview with any of the family members, and had asked Julio to consider intervening on his behalf.

The bartender thought about it for a couple of days, and then agreed to help Cameron. Julio hoped a well-written, in-depth article would prompt individuals across the state to get resilient in helping to find Mrs. Blakely and the other two women. The closer to home and real the mothers felt to readers, the stronger the pressure that might be exacted upon law enforcement officials to pull out all the stops.

When Julio raised the interview idea with Tom, he expected his boss to decline. Tom simply shrugged. "Why not," he said, well into his third cocktail.

Even though he'd grown to trust Cameron, Julio was protective of Tom and didn't want anything in the pending article about the drinking. He debated whether to proactively say something to Cameron, considering whether that would make it worse by drawing attention to something that Cameron might not notice or care about. But what if Tom downed three or four drinks during the interview itself and started slurring his words?

"Tom's doing the best he can," Julio finally said to Cameron the previous evening. "But he drinks more than he probably should. Maybe leave that out of the article?" Julio waited. Cameron simply nodded, and that was that.

Tom and Cameron spoke quietly. Tom had a Scotch, but was taking his time with it. It was 4 p.m. and the restaurant was quiet.

An attractive brunette plopped onto a bar stool. Julio gave her his full attention for the next 15 minutes, long enough to that learn her name was Susannah and that she was single.

Chapter Sixteen:

JUNE 17

James Thorne, 21, looked up from his desk as he heard his name being called out. The economics class was in the middle of an essay exam, and James had been deeply focused on a particular paragraph. His professor was standing by the classroom door with another man. The newcomer was well-dressed and clean-cut, and motioned James over.

"James, we're very sorry to interrupt," the man said to him. "Could I see you outside for a few minutes, please?"

James glanced at the professor, Dr. Rodgers, who nodded. He went back to his desk, folded his essay book, and handed it to Dr. Rodgers. Most of the other class members had looked up at least momentarily to see what was taking place.

"You can make this up later, James," the professor whispered to him, patting him on the shoulder with a somber expression on his face.

"Thanks," James said, utterly perplexed.

"I'm Bernard Walker, the assistant dean of student affairs," the well-dressed man said, shaking James's hand as they walked. "Let's head out to the courtyard if you don't mind. We've got to talk about some things."

James felt his heart starting to race. "Am I in trouble for something?"

"No, not at all, James," Bernard said. "Let's go sit over here, shall we?"

Bernard gestured to a bench in the courtyard. There were no other students milling about at the moment. They sat down on the bench together, Bernard leaning forward and looking closely at James.

"Are Gerald and Rebecca Thorne your parents?" Bernard asked softly.

James nodded. "Yes. Why?"

Bernard swallowed hard.

"I'm afraid I have some tragic news, James," he said. "We've received word that your parents have died in a car accident back home in Syracuse."

Bernard stopped talking, simply looking at James. James stared back at him, processing, trying to detect any hint in the man's face that he was kidding around. James tried to reply, but his throat closed up.

"I'm so sorry," Bernard added, resting a hand on James's shoulder as he saw the college senior's eyes fill with tears.

"Are...are you sure it was them?" James asked.

Bernard nodded. "Yes. I'm so sorry."

The tears flowed down James's cheeks. He rested his face in his hands as Bernard continued to comfort him.

Curtis Everett sat in the empty chapel on the ranch property, attempting to focus on his breathing. He'd lost track of time, the world reduced to only the counting of his breaths, and then was jolted out of his meditation as he felt his scar twitch.

Curtis often couldn't fully distinguish between his emotional and physical awareness of the scar. He reached down and started to scratch at it, and then pulled his hand away. The twitching intensified, and he yielded and gave it a good scratch, feeling his nails scrape along the fabric of his jeans.

The worn, old school photograph album was resting next to him on the bench. It was the only possession Curtis still carried with him from his old life, but he hadn't leafed through it in years. That morning, something prompted him to grab it from a drawer in his private cabin and carry it with him across the grounds of the ranch.

Curtis stared down at it, and randomly opened the album to a spot near the middle. He felt his breathing quicken as long-gone faces of family members and friends jumped out at him, frozen in time. Curtis flipped to the end of the album, where several pages remained unfilled. He wished he'd taken more pictures, not just of his family but of the woman he'd loved and then lost just before he received the scar.

The sound of the chapel door slowly opening pulled Curtis out of the album and his thoughts. Dan Ferguson approached, still limping a bit after his most recent mini-stroke, smiling and sitting down next to Curtis.

Dan gestured to the album.

"Reminiscing?"

"Just a little."

"That's not like you," Dan said. "At least not anymore."

Curtis shrugged. "I guess I'm still evolving."

"That never stops. But you've come a long way since I first found you."

"I hope so."

Dan held out his hands, his face questioning, and Curtis handed him the photo album. The older man slowly and respectfully looked through it, starting at the beginning, smiling as he saw pictures of a teenaged Curtis and pausing at certain pictures as if to fully absorb them.

"Your family had very kind eyes," Dan said.

Curtis nodded. "They were kind people."

Chapter Seventeen:

The then-13-year-old Nicky Ferrante wasn't sure how long he'd been asleep when he heard the sound of crying—actually, wailing—somewhere in the house. He stumbled out of his bedroom and found his mother Robin in the kitchen, his Aunt Josephina's arms wrapped around her. Two other men whom Nicky recognized from his dad's work were there also.

Nicky's younger sister Abby, eight, came stumbling out of her own bedroom, rubbing her eyes. She pressed up close to Nicky, putting her arm around his waist.

"What's happening?" Abby whispered.

"I don't know," he told her. "But shh. I'm trying to listen."

"Okay."

The men noticed the siblings first, then Aunt Josephina, and finally their mother. Robin Ferrante stared at her children with sad, red eyes, then held out her arms. Nicky stumbled into her grasp, followed quickly by Abby, neither of them fully understanding the situation. Nicky had the fleeting thought, "Where's Dad?"

"We'll give you two ladies some time alone with the children," one of the men said, and motioned for the other to follow him out to the living room.

"Kids, you'd better sit down," Aunt Josephina said, pulling a couple of chairs back from the small kitchen dinette. Nicky sat down, and before Abby could sit her aunt gave her a tight bear hug.

Robin was furiously wiping tears from her eyes as she sat down. She stared at the table, trying as long as possible to delay telling her children what needed to be said.

"It's your father," she finally said. "He's gone to heaven, just like your Grandpa Sal."

Nicky stared at his mother, his jaw dropping. Dad wasn't even sick, he thought. Was his mother joking? Abby seemed to accept the reality quicker, letting out a loud cry and burying her face in Aunt Josephina's shoulder.

"What happened to him?" Nicky asked.

Robin shook her head. "It doesn't matter. It doesn't matter. What's done is done."

Nicky still wasn't crying. He was too angry.

"What do you mean it doesn't matter? Of course it matters! What happened to my father?"

"Nicky, please!" Aunt Josephina said, resting her hand on his. "Your mother is in shock. She just lost her husband. Just take a deep breath."

Nicky paused at Josephina's words. She was always his favorite aunt, and he respected her.

"I'm sorry," Robin said, her voice choking, unable to look Nicky in the eye now. "I'm so sorry he did this to you. I'm so sorry he did this to us."

"Robin, that's enough for now," Josephina said. "Let's just comfort each other. We can talk about details another time."

Nicky stared into space, trying to think of the last time he saw his father and what they'd talked about. It was before school the previous day. His father hadn't come home for dinner at all last night, which was not unusual.

Especially, it seemed, on Thursdays.

Chapter Eighteen:

JUNE 18

Henry Reid stared at the dark blue hat he'd worn as a rookie cop in Brooklyn. He'd taken good care of it, allowing it to remain untarnished. After a moment Henry sat the hat back inside his desk drawer and helped himself to another cup of coffee, glancing out at his men in the cubicles while waiting for Mario to summon him.

On Henry's office wall hung a photo collage of his numerous nieces and nephews. Henry smiled. Those little faces were the lights of his life. They all lived up north except for his youngest sister Casey and her family, who moved to Ft. Myers a while back. Henry was always invited there for the high holidays and birthday parties, and spending time with family was a welcome respite from the bland, humorless life he faced each day.

If one of those nieces or nephews disappeared, Henry would move heaven and hell to find them. He felt his blood pressure rising at merely the hypothetical notion of such an incident. The perpetrators would become the most sorrowful folks on the planet, for they would have messed with the wrong uncle.

Henry heard Mario's footsteps and his boss appeared in the doorway. He noted Henry looking at the pictures and paused to appreciate them as well.

"You should invite them all here sometime," Mario said. "I'll throw them a big party. We'll get bounce houses, slip and slides, all that nonsense."

"They'd love that, I'm sure." Henry followed Mario into the boss's office and shut the door.

Mario looked at his own framed photograph of Emma on his desk.

"It's time," Mario said.

Henry pondered things for a moment. "Do you have any particular suspicions?"

Mario shrugged. "It's a short list, I think. I've been trying for weeks to discern motive and ambition. Then there's the so-called ransom letter, which could be a fake."

Seeing Henry raise his eyebrows at this news, Mario reached into his pocket for a key and unlocked a desk drawer. He retrieved an envelope with professional-looking typeface indicating Mario's name and business address. There was no return address. Henry put on his reading glasses in order to make out the circular stamp in the right-hand upper corner indicating the post office from where the item had originated. He studied the envelope a while longer, and then pulled out a letter bearing multiple creases.

Mario waited while Henry read through the typewritten letter a few times. "Well?"

Henry scratched his head, leaning back in his chair. "I think it's a false trail. They might want what they're asking for, but there's more to it."

"There's always more to it."

"They think you're stupid enough to just send me there, like some sitting duck errand boy."

"Let them think that." Mario glanced down at Emma's photo once again. "I've had to accept the likelihood that this isn't Emma's choice. For a while I wondered if she sent the letter. But then I look into my grandson Pete's eyes, and I can't imagine his mother just leaving him behind."

Henry waited. Mario had more to say.

"But she's not always well, my daughter. You catch her on a high, and everything's great: I'm the best dad in the world, Pete is the reason the sun comes up in the morning, and Russ is not such an annoying ass after all. You catch her on a low, and the sky is falling so rapidly that no one is safe."

Henry processed all of this, considering the alternative possibilities to which Mario was alluding.

"I think the best step," Mario began, "is for you to take a couple of men with you, and head down south and take a look around once again. Carefully."

Henry nodded. "If that's what you want."

"You sound a bit skeptical."

"No, I don't mean any disrespect. I just think we're clutching at straws."

"Yeah."

Henry put his glasses away. "What are you gonna tell Russ? He's gonna want to come with me, and I don't need that kind of distraction. He should stay in his lane."

"Agreed. I'll deal with Russ. I've got plenty of work for him to do around here, and I'll keep him close to me so he feels involved."

"You've fully vetted him? He's clean?"

Mario nodded. "I'm convinced beyond a shadow of a doubt that my former son-in-law had nothing to do with this." He paused. "As of right now, he might be the only person in the world whom I'm certain is innocent."

Henry raised his eyebrows again, and Mario smiled.

"Present company excluded."

Mario stood and gave Henry a hearty handshake and pat on the shoulder. "Be careful down there, and keep me posted. Use those throw away cell phones that no one can trace."

Henry chuckled. "You got any other advice, boss? Should I avoid using my corporate credit card as well?"

Mario laughed. "Always a wise guy. I'm very lucky to have you."

"I'll remember that when it's time for a raise."

"There'll be a hell of a bonus if you find my daughter and her friends."

"I'll hold you to that."

Mario watched as Henry approached the cubicles and summoned a couple of the guys to follow him into his office. He made a mental note to spend some quality time with Pete in the next couple of days. He also needed to call his ex-wife Carmen and give her some kind of update, something to keep her from continuing to call him several times per day asking if there was any news on their daughter.

Carmen's attitude toward Mario had thawed considerably across the years. Perhaps Mario's two subsequent divorces had evoked some sympathy. For years Carmen was bitter about their break-up and the affairs that led to it. When Emma divorced Russ, Carmen told Mario that he'd "failed to model positive adult relationships" for their daughter. Carmen backed off from this once Emma advised her parents that the failure of her own marriage was hers and Russ's alone.

Mario sometimes considered selling Daytona Development Corp. and moving to another state or even a different country. He'd heard great things about Ecuador and was planning to visit. Although he'd relished the spotlight for the longest time, especially with a beautiful woman draped on his arm, Mario was tired of stress and wanted a more quiet existence. Sometimes he grew discouraged when considering how many people—whether family; former friends; the government; the police; or those who had become his enemies—were motivated to deprive him of any lasting peace. But in the end Mario had to embrace life and not fear what trouble might show up on his doorstep.

Emma's disappearance had obviously halted any big plans for the moment.

Divestitures, consolidations, and explorations of South American countries would have to wait.

Mario considered whether to tell Carmen his concerns that Emma might have harmed herself and her friends. Carmen was constantly harassing Emma about staying on her medication, and worried about Pete inheriting his mother's psychosomatic issues.

He wished he still had his own parents around to talk with about Emma. They'd known little about his specific business dealings during their sunset years, simply proud that their first generation was successful in real estate. The elder Lazanos stayed in Miami after relocating there from New York before Mario was born. Back then, Miami was far from the over-crowded, over-commercialized hub it resembled today. Each time Mario visited his parents the traffic was worse, the driving was worse, and the culture in general was more transient. Mario had never wanted to learn Spanish, and got pissed when driving around certain Miami neighborhoods where all the signage was in that language.

Mario's parents had two more sons and two daughters after Mario was born, and their childhood was characterized by picnics on beaches that were easy and cheap to access. Their street was a mixture of good-natured Miami natives and other relocated New Yorkers, and dinner parties and occasional street festivals were the norm. Mario always felt like he had several sets of parents looking out for him. Mario wasn't a bad kid but if he cut school or committed some minor vandalism with his friends he was sure to get caught, because there were so many pairs of adult eyes watching.

Both of Mario's brothers left Florida decades ago, one finding joy in Colorado and the other building a thriving insurance business in San Diego. His sisters remained in Miami, caring for their parents while raising families of their own. Like his parents, Mario's siblings knew little about the details of what he did but were always grateful for the wonderful birthday and Christmas presents that showed up in the mail without fail.

Mario's cell phone starting vibrating. It was one of those sunscreen models. Mario let it go to voicemail, and then the caller—whose name was Heather—texted and asked if he needed a drink. When *didn't* he need a drink? He replied, *Yes.* Another text came in a minute later, and Mario assumed it was Heather.

Delphi. Again. Mario had been trying to gently ease her out of his life. He'd not responded to Delphi's last several texts.

Chapter Nineteen

JUNE 19

W*ow, you made a lot of money today, James,"* Uncle Everett said as they sat at the kitchen table in James's parents' house—now James's house—flipping through the stacks of cash.

"Yeah," James said with little emotion.

Everett looked closely at his nephew.

"There's still a lot of things out there in the garage that didn't sell: clothes; books; furniture; personal items. What do you think you want to do with all that stuff?"

James shrugged. "I don't know. Maybe have the Salvation Army come and pick it up. I want the house completely empty before the Realtor starts to show it."

Everett rested a hand on James's arm. After a long moment, the college senior finally looked his uncle in the eyes.

"You don't have to do this, you know, James," Everett said. *"Sell off everything. I mean, you can do whatever you want to, but it's not going to take away your memories of your mom and dad. It's not going to take away the pain."*

"I know," James said. *"I don't expect it to. I just want to be unencumbered by it all. I want to move forward. And I don't want any of this stuff, or this house."*

"Fair enough," Everett said. *"I'm here to help you, whatever you need to do."*

"Thank you. I appreciate that."

They continued counting the cash. Everett got up and grabbed a beer from the nearly-empty refrigerator. He offered one to James, who politely shook his head.

"You haven't said much about what you're going to do after graduation," Everett said.

"I'll get a job eventually," James said. *"I'm not sure with whom or where. But I'm going to travel for a little while."*

Everett smiled. "Traveling sounds nice. Where do you think you'll go?"
James shrugged again. "I have no idea. But I'll figure it out."

Uncle Sal's attitude toward Nick Ferrante had shifted a bit ever since the 21-year-old started insisting that people no longer call him "Nicky." The older man started talking more openly in front of his nephew, giving him deeper glimpses into his world of money, gambling, and women—as well as painting a more accurate picture of Nick's late father.

Some of it was hard to hear. His dad had cheated on his mother. A lot. His dad had people killed. But at the same time, the growing mythology around Nick's father was a source of pride, and the more Sal told stories, the greater the adrenaline rush of being the heir of such a street legend.

Today, however, Sal was taking things to another level. He and

Nick were joined by three of Sal's business associates, two of whom were named Jimmy and another whose name he didn't know. All three were muscular, sullen, and fierce in appearance. The five of them stood in a circle around another man, who was on his knees, bound and gagged. Nick wasn't sure how the man had gotten there, into the basement of one of the Jimmy's houses, but it was clear he had angered the wrong people.

Sal turned to Nick. "So, you keep saying you want to work for me, like these guys here do. That's right, isn't it?"

Nick nodded. He tried not to look the prisoner in the eye. "Yeah, that's right."

"And I want you to," Sal said. "I think you've got a bright future. You've got your old man's charisma but with a hell of a lot more common sense, I think. But you've got to prove your mettle first."

Sal looked at the nameless colleague, and nodded. The man reached into his jacket and pulled out a small revolver, and handed it to Sal. Sal held it up before Nick's face as the younger man's eyes widened.

"You see this guy kneeling here before us? He wouldn't hesitate a moment to kill any one of us if the tables were turned. He's too dangerous to be kept alive." Sal looked at the man, reached down and ripped the gag off of the man's face. The prisoner winced.

"Isn't that right, Martinez?"

Martinez slowly turned his face upward to glare at Sal, his eyes full of contempt. "Yeah, that's right. So finish me off, you syphilis-filled fucker."

Sal laughed. "I like your attitude," he said. "It's almost a shame we have to kill you. You're sort of fun to have around."

Sal looked back at Nick, and held the gun out to him. Nick stared back at his uncle, afraid to move.

"Go ahead, Nick," Sal said. "This is your moment of decision."

Nick locked eyes with his uncle for another moment, and then glanced at the other three men, who simply stared back at him, revealing no emotion. Finally, he dared to look down at Martinez, who smirked at him.

"Hey, kid," Martinez said. "You should kill these guys instead and let me go. Then you'll really be a big shot."

Nick glanced back at Sal, who was smiling, still extending the gun toward his nephew.

"You heard the man, Nick," his uncle said. "He's giving you an additional choice."

"It's your uncle's fault your father died," Martinez continued, and Nick was shocked that the other men were allowing him to talk like this. "He dragged your father into the underworld. So he's the one you ought to kill."

Nick was shaking. He looked back at Sal, and then down at the gun. Finally, he reached out and accepted it, nervously moving it back and forth between his palms, feeling its cold indifference.

"It's not a hot potato, kid," Martinez said, and the other men actually chuckled.

"Make your decision, son," Sal said, patting Nick on the shoulder. "You need to kill someone in this room. Just one of us. I'd prefer it be this scumbag Martinez, but I respect you enough to let you choose."

The other men remained silent. Nick was pointing the gun down and away. He took a deep breath, and looked back at his uncle.

"Cover his mouth up again," Nick said, pointing to Martinez.

Sal smiled. "Happy to," he responded, and did as his nephew had requested.

Nick took a step closer to Martinez. His right arm was trembling furiously as he lifted it and aimed the gun at the man's face. Martinez stared back at him. He moved a little closer, and pressed the front of the barrel right against the guy's forehead.

"That a boy," Sal whispered. "Right up close. That's having skin in the game, no pun intended."

Fighting the urge to shut his eyes, Nick started to squeeze the trigger. It felt like he was trying to push a boulder up a flight of stairs. He took another deep breath, and squeezed the trigger all the way.

Click.

The men roared with laughter. Nick looked down at Martinez and could tell he was trying to laugh as well. He took a step back, staring down at the gun and then at Sal, who reached over and took it from him. One of the Jimmys ungagged Martinez again and started untying him.

"You did good, nephew of mine," Sal said, giving Nick a giant hug. "You did good."

"What the hell?" Nick whispered to his uncle, not wanting the other men to hear.

"You passed the test," Sal said. "Everything is a test. Every day, every way, it's a test."

Martinez approached Nick, and extended his hand. Nick shook it, wondering if he'd ever be able to forget what the pretend victim had said about his uncle and his father.

~~~

Delphi guided her mid-size SUV into the reserved parking spot at her Boca Raton condominium. She sat in the car for a while, debating whether to leave the sun roof open. She did so, and then took a few nervous glances around as she stepped onto the parking lot.

Across the street, in a rental condo, Sarosky and Rice watched Delphi through a pair of high-powered binoculars. They'd been tailing her since she arrived the previous afternoon. Delphi hadn't done anything interesting so far; just a stop at a green market and a short walk on the beach.

She came out to her car again an hour later, dressed up, and Sarosky and Rice rushed down to his car. He casually drove a few car lengths behind Delphi for several blocks, until she pulled into a parallel parking spot in a busy shopping district. Sarosky parked as well, and he and Rice found a small table in the same outdoor seating area where Delphi joined an Italian-looking guy, probably in his 40s, wearing sunglasses.

"Look at their body language," Rice whispered. "It's not a happy gathering. I think they're bickering about something."

Delphi appeared to wipe away tears as she stood and rushed inside the restaurant. The detectives waited and watched as Italian Sunglasses made a call on his cell phone. The man quickly put the phone away once Delphi returned.

"She's not beautiful, but not bad-looking either," Rice said. "Could you date someone like her?"

Sarosky raised an eyebrow. "Come on."

"Well, at some point you have to have a semi-normal adult life again," she said, smiling.

"Yeah, whatever normal is," Sarosky said, "But aren't there women out there who aren't connected to an ongoing missing persons' investigation?"

Rice sighed. "Everyone has their baggage."

Delphi and her companion were wrapping things up.

"We gotta decide who to tail next, her or him," Sarosky said.

"We can find Adams again. I say we follow Mr. Sunglasses for a while."

Sunglasses hopped into a Lexus and took off toward the heart of downtown

Boca, through Mizener Park. Sarosky kept up, Rice calling in the tag and learning that the car was registered to a Mr. Nick Ferrante. Ferrante didn't have any outstanding warrants or other issues. Sarosky followed him into a parking garage, where Ferrante parked in a spot reserved for something called the "Palm Beach Sun Gods."

"What the hell does that mean?" Rice asked.

Sarosky parked and the detectives took a walkway connecting the garage to an adjacent office building. Once inside the lobby, they found a directory and saw that the "Sun Gods" were located on a suite in the third floor.

Rice was doing a search on her smart phone. "Listen to this," she said. "The Palm Beach Sun Gods are the resident Arena Football League team, and Ferrante is a majority owner. Do you watch Arena football?"

Sarosky shook his head. "Never. I only watch the Browns."

"I'm sorry to hear that."

"Yeah, me too."

Rice kept reading her phone. "According to his online bio, Ferrante purchased the franchise three years ago. Apparently he's been instrumental in 'bringing several high-caliber players' to the franchise. He's also married with three children."

Sarosky started walking back to the parking garage.

"I wonder what Delphi Adams was so urgently and stressfully discussing with a married sports team owner?"

Rice gave her partner a playful punch on the arm. "That's the fun part for us, finding out."

Chapter Twenty:

JUNE 20

Had it been pure nightfall and not twilight, Tom might not have noticed the stray cat as he drove towards home with several cocktails percolating through his impaired system. But he overreacted as the animal darted across the road, and plowed his car into a brick mailbox.

At first, Tom felt immediate gratitude as his seatbelt restrained him—and then was pummeled by the air bags. Everything quickly shifted from loud and crazy, to quiet and smelly but peaceful. Tom leaned back in his seat, his whole body tense and tingling, taking deep breaths.

An hour later he sat in a small cell at the Daytona Beach City Police Department, his face bruised and scraped from the airbags.

About 30 minutes into Tom's incarceration, Ben drove in silence toward that same police station. Ben had already called Beth and asked her to pick up Connor as a guest for the night. He urged his wife to tell Connor that his father was fine, and that Tom needed some time alone.

Tom was quiet as Ben drove him home. Ben asked Tom if he wanted to get some food or coffee, and Tom chose the coffee.

Sitting across the table at a Starbucks, Tom sipped black coffee and took his time before finally looking Ben in the eyes.

Ben smiled. He'd been in these kinds of situations before, usually with employees but sometimes with friends: a person messes up royally, and thinks their career or life is over. Sometimes the consequences were indeed pretty dire. Ben hoped Tom would get a sympathetic circuit judge who would look at the larger context of what was happening in his life, and go lenient on him.

Tom could replace the mailbox, and pay whatever other fine was required. He might lose his license for a short period of time, and Ben would find a way to ensure Tom got to his restaurant and back. Thankfully no one else was involved in the accident.

"They really are careful about not letting you smack your head, just like in TV shows and movies," Tom said.

"What do you mean?"

"When they shove you into the back of the police car."

"Oh, gotcha."

The aroma of coffee beans filled the air.

"Tom, how can I help? What do you need from me?" Ben asked.

Tom leaned back in his chair, and stared up at the ceiling. His face looked worn, his eyes bloodshot, his nose starting to assume that rosy tint often associated with heavy drinking.

"I don't know," he said. "Just be a friend, I suppose."

"I hope I'm that already."

"You sure are."

Ben's mind moved into strategy. *There always has to be a strategy with you,* Beth sometimes said to him in exasperation.

"I wonder if it might make sense to step away from the business for a little while," Ben said. "Bring someone in to run operations and all the shift managers. Free you up to just focus on yourself and Connor for a while, and not have to be in the weeds of things every day."

Tom didn't respond.

"I don't know what your payroll budget is right now," Ben continued. "But I know a few guys with experience and maturity who are in transition. I could send them your way."

Tom nodded. "I appreciate that. I'll consider it. You know, being in the weeds is kind of what's kept me sane: having something to focus on."

"I don't mean to be disrespectful," Ben began, "but this situation tonight, it's a little crazy."

"Yeah, I know."

"I'm not at all trying to sound judgmental or condescending," Ben said. "But this is the wake-up call. Things could have ended a lot worse tonight, for you or for some other person. Something's gotta change, Tom."

Ben reached forward and clasped Tom's hand.

"I'll get moving on these potential general managers. What I'd like you to do, in the meantime, is get some help with the drinking. Lots of other men have walked this journey before you. I'll even find out when AA meetings are taking place in the area, and I'll go with you to the first one if that helps."

Tom smiled. "Hey, I appreciate all of that, I really do. Let me think about the meeting thing, okay? That's a big step. Right now, I'll just stay off the booze and find better outlets for all of this stress." He stared at Ben, as if waiting to see if his friend would challenge him some more.

Ben knew when he'd made his point about something and it was time to pull back. "Sure thing," he said, and stood. "Connor is welcome to stay with us as long as you'd like this weekend. We'll just stay in touch."

Tom stood, and gave Ben a hug. "I really appreciate that," he said. "I appreciate everything you've done for me."

As he drove home, Ben's mind circled through a history of conversations with friends, classmates, and employees who rationalized their behavior and wouldn't embrace serious self-reflection. He felt his burden in life was to help others see what they couldn't see for themselves; and while this was exhausting, it also provided an adrenaline rush. A heaviness settled upon Ben, however, when those he had tried to help continued to screw up.

His thoughts shifted to Connor. The kid could easily become an orphan before long. The next time Tom could plow headlong into another car, and that would be it. Ben needed to spend some time that night and tomorrow really getting to know Connor, because there was a good chance of him becoming a regular if not permanent fixture in the McBride household.

Ben didn't know if Beth could handle taking care of someone else's son. His Next Gen business travel was increasing, her fitness clientele was continuing to expand, and Maddie obviously needed lots of time and attention. Ben and Beth sometimes talked about having another baby, and that would only serve to ratchet up the stress.

Chapter Twenty-One

JULY 6

The bell chimed, indicating that a customer had entered the bookstore.

"Coming!" Delphi called out from the back room, where she was trying to organize the sprawling mess of paperbacks and hardbacks she'd allowed to accumulate for the past several months. Now that she was finally on an organizing roll, Delphi was frustrated at the interruption.

She rubbed her palms together to release some of the book dust and walked into the main room, smiling until she saw the two detectives waiting for her.

"Good afternoon, Ms. Adams," Sharon Rice said. "You remember Det. Sarosky and myself, I presume?"

"Yes, of course," Delphi said. "What can I do for you?"

"We just wanted to chat a little more," Sarosky said. "I hope this is a good enough time?"

Delphi shrugged and gestured around. "Yeah, as good as any."

Rice smiled. "Well, too many people are buying online now. They don't appreciate a real bookstore anymore."

"Tell me about it," Delphi said, and motioned for them to follow her to the back room.

The three of them sat down, and Sarosky and Rice pulled out their notepads.

"I'd offer you coffee, but I still have to clean the pot," Delphi said.

"All good," Sarosky said.

"So do you have any kind of update on my friends?"

Sarosky shook his head. "No, I wish I did. Have you heard anything?"

"Of course not. I would have called you guys right away."

"That's good to know," Rice said.

Sarosky began, "Delphi, we're curious about some of your recent activities. You've spent some time down in Palm Beach County lately, visiting your condo and meeting with a gentleman named Nick Ferrante, if I'm not mistaken."

Delphi felt her eyes widen, and took a breath to settle herself down.

"And how would you know that? Are you guys following me?"

"Relax," Rice said. "We're keeping an eye on all of the book club members. Hasn't it crossed your mind that we might be worried about everyone's safety?"

Delphi frowned. "What, you think there's a serial book club kidnapper out there, and their goal is to take the entire group so they can have their own personal reading harem?"

Rice laughed. "That's clever. That would make a great movie." "Well, make sure I get full credit and royalties."

"You seemed upset with Mr. Ferrante," Sarosky continued, and waited.

Delphi sighed. "He was a business associate of my ex-husband's. He still owes my ex some money, and I'm supposed to get a portion of it; which I really need. Believe me, it's no fun having to drive three hours and have lunch with one of your ex-husband's scumbag associates."

Sarosky nodded. "I'm sure. What kind of business was your former husband in with Mr. Ferrante?"

"He was a partial owner of that stupid football team. They bought him out, but didn't pay him even close to what was promised," Delphi said. "My ex isn't the brightest bulb out there."

"What's your ex-husband's name again, if you don't mind?"

"Richard Jones. Yep, Dick Jones. Sounds like a soap opera character, right?" Delphi rolled her eyes.

"Totally," Rice said. "So is there anything we can do to help with the situation?"

Delphi shook her head. "I have no idea how you can possibly help. It's just a private civil matter. I could always hire a lawyer again, I suppose, but who wants to waste money on that when there's such a small chance I'll ever collect anything?"

Rice glanced around at the piles of books. "Do you think you guys will keep being a book club?"

"I don't know. No one has brought it up. I think we're all still shell-shocked about our friends. If anything, we'll just morph into a grief support group."

"Do you think you'll be going down to see Mr. Ferrante again any time soon?" Sarosky asked.

"He's agreed to meet with me again whenever I want to. So charitable of him."

Sarosky stood up. "Well, please let us know if you think of how we can be of help. And just be careful, okay? Keep a look out for any suspicious characters. Keep your guard up."

"Oh, my guard's been up," Delphi said. "I haven't exactly been sleeping like a baby lately."

<center>~~~</center>

His parents' house sold a few weeks earlier, and James Thorne was on his journey, backpack in tow.

James had heard a little about London from fellow Rochester Institute of Technology students who'd been there with their families. The punk rock scene was big there, they said, and it truly was an international city where you'd see all walks of people.

His friends were right, James thought as he sat on the Tube, speeding under the city. James saw whites, blacks, Asians, Middle Easterners, Spaniards, and people who looked like they could've come from any of the countries surrounding the United Kingdom. Several younger persons wore hair dyed various colors, a few of them styled in Mohawks.

Most of the fellow Tube passengers were silent, keeping to themselves, which James preferred. He found it fascinating to simply observe. Yesterday he'd purchased a small notebook in which he had begun jotting down his thoughts and observations.

Soon James exited the train and wandered into Chinatown, where he walked a few blocks before randomly picking an eatery and ordering a heaping amount of din sum. After he was done he made his way over to the theater district, considered taking in a show, but then simply kept walking.

He caught the Tube again and exited near the Thames, the famous St. Paul's Cathedral as his destination. James paid for admission and attended just enough of a tour to learn about how the locals had banded together to protect the church from being destroyed by Hitler's bombs during World War II.

James wrote a solid paragraph about that in his journal, and then simply sat under the massive dome and studied all of the stained glass, statues, and carvings. He'd never seen such a beautiful place in his short lifetime, and wished his parents were with him.

Chapter Twenty-Two

JULY 21

D id you hear what that girl said?"

Ben glanced up from his phone, which he had absent-mindedly pulled out of his right pants pocket.

"What's that?"

Beth motioned to a nearby table gaggled with teenage girls. "I heard that girl say that Michael Jackson was spotted alive in Paris."

"The late King of Pop?"

"Is there another Michael Jackson?"

Ben shrugged. "Check the White Pages, I bet there's a whole bunch of them. I think there's also a British broadcaster who goes by the same name."

"Do people still use White Pages?"

The McBrides had a babysitter at home and were enjoying their version of a date night. They'd already spent an hour in unbroken conversation, the longest stretch in many months. Topics related to either one of their jobs were off-limits.

"I still wonder how he really died," Ben said. "Did he overdose on oxygen? Is that even possible?"

"Maybe he was murdered by one of those kids' parents. It was always a little creepy, all that time he spent alone with little kids."

"Show some respect." Ben smiled.

"I still remember hearing 'Thriller' for the first time, and seeing that scary video," Beth said. "I was just a little girl. I think I ran screaming out of the room, and didn't leave my mother's side the rest of the night."

"It was pretty groundbreaking, back in the day, the whole musician-to-werewolf dynamic. These days, it's common. Over-done, really."

Ben thought they'd milked the apparent MJ sighting to its fullest potential, and hoped Beth had a new topic before they reverted into work-talk. But just then he saw the journalist Cameron Brock enter the Starbucks and settle at a small table with his laptop.

"That's him," he whispered to Beth, subtly gesturing. "That's that reporter Cameron, the one who's already interviewed Phil and Tom."

Beth glanced over at Cameron. "Yeah, I've met him, remember? I hope he doesn't notice me."

"I think all men notice you. Or, at least, they should."

Beth smiled. "Well, thank you. No, I told you how he came into the studio as soon as everything happened. I really don't want to talk to him. I'm not sure why Phil and Tom talked to him."

"He hasn't published a word yet."

Beth raised an eyebrow. "So?"

"So, I think that's a good sign. That he's not another sensational hack."

"Maybe he's just going to write a book and try to cash in on all of this," she suggested with derision.

Ben shook his head. "I don't think so. He would have done it already. Plus, Julio likes him, and he has good instincts."

"Who's Julio?"

"Tom's head bartender. Young guy, really sharp, great customer skills."

"I don't know if I'd put a lot of credibility in Tom's bartender. Tom is still drinking heavily, last time we checked. We spend more time with Connor than he does."

Ben started to pull out his phone again, and saw Beth scowl.

"You're married to that thing as much as you're married to me."

"It was healthier for me when I used a BlackBerry. Lots of antioxidants."

"Come again?"

"Blackberries are loaded with antioxidants."

"That's *blueberries,* babe."

"Well, I think blackberries are as well. I think all berries are good for you. Of course, I love you berry much."

"Enough." Beth tilted her head back slightly. "Is he watching us, acting like he wants to come over here?"

"No. He's tuning everyone else out, as far as I can tell. He's probably writing about the demise of Michael Jackson and the BlackBerry. Not Next Gen's hottest selling product by any means anymore."

"You just talked about work, so you owe me a dollar. What's the point in anyone talking to some strange reporter about their private lives?"

"Phil saw it as part of his healing. I think his therapist encouraged it."

"That doesn't sound like something a therapist would recommend."

"Have you ever been to therapy?"

Beth smiled. "Fitness is my therapy. You know that."

Ben studied Cameron from across the room. "You would add a lot of depth to the story, from a different angle. Tom and Phil know their wives as wives and mothers, but you knew them as friends, clients, readers…"

"Yeah, and if they hadn't met at my studio…"

"Beth."

"I know. So, Delphi won't talk to him either, which I think is smart. I think it's smart if we all continue to deal with this privately. These kids don't need a spotlight on them all the time. Their lives have become hard enough."

Ben finished his coffee. "Sounds like you're not going to change your mind."

"Nope. And I'm not sure why it's so important to you that I talk to him." Beth looked over at Cameron once more. "Can we leave, by the way? I don't feel relaxed any more with him in here."

"Sure."

It was too early to go home yet, in Ben's opinion. He suggested a walk on the beach, which they hadn't done alone since Beth was pregnant with Maddie. Beth sounded enthused at first, but when Ben started to drive toward the Intracoastal she said she was getting tired and maybe they should just go home and watch a movie.

Beth was quiet for a few minutes as Ben drove, and then she looked over at him.

"By the way, what's the name of Phil's therapist?" she asked.

Chapter Twenty-Three:

JULY 22

The little brunette enrolled in Phil's four-week, accelerated *Introduction to Humanities* course gave Phil a jolt whenever they made eye contact.

Amanda Bane was built like a gymnast, and her hair was stylish and cut shorter than most young women wore it these days. She looked a few years older than her peers, and sported a tiny tattoo on the back of her neck that—from a distance—looked like a lotus flower.

Phil caught himself spending extra time on Amanda's papers compared to the other 27 students. He noticed his heart racing a little when she turned a paper in and smiled. Phil also kept a lookout for Amanda when walking across campus, and even dreaded the notion of seeing her arm-in-arm with some young guy.

Snap out of it, Phil chided himself as he caught his mind wandering during an open class dialogue. He'd looked Amanda's way at least three times already, even though she'd yet to raise her hand to contribute to the conversation.

It was ridiculous to think that Amanda would "notice" him: a balding, average-looking professor in his mid-40s. But after nearly three months without Jackie, the waters that divided the land of the rational from the emotional had dried up to the point where the two parcels were becoming indistinguishable.

Phil had office hours after class; a chance to read papers, catch his breath, and enjoy a cup of coffee. He stared at a framed photo of Jackie, Audrey, and Natalie, and then tried to concentrate on a rather mediocre paper written by a kid named Michael Nielsen. His office door was open, as it usually was, but Phil heard a soft, polite knock and glanced up to see Amanda with her backpack slung over her toned shoulders.

She wore a tank top with jean shorts that were perfectly appropriate for a summer school collegiate setting, revealing her tanned, trim legs. Phil noticed another tattoo on Amanda's left ankle, which looked like a grapevine.

He swallowed hard.

"Dr. Solomon, do you have a few minutes, please?" Amanda smiled unassumingly, and took a couple of steps toward the interior of the office.

"Sure, Amanda. Come on in." Phil sat up straighter and hoped he didn't appear disheveled. "Have a seat," he added, gesturing to one of the chairs in front of his desk.

Amanda smiled and pulled the backpack from her shoulders, and Phil tried not to watch her every move as she settled into the chair and crossed her legs.

"I'm working on my final paper," Amanda began, "trying to assimilate everything we've been discussing this month. There's been so much, and it's all been incredible. It reminds me of what I saw when I was traveling for the past few years." She paused. "I spent some time in Europe and South America after high school, before starting college. I think I referenced that in one of my papers?"

"You did," Phil said. "Tell me more."

"All the extra insights on symbolism are blowing my mind. Such as the way light flowing through the cathedrals is intentional and meant something. The angles, the shadows, the architecture—it all meant and continues to mean something. I wish I'd taken your class before traveling."

Phil smiled. Amanda's eyes were green and got larger when she was excited.

"Here in the States, almost everyone goes through the motions each day with such little meaning. I used to do it a lot myself. I want to write about that in some way in my final paper, but I'm having the hardest time pulling it all together."

Amanda paused, and smiled. "Am I making any sense?"

"I've heard worse," Phil deadpanned, and Amanda laughed, un-crossing and re-crossing those amazing legs in reverse fashion. Phil saw her left hand quickly play with her hair, and this made him feel even more alive and engaged.

"You're funny," Amanda said. "I was wondering, do you think it would be ok if I gave you a rough draft of the paper a few days before it's due? Maybe you could let me know if I'm going in the right direction, or if I'm just all over the place like some stream of consciousness freakazoid?"

Phil liked how she said "freakazoid."

"That would be fine. Just email me your draft when you're ready. I think it's smart that you're reaching out to ask for help ahead of time."

"Thank you so much," Amanda said. "I really want to visit more cathedrals.

I haven't gotten to Eastern Europe yet." Phil saw her looking at the picture of Jackie and the girls. "Your wife and daughters are beautiful."

"Thank you."

Amanda touched her hair again. "You look pretty outnumbered at home."

"I've gotten used to it," Phil said.

Amanda looked around the office some more, and then stood as if to leave. She started to reach for her backpack, but then wandered over to Phil's crowded bookshelf and ran her fingers along a few of the spines.

"So many," she said, her eyes scanning the titles. "Have you read all of these?"

"Memorized every one of them," Phil quipped, and she glanced back with a smile that destroyed another layer of his impulse control.

Amanda came back over to retrieve her backpack. Phil purposefully averted his eyes, not wanting to stare at her as she leaned over.

"I've taken enough of your time," she said. "I'll email you that draft. Thank you so much."

Phil stood, and gently shook Amanda's small, perfect hand.

"Anytime," he said, and Amanda smiled a final time before leaving the office. Phil hoped she wouldn't glance back and realize that he couldn't take his eyes off of the back of her legs.

He sat back down and ran his fingers through his own hair. Phil picked up Michael Nielsen's paper and then set it aside, deciding it was time for a walk across campus.

Chapter Twenty-Four:

James's face was scraggly and his hair longer than it had been in several years. He sat at a small table on the porch of the Parisian café, his notebook open, watching people stroll past.

After trying out several cafes across the past couple of weeks, this venue had become his favorite. James arrived about the same time each day and sat for hours, ordering coffees, popular pastries, cheeses, bread, and an occasional glass of wine. He journaled several times a day, every day, and found he couldn't fall asleep easily at night without jotting down his final thoughts.

The wait staff had quickly learned James's name and where he was from, and greeted him heartily when he arrived. An attractive young server named Lenore was usually there, and James found himself looking forward to the sight of her large brown eyes locking with his as she asked for his order in her heavily accented English. He gradually learned to order in French, and could tell by Lenore's smile that this pleased her.

James glanced down at his open notebook, where he'd scribbled the day's date and a short list of things he wanted to accomplish. At the top was "write to Uncle Everett." James hadn't sent his uncle a letter in several weeks, and knew he was overdue. He'd intended to send a couple of his college friends a postcard as well.

Most of the time, however, James wasn't thinking about Rochester or the U.S. or anything related to his old life. The past felt like someone else's life now, like a dream James had awakened from as he sought to bring into the focus the fuzzy details of his true life. His destiny, he felt, was still emerging, and there was no need to rush its commencement.

"More wine, James?" Lenore's sweet voice interrupted his thoughts. He smiled up at her, realizing she'd asked the question in French.

"No, thank you, Lenore," he responded in his own awkward French.

She lingered, smiling. "We are having a party tonight, at the apartment," she said in English. "You would like to come?"

James thought about the invite for a moment. "Sure," he said. "That would be nice."

"Hand me your notebook, please," she said. "I will write down my address for you."

James did as he was told. He liked the way Lenore carefully wrote out the information, and was happy that their fingers briefly touched as she handed the notebook and pen back to him.

"I will see you at seven, then, James," Lenore said, smiling back at him as she walked away. He nodded and watched her, and then took a deep breath of resolve and started to write the letter to Uncle Everett.

〜〜

Curtis walked through the ranch's garden, awed as usual by its breadth of vegetables. Some of the residents ate meat products, but those too came from the ranch and the cattle and poultry were grass-fed and not exposed to pollutants. Curtis personally didn't favor the killing of animals, but had taught those who performed that task to embrace it as a sacred ritual done with respect and honor.

Roger, a recent arrival and about 20 years younger than Curtis, walked beside him. Roger had shown up in a drugged-out haze, barely alive. He'd lived on the streets for the past few years, the culmination of a relatively aimless life that followed a painful break-up with his fiancée and the loss of his job as a graphic designer.

Although Curtis spent most of his time with the community's leadership, he felt drawn toward Roger and wanted to mentor him. He saw potential in the younger man, despite his reactionary personality and short temper, and resonated with Roger's enduring sense of heartache.

"I lost a great love as well," Curtis told Roger when the younger man shared his story. "I thought I would never see her again, but in time I grew enough to the point where she was able to come back to me." Curtis paused, noticing a sparkle of hope light up in Roger's eyes. "I'm not sure if that will be the case for you. But perhaps you will find a new, better love. Become who you truly are, and then the best people cross your path."

As they walked, Roger pointed out the rows of green beans he'd helped to plant.

"I like seeing it all come to life," he said. "I feel like I've done something real, and not just for me but for everyone."

Curtis nodded. "This environment we're in is far more real than anything we experienced before we arrived here. All that falsehood of going through the motions, losing ourselves in jobs, possessions, clichés—I don't miss it at all."

Roger nodded. "I don't either. It got me nowhere."

Curtis continued, "When Dan took me in, I didn't realize how lost I'd become. I was angry, bitter, entitled…it took him years to calm me down. He didn't allow me to get into community leadership until after a year had passed."

"I don't know if I can be a leader," Roger said, staring down as they walked.

Curtis gently patted his shoulder. "Don't concern yourself with that right now. Just become more of you who you truly are, and the path will be clear." He paused. "And don't forget to journal every day. It's an expectation of life here."

"Okay," Roger said.

Curtis heard footsteps behind them, and turned to see Dan Ferguson himself approaching with a smile. He greeted Roger with a hug.

"Roger, do you mind if Curtis and I have a few minutes to talk?"

Roger shook his head. "Nope. I need to get back to the kitchen anyway." He glanced at Curtis. "Thank you, Curtis."

"My pleasure." Curtis smiled as he watched Roger hurry off. He felt Dan's stare, and turned to look at his mentor.

"You've been avoiding me," Dan said, with a touch of sadness. Curtis didn't respond.

Dan continued, "You're the leader of this community, and you don't owe me an explanation for your decisions or your methods." He paused. "But you're in danger of taking us in a direction where we never intended to go."

Curtis nodded. "I respect your vision. You know that. I also ask that you respect change, knowing it's inevitable."

Dan stared at the garden with admiration. "Change and growth are inevitable. We till, we plant, we water, and with grace the growth comes." He paused. "Sometimes, though, our personal ambitions hinder the greatest growth before it gets a chance to manifest."

"Give me more time, please. I have a plan. A plan for sustainability."

Dan smiled. "The only thing that's sustainable is love. Search your heart, and ensure it's filled with nothing else."

He embraced Curtis, and left him to his thoughts along the periphery of the garden they'd both worked so hard to establish.

Chapter Twenty-Five:

JULY 25

Russ knew he'd never get past the Cubists, but at that moment he didn't give a shit. Sure enough, three of them respectfully but forcefully blocked his path as Russ aggressively strode toward Mario's office.

"Mr. O'Rourke," one of them said, "I'll need you to—"

"Fuck you guys." Russ pushed his way past them, ready to fling open Mario's door.

"Mr. O'Rourke, Mr. Lazano is not expecting you right now," said the other Cubist, louder but still cordially. "You'll need to make an appointment."

"Which part of 'fuck you' did you not understand? Get your asses back in your cubicles or you'll be out on the streets. I'm a vice president of this company!" Russ shoved the two goons off of him, and managed to rap his knuckles on Mario's door a couple of times before the Cubists' muscular arms pinned him back again.

The office door opened, and Henry Reid stared at the three men. Russ watched Henry study his face for a moment, and then Henry waved his hand to dismiss the Cubists and motioned for Russ to come inside.

Russ ignored Mario's offer of a handshake.

"I've had enough, Mario. It's been nearly three months. Where's my goddamned ex-wife?"

Henry remained close to Russ, as if ensuring he wouldn't pounce on his former father-in-law.

"Calm down. Take a seat," Mario said, sitting back down himself.

"No thank you. I need to know what the fuck is going on."

"Henry, tell our friend what's going on."

Henry faced Russ, trying to stuff down his annoyance at the prick just barging in on them and acting like a surly teenager.

"What's going on is there's not a goddamned trace of Emma. Not a single one. It's as though she never existed. I'm baffled by the whole thing."

"This," Russ said, picking up the photo of Emma and Pete that sat on Mario's desk and waving it a little too close to Henry's face, "is proof that she existed. Why don't you come over and tell my son that she never existed?" He set the frame back down on the desk, not roughly enough to break it but with enough carelessness that it fell over.

Mario simply stared at Russ, waiting for him to finish.

"You're not doing enough," Russ said.

"I'm not a magician," Mario said. "I can't just make her and the others reappear out of thin air."

Russ plopped down in one of the two chairs in front of Mario's desk, and Henry settled into the other.

"I've tried to set up meeting times with both of you," Russ said, far more quietly now. "I've left messages for both of you, texted you, emailed you. You've not communicated anything back to me for weeks. Why?"

Henry looked at Mario, who motioned for him to take the lead.

"Russ," Henry began, "you've divorced from Emma. You may not have wanted that divorce, but it's the way things played out. Each of us in this room has been through it. It sucks, but it's reality. But you'd started to move on, as most men do. I think it's best that you keep moving forward, becoming the best man and best father you can be."

Russ stared back at him.

"I don't even know what that's supposed to mean."

"What it means," Mario interjected, "is that you have a chance to create a better life for yourself and Pete. A life without Emma. You're all he has now." Studying Russ's expression, Mario sighed. "Do you understand what I'm getting at?"

"Spell it out for me."

Mario lowered his head, and when he faced Russ again the older man had watery eyes. "I'm having to accept the likelihood that my daughter is dead," he said, his voice faltering. "And you're going to have to accept that as well. And so will Pete."

None of them said anything for a while. Russ was battling his own tears, emotion shifting from anger to grief, but refused to buy into Mario's certainty.

"We don't know that," he said. "There's no evidence, no body, no crime scene. Maybe she's on an island somewhere, living it up."

Mario wiped his eyes with a tissue, composing himself. He stared hard at Russ.

"Do you really think she'd just abandon my grandson, unless she was forced against her will? Or unless she didn't know what the hell she was doing?"

Russ said nothing for a while, and then looked at Henry.

"I want to help out," he said. "I want to be involved in your efforts to find her. Don't shut me out anymore."

"There's nothing to be involved in any longer," Henry said, bluntly. "Even the police have placed this on the back burner; Sarosky and Rice are just going through the motions. It's an unsolved mystery, the kind of stuff you see on TV. Except it's happened to us. It's happened to you, and to Mario. And I'm very sorry for what you're going through."

Russ glanced at Mario, who simply nodded.

"Believe me," Henry said, "if there's something to know, I'd have found it by now. There's not a lot that gets past me."

Russ sank lower in his chair, feeling deflated. Then he leaned forward, resting his face in his hands. Mario got up, walked around his desk, and tried his best to comfort him while Henry sat there impassively. After a while Russ stood to leave, and Mario walked him out and down the hall. Henry waited, and Mario looked exhausted when he returned and slammed the door a little harder than he intended.

"We have to make that deal," he said to Henry, who nodded with some exasperation.

"I know, I know," Henry said, "but they keep changing the conditions. Those guys aren't right in the head, they aren't businesspeople. They don't seem to know what they want, which only makes them more dangerous."

Mario said on the edge of his desk, and cracked his knuckles. He felt his blood pressure rising.

"If I ever come face to face with these people in the shadows," he said, "I'll kill them myself."

Henry nodded, and then tried to add some levity.

"Just like in the old days?"

"Just like in the old days."

Chapter Twenty-Six:

JULY 30

Ben looked through tired eyes at Julio, who was slammed with customers but still making it all look effortless. He had some help behind the bar tonight from a young woman with blonde pigtails, and Steve Clarke—the new general manager Tom had recently hired on Ben's referral—was checking in regularly and helping to pour beers on occasion.

It was just after 7 p.m. on a summer Thursday night, and Famoso's was a buzz. Tom wasn't there, which Ben thought was good; the less Tom was at the restaurant, the less he was at the bar.

"Ben, how goes it?" Julio shouted out as he scampered past him.

"It goes!" Ben yelled back.

Ben sipped from his glass of red wine, and reluctantly turned his eyes to the stack of business results he'd brought with him to study. He was definitely the only patron at the bar doing any work.

"What's all that stuff you're reading?" Julio asked.

Ben held the paperwork up in the air. "Numbers from my stores. Exciting, huh?"

"The best beach reading I can imagine." Julio looked more closely at the sheets of finely-crunched metrics. "So you understand all of that stuff?"

"All too well. I don't always understand why it doesn't look as good as it should, but I understand it."

Julio grabbed a wet cloth and cleaned the bar area. "It looks complicated."

"So does all of this," Ben said, gesturing to the vast collection of booze that surrounded them.

"Once you know the basics, the rest is instinct," Julio smiled. "Sort of like jazz."

"Sort of, I suppose."

"You enjoy what you do?" Julio asked him.

"For the most part, yeah. I don't enjoy this stuff, but it's necessary. I enjoy the people piece. I like helping people be successful."

Julio smiled. "I can see that in you." He nodded toward Steve, who was checking in with customers seated at the nearby booths. "Good find in this guy. He's got a lot of genuine charisma. I know Tom appreciates him, too."

"Glad it's working out."

"Hey, you're married, right? I never see you bring your wife in here."

Ben chuckled. "She thinks I spend too much time here already, I don't know that she'd let me drag her out here."

"You have kids?"

"One. A daughter, Madison. We call her Maddie. She's two."

Julio smiled. "Sounds pretty precious. And a handful?"

"A precious handful."

"Good for you, man. I hope to become a dad someday."

"It changes your life. You got a girlfriend?"

Julio smiled, almost shyly, which was endearing to see on the face of a guy who radiated confidence. "Actually, I've been seeing this girl I met in here for a couple of months now," he said. "Her name's Susannah."

"Great. You have a picture of her?"

Julio pulled his iPhone out of his pocket, scrolled through some pictures, and handed the device to Ben. Ben smiled at a close-up shot of Julio with a pretty dark-haired woman with red-highlights, both of them beaming.

"Pretty," Ben said, then added, "She's not bad-looking, either."

"You're a mess," Julio chuckled.

"Yeah. Sometimes I am."

"Not literally, of course, Mr. McBride," Julio said.

"That makes me sound old. I'm not ready to be old yet. Getting more gray hair each day, though, so harder to hide the age."

"It works on you. Hey, you got any tips for me about staying married? Once I get married, whether it's to Susannah or not, I want to stay that way."

Ben grinned. "Here's my first tip: When you tell that to Susannah, leave out the 'whether it's to Susannah' part."

"I'm smart enough to know that. Not real smart in general, but smart enough for that."

"I know. I'm flattered that you'd think I might have some answers, but I don't. I didn't even get married until six years ago, and I'm ten years older than Beth. I think I was too into my career before then. I wonder if I'm still too into it."

Julio shrugged. "But you love what you do. The people piece, I mean. And everything is about people."

Ben lifted his wine glass. "My friend, if you just remember that last thing you said, you will go far in this world."

"Thanks."

Ben frowned. "Just don't feel like you have to go too far. Sometimes the farther you go, the less of you remains."

"I bet you had a lot of girlfriends before you settled down."

Ben took on an expression of mock offense. "Why are you speaking in the past tense?'

"Hey, not my business," Julio laughed.

Ben swirled what was left of his wine, and drank. Julio pointed to the glass, and Ben nodded. He waited while Julio grabbed a bottle of Merlot and filled him up again.

"How's Tom doing?"

"Okay, I guess," Julio shrugged. "I don't see him too much anymore. I guess no news is good news?"

"I guess. Sometimes."

"In the case of his wife and the others, no news is bad news."

Ben sipped his wine. "Yeah. Definitely bad news."

"It's a crazy thing. Really crazy."

"The craziest."

"In this day and age," Julio said, noting a couple of new customers who had arrived at the bar, "how do three people just vanish like that? Google can find anyone." He stepped away to go serve his new patrons.

Ben pondered Julio's rhetorical question, enriching it in his mind. In a day and age of so many tools and resources, he thought, when technology presented so many solutions, people could still vanish not just from society but from themselves.

He glanced at his watch, knowing that he was missing Maddie's bedtime stories, and sighed in quiet defeat.

Chapter Twenty-Seven

JULY 31

Delphi broke out a bottle of Malbec. Each of the women accepted a pour except for Kari, who said she was "on a diet."

"You can have a glass of wine, Kari," Beth said. "You're working out hard each week. As your personal trainer, I give you my blessing."

Kari laughed. "Well, thanks. But I just don't want the extra calories right now."

"Diets, diets," Jackie said. "I'm so sick of that word. I want to call it something else."

"Like what?" Delphi asked.

"I don't know. 'Nutritional strategy.' Something like that. Or maybe nothing at all."

Lisa laughed. "You sound like Dr. Oz."

Emma downed her glass of wine so quickly it made her cough.

"I get tired of the sense that we 'ought' to be dieting, or we ought to be doing this or that," she said, her voice cracking a bit. "I really resonated with that statement that Robert Cohn makes to Jake early on in the book. Remember that? He says, 'Don't you ever get the feeling that all your life is going by and you're not taking advantage of it? Do you realize you've lived nearly half the time you have to live already?'"

"That's depressing," Kevlin said.

"But it's true," Jackie interjected. "Our lives are going by while we're counting calories, looking for coupons, gossiping about this or that. I don't know about the rest of you, but I want to actually live."

~~~

Detectives Sarosky and Rice sat in Dara Wilson's living room, along with Lisa Grayton, Kevlin Lane, and Liz Morgan. Beth McBride was supposed to join them but had to cancel, and Delphi Adams said she would be out of town and couldn't make it.

"We just wanted to check in with all of you, and see how you were holding up, and what you might need from us," Rice said to the group.

Each book club member glanced at the other, and no one spoke for a while.

"We need our friends back," Kevlin said, finally. "But I guess that's the obvious."

"My husband is still stressed out," Lisa added. "He wants to move out of Daytona Beach, up to North Carolina or something. Says he doesn't think the kids and I are safe here."

"Oh, there's dangerous people everywhere," Liz said.

"Yeah, especially here," Kevlin added.

"We've been searching for any kind of evidence that your group of friends was specifically targeted," Sarosky said. "So far we haven't seen anything that indicates that. This may have simply been a random incident that occurred hours away from here."

"I just don't understand," Dara said, "how people can up and disappear in this day and age. I mean, the world has gotten pretty small."

"Not small enough yet, I suppose," Lisa said.

Delphi stared across the table at Nick Ferrante. The two of them spoke in hushed, rapid tones.

The lingering memories of Delphi's deceased, Twinkie-loving, diabetic mother fueled rage inside of her at the moment. Beatrice Adams was always low on money, and Delphi hated having anything in common with her. She wanted to smack Ferrante in the face right now.

"I need my money," she said, struggling to keep her voice low. "I did what you asked me to do. I've suffered tremendously for it. Now give me what you promised."

Ferrante sipped from his Perrier. "I've told you, I don't have it to give. As soon as my client comes to his senses and follows through on the delivery, I'll have it and then you'll have it."

Delphi glared at him. "You can give me something out of your pocket, in the meantime, just like you should have done in the first place."

To Delphi's surprise, Ferrante pulled out five crisp one hundred dollar bills and handed them to her. She snatched the cash, folded it up, and shoved it inside her purse.

"Happy?" Ferrante asked.

"It's a start," Delphi said. "But a fraction of what I'm owed. Really, a fraction of a fraction."

"That's very creative," Ferrante said, growing irritated. "You sound like a real mathematician."

"I sound like a businesswoman who expects to be fully paid for her services."

In moments like this, Delphi wished she was more like her father. Sgt. Willard Adams was skilled in asking for what he wanted: he was courteous and diplomatic, but direct. In doing so the sergeant never seemed to manipulate people.

Ferrante mowed down his plate of spaghetti as if someone was going to whisk it away from him. Delphi hoped he got severe heartburn, or maybe even a massive heart attack.

"Well, I guess there's no point in talking any more today," Delphi said, leaving a half-finished salad and the bill on the table. "Enjoy the rest of your meal, and thanks for the down payment."

"Anytime, doll," Ferrante said with a mouthful of bread.

Chapter Twenty-Eight:

"Sarge, come here, you gotta see this," Officer Bennett yelled across the room to Sgt. Houseman. Houseman glanced up from the mountain of paperwork that lay before him, sighing at the interruption and yet eager for a break.

"What is it, Bennett?" Houseman asked, walking over.

"It's Sarosky. Take a look at what he's doing in the conference room."

"I hope he's not beating off."

Bennett laughed. "I think he's way too private for that. Look at the stuff he's got on the white board."

Houseman joined Bennett at the glass-paned door to the conference room, peering inside as they watched the then-20-year-old rookie cop Bob Sarosky scribbling furiously with a dry erase marker. The sergeant squinted, trying to make out the words that Sarosky had written inside of numerous circles that were connected by squiggly lines to other circles, depicting what looked like a vast web of linked ideas.

Houseman pushed the door open, and Bennett followed their boss inside.

"Sarosky, what the hell are you doing?" the sergeant asked Sarosky, who was startled and almost dropped his marker as he turned around. Sarosky smiled shyly as the two men approached the board and looked closely at it.

"Uh," he started, "I've been thinking a lot about the Radio Shack robberies. We've struck out on suspects so far, but I woke up last night and started brainstorming some possibilities."

Houseman smiled. "Yeah? Tell us what you've got here."

"This is called a 'mind map,'" Sarosky said. "Notice the three largest circles in the middle. Each represents one of the stores that were robbed within the past two weeks, *along with the street address. The lines that connect these three circles simply indicate that the stores have some obvious qualities in common, all being Radio Shacks. But also, they were each robbed in the final minutes before closing time when only two employees were left in the store and no customers were still hanging around."*

Sarosky paused, and used his marker to point at the board.

"What's interesting is the comments we received from the store employees who were working at the time of the armed robberies," Sarosky said. "Each of these stores was several miles apart, across the Akron community. They were robbed on different days. And yet, in our interviews with each of the three pairs of different employees, at least one employee from each store told us something very similar."

Rogers and Bennett looked on as Sarosky pointed to a series of interconnected circles he'd placed above the store addresses, in which he'd written the words "SIMILAR STORIES" in quotes.

"And what was that?" Bennett asked.

"Each of these employees, when interviewed separately by different police officers who responded to the scenes of the crimes, at some point in their interviews used the phrase, 'The universe spares its bright spots' when describing their relief at not being shot and killed by the robbers."

Sarosky paused, waiting.

"'The universe spares its bright spots?'" Bennett repeated.

The young officer nodded. "Yeah. If you looked in the reports that were filed, each of them from different cops, in the aftermath of different stores that were robbed on different nights, they captured that phrase in their notes. That exact phrase, from three different employees. Isn't that a quirky thing for three different people to say, in the same context but to different officers?"

The sergeant thought for a moment. "It is kind of weird. Kind of a new agey thing to say. Probably not a phrase I would use. I don't even know what the hell it means."

"So all three of them said it. Kinda strange, I agree, but how does that help us get closer to catching the suspects?" Houseman asked.

Sarosky nodded. "I spent a lot of time thinking about that phrase, because I knew I'd heard it somewhere before. It rang some kind of bell in my mind. I was driving myself crazy, trying to remember."

He smiled. "And then, I was off-duty and out for a drive, the radio playing and the windows open, and I caught something out of the corner of my eye. It was a church marquee, of all things, the kind where they often have those cheesy sayings like, 'Smile, God loves you.' Except this one said something else."

Sarosky pointed to a large circle near the top of the white board, connected by squiggly lines to the other circles below it. He'd drawn a tiny church building on top of the circle, and inside the circle was the same verbiage: THE UNIVERSE SPARES ITS BRIGHT SPOTS.

Houseman looked at his rookie beat cop. "Seriously?"

Sarosky nodded. "Yeah. I even stopped and took a picture of it with my Polaroid." He walked over to the conference table, opened a folder, and showed the picture to the other two men.

Houseman looked closely at the photograph. "What's the name of this church? 'Universal Fellowship?'"

"Yeah," Sarosky said.

"What kind of a church is it?"

Sarosky shrugged. "That was going to be my next step. See what the place is all about, perhaps get a hold of their membership list. See if, by some weird coincidence, our three different robbery victims attend services there."

Bennett frowned. "Well, even if they all happen to be members of this weird church, which I admit would be a strange coincidence—what does that tell us about the robberies themselves?"

Sarosky looked at the white board.

"It doesn't guarantee anything for sure," Sarosky said, "but my gut is telling me that if we keep peeling this onion, we just might find that our Northeast Ohio Radio Shack franchisee is the victim of an inside job…facilitated by none other than the universe's brightest spots."

The two other cops looked at Sarosky for a long while. Houseman finally smiled.

"Keep peeling, Sarosky," he said. "If things play out the way your crazy mind map is taking you, you just might be a detective a lot sooner than you expected."

Chapter Twenty-Nine:

AUG 3

Daddy, I'm getting b-b-better at solving the crosswords," Natalie said from the back seat as Phil drove, holding up the book she'd been working her way through all summer.

He glanced in the rear view mirror and made eye contact with his oldest daughter, Audrey.

"That's great, sweetheart," Phil said as he pulled into the parking lot of Vanessa Porter's counseling office. "Has Audrey helped you with some techniques?"

"Y-yes, she s-sure has," Natalie replied, smiling at Audrey.

They parked, and Audrey leaned in close to her father as Natalie skipped ahead so she could be the first to open the door.

"Dad, it's getting worse," she whispered.

"I know," Phil said. "It just came out of nowhere."

"Do you think Vanessa can help her with it?"

Phil shrugged. "I'll ask her. I hope so. I think it's just a phase."

Vanessa felt tender affection toward her two young patients as they sat together on the loveseat in her office. Audrey made lots of eye contact with Vanessa and smiled often. Natalie sat close to Audrey, occasionally glancing at Vanessa with big, dark eyes and offering a nervous smile.

"Are you ready for the new school year?" Vanessa asked them.

Audrey nodded. "I still need a new backpack. My dad is going to take us shopping this weekend, I think."

"Are you going to buy some new clothes, too?"

"Oh, yeah, you know it. And I'm starting high school, so I can't look like a middle schooler anymore." Vanessa laughed, and saw a big grin spread across Natalie's face.

"What have you girls been doing this summer?"

Audrey shrugged. "Not a whole lot. We've gone to the beach some, a couple of times with our dad and a few times with other families. A couple of my friends invited me to go to camp, but I didn't really feel like it."

Audrey looked at her sister. "Natalie's read a lot of books. She loves to read. Don't you, Nat?"

Natalie nodded.

Vanessa paused. "What have been some of your favorite books this summer Natalie?"

Natalie shrugged her shoulders in the same manner as her sister. "I-I don't k-know," she said softly. "I like to read series. I've read a lot of the N-Nancy Drew series this summer. They're f-fun."

Vanessa smiled. "Books are a great way to pass the time during the summer. It's nice to not have homework and just be able to do what you want."

Natalie nodded. "Yeah. And I've done lots of c-crosswords."

Vanessa allowed for some silence, and then directed her next question squarely at Audrey.

"What's your mother like? Can you tell me about her?"

Audrey broke into a big grin. "She's really funny. She talks in a Southern accent, which cracks up all of my friends. She's just really nice to people and cares about everyone she meets."

"She sounds wonderful."

"Yeah, she is," Audrey said, staring at Vanessa with eyes that were starting to redden. Audrey rested her hand on Natalie's lap for a moment, and Vanessa saw the little girl inch even closer to her big sister.

"How about your dad? Can you tell me a little bit of what he's like?"

"He's very sweet, and listens a lot," Audrey said, her eyes steadily growing more watery. "He's always asking us how we're doing and what we need. Sometimes he used to get impatient with us, but he hasn't done that even once, I think, since Mom left."

Audrey swallowed hard.

"I worry about him, though. I can tell he's lonely, even with us. And he looks older." She glanced at Natalie. "We don't want him to get older." Natalie nodded, looking over at Vanessa once more with those sad, big eyes.

"He r-reads to me at night," Natalie said shyly.

"That's sweet," Vanessa smiled. "I bet you enjoy that."

"Yeah."

"Natalie ends up sleeping with me a lot," Audrey said, giggling. "She comes in and asks to have a sleepover. Don'tcha, Nat?"

Natalie smiled. "Yeah."

"Is it hard for you to sleep, Natalie?"

Natalie shrugged. "Sometimes. I get s-scared."

Audrey pulled Natalie even closer. Vanessa felt herself holding back her own tears.

"When you feel scared or sad, do you ever write your feelings down on paper?"

"I do, some," Audrey piped up first. "I keep a journal. I start each day keeping track of how many days it's been since my mom left."

Vanessa waited.

"It's been exactly 90 days, as of today," Audrey continued, her voice cracking a bit.

"That's a long time," Vanessa said. She looked at Natalie, who was staring at the floor.

"Natalie, I have some blank notebooks that I keep here," Vanessa said, walking over to her desk and selecting one. "Do you want one, so you can write down some of your feelings as well?"

Natalie nodded and Vanessa handed her the notebook. Natalie flipped through the blank pages.

"We can journal together, at the same time," Audrey said. "It'll be fun."

Natalie smiled at her sister.

"You guys seem to get along really well," Vanessa said. "That's sweet."

"Sometimes we fight," Audrey said, laughing.

"All sisters do that."

"Yeah. Natalie doesn't always like it when my friends come over and I just want to hang with them alone. It makes her feel left out."

Natalie gave an embarrassed smile and looked at Vanessa.

"That's understandable," Vanessa replied.

"Our grandparents keep telling us that Mom is going to come home, that she'll be okay," Audrey said.

"What do you think?"

Audrey looked at her sister. Natalie took a long time to consider her answer. Finally, in a tiny, resigned voice, she simply replied, "I h-hope so."

Connor Blakely had seen the technique in some movie: pour ice into a glass, fill it with water, and slowly pour it on top of the person's head. He'd been trying for five minutes to wake his father up from another drunken slumber on the couch, but so far Tom had merely flicked his eyelids a few times and groaned.

The boy walked into the kitchen, wondering whether to take the chance. His dad would probably get really mad; but so what? Connor was already really mad that this kept happening, and was tired of being alone most of the time. He was mad at his mother for disappearing, and even annoyed at the McBride family for inviting him over all the time and trying to cheer him up.

Connor walked over to the ice maker in the front of the refrigerator. He hesitated before filling the glass, hoping the clatter of the ice would be enough to arouse his father from the couch. Connor stole a glance over at Tom, saw that nothing had changed, and then went to the sink and filled the glass with tap water.

As he stood over his father, the glass poised for spillage, Connor felt a tremendous wave of guilt sweep through him. He thought of all the times they'd played catch together in the back yard, and all the quiet words of encouragement his father had offered Connor: about how not being popular didn't mean there was anything wrong with him, and all the times Tom had praised his drawing.

The boy sat on the floor next to the couch, the glass in his hand, and started crying. After a while Connor went back to his room, picked up his sketch pad, and drew until he was too sleepy to hold his pencil.

Chapter Thirty

AUG 4

Pete O'Rourke had the giggles and couldn't stop them. His friends Marty and David were laughing as well, but Pete was the most out of control. He waited for his turn, and snorted as David cussed while burning his finger on the joint they were sharing.

It was another long summer day, and there was little to do but hang out and get high. Pete hadn't tried weed until the past couple of weeks, when he started going to Marty's and David's houses. After getting bored with social media, YouTube, and television, their fascination turned toward how easily they might score a bag. Weed was all over Mainland High School, the boys knew, and shouldn't be hard to find.

David's older brother, Tanner, couldn't resist inviting the boys into his room to show off a small dime bag he'd purchased. Tanner warned the boys not to blab about it, and said they were too young to smoke. An emboldened Pete told Tanner he'd tell the older boy's mother if Tanner didn't roll one up for them.

Tanner, a couple of years older than Pete but not much taller, at first glared at him with disdain. Pete waited, only slightly nervous, to see whether Tanner would smack him or simply tell him to get out of the house. Tanner did neither, but grunted, "Wait in the back yard for me. All of you."

The three younger boys worked out a deal with Tanner for beyond that day: Tanner would give them one fat joint per week to share, David would do some of Tanner's chores, and all three would keep their mouths shut. Pete and Marty felt bad for David's extra workload, and pitched in to help him fold laundry, clean the kitchen, and take out the garbage. They performed these tasks rather quickly and sloppily before rushing into the backyard and lighting up.

Pete was laughing so hard at the moment that he dropped to his knees, struggling to breathe and enduring a coughing fit. Marty held the joint out to him, since it was Pete's turn to toke, but Pete reluctantly waved him off while he continued coughing.

"You're a mess, dude," Marty said, and handed the shrinking bud back to David instead. "You really are."

"Get off his case, man," David said. "His mom's gone."

Chapter Thirty-One:

AUG 6

I see the suitcase is out again," Beth said.

She placed a handful of green peas and small chunks of chicken on Maddie's high chair. Ben finished swallowing his own bite of chicken before responding.

"I'm leaving in the morning for Dallas, remember? I told you about it last week."

Beth nodded. "I remember, now."

He waited to see if Beth had more to say. Ben didn't see any point in asking if something was bothering her.

"Daddy, where's *your* peas?" Maddie asked.

Ben smiled. "Daddy doesn't like peas."

Maddie processed this. "I like peas. Here, try." She handed him a pea.

"No, thank you, sweetheart."

"Just *try*, Daddy."

He looked at Beth, who was glaring at him. Feeling like one of his younger part-time store employees rather than the guy who managed the managers, Ben plopped the pea into his mouth.

"Mmm, yummy," he said, quickly washing it down with his glass of water.

"Good Daddy," Maddie said, and clapped.

"Good Daddy," Beth repeated, and Ben glanced at her to see if she was smiling. Negative. He shoved some more chicken into his mouth.

Neither Ben nor Beth said much to each other for the next hour. Ben took charge of Maddie's bath time, read her a couple of short books, and tucked her into bed. He sat on the edge of the tiny bed for a while, stroking the little girl's head while her eyes grew heavy with sleep.

"Maddie, Daddy's leaving early tomorrow for work," he said. "I might not be here when you wake up."

"Can I go to work with you?" Maddie mumbled, half asleep.

Ben smiled. "Not this time. But one day."

"Okay, Daddy."

Ben stood, and stretched.

"Daddy?"

"Yes?"

"One more hug and kiss?" Maddie held out her tiny arms.

"Of course." Ben held her tightly, and Maddie gently patted his back. He loved when she did that.

Beth was washing her face and rubbing off makeup. Ben approached her and gently wrapped his arms around her front and kissed her neck. Neither spoke as they moved slowly to the bed. After making love, Beth laid her head on his chest. He waited, knowing she had lots on her mind. But soon Beth was breathing deeply, holding her thoughts close as she slept.

Chapter Thirty-Two:

AUG 7

James had spent the past week exploring the Peloponnese Peninsula in southern Greece, often taking hours at a time to stare out at the Gulf of Corinth as he continued to journal.

The area's combination of mountains and water was quite lovely, and James imagined himself staying forever in this place where the Greek war for independence had started in 1821. But he'd fancied that about each European city he'd visited so far in his post-college graduation trek, paid for by the proceeds from his late parents' estate.

The peninsula was said to have been inhabited since prehistoric times, with its name deriving from the Greek mythology surrounding the hero Pelops. Pelops conquered the entire region, and hence the name Peloponnesos: "Island of Pelops."

Today, James was exploring the Temple of Apollo Epicurius at Bassae, which scholars claimed was built sometime between 450 and 400 BC. His private tour guide, Thanos, was dropping bits of knowledge and trivia every couple of minutes as they walked. The man was perceptive enough to know that James needed intervals of quiet, so he could reflect and jot down observations.

"What's most interesting about this temple," Thanos said, "is that it is aligned north-to-south. This differs from the majority of Greek temples, which are aligned east-to-west in order to face the rising sun."

James nodded, realizing he had little sense of which direction he was facing at any given time during his extended sojourn across Europe. In general, he was gradually moving toward the eastern hemisphere.

"I wonder why that is?" he asked Thanos, who simply shrugged.

"Another unusual feature is that all three of the classical orders of ancient Greek *architecture are found here," Thanos continued, pointing to the structure. "You have Doric columns forming the peristyle. Ionic columns support the porch, and you'll see Corinthian columns inside."*

James took a moment to jot that down in his journal.

～～～

Volusia County Schools were set to open. As Tom studied the list of supplies that Connor needed for his sophomore year, he grew annoyed that school started in the middle of August when it was still quite summer and quite goddamned hot.

Tom sat at a small table near the rear of the Ocean Deck, the beach just a few yards away, sipping from a glass of Jack Daniel's on ice. Nearby, a group of college-aged volleyball players enjoyed a pickup game in the sand pit.

He was at Famoso's very seldom these days. Steve had things under control and business remained steady. Tom valued his privacy, relaxing and drinking without needing to engage in constant conversation or worry about others' opinions on how much he drank. The Ocean Deck had become a consistent place to park himself, especially in the middle of the day when it wasn't too crowded. Sometimes Tom took a long walk along the beach to clear his head.

Tom was grateful to still have his driver's license and the freedom to get around, having paid a fine and endured a tongue-lashing from a compassionate judge. He made sure there was always plenty of "padding" between his drinking and driving, and the walks on the beach were especially helpful for ensuring legal sobriety.

He noticed a familiar face across the restaurant, near the stage where a reggae band played most nights. Phil Solomon had just sat down at a table with a pretty, dark-haired young woman.

Tom felt guilty that he'd made no effort to reach out to Phil during the past couple of months. Phil had left him a couple of voice messages that Tom hadn't returned. Tom intended to call back, but the time and mood never felt right.

He wondered if Phil and Ben McBride were close, and if Ben was as wrapped up in Phil's life as he was in Tom's. Ben was a good guy and Tom owed him a lot for his influence with the justice system on Tom's behalf; but Ben's insistence on helping had become stressful. Thankfully Ben was very busy at work and traveling more, calling Tom and dropping by the Blakely residence less and less often.

Then there was Russ O'Rourke. Tom hadn't talked to him in a while, and wondered how Russ was handling things.

Tom wanted to pay his bill and walk on the beach, but really needed to piss. Heading to the bathroom near the front entrance would mean walking past

Phil's table. Phil was engrossed in quiet conversation with his female friend and didn't see Tom walk past. After relieving himself and washing his hands, Tom stared into the bathroom mirror and debated whether he looked drunk.

Phil noticed Tom as he approached the table. Phil stood and they shook hands, both men feeling a bit awkward. Phil introduced Amanda Bane to Tom. The men made small talk for a couple of minutes regarding children and jobs, but didn't address the elephant in the room.

"It was good to see you," Tom said. "Let's keep in touch more."

"Agreed," Phil replied. The men locked eyes for a moment, and then Tom turned to Amanda.

"Nice to meet you, Amanda."

"You, too."

Tom headed down to the beach, and Phil sipped his iced tea as Amanda finished her thought process about the classes she'd chosen for the fall semester. This was the third time they'd gotten together outside of class.

"Phil, did you hear my question?"

Phil had encouraged her to call him by his first name, which he preferred from everyone. "Dr. Solomon" sounded too erudite and stiff, and definitely way too Jewish.

"I'm sorry, what did you say?"

"I asked how you know him. How you know Tom?"

"Oh." Phil considered his answer. "Our wives are friends."

Amanda nodded. He could tell she had more to say.

"Phil, I've heard about your wife on the news," she said. "I'm really sorry. Do you have any idea where she is?"

Phil shook his head. "Unfortunately, no."

She smiled sadly.

"Tom's wife was with her. Kari Blakely."

"Oh my god."

"And another woman, Emma O'Rourke. They met at the gym together, a little fitness place. They hit it off, and formed a book club. Then, they decided to take a weekend adventure together."

Amanda gently patted his arm, and Phil felt a jolt of excitement. "It's okay," he said. "There's nothing any of us can do but wait and hope."

"How are your children doing?" Amanda asked.

"About as well as expected. Maybe better than expected. They've really blown me away, how strong they are. They're stronger than me, I think."

Amanda wiped tears off of her cheeks. "You've got a lot on your shoulders.

I'm amazed at how you taught classes all summer. No one could have guessed what you were going through."

Phil laughed. "Except that it's been all over the news and social media."

"Right."

"The public is losing interest, though. My girls and I don't have that luxury."

"Are the police still investigating?"

"As far as I know."

They sat quietly for a few minutes.

"Hey, you know," Amanda began, "I'm good with kids. I can babysit for you, whenever you need to get out of the house at night. If you think that would be all right, of course."

"That sounds really good. I appreciate that, Amanda. My parents live here, but the girls might like a change of pace."

"Just want to help you out in some way. After all, you've helped me a lot." Amanda smiled and patted his hand, and as her eyes sparkled in the light Phil thought that she'd never looked more beautiful.

Chapter Thirty-Three:

AUG 9

Beth asked Vanessa to repeat the question.

"Tell me more about why you've decided to own this."

Beth shifted her weight. It was her first session with Vanessa, after many weeks of contemplating reaching out and setting up an appointment.

"I don't know. I guess someone has to, and I'm the closest thing to a cause."

Vanessa nodded. "So there has to be a cause, in addition to what actually happened to your friends?"

"I suppose not," Beth said. "But I also feel guilty for not feeling more grateful. More grateful for my husband, for my child, for the fact that I didn't go on that trip with them even though they wanted me to."

"If you were feeling more grateful about the life you have, what would you notice? What would be different?"

Beth considered this.

"I'd have more patience with my husband Ben," she said. "I wouldn't get upset when he has to work late or go on a trip. I'd spend more time on the phone with him when he calls me from a hotel, when I can tell he really wants to hear about my day and about Maddie."

Vanessa jotted down some notes.

"Would it be possible to be both grateful and imperfect? Can those two co-exist?"

"I'm sure they can," Beth replied. "I guess they already do in many ways. Maybe I just need to accept that. But I want Ben to see that I'm grateful. I want to show him that, and not just use my frailty as a constant excuse."

"I get that. How can you tell whether Ben's grateful?"

Beth smiled. "He thanks me a lot for the way I care for Maddie and for the house. He's pretty generous with the hugs, kisses, and flowers."

"Sounds like a great guy."

"He is."

From his hotel room on the 27ᵗʰ floor, Ben could see the sparkling lights of Chicago's Michigan Avenue. Downtown Chicago was always one of his favorite places to go on business, with its energy and endless sea of young professionals.

This particular business trip involved a two-day motivational seminar, featuring an all-star lineup of best-selling authors who doubled as popular speakers. The first day had been rich with content and packed with interesting peers from across the country.

Ben's adrenaline was still high from the events of the last hour. At the hotel bar, he'd struck up a conversation with a middle-aged African-American bartender named Drake. Then Allison, a young woman with strawberry blonde hair whom Ben recognized from the seminar, joined their conversation. As Drake got busy with other patrons, Ben and Allison chatted with no small amount of humor and quips.

Allison was a sales leader for a cosmetics company, based in suburban Dallas. She was married with two young children, and attended two or three of these kinds of events each year. Allison had finished her drink and Ben, without thinking through the implications, told her to order another one on him. Soon they moved to an empty pub table and continued their conversation.

His new friend complained humorously but rather excessively about her husband, Ethan. She was toned and very health conscious, which reminded Ben of Beth, but also very gregarious and optimistic—which didn't remind him of Beth these days.

"Maybe we can sit together tomorrow," Allison had said. "That could be fun. We could quietly make fun of everyone else."

"Yeah, that could be a blast," Ben said.

"I don't fly out until the morning after tomorrow. What about you?"

"I don't either."

Allison beamed, and touched his arm. "Awesome! We can do this again tomorrow night."

They'd said goodnight, and Ben was tempted to half-jokingly asked for her hotel room number. He didn't know what would have happened after that, but as he sat in the window his mind spun possibilities. It took him a long time to fall asleep.

The next morning, Ben and Allison found each other during coffee time before the seminar began and sat together. Lunch was more of a group setting that didn't afford the same depth of conversation, but after the event was finished they walked a few blocks down Michigan Avenue to a delicious deep dish pizza joint and drank some good Cabernet.

"It kind of sucks," Allison began, as they walked back to the hotel, "that this is the last time we'll get to hang out together."

"Yeah," Ben said. "It's a bummer."

"Life is too short."

"And we have no actual idea how short or how long. How crazy is that?"

She laughed. "So crazy."

They entered the hotel lobby and walked toward the elevator. Ben pressed 27 and Allison pressed 35. When the car stopped at 27 and the elevator door dinged open. Ben held the button to keep it from shutting again and Allison laughed.

"I guess this is where we hug goodbye," she said.

Ben nodded and they embraced just long enough for the elevator door to shut again. They laughed. Allison's perfume was nice, and the hug felt nice too. The elevator started up again, on its way to 35.

"You're making me ride all the way up to 35?" Ben asked Allison. "That's cruel."

"I know, it's so out of your way. Hopefully the hug was worth it."

Ben could smell her perfume on him. "Sure it was."

The elevator arrived at 35 and the doors opened. Ben held the button in order for her to step out, but Allison didn't move.

"I have an incredible view of the city from my room," she said, moving closer to him. "Just breath-taking. Would you like to see it for a minute?"

Allison smiled, and the effort she made to look both innocent and seductive caused Ben's head to pound.

"It sounds really nice," he said. "But I should probably take the long ride back down to the 27th floor."

Allison nodded. "If you must," she said, and stepped out of the elevator before glancing back with a final smile. "My cell phone is on the business card I gave you, in case you change your mind." And with that, Allison turned and disappeared from sight as the door closed.

A few minutes later Ben sat in his hotel room window once again, his cell phone in his hand. He found Allison's card. Ben stared out at Michigan Avenue, and dialed.

"Pick up, please, pick up," Ben whispered into the phone.

"Hi," a familiar female voice finally answered.

"Hi," Ben said to Beth, and fell onto the nearby bed while holding the phone against his ear. "Maddie sound asleep?"

"Like an angel." Beth paused. "I was hoping you'd call."

Ben smiled, both relieved and guilty. "I was hoping you'd answer."

Chapter Thirty-Four:

AUG 10

Delphi said goodbye to her final customer of the day, and locked the front door of The Oracle. She straightened up the shelves for an hour or so before heading out to her car. It was getting dark.

Not long after starting the drive to her townhouse, Delphi noticed the car behind her. She couldn't make out the driver's face and the vehicle itself was unfamiliar. Delphi sped up, reaching for her cell phone, prepared to dial 9-1-1 if necessary. She passed her neighborhood and continued driving, heading in the direction of the Daytona Beach Police Department.

She cruised through a yellow light, and looked into her rearview mirror. The car had stopped at the light. Delphi felt a huge surge of relief, but continued toward the police station just in case the car caught up with her.

It didn't. Delphi sped past the station on U.S. 1, and studied the upcoming intersections to figure out which one would be the easiest to take and backtrack home. She quickly selected the first available side street and then activated her smart phone's maps application. For the next several minutes, Delphi drove the circuitous path directed by the application's computerized voice.

She let out a deep breath when she reached her neighborhood, and entered the gate code with a final couple of nervous glances into her rearview mirror. Delphi pulled into her driveway, pressed the remote control attached to her overhead sun visor, and her single-car garage door dutifully opened.

Just as Delphi put her SUV into park and hit the remote again to close the garage, her phone rang. She was distracted just enough by the call to not turn off the ignition.

Unknown Caller. As Delphi debated whether to answer, her vehicle still running, a pair of hands reached forward and wrapped a white, soaked cloth around her face. The cloth suctioned firmly to her mouth before Delphi could scream, and then the same hands pinned her arms down long enough for Delphi to lose consciousness.

The car still running in the closed garage, the man who'd been hiding under a large blanket Delphi left in her back seat scampered out of the car and through the door that led to Delphi's kitchen. He shut and locked the door behind him, and then traveled carefully through the inside of the townhouse to the front door, which he locked behind him using a special tool.

The man walked briskly to the sidewalk, and continued to the outside of the neighborhood gates until he reached a waiting car and vanished into the night.

~~~

Mario was awakened near midnight by Henry. It was either really good news or really bad news, Mario assumed.

"The Adams girl is dead," Henry said.

Mario was surprised by the wave of grief. Delphi had been a pain in the ass, but there remained a sweet spirit inside of her. He plopped down into an easy chair. Henry offered to fix him a drink, but Mario waved him off.

"What happens next?" Henry asked.

Mario shrugged.

"We wait."

~~~

Each morning in the ashram, James woke up well before 6 a.m. in order to attend the first Satsang, which in Sanskrit meant "communion with truth." Devotees gathered to imbibe the master's transforming spiritual discourses, with the goal of emerging renewed and inspired for that day's leg of the continuing spiritual journey. James and the others, led by the guru named Raji, read and listened to scriptures, discussed their potential meanings, and then had a period of silent meditation.

Afterwards James joined the others for tea, and then participated in the asana class that involved practicing various yoga positions. Breakfast—vegetarian, of course—was served in the latter part of the morning. There was more tea time in the early afternoon, followed by a lecture from the guru, another asana class, and then a vegetarian dinner. The evening Satsang occurred at 8 p.m., and by 10:30 p.m. James was usually asleep.

James sat with Curtis, a 40-ish South African native who'd taken the younger man under his wing when he arrived at the ashram, as they sipped tea one afternoon. James didn't know Curtis's last name and never thought to ask.

"How would you replicate all of this in the 'real world,'" Curtis asked him, "all of this around us?"

James looked closely at his friend. "All of this routine? This lifestyle?"

Curtis nodded.

"I don't know. I don't know that you could. Maybe incorporate pieces of it. But not all of it. People have too much to get done."

"That's the problem. You can't export this into industrialized civilization. The world is a messed up place, my friend."

James smiled. "Well, we knew that."

He thought more about Curtis's remarks.

"I'd like to try some day," James said. "To incorporate some of it. To experiment, and see if people can adjust."

"Maybe I'll join you," Curtis smiled. And then, as an afterthought, "Or maybe you'll join me."

Chapter Thirty-Five

DEC 5

Kari," Jackie said, "you keep wanting to do this or that to your body, or change Tom into being this or that. Or move somewhere where life will be more fulfilling. You remind me of Robert Cohn sometimes. Jake tells him, 'You can't get away from yourself by moving from one place to another.'"

Kari took a long sip from her third glass of wine, and some dribbled onto her chin because she was too eager to respond.

"I'm just joking around, mostly, when I say those things," she said. "I know that you can't escape from yourself. I just think that if you're not fully happy with yourself, you should do something about it."

"So do something," Delphi said. "Don't just complain all the time."

Kari shot daggers at Delphi. "Am I complaining all of the time?"

"Quite a bit of it."

"Do you want me to stop coming?"

Emma touched Kari's arm. "Don't be ridiculous," she said. "This book club is where we can just be ourselves, with our imperfections."

"Yeah, well apparently some people think I'm too much of a complainer."

Delphi sighed. "Kari, don't be offended by that. I'm a complainer, too. I guess I get irritated when I see it in other people because I see it too much in myself."

"Have you guys noticed," said Beth, hoping to change the subject, "how this book has no real narrative? It's like stuff just happens and people say things, but I have no idea where it's going."

"It's going to Spain," Jackie said. "And we're going, too. Figuratively."

"We really should go somewhere together," Delphi said.

"Merry Christmas," the stranger said.

"Merry Christmas to you," Curtis Everett replied to the man who'd driven up to the ranch gates. "What can I do for you?"

The man had thinning blonde hair. He gestured out the driver's side window toward the vast expanse of property that lay beyond Curtis.

"I'd heard this property was maybe for sale. I was hoping to take a look."

Curtis shook his head. "No, sir, you're mistaken. I believe there are a few other large parcels that might be on the market. You could take a look, tell them I sent you." He reached into his front pocket and handed the man a card that simply read:

Curtis Everett

ORGANIC PRODUCE

877-471-1200

The man studied the card for a moment. "Organic produce," he said. "Interesting."

"We sell at all the local farmers' markets. Come give us a try sometime. We're the best around."

"I sure will. You grow everything on site here?"

"Everything."

"That's neat."

"We deliver to people's homes also, if the order is large enough," Curtis added. "All they have to do is call the toll-free number."

The man nodded. "Well, I'll spread the word. Do you have a few more of these cards?"

Curtis handed him several more. "I sure appreciate it," he said. "It was nice to meet you, Mister…?"

"Layman," the man said. "Scott Layman." Scott produced one of his own cards, indicating a real estate brokerage business. "If you're ever looking for more pieces of land for expanding your business, I'm the guy to call. I know this area well."

"That's good to know," Curtis said, studying the card.

"I may order some vegetables from you before New Year's. I'm going to make one of those clichéd resolutions about eating better."

Curtis laughed. "We could all stand to do that. I look forward to your call."

The men shook hands a final time, and Curtis watched Scott Layman drive away before hopping back into a golf cart and cruising across the ranch.

Sarosky, why are you still here? It's Christmas Eve. Go home."

Sarosky was absorbed in his laptop. "I will in a minute. Why don't you go, though?"

Police Chief Higgins shrugged. "I don't feel right being home when I've got some of my folks out there, protecting people going to Mass from getting run over by sad drunks."

"Understood."

Higgins sat near Sarosky.

"You and Rice still at it with the book club girls, huh?"

"Still at it."

"It's beyond our league now, pal. If the feds can't find them with their resources, no way we can."

"The feds aren't doing squat. No one's taking it personally."

"But you are."

"Yeah, I guess I am."

"That's dangerous. At worst. At best, it's disheartening."

"Understood again, on both counts."

Higgins glanced at his watch. "Why are you making your parents spend Christmas Eve alone?"

"They're not alone. They have each other. I'm alone."

"They want you with them."

"They're probably asleep by now. They go to sleep by 8 every night."

"Where's Rice at tonight?"

"Off with her family in Gainesville. Where she should be."

"Good for her." Higgins sighed. "Holidays are tough. You love them as a kid, and when you grow up all you think about is who's not there anymore."

"Yeah," Sarosky replied.

"I'll leave you alone now. If I don't see you again, Merry Christmas, Detective."

"Merry Christmas, Chief."

~~~

Across town, Cameron Brock and his partner Nelson walked into Famoso's, invited by Julio to a private party. Cameron smiled upon seeing Susannah clinging to the bartender's side.

"Cameron, my man!" Julio gave him a bear hug. He looked at Nelson. "You must be Nelson? Welcome! Thanks for coming."

Susannah gave them both a big hug, and promptly made sure they each received a glass of wine. Cameron glanced around at the crowd. "So, who are all these people?"

"A few regulars," Julio said. "A few friends of Susannah's. A few friends of mine. Okay, more than a few friends of Susannah's."

"I have a lot of friends," she shrugged.

"They all have really good hair," Nelson said, pointing to a couple of the women.

"Those are two of my co-workers. Gina there does my hair. She's the best."

"And who's that hottie?" Nelson asked her, pointing to a handsome blonde man who was dancing with one of the hairdressers. "Does he work with you, too?"

"What gave it away?" Julio smirked, and Susannah pretended to smack him.

"Don't stare," Cameron said to Nelson, half-kidding, half-serious. He looked at Susannah. "Nelson has slutty ambitions. But I love him anyway."

"Hey, man, I've got a New Year's Resolution for you," Julio said to Cameron. "Finish that freakin' article."

"Totally," Nelson added. "How much longer do I have to hear about that rambling monstrosity?"

"You haven't even read it," Cameron said.

"I'm waiting until it's finished."

"Well, it won't be finished until Beth McBride talks to me."

Julio sighed. "We'll still be arguing about it next Christmas, then."

"Have a little faith in me."

"Hey," Julio said, "you're the best journalist I know."

"I'm the only journalist you know."

Julio looked at Susannah, and caressed her forehead. "You feeling better than you were this morning, baby?"

"Yeah," she nodded. "Not sure what was coming over me."

~~~

"Mario, that's like the most beautiful tree ever," said Rayna, a leggy brunette who was new to the Daytona modeling scene during the past few months. "Like, it ought to be in Rockefeller Center or something."

Rayna and the dazzling blonde Heather took turns gushing about the tree. Trying to ignore them as he sipped on some egg nog, Pete O'Rourke looked at his father Russ and rolled his eyes. Russ grinned.

"The tree is my favorite part of all of this holiday madness," Mario said, drinking from his own egg nog.

"Aw, just like the Beast!" Rayna declared. Everyone turned to look at her with puzzlement.

"Pardon me?" Mario asked politely.

"You know, the Beast in *Beauty and the Beast.* Before he was turned into the Beast, the tree was always his favorite part of Christmas."

Pete stifled a laugh. Henry Reid, invited but not participating in the tree decoration, stood at a respectful distance and remained stoic-faced.

"Oh yeah, she's right!" Heather exclaimed. "I remember my mother reading that to me."

Mario smiled.

"I've been called a beast before, but not nearly as kindly."

Heather squeezed his arm. "I'll bet you have."

"Did you ever read that story to Emma when she was little?" Rayna asked Mario with the best of intentions.

Pete glared at her, and it took Rayna a moment to realize that her perfectly legitimate question was dripping with severely illegitimate timing. Henry quickly glanced about at the faces in the room, and drank more of his Scotch on the rocks.

"So!" Russ said loudly, holding his glass of egg nog high in the air. "Who's ready to enjoy some appetizers in the dining room?"

After dinner, Heather begged to watch *It's a Wonderful Life* and

Mario volunteered his grandson to "entertain the ladies." Pete shot daggers at his grandfather, and then reluctantly obeyed as he went into the media room and turned on the massive flat screen television. Rayna and Heather marveled at

127

the home popcorn machine as Pete fired it up. He gave each of them a box, and found he didn't mind them nearly as much as they settled on either side of him.

"Do you like romantic movies, Pete?" Heather asked him, stroking his arm.

"Only when I'm drunk," Pete deadpanned, and the girls laughed like it was the funniest thing they'd ever heard.

"Hey," Russ called into the media room, "make sure you behave yourself, kiddo."

Rayna turned and waved Russ toward them. "Why don't you join us, honey?"

Russ shook his head. "I've gotta talk some shop with the old man."

Rayna made a fat lip. "Party pooper. Mario's always talking business. Even on Christmas Eve."

"Shh!" Heather said. "I'm missing some of the dialogue."

Dialogue? Pete thought.

"I'm really sorry about your mother," Heather whispered, pressing close against him. "It must be really hard this time of year."

"Thanks," Pete said, hoping she wouldn't go on and on about the subject.

"I don't think I'll ever get to be a mom," she continued. "I'll probably be an old maid someday, still hoping to be a famous actress."

Pete glanced at Heather. She smelled really good. He was tempted to take a selfie with both women squeezed against him and send it to all of his friends, none of whom were likely watching a movie with bikini models on this most sacred of evenings.

Russ joined Mario and Henry in the study. They were drinking straight liquor now, Scotch for Mario and Henry, and Captain Morgan for Russ.

"Nothing still?' Russ asked with little energy and even less optimism.

"Nothing." Henry shook his head.

Russ lifted his glass of booze. "To Emma. And days of Auld Lang Syne and all of that."

Mario and Henry dutifully lifted their glasses, and the three men drew closer. *Clank, clank, clank.*

"After Delphi died," Mario said, "we stopped getting the phone calls. That's been four months."

Russ nodded. "Yeah. I know. I'm sorry about her, Mario. I know she was very close to you at one point."

Mario nodded. "Thanks. Yeah, she was a loon, but there was something very loveable about her."

"She must have been in a lot of pain, to take her own life."

"A whole lot of pain." Mario added.

Russ glanced at Henry, who shifted his weight uncomfortably. Russ was drinking just enough to amplify his naturally bold, direct personality.

"You sure it was suicide, right?"

Henry frowned. "Come on, Russ."

"I'm only asking."

"That's what the police concluded," Mario said.

"Since when have you held a ton of faith in the police?"

Henry took an irritated step toward Russ. "Enough, O'Rourke," he said, and lifted his glass again. "Merry Christmas. And Happy Almost New Year."

"We'll see if it's happy," Russ muttered, downing the last of his Scotch. He headed straight over to the home bar to get a refill.

Mario moved closer to Henry. "What did your person tell you this afternoon?" he whispered.

"That nobody can even get near our source. They say they still don't even know his name. Everything is done through layers, two or three deep."

Mario waited.

"We're not dealing with a rational person here. Whoever they are, they aren't motivated by money. They're not business people."

"I'm not motivated by money in this case either."

"I know."

"Keep digging," Mario said. "Give my grandson a late Christmas present."

"Of course."

Russ ambled back into the room.

"Just checked on our boy, Mario. You've got competition with the tits on sticks."

Mario smiled. "He can have them. He's going to inherit everything one day anyhow."

Chapter Thirty-Seven:

DEC 31

Tom and Connor were the last to arrive at the McBride home for their "casual" New Year's Eve party. Connor was nervous as they greeted the other invitees: Phil, Audrey, and Natalie; Russ and Pete; and Julio and Susannah. Pete and Connor awkwardly shook hands as their fathers greeted each other.

Beth was an energetic hostess, bustling around as a cheerful Maddie—sporting a tiny plastic tiara that displayed *2013*—worked the crowd with her charms. The dining room table was beautifully adorned with appetizers, and an adjacent table contained every non-alcoholic beverage imaginable.

Tom smiled. They were having a "dry" New Year's Eve party for his benefit. *Not necessary,* he thought, but a kind gesture and a bit of a sacrifice for the others.

Ben invited the kids into the den, where they found their own hefty supply of snacks and sodas. Maddie hopped onto Connor's lap, and Pete asked Natalie to decide which movie they should watch as Ben held out several DVD options. She selected *Ramona and Beezus*. Audrey and Pete made eye contact for a moment, and she smiled.

Ben hung out with the kids to get them settled, and as he left he wondered whether they'd talk to each other about their missing mothers. He joined the adults in the living room. After about ten minutes of small talk, Ben looked around to ensure none of the young people had wandered back over to eavesdrop, and then nodded at Beth.

This is not a good idea, Ben thought.

"Everyone, I really appreciate you being here tonight," Beth said. "Ben and I care very much for each of you. It's been a very tough year, and we really wanted to all be together as we go into 2013 with a hopeful spirit."

"Thanks for inviting us," Phil said. Tom and Russ nodded. Julio, sitting near Tom, gently patted his arm.

Beth turned her attention fully to Tom, and Ben hoped Maddie wouldn't come bouncing in at that moment.

"Tom, I'm especially glad you're here," Beth said. "We've been really worried about you, and we want to help."

"I appreciate that," Tom said, hoping Beth would change the subject.

She continued. "No one can blame you, or Phil, or Russ, for feeling the things you're feeling. But we're all begging you to think about Connor, and your business, and your own health and well-being."

Beth paused. Russ shifted uncomfortably; he didn't particularly want to come tonight, and certainly didn't want to be a part of this quasi-intervention. Ben had asked Russ to participate to "show solidarity." Ben was a great guy, Russ could tell, but the "solidarity" concept was corporate bullshit and overall this felt like poor taste.

"I appreciate that," Tom repeated.

"Tom," Ben joined in, "we're not trying to judge you, just share our observations. Each of us here has noticed that your drinking has been excessive. I know that you tried to stop drinking after the accident, but you've not been able to. You don't have to go through this alone, and so I'm asking you to consider a treatment facility or an AA group. And I'm ready to help get you situated at either one."

Ben waited. The room felt tense. Tom was looking down.

"What do you think?" Beth asked Tom.

Tom gave everyone a quick glance and forced a smile. "I appreciate your intentions in doing this," he said. "But I doubt this is really how you wanted to spend your New Year's Eve, having a dry party for the sad alcoholic."

"I wouldn't want to be anywhere else," Julio said, and Susannah nodded enthusiastically.

"But," Tom continued, "it's a bit embarrassing. And I'm more comfortable initiating these kinds of conversations myself, in private, with just one or two persons." He looked at Ben. "Know what I mean?"

Ben nodded. "Yeah, I do. But we've had those. The situation hasn't changed."

"I suppose it hasn't," Tom said. "But this is my decision, in the end. And things are going better for me. The restaurant is doing well, Steve is doing a great job. I'm not driving around plastered, and I'm spending a lot of time with Connor."

"Connor tells us you drink every night, until you pass out," Beth said, trying not to sound judgmental.

Tom stared at her, and then at Ben. "So is that what happens when my son visits here? An interrogation?"

"Absolutely not," Ben said. "He brings the subject up. We don't ask him about it."

"Connor hasn't said a word to me about it," Tom said.

"He probably doesn't want to make you feel bad," Beth said.

"This here makes me feel bad. This here, tonight."

Phil spoke for the first time. "That's kind of the idea, Tom."

Russ jumped in as well, more out of a sense of obligation than conviction. "Hey, Tom, you gotta live your own life at the end of the day. But your life affects others. So your friends here, they just want to help."

"You're a great guy!" Susannah added with too much enthusiasm, and Tom had finally had enough. He stood.

"I need to go for a walk," Tom said, and left out the front door. He walked briskly down the sidewalk, observing house after house still lit up with Christmas bulbs and multiple cars parked in driveways. He doubted a single other house was dry that night, and wished he'd chosen a different party with no well-intentioned sympathizers in his face.

Back inside the den, Pete kept making Audrey laugh by quietly making fun of each of the Ramona and Beezus characters. Natalie gave the movie her full attention, and Connor was half-watching while balancing his sketch pad on his lap.

"What are you drawing?" Pete asked him at one point, and Connor held up a drawing of a dog on the side of a mountain.

"That's really good, Connor," Audrey said.

"Yeah, it is," Pete said.

"Thanks." Connor looked back at his sketch pad, and kept drawing.

Audrey and Pete were sitting next to each other on the couch, Natalie on the other side of Audrey. Pete liked how the older Solomon girl smelled.

"Do you like to body surf?" he asked Audrey.

She shrugged. "I'm not sure if I ever have."

"You've never body surfed?"

Audrey laughed. "You mean, like ride a wave into the shore? I'm sure I have, but it's not like I do it regularly. I don't go to the beach a lot, because I sunburn too easily."

"You should come body surfing with me sometime. It's a blast. Even when I'm just hanging out in the ocean, floating and treading water."

"Maybe I will," Audrey said.

Natalie whispered to Audrey, "I-is he asking you out on a date?"

Pete smiled at Audrey's embarrassment. "You can come too, Natalie."

"Cool," Natalie said, and turned her attention back to the Quimby family.

Chapter Thirty-Eight

JAN. 10, 2013

This is Lt. Carlson from the Daytona Beach Police Department. We have your son Pete."

Russ asked the lieutenant to repeat himself, which he did.

"What's he doing there?"

"He and a friend stole some items from the flea market."

Fuck, Russ thought. "I'll be right there."

Russ was road rage personified, cursing out loud at drivers who were too slow or too fast or too timid, or just too much of anything he couldn't tolerate. He pulled in hurriedly to a visitor's spot and slammed the car door.

Pete wouldn't look at him, which pissed Russ off even more, but he held his cool inside the police station. Russ said nothing as they walked out to the car, and once inside he kept his voice calm.

"They said you stole a bunch of baseball caps from a table. Was it your idea?"

Pete didn't say anything.

"Was it, Pete?"

Pete shrugged. "I don't know. We just did it."

"You just *did* it?"

"Yeah."

In the rearview mirror, Russ saw Pete frown.

"Where are we going? This isn't the way home."

"We're not going home."

"Where are we going?"

"I'm going back to work. You're coming with me."

Pete glared at his father in the mirror. Russ wanted to punch him.

"I don't want to come with you."

"I didn't ask you what you wanted. By the way, I didn't want to go to the goddamned police station in the middle of the day, on your last day of winter break."

Pete folded his arms and sulked. Russ wondered if the kid would even get out of the car once he parked at the office, and whether Russ would have to drag his ass inside. But Pete got out, albeit slowly, and walked several steps behind his dad.

Once again, Russ approached the Cubists without a scheduled Mario appointment.

"Mr. O'Rourke…"

"Tell Mr. Lazano his grandson Pete is here to see him."

The Cubist glanced at Pete, looked him up and down, and motioned for them to wait. He went into Mario's office, and a couple of minutes later emerged with the man himself.

"This is a nice surprise," Mario said, looking at Russ more than Pete. "Come on in."

Russ passed Mario without shaking his hand. Mario gave his grandson a hug, and Pete returned it with a small gesture of enthusiasm.

As soon as the door closed, Russ went back into rage mode.

"He's your problem now," he said, pointing to Pete as his son sunk into the chair across from Mario. "He's following in your footsteps, so you take care of him."

Mario stared at Pete, and then at Russ.

"I'm not understanding."

"Tell him what I'm talking about, Pete."

Pete stared down, keeping his mouth shut. Russ didn't bother to wait.

"He got arrested for stealing some fucking baseball caps from the flea market. He and his friend thought that would be fun, apparently." Russ paused. "Actually, I don't know what the hell they were thinking. I don't know what you're thinking anymore, Pete."

He starred at Mario. "You understand the mind of the criminal better than I do, Mario. So take him under your wing, and at least make him a higher class of criminal than someone who steals worthless crap from white trash."

Pete glanced up at his grandfather, who was simply rocking back and forth in his desk chair and looking at Russ.

"Maybe you should leave us," Mario said. Russ, knowing he'd more than pushed his luck with the old man, turned and left without another glance at Pete.

He trudged back to his office, ignoring his assistant Becky, trying to figure out where he'd left off before the call from the police. Focus and motivation eluded him, and Russ decided it was probably time to look for a different place to work.

~~~

"Do you want to sleep with her?"

Vanessa Porter posed the question with no hint of accusation or expectation. Phil glanced at her, knowing that it would be impossible to hide his feelings regardless of his answer.

He imagined Amanda, with her youthful spirit, curious mind, and toned body.

"I do," Phil said. "I feel very alive around her. I like connecting with her. I want to keep connecting with her."

Vanessa nodded. "Has the relationship grown physical? Is that why you're bringing the topic up today?"

"It has not."

"But you think it could if you wanted it do."

"I don't know. She might look at things totally differently. This might all be an illusion for me. Amanda might smack me if I tried to kiss her."

Vanessa laughed.

"I wonder,' she said, "if Amanda was closer to your age, and not one of your students, what you'd be thinking right now about being so attracted to another woman?"

"You mean, would I feel just as guilty because it's not Jackie?"

"Correct."

"Good point. Not as guilty. But still guilty."

Vanessa waited.

"Price of being Jewish. We breed guilt."

"There's help for that, you know."

"Yeah. Isn't that why I'm here?"

"I'll try my best, but I'm not certified in Jewish Guilt," she said. "I'd be happy to refer you."

"Let's see how far I get without slaying that particular demon, and then we'll catch it off guard."

"Deal," Vanessa said. "So tell me, who initiates contact usually, you or Amanda?"

Phil thought through the past six months. "She does, usually. But I make sure I'm available when she reaches out."

"What's the risk if you weren't available?"

"I guess she'd do something else for a couple of hours."

"*With* someone else?"

"Perhaps. I don't know."

"Does she have a boyfriend?"

Phil shifted his weight. "I don't think so. She's never mentioned one."

"And she knows about your personal situation?"

"Yeah. She's been very respectful about it. Doesn't ask me a lot of questions, but I know she cares."

Vanessa waited.

"I don't want to hurt her."

"Understood."

"I don't want to hurt *me*," Phil added.

Chapter Thirty-Nine:

JAN. 21

This time, Connor poured the ice water all over his passed-out father.

Tom jumped, cussed, and frantically wiped the excess water and cubes off of his face and neck. He blinked his eyes several times and glared at Connor, who stood trembling with the empty glass in his hand.

"Connor, what the hell!"

"Don't talk, Dad."

"What?"

"Don't talk. You need to listen to me right now."

Tom took a deep breath. He sat down, away from the portion of the couch that Connor had drenched.

"Ok, Son."

Connor paced around. "I want to go live with the McBrides. You don't care about me."

"That's not true. I care very much."

"You don't. You don't show it."

Tom felt stupid defending himself, so he just sat and listened.

"You drink every night until you pass out right here. You don't care what I'm doing during that time. You don't help me with my homework. You don't know if I'm even in the house. You don't care. All you care about is that restaurant, and drinking."

Connor was stumbling over his words. The shaking intensified, and tears were flowing down his cheeks.

"The McBrides and the other fathers talked to you on New Year's Eve. They begged you to get help. That's been weeks now, and you haven't done anything."

Tom stared at the floor.

"Mrs. McBride said for me to call her if I needed anything. I'm calling her in the morning, and asking her to come get me. I'm going to pack a bag. If you try to stop me, I'll call the police."

When Tom looked at Connor in disbelief, his son added, "I mean it. I love you, Dad, but I can't take this anymore."

Connor could no longer speak, he was trembling so badly. He melted into tears and sat down on the floor. Tom watched him for a moment, and then sat beside him. Not sure whether the boy would shove him away, Tom put an arm around Connor and pulled him close. Connor simply continued to sob and Tom hugged him tighter. He buried his face in Tom's chest.

After a few minutes the sobbing subsided and Connor rested against him, saying nothing. Tom remembered when his son would fall asleep in his arms, the early years when Connor adored him and Kari was around and Tom couldn't have imagined himself ever becoming a drunk.

A drunk. He'd said it in his mind for the first time.

"You don't need to leave," Tom said gently. "I won't drink anymore."

Connor didn't respond, and Tom decided that elaborating would diminish the simple commitment of those last four words. He stood, and helped Connor to his feet. Arm around him, Tom walked Connor to his bed and tucked him inside the covers. He kissed him on the forehead, and sat on the edge of the bed as Connor drifted off to sleep.

After a few minutes, Tom quietly left the room and went to the kitchen. He found whatever bottles of whiskey, rum, and tequila were still around and put them in a big garbage bag. Tom started to take the bag out to the trash can in the garage, and then removed the bottles and poured the contents into the kitchen sink. He returned the bottles to the bag and gently plopped it into the big plastic receptacle.Back at the sink, Tom turned on the hot water and watched it chase the booze down into the pipes.

He wanted a shower, and turned the water as hot as he could stand it. Tom closed his eyes and let the water pound his chest for a while, and then turned around and did the same for his back. Tom remained in the shower until he was too exhausted to stand.

Chapter Forty

FEB. 10

It was a warm Daytona Beach morning. James stood at a phone booth located outside a convenience store along A1A.

"It'll all work out, Uncle Everett," he said into the receiver. "You can relax."

"I just can't believe you spent almost all of that money," Everett said, relaxing in his recliner at his home in Rochester. "At least it sounds like you had a great time and saw the world. What are you going to do next?"

"Get a job."

"Doing what?"

James laughed. "Doing whatever. I have a business degree from RIT, remember."

"Do you remember anything you learned?"

James watched as a car full of beach-bound women pulled into the parking lot and laughed their way inside the store.

"From college or from my traveling?"

"Well, I was thinking college. But I guess it really doesn't matter now at this point, does it?"

"Nope."

Everett paused. "I have a question for you. Why Florida?"

James shrugged. "Why not? It's warm. It's sunny. And I hear it's pretty cheap to live here."

He glanced across the busy road, and noted a two-story office building with the words DAYTONA DEVELOPMENT CORPORATION in giant letters across the top.

"I'll find something good to do. I've learned you can't take anything for granted, Uncle Everett, and you can't plan anything. Each day unfolds new possibilities."

Everett chuckled. "Sounds like some of that Eastern mumbo-jumbo you picked up over there in India. But you know yourself better than anyone."

James smiled. "I want you to come visit when I get settled into an apartment. You could use some fresh, warm air."

"Yeah, I'm sure I'll fit in just perfectly down there," Everett said. "Thanks for calling, Son. I love you."

"I love you, too."

James hung up, took a glance back inside the large store window to see what the pretty girls were up to, and then shifted his gaze back upon the building across the street. He grabbed his rucksack and started walking.

Julio was uneasy about the two men who sat down at the crowded Famoso's bar. One was stocky with a massive neck and greasy, slicked back, thinning hair. The other was younger, with spiky blonde hair. Greasy Neck ordered a shot of Patron for each of them, and Julio felt their eyes following him as he served other customers.

When they made eye contact again, Greasy Neck motioned Julio over.

"Where can we find Tom Blakely?"

Julio glanced over at Spiky Blonde, who just stared at him with a goofy expression. He looked back at Greasy Neck.

"He's not here right now. Did you want to speak with my manager, Steve?"

Greasy Neck shook his head. "No, I'm not interested in Steve. When does Tom come in usually?"

"I don't know. He's not here very often."

"How can we reach him?"

"Through Steve."

"I don't want to talk to Steve."

Julio was irritated. "Then you'll have a hard time getting a hold of Tom. Can I get you gentlemen anything else, or are you ready for your check?"

Greasy Neck finished his shot, and shoved the glass over to Julio, who took it. "Another," the man grunted. Spiky, as if on cue, finished his shot as well and held up his index finger. Julio poured another shot and moved on to other customers once again. He saw Steve working the crowd, and debated whether to say something to him.

"That's a shame about Mrs. Blakely," Spiky said to Julio. "Does Mr. Blakely have any idea where she is?"

Julio considered his response.

"You'll have to ask him. It's none of my business," Julio said.

Greasy Neck tossed some cash onto the bar. He gestured to Spiky that it was time to go, and handed Julio a business card. "Please give this to Mr. Blakely," Greasy Neck mumbled, and the two men headed out.

Julio collected the cash, watching the men exit the restaurant. He glanced at the card, thought about Susannah, and felt worried.

Chapter Forty-One:

FEB. 14

The low ocean tide gave Phil and Amanda a long, flat stretch of sand to walk along.

They hadn't reached the holding hands stage, but the emotional intimacy and sexual tension thickened on each occasion they were together. The fact that it was Valentine's Day wasn't mentioned; they'd simply made plans to walk on the beach and grab a bite to eat.

"Now that I've started, I don't want to ever finish school," Amanda said. "It just seems like you graduate into the grind and that's that."

Phil smiled. "That's that, huh?"

"Yeah. Who needs that? Not me."

"You don't have to leave school, if you become a professor."

"That's true," she said.

Amanda stooped to examine a few sea shells that were lodged in the sand. She pocketed one of them.

"Do you collect those?" Phil asked.

"I have some going back to when I was very little. I like to hold them up to my ears and hear the ocean."

"That's cute."

"Maybe I worry that if I just become part of the grind, I won't ever hear the ocean anymore, or anything else peaceful and mysterious," Amanda said.

"You've got to pay attention to your heart. Not everyone has to go into the business world. I never have, and I sure haven't missed out on anything."

"Even the higher pay?"

"Even the higher pay which comes with a higher price tag."

The sun was sinking lower to the west, over the beachside condominiums.

"I was wondering something, Phil. Something about Jackie."

Phil tensed a little.

"Yes?"

"You've said a couple of times recently that you don't believe Jackie is still alive. And I was wondering if you might want to do something symbolic, something to give you more closure. Like a memorial service."

Phil reflected on the idea. He envisioned a synagogue full of mourners and a cantor singing passionately, while an empty casket rested in the front of the temple. Or more likely it would be a Protestant church, since that was Jackie's background and her parents would probably prefer it that way.

"I hadn't thought about that before," Phil said. "I guess that would be a big step."

"Yeah, especially for the girls. It might be too soon, still. But something to think about."

Phil watched a sand crab burrowing its way out of sight.

"It's important to recognize big life changes, to commemorate milestones," he said. "That's something we've lost in the modern age, the significance of rituals at key seasons of life."

"Kind of like your daughters' bat mitzvahs?"

He nodded. "Exactly. But there's many more things that can take place in a person's life, to help someone notice the significance of things."

"I blame the grind, once again."

"As you should. Human beings, especially in the west, have become so busy doing life that we've forgotten to observe its meaning along the way."

Amanda stopped walking and took Phil's hand. Hers was cool and smooth, and she smelled nice.

"You get me," Amanda said. "I really appreciate that." She gave him a soft kiss on the cheek, and then released his hand.

It was just a simple kiss, but to Phil it felt like one of those big milestones.

Across town, Julio arrived at Susannah's apartment and was blown away by how she looked in her red dress. She smiled, noticing his inability to form coherent words or remove his eyes from her significant cleavage. Susannah wrapped her arms around Julio and kissed him.

"They look bigger, don't they?" she whispered in his ear as they pressed close together, rubbing and caressing, her apartment door still open.

Julio laughed. "Well, yeah, they do. They were already pretty perfect."

They went inside, and she fixed him a cocktail.

"None for you?" he asked.

"Not right now."

They sat entwined on the couch, making out, and Julio caressed her neck and shoulders.

"Did you have them done?" he asked.

Susannah gave him a mischievous stare. "I was waiting until Valentine's Day to tell you."

"To tell me that you got a boob job?"

Susannah shook her head. "No, silly. To tell you that we're going to have a baby."

As Julio stared at her, Susannah slid the dress off of her shoulders and revealed her bare breasts.

"These are mommy boobs," she smiled. "Do you want to enjoy them while they're still all yours?"

Julio pulled her close and kissed her deeply. Susannah found it adorable when tears started to flow down his cheeks, and rubbed her breasts against his face. Knowing she was pregnant led Julio to automatically want to be cautious, but Susannah climbed on top of him and rode him with more ardor than he'd ever experienced with her.

"Wow," he whispered afterwards, as she rested against him. "Just wow."

"Wow for what in particular?"

"Wow for all of it."

"It's pretty exciting, isn't it? And scary."

He caressed her back. "Yeah, it's scary. But it'll all be okay."

Chapter Forty-Two

FEB. 15

Ben greeted each of the Florida Region district managers as they flowed into his Orlando office. They'd all congratulated him through phone calls and emails, but this was his first time to see them in person since his promotion to Florida Director. He'd earned their respect and friendship as a peer, and Ben hoped the enthusiasm they were demonstrating would be sustainable—especially when results weren't good and difficult conversations had to take place.

He smiled as the group enjoyed coffee and doughnuts. The previous year's fourth quarter results had just been announced, and Next Gen showed upward movement in customer additions and reduction in customer losses. Billions were being invested to expand the network. Ben saw his new role as a huge opportunity to build on that momentum by energizing the front line employees across Florida.

Ben had bought them each a book. He'd written a personal note inside the cover of each copy of Peter Block's *The Answer to How is Yes*. This was one of Ben's favorites but not commonly known in business circles. Block wrote about exploring possibilities through vibrant conversations, while refusing to shut down new ideas before they could be thoroughly discussed. Beth had cautioned Ben against choosing the book, saying it might be too "out there" for this particular team, but Ben wanted to take the chance.

"This book is all about saying 'yes' to creative ideas and new approaches," Ben told the group. "I'd like us to refer to it regularly across the next several months. As you read it, jot down your observations and your ideas for the business. Every idea is valid and will be discussed. We're not just going to sit here and run through the numbers whenever we gather."

Just then Ben's cell phone vibrated, and he glanced at the display. *Beth*. He'd call her back during a break.

"This looks really interesting, Ben, thank you," said one of the managers, Paul Butterfield from Tampa.

"It's not something I would've ever thought to read on my own," added Mary Alger from Jacksonville.

"Just be open to what Block writes," Ben said. "You might not love this book the way I do, and that's okay. Just be open to some new ideas."

His phone vibrated again, and Ben was ready to turn the damn thing off. It was Beth again. She didn't leave a message the first time, and it was unusual for Beth to call him repeatedly while he was at work.

Ben didn't answer, but decided he needed to call her back. He glanced about at the group, disappointed that he would have to break the momentum of the conversation. He excused himself and went into his office and called Beth. She was crying.

"Maddie hit her head at the playground, and they think she might have a concussion. They called an ambulance. I'm meeting them at Halifax Hospital."

"What?" Ben had understood, but was still processing the news.

"She fell at Mother's Day Out," Beth added hurriedly, her voice cracking with tears. "I'm scared, Ben. Can you head over here?"

"Of course. It'll take me about an hour. I'll leave right now."

"Thank you. I've got to go." She hung up.

Ben grabbed his car keys and rushed back into the conference room. The group grew quiet as he stood there.

"Team, I apologize, but I need to leave. My daughter's had an accident at day care, and she's at the hospital in Daytona."

"Ben, go, it's okay," Mary said, standing up. "Go be with your family. We'll continue to meet, and we can fill you in later."

He nodded. "Thank you so much. Would you mind leading the discussion, Mary?"

"Not a problem," she said. "Now go."

A couple of the other district managers stood and patted him on the back as he headed out. "Let us know if she's okay," said Jorge from Miami.

Ben navigated traffic to Interstate 4 and headed east toward Daytona. He called Beth about halfway through the drive. She said the nurses were preparing to take Maddie for an MRI. Beth was nervous about how the little girl would handle it, but Ben reassured her that Maddie was brave and would think it was fun.

By the time Ben arrived at Halifax Medical Center, the MRI was completed and the staff was wheeling Maddie back to the ER, Beth at her side. Beth rushed into Ben's arms as Maddie screamed, "DADDY!" A nurse gently prevented her from jumping out of her mobile bed.

He kissed Maddie gently on the top of her head.

"You fell down, sweetheart?"

"Yes, Daddy. They took pictures of my brain. I can't wait to see them."

Ben laughed. "I can't wait either. You just relax and try not to move a lot, okay?"

"They keep saying that."

"They're very smart. Don't fall down like that, okay honey?"

"Okay, Daddy."

One of the nurses smiled. "She's a very sweet, brave girl." Ben put his arm around Beth.

"Thank you so much for leaving work," she said to him. "I'm really sorry, I know it was your first meeting with your team."

"Please don't be sorry. This is so much more important."

The concussion was mild, but the doctor wanted Maddie to stay overnight for observation. A short while later, they caravanned up to the children's wing. Maddie was excited to have her own room with a television. There were a couple of large recliners off to the side, where Ben assumed he and Beth would spend the night.

As expected, Maddie was treated like a celebrity and loved every minute of it, eating French fries, ice cream, and popsicles. Ben and Beth sat through several hours of *Dora the Explorer* and *Good Luck Charlie*. In the early evening they flicked off the television, and Beth crawled in next to Maddie and read her a couple of stories from a stack of children's books. Ben scrolled through his phone and responded to texts from district managers asking how Maddie was doing.

Once Maddie had drifted off to sleep, Ben and Beth sat in their respective recliners. Ben reached over and took her hand, and she squeezed his and held onto it.

"Shame that this was needed for us to spend so much quality time together," Ben said.

"Yeah, really."

"I know it's been a marathon. I don't know when it'll let up. But I do know that I want to be home more."

Beth nodded. "I'd like that. And I promise, I don't blame you for how busy your job is. I'm grateful for how you provide for our family."

"Hey, I'm grateful for what you're doing, too. You take great care of Maddie, and you're running a successful and growing business."

"I guess neither of us is to blame for the crazy schedules."

"Nope. We're not to blame. We're just living life, trying our best."

"You mean our 'bestest?'"

"As Maddie would say." Ben leaned over and gave his wife a kiss on the cheek.

"I was really scared when they called me this morning. I didn't know how bad it was going to be."

"I was scared, too, when you called me."

Beth sat up, rubbing her eyes. "I think I take Maddie for granted too much. I'm just doing my thing, shuffling her from Mother's Day Out to babysitters and back, and just assuming that she's indestructible. But she's not." Beth was crying again. "No one is. Including us."

Ben rubbed her shoulders. "I know."

"I don't want her to get lost in that shuffle. She's not going to be tiny very long. Pretty soon she'll be gone all day, every day, and we won't be the only big influences in her life anymore."

"She seems taller and smarter every night when I get home from work," Ben said.

I think I need to hire some help at the studio," Beth said. "Perhaps it's time."

"As well as a housekeeper?" Ben grinned.

"That's a great idea," Beth smiled. "I'm thinking about another personal trainer who can teach some of the classes, so I don't always have to be there. Give up some of the revenue but get some quality of life back."

Ben nodded. "And perhaps grow the business even more."

"Exactly."

"I like where you're going here." He began to massage her neck and shoulders more firmly, and Beth leaned back toward him.

"Come join me over here," Ben said, and Beth stood and crawled into his recliner, leaning back against him as he continued the massage.

After a while he simply wrapped his arms around her and could tell she was drifting off to sleep. He loved the smell of her hair. Ben wanted to lose himself in the moment of just being with Beth, but that distracting pang of guilt got in the way once more. He could still see Chicago in his mind, and Allison's face.

T he book club members were making progress on *The Sun Also Rises* and making even more progress on the wine.

"Tom reminds me of how Jake describes Brett," Kari said. "'She only wanted what she couldn't have.' That's Tom. As soon as he buys one business and runs it for a while, he wants to move on to something else. He's never satisfied."

"But in the book Jake adds that that's how people are in general," Emma said. "We're never quite satisfied."

"Ben talks that way when he's describing the executive team of his company," Beth said. "They always want them to drive the sales numbers higher and higher. That's understandable, for a for-profit company. But they don't stop and celebrate when they hit or even exceed their goals. They jump right back onto the hamster wheel."

"Well, my father and my ex-husband are the same way," Emma said. "But they're extreme examples, I think. A lot of people can be reasonable about their expectations."

"Phil is very reasonable," Jackie said. "Mr. Even-Keeled. He's a simple guy with a lot of depth and smarts. I lucked out."

"You sure did," Delphi said. "All of you lucked out, in my opinion."

"Thanks for meeting me, Detectives," Ben said, shaking hands with Sarosky and Rice. "Have you had lunch here before?"

"Once or twice," Rice said, glancing about at the other Famoso's patrons. "As I recall they have sensible portion sizes." Everyone chuckled.

The waiter took their drink orders. Sarosky eyed Ben curiously.

"So what can we do for you, Mr. McBride?"

"I just wanted to check in again and remind you that my company is eager to keep finding ways to support the case," Ben said. "I have volunteers from each of my stores that continue to visit shopping malls, and other crowded public places, passing out the flyers."

"We really appreciate that," Sarosky replied.

"I have other employees that are monitoring the Facebook and Twitter pages that have been set up, just to see if anything strange pops up there," Ben added. "I'm sure you get all kinds of weird leads that come in by phone, and maybe some of that will show up on social media also."

"You think like a detective, Ben," Rice smiled.

The waiter returned. Ben ordered a chef salad. Rice asked for the same, while Sarosky ordered a club sandwich.

"Ben, we hear from you more than the actual husbands of the missing women," Sarosky said casually. "Have they asked you to be their liaison to us?"

Ben smiled. "Not formally. I just know they have their hands full, and I want to help streamline things for them." He paused. "Plus, my wife Beth is always talking about the situation, as you can imagine."

"I'm sure," Sarosky said. "Remind me—did you know any of the missing women particularly well?"

Ben shook his head. "No. I've learned a lot more about them since they vanished, unfortunately."

Sarosky nodded, sipping from his Diet Coke.

"Well, I sure appreciate you being such an advocate for them and a friend to their families," the detective said. He looked at Sarosky for a moment longer, and then glanced at Rice.

For the rest of their lunch the three talked about matters beyond the book club case: life as a detective, the wireless business, the weather. Ben paid for the meal and bid goodbye to the detectives.

Once in the parking lot, Sarosky lit a cigarette. Rice caught her partner watching Ben as he got into his car and drove away.

"Why do you seem troubled by him?" Rice asked him.

Sarosky took a long drag on the cigarette and turned the ignition.

"I don't know."

Chapter Forty-Four

MARCH 20

Mario sniffed and swirled his freshly-poured glass of wine. It was late afternoon, and Famoso's was still fairly quiet. He looked across the table at the twenty-something man seated before him, and smiled.

"I want to retire young, I'm pretty sure. Relatively young, that is, since I'm already in my 40s. But I don't think my youngest daughter is going to want to be involved in my work. She's not interested."

James nodded, waiting to speak because he could tell Mario had more to say.

"I want you to learn as many different aspects of the business as you can," continued the CEO of DDC. "I'm going to keep stretching you. I like what I see in you. You work hard, you're smart, and you always think of how you can help others to be successful."

"Thank you, Mr. Lazano."

"I've told you a million times to call me Mario."

"Okay."

Mario sipped his wine. "You've traveled the world, and hopefully gotten a lot of that wanderlust out of your system. You'll meet a nice girl before long and start a family. And if all goes well, in about 10 years or so, maybe less, you'll run this place."

"I really appreciate your confidence in me."

Mario shrugged. "Well, it's well deserved. Just keep telling me what you need, how I can help you to continue to be successful."

"Certainly."

Mario glanced at the menu. "I hope you like this place, since I own it."

James chuckled. "I'm sure I will."

"Oh, there's one more thing," Mario said, looking back at James, more serious now.
"What's that?"

"There's some people I'm trying to ease out of our network. Don't worry about names or details, I'm taking care of it. But I don't want you to ever get mixed up with these folks. They're bad news, and you're too good a person."

James nodded. "Okay."

"What I do need you to do is come to me right away if someone shady approaches you. If you get a red flag about a conversation, or a request, from whomever and whenever. Make sense?"

"Makes sense."

"Good man." Mario looked back at the menu. "So, what are you going to order for dinner?"

～

Scott Layman remained curious about the organic produce ranch ever since his impromptu visit and chat with Curtis Everett. He purchased green beans, lettuce, and tomatoes from Curtis's salespeople at the area's largest farmer's market, and thought the quality was superb.

He'd called the toll free number on Curtis's card, and left a message with a very friendly woman named Sally for Curtis to give him a call regarding the possibility of a tour. Curtis called back several days later, and the two had a nice chat about the advantages and challenges of growing produce in South Florida. Scott said he'd love to tour the ranch, and Curtis said that could be worked out but "needed a few days to arrange everything."

When Scott showed up on a warm March morning, a young man named Roger was waiting for him at the gate with a golf cart. Roger wore a green polo shirt and light-colored khakis, and explained that he worked there as one of the supervisors. Roger asked Scott a few questions about his own profession as the two built a light rapport.

As they rode in the golf cart, the heart of the property came into view for Scott. He saw a massive section of gardens to the far left. To the right, near a lake, was a one-story brick structure that resembled a small lodge. Straight ahead, still pretty distant, was a large warehouse type of structure with a couple of trucks parked next to it, and beyond that what appeared to be a couple of dozen cabins.

Each section—the gardens; the lodge; the warehouse; and the cabins—was surrounded by its own tall, black chain link fence. As they traveled deeper into the

152

ranch, Scott noticed that each fenced-in section had a couple more golf carts parked in the front, and each golf cart was occupied by a man dressed like Roger. Scott couldn't quite make out their faces, but had a subtle sense they were observing him.

Roger drove them toward the garden. Near the front gate of the garden fence, Curtis stood next to a couple of parked golf carts, each occupied by men. Curtis smiled and walked forward to greet both of them.

"Thanks for coming out," Curtis said. "And thanks for being a customer."

"My pleasure," Scott said. "Wow, there's a lot back here."

"It's a pretty big operation. We'll start our tour with the garden, and then make our way clockwise around the property. Does that work for you?"

"Sure. Whatever is most convenient for you and your staff."

As they walked past row after row of leafy produce, Curtis gave a high-level description of what was there. Scott tried to keep track of it all, but it was like trying to catalogue the produce section of a local Kroger or Albertsons.

"How did you get into this business?" Scott asked.

Curtis laughed. "I was in the financial world, and dealing with stress and abstraction all day long. I wanted something simple and tangible. What's more tangible than all of this? Although it's a lot of work, it's very rewarding."

"I imagine so."

They left the garden and Curtis drove them to the outside of the large warehouse building, explaining the distribution process for how the produce got to the markets and private customers. Curtis took Scott inside and showed him a small office located near the front of the building.

"This is where I work," Curtis said. "And this is my assistant, Sally. I believe you spoke with her on the phone."

Sally was a skinny woman with an extremely short haircut. She smiled at Scott. "Wonderful to see you."

Curtis didn't linger in the office, but took Scott back to the golf cart. They drove to the section of fenced-in cabins.

"Our employees live on site," Curtis said. "They work a lot of hours, and it's comfortable for them to not have to drive back and forth. We provide everything they could possibly need."

Scott was surprised. "Interesting. Everyone who works here lives here?"

"Everyone. It's part of the job description."

"Are there families with children here?"

"Just a couple. The children are home-schooled. Most of our employees are single men, though." Curtis paused. "I like to find people who've never quite fit in anywhere else, and give them a job and a home. So they can finally belong."

"That's neat."

"It's more effective than most of your traditional social services agencies."

Curtis slowed the golf cart down in front of the cabins, but didn't park. The observing men in the other golf carts smiled and waved. "We won't tour the cabins, since they're people's private homes. But hopefully this gives you a general feel for our community."

Scott nodded. "Sure."

They proceeded toward the lodge, which Scott assumed would be their last stop.

"This is kind of a multi-purpose building," Curtis said. "It's a place where we can all gather and celebrate being a community together."

"Who are the men in the golf carts at each area?"

"They're responsible for ensuring the residents get any help they need. They take different shifts."

Curtis's cell phone buzzed. He stopped the cart and answered. "I'm not expecting anyone else today," Curtis said to the caller. "Did they give their names?"

Curtis listened to the response. "I'll be there momentarily." He put the phone away and smiled at Scott. "I've got a couple of external partners with whom I'm having a bit of a misunderstanding. They're very persistent. You see, it's not all paradise here."

Scott chuckled. "Can't escape from human nature, can you?"

"Never. Do you mind if we end our tour now? It's been a pleasure having you here, and you're welcome back anytime."

"I don't mind at all. I'd like to talk further about how we might do business together."

"I'd like that as well."

Curtis sped up and headed toward the front of the ranch. Scott saw a car parked next to his. Two of Curtis's employees stood between the car and the closed gate. As Curtis and Scott approached, the men opened the gate and then closed it after them. Curtis escorted Scott to his own car.

"Thank you again," Scott said.

"Thank you. Be well."

Curtis watched Scott drive off, and then approached the other car, flanked by his two employees. The driver rolled down his window.

"Gentlemen, I wasn't expecting you. I'm going to have to ask you to leave, and call my assistant Sally to make an appointment."

Mario leaned back in his chair, studying a couple of 8x10 black-and-white photographs and waiting for Henry to give his update. Henry flipped open a small pad of paper, and then put on his reading glasses and scanned his notes.

"The two of them seem to be regulars at Arena Football events," Henry said. "They go to the big games. Looks like they work security."

"Security for whom, exactly?"

"Still trying to piece that together."

Mario placed the photos back into the manila envelope that Henry had given him.

"What makes them stand out from the others?"

Henry shrugged. "Mainly because they're not one-offs. They were seen talking with Delphi in a restaurant not long before she was found dead. They've visited Tom Blakely's restaurant, looking for him. That's two separate, seemingly unrelated points of contact they've made with persons bearing very close ties to our missing ladies."

"Julio's being pretty thorough?"

"He's doing his job well. We get the names of every person who uses a credit or debit card to buy anything at the bar. So far, he's been able to do it without that Steve fellow noticing."

"Or Tom?"

Henry nodded. "Especially Tom. Tom's barely even running the business anymore."

"What else are these two up to?"

"We just started tracking their phones a few days ago. They've been up and down I-95 a lot, and are mostly in South Florida. There's one place that they visited that doesn't align with their other activities, though."

"Yeah? What?"

"An organic produce farm. Registered owner is a Dan Ferguson."

Mario considered this. "Organic produce? They stop to pick up some healthy apples or something?"

"Who knows?"

Mario paced around for a bit.

"Did I ever tell you that I once owned Tom's restaurant, Famoso's? It was quite a long time ago."

Henry shook his head. "I don't think you've mentioned that."

"It's a small world, I tell you. Especially this town." Mario glanced at his watch. "I need to go meet with Russ."

"Business?"

"No, unfortunately, I wish it was. Family."

Henry turned to go. "I'll tell the guys to get the car for you."

Phil had been to a few nice holiday parties during his years in Daytona Beach, but hadn't entered a house quite as extravagant as Mario Lazano's. The security detail treated him like an honored guest. He arrived shortly before Ben and Tom, who were equally impressed. Russ showed up next, polite but subdued. They were provided with drinks in the den, Tom asking for a club soda, and waited for Mario.

Mario was graceful as he greeted each of his guests, ensuring they were being well taken care-of and feeling at home. Finally he sat down, and the others did as well.

Everyone looked to Phil, who'd requested the get-together.

"I really appreciate everyone's time this afternoon," Phil said. "Mario, thank you for opening up your home to us."

Mario nodded. Phil took a deep breath.

"It's been almost a year since Emma, Kari, and Jackie disappeared. The police haven't been able to learn anything. Whatever we've tried to learn on our own has been fruitless as well."

Phil saw Russ glance over at Mario, but Mario kept his gaze on Phil.

"I've spent a lot of sleepless nights, as I'm sure each of you has as well. In more recent weeks, I've come to realize that it's time to formally say goodbye. As much as I don't want to, it's time."

"What does that mean, exactly?" Russ asked.

"I think we should have some type of non-denominational memorial service," Phil said. "Something where family and friends can pay their respects, that gives us all a little bit of closure."

No one else spoke. Russ stared at Phil for a moment and then glanced once more at Mario, whose face was impassive. Ben saw Tom lower his head.

"Everything is so open-ended," Phil added. "I think we need something, something simple, to recognize our loss."

"It's too soon," Russ said. "We've got some leads that we're still pursuing. Don't we, Mario?"

All eyes turned to their host. Mario offered a sad smile.

"I appreciate Russ's optimism," he said. "It's one of his greatest strengths as a business person. Unfortunately, I can't back up his hopefulness with any kind of information. Some of my best people have lifted up every possible rock to see what's underneath, and they've found nothing.

"I'm sorry," Mario added, looking each man in the eye one at a time.

Ben touched Tom on the shoulder. "Tom, what do you think?"

Tom took a sip of his club soda. "I don't know. I guess we should do it. I don't know what else to do at this point."

"Ben, what are your thoughts?" Phil asked. "You've been a great friend to all of us through this, and we're grateful for that."

"Thank you," Ben said. "I hadn't considered the idea before. I think it's definitely worth thinking about. It's a very personal decision for each of you to make, though. I don't know what I would do, if Beth"—Ben felt his throat grow tighter—"if Beth were in this situation as well."

"What about the kids?" Russ asked. "Are we expecting them to stand up there and talk about how much they loved their mommies, assuming that they're dead? And basically tell them we've given up hope?"

Everyone in the room shifted with discomfort. Mario waited to see if anyone else would respond, then looked at Russ.

"Russ, I don't think that having a service means we've given up hope. Hope will always live on inside of our hearts. It means that we're recognizing our loss, and celebrating our love for these three wonderful women." He paused. "And of course I think the children should be included. They need this as much as we do, even more. Children, grandparents, sisters, brothers, friends; everyone who loves them."

Mario looked over at Phil.

"Phil, give the others here some more time to think about whether to do this, please. In the meantime, perhaps you can start putting together some ideas and details."

Phil nodded. "Sure."

"I'm happy to help you with that," Ben said.

"Thank you."

Phil waited to see if others had more to say, but the group remained silent. Finally Mario stood, and each man said their goodbyes.

Tom's gritty willpower had finally reached its breaking point as he drove away from Mario's estate. He pictured Connor waiting for him, ready to inspect and ensure he hadn't been drinking.

He knew that a familiar liquor store was coming up on his right. Tom could swoop in there, grab a small bottle of whiskey, and leave it inside the car or somewhere hidden in the garage until Connor fell asleep later that night. Then, Tom fantasized, he could retrieve it and sneak it into his bedroom.

Tom pulled into the liquor store parking lot. He kept the engine running for a while, looking at his reflection in the rear view mirror. Tom shut off the ignition, and then slapped the steering wheel hard with both palms. He stared down at his reddened flesh, fighting back tears.

Chapter Forty-Five

MARCH 30

Ben gave Beth a hug and kiss as she left the house. Although she'd finally agreed to speak with Cameron Brock, she remained nervous and hesitant. Everyone else seemed to like the guy so much, however, and she couldn't think of any more rational reasons to say no.

Cameron was waiting inside Starbucks when Beth arrived. He offered to buy her coffee, but she politely declined and purchased her own. They sat together, and Beth noticed he had a pad and pen on the table but was making no effort to use them.

"So you finally got me," Beth said.

Cameron smiled. "Finally. The story will now be complete."

"Or open-ended. Kind of like the situation."

"Yeah. Very much so."

Beth folded her arms and studied Cameron closely.

"Are you just really charming, or is the sincerity and compassion for real?"

Cameron shrugged. "You'll have to decide for yourself. You'll know a lot more a couple of hours from now, I suppose."

"Okay, fair enough. How do we get started?"

Cameron flipped open the pad of paper. Beth saw handwriting, but couldn't immediately decipher it.

"Can we start with the big picture, of the themes that have been emerging throughout my conversations with everyone else? That will help provide some context for our discussion."

Beth nodded. "That's fine, although I think I have a pretty good feel for the context. I've been living it."

"Keep an open mind, is all I ask you. You've been living it, but you haven't been sitting in on these one-on-one conversations I've been having with your friends and husband."

"Yeah, Ben said he'd talked to you as well. Guess I didn't have any more choice after that."

"You always have choices. People always have choices."

Beth unfolded her arms and leaned forward. "Okay. Give me the context, Mr. Reporter."

Cameron flipped through his notes.

"This is a story about unmet expectations," he said. "We live with them every day: our expectations about how things should be. We learn to practice such expectations early on: what kind of grades we should get; what kind of job we should get; what kind of person we should marry; what kind of children we want to have."

"Seems pretty simple enough. A common human experience," Beth said.

"Yep. So much, that most of us fail to see how entwined we are with our expectations. They become part of our DNA. We eventually can't separate reality from what we expect reality to be."

Beth pondered this. "Deep stuff, Mr. Reporter."

"Yeah. A lot of things that are hiding in plain sight end up being pretty deep."

"So what's unique here about the common human disease of expectations?"

Cameron scribbled a little on his notepad.

"What's unique here," he said, "is that we have a train wreck of expectations not being met. Most people are realistic enough to not expect to have a perfect marriage, and expect to have some difficulties and twists and turns along the way. But no one expects their spouse—or ex-spouse, for that matter—to up and disappear one day."

Beth nodded, waiting for more.

"And what I'm finding, from talking with the others," Cameron said, "is that this colossal life event is making them much more tuned in to the smaller expectations they cling to every day. Some of them are realizing how addicted they are, for lack of a better word, to expectations, and how they medicate themselves when they even sense that expectations aren't being met. Even subconsciously."

Beth began considering her own expectations: *For she and Ben to get along; for Maddie to be healthy and develop at a normal or accelerated pace; for her fitness business to keep growing; for her to stay healthy and fit herself...*

...for Emma, Jackie, and Kari to return home.

"I get it," she said.

Cameron leaned back and sipped his coffee. "Let's come back to context a little later, if that's ok. I'd like to learn a little more about you."

"That's fine. You probably know some things already." Beth smiled.

"Tell me about how you met the other three women, if you could."

Beth replayed the scenes in her mind.

"Each of them showed up at my new fitness club in the early weeks," she said. "I had never met any of them before. They were part of the original core, and seemed to hit it off right away. Three very different personalities, but they bonded over fitness, I suppose."

Cameron waited for more.

"Dephi Adams was part of the group as well. They would linger after class and chat, and were friendly toward me also. I can be a little more on the reserved side and very business-oriented, but of course I want to get to know my clients. So I started to consider them to be my friends as well.

"They were really motivated to build more muscle tone and strength and lose a few pounds. It seemed that the stronger the friendships grew, the more motivated they became, and the more motivated I was to make the whole thing a success."

Beth saw Cameron jot down a few key words here and there, but he mostly maintained eye contact with her.

"They would occasionally go out for coffee or a drink after class, and invited me now and then. I often needed to get home, but sometimes I went along. During one of our little social hours, Delphi was talking about the challenge of keep her little book store going; and the topic of books and reading in general came up. Jackie started talking about how much she used to love reading fiction growing up. "So," Beth continued, "we decided to start a book club, and Delphi offered for us to meet at her store after hours to give it some atmosphere. I was probably the last to jump on board; as I said, I'm kind of reserved, and I always found the idea of book clubs a little pretentious. Like, I pictured a large group of women—probably women—sitting around and trying to act so scholarly about what a book meant and didn't mean, what an author did well and did wrong, what genre it was and what symbolism was in there and all that other bullshit that the author probably never intended. All the while missing the fact that the author, however imperfect her work, had done something they had likely never done, and that is actually *written* a goddamned book."

Cameron smiled. "A lot of journalists miss that fact also, especially critics."

Beth laughed. "For sure! Those who can't, write about others who can." Her eyes grew wider. "Oh, shit, I wasn't trying to offend you. I'm sure you're a very good journalist. I was speaking more to people who seem to thrive on nit-picking others."

"I knew what you meant, and I'm not offended. It's not easy to offend me."

"That's good," she smiled.

"But you became part of the book club anyway," Cameron noted.

"I did," she said. "I liked the ladies a lot and they were my clients, and so it was hard to say no. I mean, I could have easily said I was too busy with my business and my daughter to take on one more thing; and they would have totally understood. But to be truthful, I hadn't been doing much reading myself lately besides Maddie's little toddler books, and I thought it could be a good catalyst for me. Keep my brain from going to complete mush, you know?"

Cameron smiled. "So how did you all decide what to read first?"

"That's where I thought we would spin our wheels. I pictured the group of us unable to choose, considering too many options because no one would want to shoot down someone else's idea. I wondered if Delphi would finally grow impatient and just strongly recommend something, since she knew books better than any of us combined.

"Finally, Emma O'Rourke had a great idea. She grabbed a couple of cocktail napkins, and gave one to each of us and told us to write down our top choice for a book based on what we'd talked about. Then, she asked us to fold our napkins in half, and set them in the middle of the table."

"Very suspenseful," Cameron said.

"Totally. When our server stopped by to check on us, Emma asked her to reach down and select one of the cocktail napkins, unfold it, and read what it said. The server obliged, and we had our book choice."

"Interesting. Random selection within a tightly controlled environment."

"We decided that we would do that for all of our book choices." Beth suddenly teared up, which she hadn't wanted to do while speaking with Cameron. "And then they went on the trip, and that was that."

Beth was surprised at her own abruptness in wrapping up the story.

"Were you and Delphi supposed to go on the trip also?"

Beth shook her head. "Delphi offered the girls her condo, but she couldn't leave her business. I couldn't leave mine, either. They…"

Cameron waited. Beth was staring down, and wiped her eyes.

"They almost cancelled the trip, suggesting they wait until another time when all of us could go. But we insisted they go. Especially Delphi. So they went."

Beth excused herself to go to the restroom. She dried her eyes a little more and fixed her makeup. Cameron asked if she wanted something else from the coffee bar when she returned, and she thanked him but said no.

"What's it been like for you, wondering what would have happened if you'd gone on the trip as well?" he asked her.

"I have this image in my mind—speaking of expectations—that I could have done something if I was with them. Saved the day, I suppose. I don't know exactly what I would have done, since I have no idea what happened. But somehow, perhaps, the larger our number, the more strength we would have to fight off whatever or whomever came against us."

"Did you and Delphi process a lot of it together?"

"We did at first. We would get together for lunch or coffee. But then I started seeing less and less of her. She stopped coming to class and returning calls. I decided to let her have her space."

Beth teared up again. "And then they found her in her garage."

Cameron waited for Beth to continue.

"I didn't see that one coming either," she said. "I have no idea what else was going on in her life. Delphi was a little off-beat, but that was just her style. I can't imagine what it must feel like to get to the edge of absolute hopelessness, and then plunge headlong into it."

Beth looked at Cameron. "I suppose that's the ultimate example of unrealistic expectations. You never expect, especially when you're young, to become so desperate that you take your own life. It's like the place where all the big and large unmet expectations just drown you."

"That's an interesting way to put it," he said.

"I've had bad-enough survivor's guilt, with the three of them disappearing," Beth said. "Now, Delphi is gone, truly gone, and I don't even have a fellow 'survivor' to process it with any longer. I'm not really that close to the other book club members. My husband can only take so much of me talking about the subject. I finally started seeing a therapist, and she's helped a lot. I've been able to shift my energy away from my own emotions, to truly trying to help the other family members."

"Is there one particular family to which you've especially bonded?" Cameron asked.

Beth reflected for a moment. She didn't know how personal the other men had gotten with Cameron.

"Connor Blakely," she said. "He's a marvelous young man. So bright, so talented. He's an artist. His father Tom…has really had a tough time with things, and we've sort of taken Connor under our wing. He loves our daughter Maddie, and she absolutely adores him. He's like a big brother to her."

Cameron smiled. "What kind of art does he create?"

"He likes to sketch. He carries this sketchbook around with him all the time. He sketches animals, especially dogs."

"That's really cool."

"Yeah, he's good. He'll study a photograph of a dog and recreate it on paper. Or he'll just make it up inside his head. Maddie loves it; she has like 15 of his drawings in her room."

Beth smiled. If any good had come out of this tragedy, it was that she'd made the most of the chance to connect with another child. And Maddie had benefited as well.

"Have you interviewed any of the kids?" Beth asked.

Cameron shook his head. "No. I met the Solomon girls when I visited the house, but I'm not going to formally interview any of the children. It's hard enough for the adults to talk about."

"Makes sense."

Beth gave Cameron a sheepish smile. "I'm sorry that it took so long for me to agree to talk to you. The press has kind of a bad reputation, as you know. I lumped you in with all of them."

He laughed. "It's okay, I get it. I'm just grateful that we've had this time together this evening. You've added a lot to the story."

"Do you like what you do?"

"What, journalism? Sure, I like it well enough."

"Don't most journalists want to be authors or screenwriters?"

"Don't most personal trainers want to be models?"

Beth laughed. "Touché."

Cameron set down his pen. "There's times when it gets really old. You have to tolerate a lot, and wade through a lot of boring, unimportant crap. Most of what I produce feels very assembly line in nature, covering a beat and meeting a deadline because the print and Web products need content. I enjoy working on larger, more introspective pieces that I come up with."

"Sounds like you might be better suited for a good magazine or journal," Beth said. "They have more of those kinds of articles, don't they?"

"Usually." Cameron shrugged. "We'll see where the road takes me."

Beth glanced at her watch. The conversation felt like it was wrapping up.

"So you're not going to make us look like freaks?"

He smiled. "You *are* freaks."

"Yeah, I know, but you don't have to tell anyone."

"I won't tell if you don't."

"Deal," Beth said.

✦≈✦

"I hope this is a good time?" Sarosky asked Ben as he answered the front door.

"Certainly," Ben said, inviting the detective inside. "I'm just hanging out with my little girl while Beth is out on an errand." He decided not to mention that his wife was meeting with Cameron Brock.

"Well, hello again, Miss Maddie," Sarosky said as Maddie bounced up to greet him. "I'm Mr. Sarosky. We've met before."

"Hi, Mr. Sarosky!" she said, and then ran off as quickly as she arrived.

"I won't take long. Just had a question."

"Sure. Would you like some coffee?"

"No, like I said I won't be long."

"Ok. Let's have a seat here in the den."

Sarosky followed Ben into an area in the back of the house loaded with couches and recliners. A large flat screen television was mounted on the wall.

"We've spent a lot of time, as you would imagine, going through the phone call and text records of the missing women," Sarosky began. "We've built a whole database of people they were frequently in touch with, as well as created a category for 'one-offs': people they might have communicated with once or twice in six months preceding the disappearance."

Ben nodded, waiting for more.

"Your wife Beth was one of those frequent contacts, which makes sense," Sarosky continued. "But we also noticed a couple of phone calls and texts between Emma O'Rourke and your cell phone number."

Sarosky paused. Ben waited for more.

"Do you remember what you might have talked or texted about with Emma?"

Ben rubbed his chin. "I'm trying to recall. Do you remember how long ago it was?"

"In the couple of months leading up to the disappearance."

Maddie came running back into the room and hopped onto Ben's lap. She beamed at the detective.

"This is my daddy," Maddie said.

"I see that," Sarosky said. "Is he your buddy?"

"He's my best friend," Maddie said, and kissed Ben on the cheek. Ben gave her a tight hug and whispered for her to go play in her room.

"Okay!' she said, and took off again.

"Is she always that compliant?" Sarosky asked.

"No way. She's on her best behavior for you," Ben said. "Now, back to your question. It was almost Beth's birthday. Emma and some of the other book clubbers were looking for ideas on what to get her, and what kind of restaurants she likes. Emma, as I recall, reached out to me to get some ideas."

Sarosky nodded. "Makes sense. Go straight to the source of the one who knows her best."

"Exactly. I think they ended up getting her a gift card to Macy's or something, and took her to lunch. I can't keep track of the details."

Sarosky stood. "Well, I appreciate the additional information." He smiled at Ben as they shook hands, and then headed to the front door.

"Say," Sarosky said, turning back to face Ben, "any of the other ladies call or text you about ideas for Beth's birthday, or for any other matters?"

"I don't think so. I guess your phone records would tell you for sure, though."

"Sounds good," Sarosky said. "I'm sure I'll speak with you again soon."

Ben stood in the open doorway and watched Sarosky get in his car and leave. He heard Maddie's footsteps coming from across the house, and turned just in time for her to leap into his arms.

Chapter Forty-Six

APRIL 1

Dean Stuart Sanderson of the University of Central Florida's College of Arts and Sciences hated these kinds of confrontations—even more than he hated the nonstop faculty and executive team meetings that clogged up most of his week. These particular job essentials made Stuart yearn for the classroom once again, and for more writing and research time. Some people were cut out to be bureaucrats, and others most definitely were not.

So when Phil Solomon showed up at his office as requested, Stuart felt awkward. He didn't grow up believing it was his business to tell another man whom he should or shouldn't date. In his graduate school days, especially, when Stuart had long hair and smoked weed, he wouldn't have dreamt of becoming one of the "suits."

"Phil, thanks for coming by," Stuart said as Phil sat down. "I want you to not take this personally. Please just know that I'm doing my job as dean, okay?"

Phil nodded, wanting Stuart to just get to the punch line.

"There have been some complaints," Stuart continued, "from a couple of your faculty peers about how much time you're spending with a female student named Amanda Bane. From their perspective, it's inappropriate. Do you know what I'm talking about?"

This was the kind of conversation Phil had dreaded and hoped would never take place. He'd tried to be as professional as possible during his visits with Amanda. He hadn't gone to her apartment or had her over to his house. Phil and Amanda always hung out in public, like friends do.

"They don't think I should be friends with Amanda?" Phil asked, trying his best to stay calm and nonchalant.

Stuart shrugged. "It's not so much that, but they think it looks like there's much more than friendship going on. And they worry that students are gossiping about it. I just don't want you to lose any credibility, and I don't want you or the school to be at any legal risk should Amanda...you know, one day feel scorned or something and do something retaliatory."

"Retaliatory about what?"

This sucks, Stuart thought. "You know. If you guys break up or something, or she doesn't get the special treatment she thinks she's entitled to, or something like that. You can never predict how these things will pan out."

Phil was annoyed. "We don't have a romantic relationship by any means. We're simply friends, and we talk about books and careers and life. If it will make my peers feel better, I'll speak directly with them and hear their concerns."

Stuart shook his head. "I don't think that's the ultimate problem. It's the students out there and their potential perceptions. I don't see how you can address that, unless you simply don't give them any more fodder."

"So what are you suggesting?"

"It's pretty plain and simple. Don't spend any more time with Amanda outside of a normal academic context. Then the kids will get bored with the topic and move on to something else. Everybody wins."

Phil studied Stuart, to make sure the Dean was serious.

"I know it's been tough for you, Phil," Stuart said, leaning forward on his desk. "Anybody would get lonely after a while and seek some companionship. Just do it outside of the campus, okay, or at least outside of the student body. I'm just trying to protect you, and protect the school."

Phil nodded. "Okay."

Stuart smiled. "Okay. Thanks for making this easier."

Phil walked back to his office in a depressed daze. He and Amanda were supposed to meet for dinner that night. What if some other students were at the restaurant and spotted them?

Fuck the students, he thought. *Let them think whatever the hell they want for one more night.*

At dinner, Phil kept delaying the topic he needed to bring up. Amanda was in a great mood, talking about some calculus test she had aced and how she couldn't wait to get all of the math and science courses out of her way and focus on humanities. Phil had inspired her to become a professor, she said.

Phil slowly broached the subject of his conversation with Stuart, launching off of what Amanda was saying about her professorial aspirations. He noted how being a professor wasn't glamorous. There were politics, Phil said, and academic people could be just as petty and simple-minded as people anyplace else—perhaps even worse.

"It's not surprising," Amanda responded. "My peers can be pretty simple-minded. They don't know anything about our relationship. It's all perception, but I guess perception is always the problem."

Phil nodded. "Yeah. The world is full of screwed up perceptions."

"So," she began, "there's an easy solution. Just come hang out at my place when we get together. My roommate Jill is super cool and she won't gossip to anyone. I've kept plenty of her secrets, God knows."

Phil hadn't expected this alternative suggestion. He'd assumed, knowing Amanda as he did, that she would simply get it and, out of concern for him, insist they stop hanging out altogether.

"I don't know, Amanda."

She leaned in closer to him. "Phil, let's be frank. Life has dealt you a shitty deal. I know that our friendship means a lot to you, and that it's helped you get through this. Do you really think it's fair to punish yourself?"

"I don't think *any* of this is fair."

"Good."

"I've got enough problems without losing my job, though."

"You won't. You've done nothing wrong."

Amanda smiled. Phil's resolve was melting.

"Why don't you come over tonight? We can talk some more, in an atmosphere where you can be fully relaxed."

"The babysitter is only there until 8. I need to get home to the girls."

"This weekend, then?"

"Perhaps." Phil felt silly that he'd even addressed the topic of Stuart's warning. Discussing it out loud made it feel trivial. Suddenly Amanda's hand was on top of his on the table, rubbing it gently. She casually pulled it away after just a few seconds, but the sensation of her touch combined with her quiet smile were enough to get Phil's heart racing once again.

Chapter Forty-Seven:

APRIL 16

First United Methodist Church of Ormond Beach was a pretty cluster of Spanish-style buildings along Halifax Avenue, nestled between the river and the Atlantic. Ben and Tom found the education building where the meeting was taking place. Tom was in no hurry to go in, and Ben wondered if he was hoping they were at the wrong church.

"You okay?" Ben asked.

"Yeah. You sure you want to go inside, too?"

"Why not?" Ben smiled.

They found a sign directing people to the meeting location, and walked into a room of mostly men who were drinking coffee and quietly socializing. It looked like any other kind of get-together of any other organization or club. A friendly, middle-aged man standing behind a folding table greeted them and jotted down both of their first names on decal name tags. Ben and Tom dutifully slapped the tags onto their chests, and stuck together as they found the large circle of folding chairs and occupied two of them. A few other people came over to say hello, but no one asked any questions.

A tall, lanky man with curly, black hair and "Rory" on his name tag finally called the room to order. Ben recognized his name and voice from the telephone, when he'd called to inquire on Tom's behalf.

"Good evening. I'm Rory, and I'm an alcoholic. I've been sober for four years, three months, and eleven days. I'd like to give a special welcome to new attendees and have you introduce yourselves."

Tom looked about the room, waiting to see if someone else would raise their hand first. No one did.

"Hi, I'm Tom," he said, and Rory smiled. Eleven other pairs of eyes were resting upon him. "I'm pretty sure I'm an alcoholic."

"Welcome, Tom," the group said in unison. *Just like in the movies.* Tom smiled. He'd gotten through the hardest part, he hoped.

Ben nodded to the room as he stood. "Hi, I'm Ben. I'm here to support Tom," he said.

"Welcome, Ben."

The focus quickly shifted to the heart of the meeting itself. Rory secured volunteers to read sections from the *Alcoholics Anonymous* book that everyone else had in front of them. While this was taking place, Rory got up and found a couple of extra copies for Tom and Ben, and directed them to the appropriate pages.

At one point, Rory pointed to a poster on the wall. "Let's be sure to keep our meeting guidelines in mind," he said, smiling. Tom glanced over at the poster. *Keep confidentiality. Make "I" statements. Stay in the here and now…*

The here and now, Tom repeated silently, and realized his mind had been drifting. He glanced at Ben, who seemed engrossed in every detail of what the other attendees were saying.

"Who would like to share a topic?" Rory asked the group.

One of the women raised her hand. She was well-dressed and could have easily been one of Ben's district managers, Tom thought.

"I'm Susan, and I'm an alcoholic," she said, and Tom smiled at the sound of his own mother's first name. "I've been sober for seven months and eighteen days." Susan paused as the group responded with gentle applause.

"I get really pissed off sometimes at the double-standard of what society expects."

The group waited for more. Rory encouraged her, "Go on, Susan."

"At events and social gatherings, people look at you funny or give you a hard time if you say you don't drink. And then, if you drink excessively, like each of us in this room has suffered from doing, you're labeled a drunk."

Susan paused, glancing around the room, saw several other members nodding.

"I guess I don't know how people live in the middle, drinking 'socially,' without going to the extreme dependence that we've gone to. Who are these 'normal' drinkers, and do they really exist?"

"Interesting," Rory said as the group processed Susan's observation and question. Ben perceived that he was, in fact, one of the "normal social drinkers," but didn't want to announce that to the group. He'd no idea how to explain why he could "live in the middle." It was simply all he'd ever known.

"I'm Bruce, I'm an alcoholic and have been sober for two months," said a man in his 60s. "I know what Susan is saying. For decades I thought I was just a social drinker. But then, as my health declined I realized I was drinking a lot more than everyone else around me. I'm not sure when and how I crossed that ambiguous line, though. Or why others around me didn't."

"That's a powerful image, Bruce," Rory said. "That 'ambiguous line.' Thank you for sharing that."

Rory waited to see if anyone else had something to contribute.

"We've talked about this some before," Rory finally said, "about how people who don't seem to have a problem with alcohol might have problems in other areas that we don't see. And how every individual, alcoholic or not, could benefit from embracing the principles that we talk about here in AA."

Rory smiled at Susan.

"I guess what I'm trying to say, Susan, is that your length of sobriety, and the fact that you're practicing these principles, demonstrates that you're learning to live in the middle. You're finding the answer."

Susan smiled as several group members voiced their agreement. Tom and Ben listened as a few of them contributed their own perspectives on being surrounded by social drinkers, and the awkwardness of telling "persistent" people they didn't drink because they were alcoholics.

Tom raised his hand.

"Tom?" Rory asked.

"I guess I was one of those social drinkers for the longest time," Tom began. "I truly don't think I drank excessively until the past year. But as I'm listening to this conversation and reflecting on things, I realize that I had another addiction, and that was my work."

Ben listened closely.

"I'm kind of an entrepreneur," Tom continued. "I've owned several businesses, and each time I've had to wear a lot of hats. It's a lot of hours. A lot of intensity. I've been driven to succeed, and I think that drive was extreme on many occasions."

Tom glanced at a few of the faces, to ensure people were tracking with him.

"My wife left a year ago," he said. "That's when I faced the double stress of running my current business and taking care of my son Connor. That's when drinking became my escape. Gradually, it replaced work as my addiction."

Tom paused, then added, "I guess what I'm realizing tonight is that my *personality* is addictive. That I have this tendency to latch onto something and go to the extreme."

He sat back, and waited. Ben was grateful that Tom had opened up so quickly to the group, and thought what he'd shared was profound.

"Tom, first, thank you for your transparency," Rory said. He glanced around at some of the others. "I think what Tom has said is very important. We admit that we're powerless over alcohol. However, as we peel back more layers, we find that the real challenge is we're powerless over *ourselves.* That's why the program itself is so powerful and has worked for so many decades. It transforms the entire person, not just the alcoholic in us."

Tom's sharing and Rory's follow-up inspired several others to discuss how AA had helped them to acknowledge and persevere in the face of such "powerlessness." Ben's mind was drifting to his own approach to work. He pictured the many occasions where Beth had complained he was gone too much, taking too much work home, and too "identified" with his profession. Beth sometimes claimed that Ben had no true "hobbies."

The hour was nearly finished. After securing a leader for the next meeting, Rory asked the group to stand and hold hands. Ben noticed that Tom's hand was damp and cold from nerves. Rory directed them to the "Serenity Prayer" that was also affixed on the wall.

"God, grant me the serenity to accept the things I cannot change, the courage to change the things I can, and the wisdom to know the difference," a cacophony of voices, including Ben's and Tom's, dutifully recited.

Ben and Tom started to release their hands from each other and the persons on either side of them, when the rest of the group suddenly tightened their grips and chanted, "KEEP COMING BACK! IT WORKS IF YOU WORK IT!"

Most of the group members walked up to Tom and Ben and introduced themselves as the meeting broke up. Rory hung around, waiting for the others to leave, and then gave Tom a slip of paper with his phone number.

"Please give me a call when it's convenient for you," Rory said. "One of the secret ingredients to success with AA is having a sponsor: a person with a few years of consecutive sobriety who's there for you as you need them. I'd be delighted to sponsor you, if you'd like."

Tom glanced at the piece of paper and inserted it into his wallet, thanking Rory.

"Hope to see you next week," Rory said.

Tom and Ben walked quietly to the car. Neither spoke for the first several minutes as Ben drove.

"Thanks again for coming with me," Tom said, staring out the window. "I'm going to go back. I'll go back alone, though. I can do this."

Ben smiled. "Sure thing. I really got a lot out of it myself."

The serenity to accept the things I cannot change, Ben kept hearing in his head as he drove home. Ben gave Beth an extra tight hug when he arrived. Maddie was asleep. He shared a brief summary of the AA meeting, careful not to mention the first names of anyone who was there, and told her "it was like opening a window into a parallel universe."

"These brutally honest conversations are happening in little rooms in every city across the world, every night," he said. "And hardly anyone knows about it, except for the people who are there. It's pretty amazing, really."

They sat on the couch together. Beth caught Ben up on her day and Maddie.

"I've been thinking about what you said Phil brought up recently, about the memorial service," Beth said. "I think it's a good idea. I think the families need something like that."

"I do, too."

"I want to help Phil put it together. I don't think he should have to do it alone," Beth said.

"I'm sure he'd appreciate that."

"He said he thought it should be non-denominational, right? Not overtly religious?"

"Yes."

Beth leaned against Ben. "It should be led by someone who knows the families well, who can really empathize and tie things together at the end."

Ben shot her a strange glance. "Are you implying that you think I should do it?"

She frowned. "Umm, no. I mean, you do know the families well and I think you'd do a great job, but I was thinking more about someone who isn't too emotionally involved."

"Oh," he said.

"I was thinking about Cameron, the journalist."

Ben waited for more.

"He's talked in depth with the immediate family members, with the exception of Russ O'Rourke and Mario Lazano, who declined to be interviewed," Beth said. "I can tell he really cares. His article is about to come out, and so he's really become the person who can tell the story comprehensively and even objectively."

"Do you think his employer would let him do something like that?"

She shrugged. "I don't know. I think it would reflect well on the newspaper, and that he'd be representing them in a very positive light."

"Should we wait to see the article first?" Ben asked, grinning.

Beth laughed. "Maybe."

He caressed her cheek, and then her hair, and gave her a gentle kiss.

"I was thinking tonight about what you've said a couple of times: that I don't have any hobbies outside of work."

Beth nodded. "Yeah."

"I guess I work so much that I'd feel bad about spending time on a hobby, like golf or whatever, when I could be spending time with you and Maddie."

She grinned. "Well, if you worked less, you'd have time for us *and* hobbies." Beth leaned forward and kissed him back.

"Now I'm a director. Even more responsibility. Shit."

"Shit is right," she said, drinking her wine.

"It's a Catch-22. Everything costs so much money, so you have to be successful and make a lot of money. Success comes with a hefty price tag of time and energy."

"Unless," Beth said, "we simply want less. Then less money is required."

"You can only want so much less," Ben said. "What would you want to take away from Maddie that other children have? It's only going to get more expensive as she grows."

"And especially if we have another baby."

Ben feigned a heart attack, and Beth chuckled.

"Yeah, it is a pretty stressful thought," she said.

"Has Maddie said she wants a brother or sister yet?"

"Not yet, but I'm sure it's coming any day now."

Ben yawned and stretched. "I don't even know what hobby I'd take up. I don't have the patience for golf. I don't know if reading is a bona fide hobby. Maybe I should get a jet ski."

"Will you let me drive it sometimes?"

"Of course."

"You could come workout at my club. That could be a hobby, too."

He ran his finger along Beth's arm, admiring her muscle tone. "That wouldn't be a hobby. That would be torture. But you'd love that, I'm sure."

"You could stand to exercise more," Beth said. "Not to lecture you or anything."

"I prefer power-walking."

"Walking is great. Especially when you actually do it."

"I'll start tomorrow morning."

"It's a deal." Beth snuggled into his chest, exhausted. "We should go to bed. Thank you for going with Tom to the meeting. I'm sure that must have been a little awkward for you."

"It was a lot harder for Tom, I imagine."

A little while later Ben lay in bed, groggy but his mind still going strong. Beth had already fallen asleep. He thought through the AA conversation, and wondered if anyone in the room had any idea that Tom was the Tom Blakely whose wife had been all over the news and Internet. Certain lines kept replaying in his head: *Powerless…the wisdom to know the difference…*

Ben wondered whether a guy who worked all the time and didn't have any hobbies needed a support group as well.

Chapter Forty-Eight:

MAY 5

It was the first time James had been invited to Mario's home. He was suitably impressed, but few houses built in the 20th Century had the same appeal to James after what he'd observed and visited during his years abroad.

DDC's full management team was gathered in the parlor, and a couple of well-dressed men were serving everyone heavy hors-d'oeuvre and wine. James had done well in his two-year tenure with the company, and was no longer referred to by the others as "The Rookie."

He was sipping from a glass of Cabernet when Mario tapped him on the arm. James turned to see his boss standing with an attractive young woman with dark hair and eyes.

"James, this is my daughter Emma. She's a senior in high school," Mario said. "Emma, this is James Thorne, who works with me."

"Nice to meet you, Emma," James said, gently shaking her hand.

Emma smiled and nodded. "Nice to meet you too," she said, and then without another word headed across the room and out the front door of the house. James deduced that Emma was long past the thrill of being introduced to her father's business associates.

Mario gathered the crew together for a toast. A little while later, James peered out the front window and saw Emma sitting by herself on a stone bench in the large garden. He quietly slipped away from the crowd and opened the front door.

"Mind if I sit?" he asked Emma.

She glanced up, surprised, and then shook her head. "No problem."

"This is a great spot here," he said, sitting next to her on the bench.

"Yeah. I come out here a lot."

"You like gardens?"

Emma shrugged. "I don't know. I just don't like being around my father when he's acting like the life of the party."

She shot him a glance. "I guess I shouldn't tell that to you. You work for him. You probably think he's wonderful, like everyone else does."

James nodded. "He's been good to me, that's for sure. But nobody's perfect."

"Yeah, that's for sure also."

Emma studied him for a moment.

"You seem a lot younger than most of the people who usually work for him. And not nearly as creepy, too."

James laughed. "Well, thank you on both counts."

Cameron Brock's article was published on the front page of *The Orlando Sentinel*, with the headline, "One Year Later, Book Club Families Wait and Hope." High quality photographs of Emma, Jackie, and Kari accompanied the text:

DAYTONA BEACH—*Phil Solomon has his work cut out for him this morning.*

He's cooking eggs on the stove while putting together peanut butter and jelly sandwiches on whole wheat bread. Phil asks his daughters Audrey and Natalie how much of each—the peanut butter and the jelly—they want on their respective sandwiches, and each girl describes a different amount while dividing her attention between her father and her smart phone.

Next, Phil negotiates a fruit to include alongside a sugary snack in the girls' lunches. They debate the pros and cons of apple slices, oranges, and grapes. Natalie, the younger of the two at age 12, mentions how the grapes tasted "sour" the day before. Audrey, 15, shakes her head, rolls her eyes, and tells her sister, "You're imagining things again."

Phil manages to get the eggs served, the lunches packed, and the girls off to school—all without skipping a beat. Somewhere in the midst of the action, he gets himself ready for another morning of teaching humanities classes at the Daytona Beach campus of the University of Central Florida.

Such activities of a working dad are far from unique, in this era of two-income families and single parenting. But what's distinct about Phil and his daughters is that wife and mother Jackie Solomon is not at work, and is not divorced nor estranged from her children's father.

She's been missing, for a year.

On the evening of May 3, 2012, Jackie and her friends Emma O'Rourke and Kari Blakely, all residents of Daytona Beach, left for Palm Beach County on what was to be a "girls' weekend" at the SunFest music festival They were to stay at a Boca Raton condominium belonging to another friend, Delphi Adams. The three women apparently arrived at the condo, texted home late that night, and then were not seen or heard from again.

"I try to help my daughters make sense of it," Phil observes over coffee. Nearby is Phil's tattered copy of Viktor Frankl's classic work Man's Search for Meaning, a gift from his father. "But I can't make sense of it myself. It's not what you expect to happen in your family, or in your life."

Law enforcement authorities cannot make sense of it either. Police report no signs of forced entry into Adams' Boca Raton condo. All of the women's items—most of them still in travel bags—were left undisturbed, including purses and cell phones. No fingerprints other than Adams' were found inside the condo. Police have found no witnesses, and repeated police interviews with Adams and the three mothers' immediate family members produced no clues of their whereabouts.

The three women, along with Adams and five other Daytona residents, were part of a book club that met twice per month at Adams's used bookstore, The Oracle, which closed after Adams's death late last year. They first met at a fitness studio owned by Beth McBride, who was also part of the book club. The group had just finished reading Ernest Hemingway's classic, The Sun Also Rises.

Tom Blakely, Kari's husband and father to their 15-year-old son Connor, is the owner of the Famoso's restaurant on the Daytona beachside. Like Phil, Tom is juggling a demanding job with the responsibilities of unexpected single parenting.

"I was fortunate to find a great general manager to run the restaurant last year," Tom says. "It's taken some of the stress off of my plate. My son Connor is an amazing human being. He's an artist, and he's been expressing a lot of his feelings through drawing and sometimes painting. I wish I had his gifts."

Emma O'Rourke is divorced from Russ O'Rourke and the two have a son of their own, Peter, also 15. Russ declined to be interviewed for this article, as did Emma's father, real estate developer Mario Lazano.

Beth McBride had been invited to join the women on the trip. She observes how she's battled a mixture of grief, guilt, and relief across the past year.

"I have this image in my mind…that I could have done something if I was with them," Beth says. "Saved the day, I suppose. I don't know exactly what I would have done, since I have no idea what happened. But somehow, perhaps, the larger our number, the more strength we would have to fight off whatever or whomever came against us."

Beth and her husband, Ben, have done their best to provide support and encouragement to the men and children left behind without answers. Ben, an executive with the wireless company Next Generation, notes he could have easily been in the other men's shoes—and doesn't know if he could have handled it as well.

"They're very strong guys," Ben says. "They're each coping in their own way, doing the best they can. It's a very lonely existence for them. There's a lot they do behind the scenes to keep everything in motion."

The families sometimes socialize together as a group, having gotten together for this past New Year's Eve. Holidays such as Christmas and Hanukah were especially tough.

"There's no way to pretend the void isn't there," Phil concedes. "I find it's better to talk about it with Audrey and Natalie, rather than try to dance around the subject."

Phil says he's engaged the services of a therapist, both for working with his daughters and for himself. Tom says a close-knit group of friends and very supportive employees have made all the difference for him. He also leans heavily on quotes from Frankl's book, such as, "When we are no longer able to change a situation—just think of an incurable disease such as inoperable cancer—we are challenged to change ourselves."

"I wish there was some lesson in all of this that I could offer," Tom says. "But there's not. I don't know how you prevent something like this from happening. The lack of closure, the lack of knowing any details; that keeps me up at night."

While the case remains open, a Daytona Beach Police Department spokesperson admits there are no new leads to follow up on at the moment.

Beth, when asked if she has a message for whoever is responsible for the women's disappearance, offers the following:

"Think about their children," she pleads, tears in her eyes. "These children deserve to have their mothers back. Let them come home. And if you've taken their lives, let their families know so they can properly say goodbye. Find some humanity within you, and think about these four children who've been abandoned and deeply saddened."

∼∼∼

The Associated Press immediately picked up the article, as did *USA TODAY* and *The New York Times*. Social media exploded with links, updates on Facebook pages, and countless re-tweets. All of the Central Florida-based television stations ran updated pieces the same day, along with several South Florida stations.

Producers from *CNN, Fox News, Inside Edition, The Today Show, Good Morning America*, and *CBS Early Show* called Cameron before the day was over, requesting him to appear on their respective broadcasts. Several national and Sirius radio shows phoned as well, and emails poured in from numerous Web sites, blogs, and YouTube channels. Cameron responded to none of them, but saved an intriguing voice mail from NPR.

Media members also attempted to call the men's houses and each of their respective places of business. Ben fielded call after call from various store employees from across Florida, saying that television shows kept calling and asking for him. Ben patiently thanked each of them, and by 3 p.m. had started letting those calls go to voice mail.

Two different book clubs used their Instagram accounts to post pictures of the missing women. On Twitter, the hashtag *#BookClubWidowers* emerged before the day was over. Cameron found that annoying, and was grateful his editors hadn't used something like that in the headline.

Anticipating that television reporters would show up at their doorsteps on the day of publication, Ben and Mario planned ahead for the families to gather at Mario's well-guarded home beginning at breakfast time. It was an expanded version of the New Year's Eve party hosted by the McBrides, except Mario didn't make any attempt to dismantle his well-stocked home bar. Henry Reid was dispatched to talk to news crews each time they arrived, politely turning down their requests to speak to Mario and asking them to leave. Most did a "live shot" from across the street, and then packed up their gear and departed.

"Any regrets?" Ben asked Beth as they watched Mario sit on his living room floor and play Legos with Maddie.

"About speaking with Cameron?"

"Yeah."

"None at all. I'm really glad my picture isn't in there, though."

Audrey, Natalie, Pete, and Connor hung out in Mario's media room, and spent much of their time tapping away on their phones.

"We still need to go bodysurfing together," Pete reminded Audrey, and she smiled.

Russ attempted to make small talk with Pete, but his son had little to say to his father these days. Mario said the boy was enjoying living at his house, and that they could continue taking things a day at a time. At one point Pete went off to his room to play video games. He texted Audrey a few minutes later, and she joined him and suggested they leave his bedroom door open.

The one visitor who was allowed into Mario's home that day was Rory, Tom's new AA sponsor. Rory knew the article was coming out, and called Tom to check on him that morning. Tom invited Rory to come over, checking with Mario afterwards to see "if that was okay." Mario shrugged and mentioned it to Henry, who scowled and pulled Tom into a private room for several minutes to grill him about Rory.

Cameron and Nelson spent the day in downtown Winter Park, enjoying brunch and the sunshine. Nelson read the article word for word, and told his partner he was very proud of him. Julio Ramos called Cameron to congratulate the journalist on a well-written piece. Susannah, who'd gotten past the bouts of morning sickness and was "one hot pregnant lady," according to Julio, passed along her compliments as well.

Phil texted Amanda with a link to the newspaper's web site. Sitting in her apartment, Amanda smiled at the article's descriptions of Phil as a father wearing all of the hats. She longed to meet the Solomon girls.

Sarosky read the print version of the article at his breakfast table, joined that morning by his elderly parents. Sarosky's mother remarked how pretty each woman was. Sarosky and Rice had politely declined to speak to Cameron for the article, and any calls from reporters were going straight to the Daytona Beach Police Department's media relations line.

Mario's guests waited until dark to depart. The television crews had lost interest at that point.

Phil and Tom arrived home with their children, gearing up for a new week of packing lunches and cooking meals, and Russ headed to his beachside condo alone and unsettled. Maybe someone would emerge with information now that a new article had come out, he thought.

Chapter Forty-Nine:

Russ's cell phone started vibrating around 11:45 p.m. that same evening. At first the noise was part of a dream he was having about the beach, sitting in the sand and staring up at an approaching helicopter. The copter was over the ocean and getting closer to the shore, the whirl of its propellers drowning out any other imaginable sound.

It's the goddamned phone, his consciousness finally informed him.

"Shit," Russ said, and his first thought was that Mario was calling to tell him Pete had screwed up again. But Russ didn't recognize the local 386 area code number. He was inclined to ignore the call, but decided that wasn't a good idea.

"Yeah, this is Russ."

"Russ, it's me, Heather."

He sat up, rubbing his eyes. "Who?"

"*Heather.* You know, Mario's friend. I've been trying to reach Mario, but he's not answering the phone."

Growing irritated, Russ recalled that Heather was one of those stupid sunscreen models Mario hung around with to prove he was still as viral a man as ever.

"So why the hell are you calling me? And how did you get my number?"

"You *gave* it to me. Don't you remember? It was at one of Mario's parties last year. I think you were pretty drunk, and you kept saying how good I looked in my little red dress."

"Yeah, I'm sure you're right," Russ said. "So what do you need, Heather?"

"I have to reach Mario, but he's not answering. There's a couple of guys here in my apartment. We were all hanging out down at the pool. We've been partying up in my place for the last hour or so, you know, doing lines and some of that stuff."

"Yeah, I gotcha. Why do you need Mario so badly?"

"Because these guys say they have information on Emma. And that they'll only give it to Mario himself, in person."

Russ almost dropped his phone.

"Can you repeat that?"

"They say they know something about where Emma is, but they'll only tell it to Mario directly. She's your ex-wife, right? Maybe they'll tell it to you." Heather paused, and Russ heard voices behind her. "Oh. No, they're shaking their heads; they'll only give it to Mario himself, face to face."

"Heather, who the fuck are these guys?" Russ asked, pacing around his bedroom. A coked-up wannabe model with suspect intelligence wasn't his idea of a reliable source.

"Their names are Morton and Freddie," she said. "We met tonight at the pool. They've just moved into the apartment complex."

"And how the hell would they know anything about Emma? Were you telling them about her?"

"No!" Heather protested. "I didn't say anything about any of that mess. They just brought it up. I don't know how they even knew that I know Mario!"

"All right, all right. Just stay put there, okay? Don't let those guys leave. I'll get a hold of Mario somehow. Call me if they take off, okay?"

"Okay, thank you!"

Russ hung up and considered his next move. If Heather was telling the truth and had her story straight, it was very weird that two guys would just show up out of the blue, start talking about Emma's disappearance, and demand to speak with Mario. The more plausible reality was that Heather was too fucked up to remember all the events of the evening, and the partiers had probably talked about the media sensation that had flared up that day around the three missing women. But who were these two guys, and did they really think that someone like Mario Lazano would just come over for a chat?

His call to Mario went straight to voice mail. "Shit!" Russ got dressed, grabbed his car keys, and headed outside.

On the way to Mario's, Russ wondered if the guys at the gate would even be willing to disturb the old fart. The graveyard shift guards bore unfamiliar faces. They listened as Russ explained he had an important message to give Mario. Next, they motioned Russ out of the car, thoroughly looked at not just his driver's license but through his wallet in general, and consulted a tablet computer.

"I'm calling Mr. Reid, we'll have him come out and make the decision," one of them said, pressing a button on his cell phone.

Russ listened as the guy spoke with Henry, whom Russ was certain would be even less pleased to see him than Mario.

"Mr. Reid is on his way down," the guard said.

Henry was cursing out loud as well as he wrapped himself in his bathrobe, grabbed his glasses, and found a pair of slippers. He missed having his own place, even though Mario's house was very luxurious and Henry had everything he needed. Hell, Henry missed having his own *life,* period, where you go to work and when you go home your work is over and you get some space. But this was the life he'd chosen, and it was business 24/7.

As Henry approached the guard shack, the sight of Russ O'Rourke pissed him off even more.

"What can I do for you, Russ?" Henry asked, motioning Russ over to him and away from the guard shack. As they walked toward the house together, Russ recapped the phone call from Heather.

"That's crazy," Henry said. "There's no way I'm sending Mario over to that bullshit. She's high and doesn't know what the fuck she's saying."

Russ nodded, impatient. "I know, I know, that was my first inclination. But my gut tells me this is worth checking out. Sometimes you gotta trust your gut, Henry."

"I trust my gut a lot. I trust this even more," Henry said, patting the pocket of his bathrobe, where Russ assumed Henry had his pistol. *Even in the middle of the night, the guy is packing.*

"We should at least give him the choice, the choice of whether to go or at least call her back."

Henry folded his arms, standing between Russ and the front door. "Who's going to go upstairs and wake him? It's not going to be me."

"I'll do it."

"Great choice. It'll be your ass."

Russ shrugged. "My ass is already on the hot seat, so I might as well annoy him some more."

"Your decision."

As they headed upstairs, Russ hoped Pete was sound asleep in his bedroom. He didn't want his son getting mixed up in this conversation. Russ knocked softly on Mario's bedroom door. After a minute or so, he knocked again.

"Pete?" Mario called out.

"No, Mario, it's Russ."

185

Silence. After about 30 seconds, a bathrobe-clad Mario opened the door and looked at Russ, then glanced beyond him at Henry.

"What can I do for you, Russ?"

Ten minutes later, Russ and Mario sat in the backseat of Henry's sedan as he drove across town. Mario called Heather before they left, but she refused to answer his probing questions over the phone and begged him to come over.

"She doesn't sound like herself," Mario said. "I think she's under some kind of duress. We'd better go and see who these jackasses are."

During the drive, Henry and Mario debated whether Mario should even get out of the car. Mario said he had no fears about going up to Heather's apartment, but Henry finally insisted on going up alone first to check things out. Henry wished he'd brought another guy with him, but Mario didn't want to take any men away from the house while Pete was there alone and asleep.

"Love how they label these 'luxury apartments,'" Russ said as they pulled into the parking lot. "Anytime you're renting, it's not luxury."

Mario directed Henry toward Heather's building, and after parking in a visitor's spot Henry remained in the car. He glanced at Mario in the rear view mirror. "You sure you think this is worth checking out?"

The boss man nodded. "Yeah. Just make sure she's ok, and if you think I need to come up then come back and get me."

"You want me to come with you?" Russ asked.

Henry shot him a glare. "No, thanks." He tossed Russ the car keys. "Just in case you need them."

Heather lived on the third floor. As he approached unit 314, Henry made a mental note to tell Mario it was time to stop associating with women who were without significant means. They were too unpredictable and needy.

He knocked on the door, and instinctively felt the portion of his jacket that covered his holstered pistol. After a few seconds Heather asked who it was. She didn't open the door right away.

"Where's Mario?" she called out, her voice cracking.

"Just open the door, Heather."

"They said they wanted to see *Mario!*"

Henry was ready to kill the stupid bitch. He waited.

"Okay, they said I can let you in."

Jesus, he thought, *it's your own fucking apartment.*

Heather opened the door. Her face was flushed, her hair a mess, her eyes bloodshot. She was wearing a little tank top and the shortest jean shorts that were still legal.

Henry walked past her into the apartment. A couple of men were sitting at her small glass dining room table. As they stood, Henry quickly recognized them.

"Guys, what the hell is going on?" he asked, but the only response was the bigger of the two pulling a gun and pumping three silenced bullets into Henry's chest. As Henry collapsed to the floor, the smaller man grabbed a screaming Heather and pinned her arms behind her back. The gunman approached her, pressed the barrel against her forehead, and pulled the trigger.

Out in the parking lot, Mario and Russ waited in the backseat. Russ could feel Mario growing impatient. Mario's phone buzzed with a text message.

"It's from Henry. He says to come on up."

Mario stared out the window for a moment, and then looked at Russ.

"Get into the front seat and drive us away."

"What?"

"Russ, just do it," Mario said. "Now, Son."

Russ hopped out of the back and into the driver's seat. As they left the apartment complex, Mario stared out the back window.

"I don't get it," Russ said as he drove. "Why did we just leave him there like that?"

"There's no way Henry sends me a text message like that. He would have come down."

"So who sent it?"

"Not Henry. Henry's dead."

Russ almost ran into a car parked on the side of the road. He stared at Mario in the rearview mirror.

"Get back to the house as quickly as possible," Mario said.

Chapter Fifty:

MAY 6

There he was, down by the shoreline as dusk settled across the horizon, just as he'd promised.

She hadn't been followed; she was certain of this. 17-year-old Emma took a deep breath, hoped her makeup was perfect, and removed her sandals as she walked onto the beach. The sand felt cool and seductive between her toes, and she was happy. It was a breezy evening, and Emma's summer dress clung lightly to her, helping her to feel flirty and free.

As soon as she reached James Thorne he swooped her into his arms and kissed her powerfully, pulling her in tightly. She'd never been kissed in that manner before, having only made out with boys her age. The ocean crashed violently against the shore.

Emma wanted to be wrapped around James as closely and permanently as possible, and responded to his hands moving across her body by reciprocating with hers. Soon James was leading her to the tiny beach cottage he'd rented for the weekend, and once inside they practically ripped off each other's clothing.

Russ stayed huddled up at Mario's house throughout the night and into the morning. Nearly all of the Cubists were at the property now, and one of them—a tall, dark-haired guy named Ethan—appeared to be in charge. Russ and Mario sat in the study, each occasionally dozing off in between proposing theories as to what had happened.

When Pete came downstairs around 9:30 a.m., he was surprised to see his father. Russ and Mario had already rehearsed this. Mario had requested Russ to come over so the three of them could spend some time together that day. Pete asked if they were going somewhere, but Mario said they were going to stay at the house. This didn't interest Pete a great deal, and he sulked back to his room.

The men passed the day watching movies, eating, and playing poker. The guards drifted in and out of the house. At one point in the late afternoon, with Pete back in his room and out of earshot, Russ asked Mario what he knew was a stupid question.

"No chance of you calling the police, I guess?"

"That'll open up a can of worms so big I'll never be able to squeeze them back inside."

"So what do we do?"

"We wait."

"Wait for what?"

Mario shrugged. "To see what happens."

Nothing happened that evening. Mario prepared a guest room for Russ. Pete, perplexed that his father was sleeping over, came in as Russ was settling in for the night.

"Dad, it's really weird that you're spending the night."

"Yeah, I know. It's just something I need to do tonight."

Pete showed no signs of leaving. Russ was exhausted.

"You and Grandpa are working on something big together. Something's going on. Something related to Mom."

"What makes you think that?"

"I just have a hunch. I think something has happened. I want you to tell me."

Russ studied his son for a moment. He wondered how many of Mario's conversations the kid had overheard during the past few months. He dreaded what Pete or his friends had read on the Internet. There was scant wisdom in treating Pete like a little boy any longer, but he wasn't yet a man.

"Shut the door," Russ told him, and Pete did so.

"The stuff we talk about stays with us. You understand?"

Pete nodded. "Yeah."

"You don't talk about it to your grandfather. Or your friends. Or with the Solomons, or the Blakelys, or the McBrides."

"I get it."

Russ began to talk in a whisper.

"Your grandfather has been mixed up with some dangerous people over the years. I don't think he ever intended to. But once you become successful and make a lot of money, sometimes you start getting too ambitious. When you get involved with dangerous people, inevitably some of them become your enemies."

"Do you think some of Grandpa's enemies took Mom in order to hurt him? Do you think they killed her?"

Pete was trying not to cry, trying to be macho, and Russ wanted to give him a hug.

"I don't know. I sure hope not. But there were some men last night who tried to get Grandpa to go meet with them. They claimed they had information about your mother. I don't know if they were telling the truth or not, but they planned to kill your grandfather when he got there to meet with them."

"But Grandpa's okay. So he didn't meet with them?"

"Mr. Reid insisted on meeting with them instead. But Mr. Reid never came back. So your grandfather and I came back here, and we're not sure what's happened."

"Do you think Mr. Reid is dead?"

"Yeah. Unfortunately, I do."

Pete processed this.

"His job was to protect Grandpa, wasn't it? Him and all these men that are always at the house? Grandpa always told me that the men were there so no one would steal anything, that he had a lot of nice things that he wanted to be able to give to me some day, and he didn't want them stolen."

Russ smiled. "Well, I'm sure he does plan to give you a lot of stuff someday." *And money,* Russ thought.

"But they're really here to protect Grandpa."

"Yeah. I think that's right."

"Will Grandpa still be safe now that Mr. Reid is dead?"

"Absolutely. Grandpa has a lot of people around him to keep him safe."

"What about you, Dad?"

"What about me?"

Pete's eyes were definitely watery. "Are you safe? Is someone going to try to hurt and kill you?"

"I'm safe. No one cares about hurting me."

"I don't believe you. You work for Grandpa. I want you to stay here with me and with Grandpa."

"Pete, I can't do that. I have a home of my own. Our home. If it makes you feel better, you can come back home with me now."

Pete looked panicked. "No way. I'm not leaving here. It's safer here. And I don't want you to leave either."

"Let's talk about it in the morning some more, okay Pete? I'm really exhausted. You need to get some sleep, too."

"You promise me you won't leave during the night?"

"I promise."

Pete sat up and went toward the door. "You promise?"

"I promise again."

Russ lay awake for the next hour, despite his physical exhaustion. He replayed episodes from his earlier years, before and after meeting Emma. There were too many decisions to second-guess.

He'd finally fallen asleep when a persistent knock at the bedroom door snapped him alert. *Shit, Pete's still awake.*

"Come in."

It was Mario whose face greeted Russ instead. "We've got some company downstairs. That detective, Sarosky."

Mario, Russ, and Sarosky sat at the small round table in Mario's kitchen. It was nearly 1 a.m.

One of Heather's friends had gotten worried when she couldn't reach her all day yesterday, the detective explained. The friend had a key, and finally went over to Heather's apartment last night and discovered the carnage.

"At first glance it appears to be a murder-suicide," Sarosky said. "Heather had a single, fatal, close-range gunshot to the head. There was a gun lying next to her, full of her fingerprints. Across the room was Mr. Reid, with several shots to the chest. All the shots were from that single gun."

Mario remained impassive.

"Mr. Lazano," Sarosky said. "I don't mean to sound insensitive, but this is the second one of your lady friends who's turned up dead in the past year."

"I'm well aware of that, Detective."

"Both through apparent suicides."

"Got it."

"If there's any information that you think would be helpful to me, this would be the time to share it."

Mario sipped from a coffee mug. He asked the other men if they wanted a refill, but they declined.

"Detective, I wish I had such information. I'd gladly share it."

"I'm sure you would. You can start by telling me why Henry Reid was at your lady friend's apartment in the first place."

"It's not unusual for Henry to go over there."

"Were they romantically involved?"

Mario shrugged. "I have no idea. I didn't ask Henry about his personal affairs."

"What was his exact job with your organization?"

"He was my advisor."

"Advising you on what?"

"The business."

Sarosky pointed to the window. "And these other men, that guard your property. What's their job with the business?"

"They protect the property. It's a nice property, you know."

"I've noticed."

"There's a lot of crime in this city."

"I've noticed that, too."

Russ liked Sarosky. He wanted to tell the guy a hell of a lot more, but was letting Mario take the lead; for now, at least.

"You can expect more visitors from the news media," Sarosky said. "This will probably go public in the morning, if it hasn't already. I think the tabloids are going to set up permanent shop here, at this point."

"They can do whatever they want."

"This can't be good for business, Mr. Lazano," Sarosky said. "Your daughter is missing. Your ex-girlfriend killed herself in her garage. Another girlfriend, or whatever she was to you, might have killed your top 'advisor' and then herself." He paused, as if waiting to see if Mario would get angry with him. "Don't you think that's too many coincidences, too many events in a short period of time to not be connected in some way?"

Mario stood up, but didn't make a move for the coffee pot. Russ recognized this move as an indication that the meeting was over.

"Detective, am I under arrest?"

"No, Mr. Lazano, you're not."

"Am I a suspect in any of these cases you're referring to?"

"Not at this time."

"Then I would like to excuse you, and to get back to sleep. Unless you have some information about my daughter that would be helpful for me to know, I'm not sure there's any point in continuing this conversation."

Sarosky stood as well.

"I suppose there isn't. But you know how to reach me, Mr. Lazano, if you have some information that would be helpful for me to know." Sarosky glanced at Russ. "After all, the three of us want the same thing, don't we? For Mrs. O'Rourke to come home safely."

Mario and Russ returned to the kitchen after escorting Sarosky back out to the guards. Mario looked like he'd aged ten years in the past day, Russ thought.

"I can't believe those bastards killed her also," Mario said.

"I'm your Henry now," Russ replied.

"What?"

"I'm taking Henry's place, as your new head of security."

Mario laughed. "You should go back to sleep."

"I'm serious."

"I don't remember offering you the job," Mario smiled.

"I'm not asking you."

"Russ, that's enough. I'm going back to bed. You're welcome to anything you find in the refrigerator." Mario turned to leave.

"Here's the deal. The alternative is that I go to Sarosky and fully cooperate with him. I'll share all of my insights and observations and suspicions from across the years. The police and FBI will be so far up your ass you won't be able to take a shit any longer."

"Don't make threats like that, Russ. It's below your dignity."

"I don't give a shit about dignity any longer. I want my kid's mother back."

Mario leaned against the kitchen doorway. "Do you even own a gun, Russ? Have you ever fired one?"

"I'm pretty sure there's a few here I can borrow and practice with."

"You're a marketing guy. How do you expect these men out here to do what you ask them to do?"

"Because you're going to tell them to."

"And what then? How do you plan to accomplish what Henry couldn't do?"

"I don't know yet. I'm going to take it a step at a time."

Mario shrugged. "Go on."

"I'm going to stay here. I need to be with my son. And I need to protect you. You're going to work out of your home from now on. I don't want you to leave the premises."

Mario chuckled. "You're grounding me, Russ?"

"I'm serious, Mario. Whether these guys know where Emma is or not, clearly they planned to kill you the other night. They're ruthless, and they don't care who gets in their way. They'll try again. We need to strengthen the security end of the business, and I'm going to head it up and do that for you."

"It doesn't sound like I have any choice in the matter."

"You don't."

"Very well. Tomorrow, arrange for some of the men to go to your condo and get whatever things you need. I'm going to sleep."

And with that, Russ was left alone in the kitchen with his thoughts—and the draining realization that he had no idea what to do next.

Chapter Fifty-One:

JUNE 1

Nick Ferrante was in his 30s when he received the phone call from George Patapos, offering insights about Ferrante's late father. After giving it considerable thought, Ferrante drove up I-95 to Daytona Beach, where a frail-looking but well-groomed Patapos greeted him at a retirement community villa.

Patapos offered Ferrante coffee but he declined. It was painful enough to watch the man move around, and Ferrante certainly didn't want Patapos waiting on him. They settled into the small living room, complete with white couches and an immaculately clean glass coffee table.

"You'll forgive my condition," Patapos said. "I'm suffering from bone cancer. My doctors tell me I don't have a lot of time left, but I'm putting up the best fight I possibly can."

"I'm sorry to hear that," Ferrante said. "Maybe you'll prove your doctors wrong."

Patapos smiled. "Maybe." He sighed. "But nonetheless, I'm seeking to get my affairs in order. And tie up some loose ends."

Ferrante nodded, and waited.

"Back in the late 1970s, when you were a young boy, I did some legal work for your father and his business partners," Patapos continued. "Did your mother ever mention my name?"

"No. She never really talks much about my father, or when we lived up here. I think it's too hard for her."

"Understandable," Patapos said. "And I'm sure it's difficult for you as well, coming up here like this to see me."

Ferrante shrugged. "I'm fine."

He waited. Patapos sipped from a glass of iced tea.

"Our work together grew more extensive, and soon I became your father's regular legal counsel. I handled all of his company's transactions, including the paperwork when your father and his partner added myself and another man as minority owners in the company."

Ferrante waited as Patapos had a coughing fit. It took the old man a moment to prepare himself to continue.

"Who was the other man?" Ferrante asked, and then again had to wait patiently while Patapos nearly coughed up a lung.

"Lazano. Mario Lazano. You ever heard of him?"

Ferrante chewed on the name for a moment.

"No," he said. "But next time I see my mother, I'll ask her if rings a bell."

The parking lot at the University of Central Florida's Daytona State College campus was overrun with police and media presence. Hot sunshine baked the asphalt. A small army of men dressed in blue blazers and khakis patrolled the property, the majority of them forming a perimeter around the large lecture hall.

The media focus had shifted from intense to downright crazy after the alleged murder-suicide involving Mario Lazano's key associate and one of his gal pals. The fact that the homicides occurred the same day as Cameron Brock's viral feature article led to wide and divergent speculation. Delphi Adams's apparent suicide was brought into the mix, based on sources who'd informed some reporter that Delphi had a romantic relationship with Mario. *#BookClubWidowers* continued to stick, and Cameron wouldn't have been surprised to see gypsy vendors hawking cheap t-shirts bearing the phrase.

Phil arrived hours before everyone else, even before Russ and his security detail, to ensure logistics were in place. He kept a copy of the approved guest list in his suit jacket, as did every single member of security. The list included family and close friends, as well as Dean Sanderson and a few faculty members with whom Phil was particularly close.

The service was scheduled to last an hour, and would be followed by a reception in an adjacent room with catered finger foods and beverages. The caterers were fully vetted by Russ and his people, who were also planning to keep close watch on everything that was prepared and served.

The stage included a simple podium in the middle front. There were also three large easels, each supporting a blown-up color photograph of Emma, Jackie, and

Kari, respectively. The easels were surrounded by several large bouquets of flowers. The stage had the look of a memorial service, absent any caskets.

Phil was thankful that the police were being cooperative and making some resource investment that day to ensure order, protection, and privacy. They kept a respectful distance from Russ's men, who in turn were careful to not draw extra attention to themselves through any obnoxious or threatening behaviors. Detectives Sarosky and Rice arrived early as well, and Phil found their presence especially comforting.

Ben and Beth, the event's official greeters, showed up not long after Sarosky. They'd left Maddie with a babysitter so they could give their full attention to the guests. Ben and Beth also had the invite list, along with a one-page collage of family photographs, so they could more easily recognize parents, grandparents, siblings, and so forth.

Mario wanted to join Ben and Beth in the front and greet everyone also, but Russ insisted he stay as far inside the lecture hall as possible surrounded by detail. If some asshole did manage to get into the building and attempt to take a shot at the old man, Russ cautioned, Mario shouldn't position himself front and center like a sitting duck.

Russ still hated the whole idea of a memorial service. He was only attending because of his new self-appointed role as head of security. Russ didn't want to listen to everyone eulogize his ex-wife and the two other women, and couldn't bear the thought of having to repeat the whole charade one day if their dead bodies were found. Russ would never say this to Pete or even to Mario, but the ruthlessness of the men who'd murdered Henry and Heather wasn't a good sign.

Cameron arrived with Nelson, and Beth gave them both a hug. It wasn't hard for Cameron to talk his editors into letting him facilitate the service, since the journalist had—at least briefly—attained a reluctant celebrity status. He'd continued to turn down every interview request with the exception of NPR, which was scheduled for that afternoon.

Phil's parents, Joseph and Rachel, were among the first guests to arrive. They each held the hand one of one of their granddaughters Audrey and Natalie. They were a dignified, older Jewish couple, whom Ben and Beth had met several times before. Joe was a retired dentist and a Daytona Beach native. Rachel was very active in their temple and the couple had lots of friends in the area. They were still in relatively strong health, and had provided invaluable support to Phil and his daughters across the past year.

Phil's sister, Esther Solomon Berger, arrived a few minutes later with her younger sister, Janice Solomon. Both women had left Daytona years ago, Esther to Chicago where she'd gone to school and met her husband David, and Janice to New York City where she worked in publishing. None of the three Solomon children, including youngest sibling Phil, remained active in their Jewish religion after leaving home. The elder Solomons often remarked with sadness that this had become the norm of the younger generations.

One thing that remained, however, was the Solomon family's rich and vibrant conversations around literature; the arts; philosophy; and politics. Phil and Joe had always been close, and Phil had even confided in his father about his friendship with Amanda. Both made a pact to not tell Phil's mother who, Joe conceded, "Would stir up too much drama about it."

The Solomons embraced Jackie Solomon's father, Earl Thompson, when he arrived. Earl, divorced and battling diabetes, had only come down from South Carolina once in the past year. He was a quiet man who enjoyed fishing and hunting, but had done very little of either in recent years. They also hugged Jackie's mother, Melinda Franklin, who came in with her oldest son Ronald and youngest daughter Shelly.

The remaining book club members showed up as a group, and Beth embraced each one of them. Kevlin gave Ben a lingering smile as he shook her hand.

Mayor Rinaldi and Chief Higgins were present as well. The mayor had told the families he didn't intend to speak, but wanted to show his support. Sarosky bet Rice a free dinner that Rinaldi wouldn't be able to restrain himself from taking the microphone.

A small group of security escorted Emma's mother, Carmen Lazano, into the building. Carmen hated coming back down to Daytona, and Russ was annoyed that she'd not seen Pete once since his mother disappeared. He was relieved that Emma's expatriate older sister Jacqueline, who never liked Russ, hadn't made the trip from Spain.

He watched as Mario spotted Carmen and quietly approached her. The two shared a light embrace, with Mario giving her a gentle kiss on the cheek. They sat together near the front of the auditorium, surrounded by security but given enough space to share private conversation.

Russ told his own parents to not worry about coming down, but they insisted. His father Patrick, an Irishman through and through if there ever was one, gave Russ a bear hug that showed he'd lost none of his muscular strength at age 70. Mother Rosary, whose Italian heritage made for a volatile but loving household for anyone growing up O'Rourke, clung to her son to the point of embarrassing him.

Ben and Beth greeted Stephen and Susan Blakely, who'd flown in from Tom's native San Diego. The two retired accountants were quiet and reserved, fitting every inch of the stereotype, and Ben recalled Tom talking about the rigid household rules he'd endured growing up. They didn't make small talk and quickly found seats together near the back of the auditorium.

Kari Blakely's parents, Jack and Lisa Bell, still lived in nearby Deltona. Each was carrying their Bible, and they thanked Ben and Beth profusely for helping out with the service. Lisa asked Beth if it would be okay if she said a prayer during her time to speak, and Beth assured her that she could do whatever felt right. The Bells were joined by sons Thomas, Stephen, and Michael, and their own spouses and young children.

"That baby's growing fast in there!" Beth exclaimed as Julio emerged with the pregnant Susannah. Susannah patted her stomach and smiled.

"Are you ready to be a dad?" Ben asked Julio.

"Were you ready?"

"I'm still not ready."

"That's scary," Beth said, "especially since I want another one."

"Aww!" Susannah said. "Little Adriana Rose will have a friend."

By 11 a.m., all of the expected guests had arrived. So far there had been no incidents of uninvited media or any other creeps trying to crash the party. As Russ paced the outside of the auditorium, he saw a couple of news crews doing live camera shots or pieces to be aired later. Sarosky approached Russ on his way back into the auditorium. The detective planned to attend the service out of respect to the families.

"Your ex-father-in-law could make this a lot easier if he'd cooperate with me."

Russ kept studying the parking lot, not bothering to look at Sarosky as he responded.

"Mr. Lazano has nothing else to tell you. Just keep doing your job, and I'll do mine."

"We have the same goal. We should work together."

"We have one of the same goals. You might have other objectives that aren't aligned with ours."

Russ turned his back on the detective and started to walk the perimeter once again. Sarosky went inside, met up with Rice, and found a seat in the back near Kari's parents. He nodded to them, and they recognized him and smiled.

Cameron was nervous as he walked up to the podium on the auditorium stage. He hadn't done a lot of public speaking, and wasn't used to being the center of attention. Being a good writer didn't translate into being a good talker. Nelson had tried his best to pump up his confidence, and even offered to practice with him but Cameron had declined.

"Good morning," Cameron began, quickly scanning the faces of the crowd and trying to slow his pace of speech. "My name is Cameron Brock, and I want to thank each of you for coming today. We're here to celebrate the lives of three very special women, and I feel honored and humbled to serve as your host."

Cameron paused, allowing for some silence that was punctuated by a few coughs amongst the audience. He saw a couple of the older ladies already wiping away tears. The room was warmer than Cameron would have preferred.

"Emma, Jackie, and Kari were living life to the fullest," he continued. "They were wives, mothers, and friends. They loved to read and workout together. They planned a fun trip that was to be the first milestone of many special times together.

"We're not here to say goodbye, because it's impossible to fully say goodbye when there remain so many questions. Rather, we're here to comfort each other and acknowledge our collective loss, as we share memories and seek to find hope for the future."

Cameron initially focused his attention on Emma, inviting up any family members who wanted to speak. Mario glanced at Russ and Pete, who both sat cross-armed and expressionless. They didn't make eye contact with him or indicate any sign of getting up. He looked at his ex-wife Carmen, who fought back tears as she stood and slowly ambled to the microphone, Cameron helping her up the short flight of steps.

"My daughter Emma is a very strong-willed woman," Carmen said, her voice shaking. She glanced down at Mario, who smiled. "She was always that way. No one was going to tell her what to do. She worked hard, and made a good life for herself. She was a good attorney, and a wonderful mother."

Carmen paused a minute to compose herself.

"I'm outraged by some of the things I've read in the tabloids, about how Emma might have been responsible for her own disappearance. How she might have run off with some man to some island, or was holding her friends for ransom; or, worst of all, how she might have killed her friends and then herself."

Russ glanced at Mario, who was looking more uncomfortable by the second, and saw Pete watching Audrey as the teenage girl stared at the floor in front of her.

"I know my daughter," Carmen continued, "and wherever she is, she's fighting to come home to her son. She's being resilient. She's not dead. I can feel it. I can feel her life within my heart. She's out there. They're all out there."

Carmen began to sob, and Cameron tried to comfort her as he helped her back down the steps. Mario put his arm around his ex-wife, and she buried her face into his shoulder and continued to cry.

Audrey and Natalie insisted on coming up with their father to speak. Phil shared first, telling the audience how hard life was without Jackie and what a wonderful best friend, spouse, and mother she'd always been. He adjusted the microphone for Audrey, who had everyone in stitches and tears as she told old stories about getting in trouble with her mother for coloring all over the wall with lipstick and once cutting off most of Natalie's hair.

When it was Natalie's turn, Phil adjusted the microphone again and Audrey took her little sister's hand.

"I m-miss my mommy very much," Natalie said. "I write her letters, and my d-daddy is saving all of them so he can give them to her when she comes home. I-I wish I knew where she was, so I could mail the letters to her now."

Phil embraced both his daughters for a long moment. Audience members smiled at the girls as they went back to their seats, and each of their grandparents hugged them.

Jackie's father Earl also garnered laughter as he shared short anecdotes about his daughter's Brownie and softball days. His little girl proved a persuasive cookie saleswoman as she went door to door. Jackie was a loud presence in the infield as shortstop. She stood up to any bully who picked on her friends, and had a special heart for new kids who arrived at school or in town. She loved Phil and their girls, Earl said, and he choked up when admitting that he got both excited and scared each time his phone rang.

When Cameron shifted the focus to Kari Blakely, Jack and Lisa Bell held hands before the microphone and asked the audience to bow their heads in prayer. Cameron lowered his eyes and quickly glanced out at the sea of faces, most of whom—praying people or not—obliged with the Bells' request.

"Heavenly Father," Jack began. "You giveth and you taketh away. You gave us Kari, and she was a shining light for all to receive during her time with us. You've taken her from us, Father, as least for now, and we thank you for the gift of your grace during our time of mourning."

Jack paused and moved aside so Lisa could have a turn.

"Lord Jesus, you are the great physician. We ask that you heal our hearts, that you heal our pain. Let this be a wakeup call to any of us who has not yet bowed the knee to accept you as Lord and Savior. Help us to realize the folly of a life spent without you. Be with these three wonderful women, my Lord, and put your hedge of protection around them. Let them feel the comfort of thy presence, my Lord. We know that all things work together for good, for those who know Christ and are called according to his purpose."

Lisa's prayer continued for at least three more minutes. Cameron saw audience members shuffling and a handful trying their hardest to keep their eyes shut.

Tom and Connor hugged both of Kari's parents as they left the stage. Now at the podium himself, Tom looked to the back of the room where Rory was sitting. Rory gave him a thumbs up, and Tom knew the brutal honesty he was about to share would make some people uncomfortable.

"Kari and I didn't have a perfect marriage by any means," Tom said. "We often didn't get along very well. We didn't listen enough to each other. But we loved each other, and we wanted to work things out. The best years were still ahead for us, and I feel cheated out of those years. I feel cheated for Connor, who's my best buddy and one of the sweetest people I've ever known."

Tom and Connor embraced, and Tom encouraged him to speak into the microphone. Connor tried several times to get started, but stumbled over his words repeatedly and finally gave up. He and his father walked arm-in-arm back to their seats, Connor's eyes downcast.

Among the remaining book club members, only Dara had it within her to get up and speak. She stood silently before the microphone for a long moment, her eyes closed, choking back tears.

"I love you all," Dara finally managed to say. "Please come home."

Cameron waited as the auditorium grew silent, and then returned to the podium.

"There's some special people I'd like to thank today," Cameron said in his closing remarks, just before noon. "I want to thank Ben and Beth McBride, close friends of the family. They greeted all of you when you arrived, and they've stood by these family members for the past year and offered their home, their time, and their resources." Cameron asked the McBrides to stand, and they smiled with slight embarrassment as they were greeted with polite applause.

"I also want to thank Julio Ramos," continued Cameron, pointing to Julio and Susannah. "Julio works at Famoso's restaurant, and he's been a great source of comfort to family members as well. In addition to being an outstanding employee, he's a listening ear and a non-judgmental spirit." More applause followed, and Susannah gripped Julio's arm and kissed him on the cheek.

Cameron closed by thanking everyone for attending, and invited them to join the reception. He found Nelson, who gave him a hug.

"You were awesome. You were just right."

"Thanks," Cameron said. "I'm drained."

"I bet. Come on, let's get something to eat and drink."

Ben and Beth stuck together and circulated throughout the reception hall, chatting more at length with several of the guests and listening to more anecdotes. They saw Carmen trying her best to love on her grandson Pete. The Bells asked the McBrides where they went to church, and the Blakelys sat with Connor as he shyly showed them the sketch pad he carried everywhere he went.

Mr. and Mrs. Solomon told their granddaughters how proud they were of them for getting up and talking. Rachel asked Natalie if she could read any of those letters she'd written to her mother, and Audrey was impressed when her little sister shook her said and simply said, "T-they're for Mommy's eyes only."

Patrick O'Rourke was livid about the comments from Carmen Lazano. "What the hell was she thinking?" he complained to Russ. "The kids don't need to hear shit like that."

"Just let it go, Dad," Russ said. "She's who she is. Believe me, I wasn't thrilled about it either."

Many of the guests gathered around Julio and Susannah, offering their congratulations on the impending birth. Lisa told Susannah that her baby was "a gift from God," and a sign that "new life arises even in the midst of ashes." She invited the couple to come visit her Deltona church some time, and promised that she could arrange a lovely baptism if they wanted to join the congregation.

Sarosky and Rice were stopped by a few of the family members who figured out who they were and wanted to know the latest on the investigation. Sarosky saw their predictable disappointment as he repeated the same lines he'd been saying for the past year. He and Rice said goodbye to Rinaldi and Higgins as well.

"You owe me a dinner," Rice whispered to Sarosky, smiling.

After a while, Sarosky wandered back outside into the heat while Rice stayed to interact with the guests. A small contingent of news media remained, hoping to toss a few questions at the guests as they departed. Russ's men were still lining the perimeter, their shirt collars stained with sweat. Sarosky felt bad for them, as well as for his fellow police officers who remained in the parking lot and on the sidewalk at full attention.

As guests left, part of the security detail broke from the perimeter to escort them to their vehicles while the police watched. A couple of reporters shouted out questions that were ignored.

The Solomons and McBrides were the last to leave. Phil's parents insisted that Ben and Beth join them for dinner soon, and said they wanted to see Maddie as well.

Ben took Phil aside and asked him how he was feeling.

"I don't know. Nothing really feels any different as far as the situation, except that it was wonderful to experience all of that love and caring."

"Your girls did a wonderful job."

"They sure did."

Phil embraced Ben. "Thanks for making everyone feel welcome.

You've got a gift for that, Ben. You're always the most encouraging guy in the room."

Ben laughed. "I'm not sure if that's true. But thank you."

Ben and Beth drove home in silence, both eager to scoop Maddie into their arms. Beth began to softly cry.

"I wanted to get up there and share," she said. "I just couldn't."

"It's okay. There were no expectations of anyone. You did your part. I was proud to be next to you."

Ben squeezed Beth's thigh, and she took his hand.

Chapter Fifty-Two:

JUNE 29

'll pick you both up back here in two hours," Phil said to Audrey and Pete after he finished paying for their hamburgers, fries, and soda. He gave Audrey a hug.

"Okay, Dad," she said.

"Thank you, Mr. Solomon," Pete said in his most polite voice.

Phil was nervous as he drove away. It was Audrey's first real "date" with a boy, and he'd wished Amanda was there with him to size up the situation. But very little could go wrong, he surmised, since the plan was pretty structured: drop them off at the beachside McDonalds at noon, and pick them up in the same place two hours later after they've carefully crossed A1A and hung out on the beach. A very crowded beach.

He dialed Amanda.

"Is the deed done?" she asked.

"Part one is done," Phil replied.

"Did you get me a Big Mac?"

"Would you actually eat that?"

"Gross. No."

Natalie and Pete grabbed their to-go bags of food, along with their beach towels, and headed outside. Audrey expected Pete to just want to run across the lanes of traffic when he saw a quick opening, and was pleasantly surprised with Pete's cautiousness and his obvious interest in making sure she was safe. A few minutes later their feet were in the sand, and they found an open spot down near the shoreline to lay down their towels.

"Can you help me put some of this on my shoulders and back?" Audrey asked Pete, after she'd removed her outing clothing to reveal an athletic swimsuit that covered most of her stomach. "As you can see, I'm pretty pale."

Pete laughed. "Sure. I probably need some of that myself."

"You're more tanned than I am," Audrey said. "I can tell you come down here a lot."

"I don't have anything else to do with my time," he said, smiling. "Except for get into trouble."

Audrey smiled back at him as Pete handed her the bottle of lotion. "No trouble for you today, sir," she said, and motioned for Pete to turn around so she could apply the lotion to his own shoulders and back.

"You know, the water is going to wash this stuff right off. We're probably spinning our wheels."

"Oh well," she said. "It's the effort that counts, right?"

"That works," Pete said.

Shortly thereafter Audrey followed Pete into the shallow waves. It was close to 100 degrees outside, and the foamy water felt great.

"Okay, watch me ride the first couple, and you'll catch on," he said. "Trust me, it's easy."

"Yeah, maybe for you," she said. "I'm not super-coordinated."

She watched as Pete swam further out, toward where the waves first began to form. He waited patiently, appearing to watch for just the right break, and then without warning dove his body forward and was briskly carried toward the shore. Audrey applauded as Pete trudged back out toward her, smiling.

"That's it?" she asked.

"That's it. Nothing but your body becoming one with the ocean."

"Nice," Audrey said. "I think I can handle it."

"Well, come on then," Pete said, and started to swim out to sea again. This time she followed him, and they treaded water for a while as Pete searched for that next perfect wave.

"How about that one?" she asked.

"Nah, it's running out of steam too early," he replied.

"That one there?"

"Doesn't feel right."

"How can a wave not 'feel right?'"

"You'll know soon enough," Pete said. "Comes with experience."

"Ahh, I see," Audrey said.

"Here we go!" he suddenly exclaimed. "When I tell you to dive, dive!"

"Okay!"

"Get ready….not yet…ready…"

"Now?" she asked.

"No. Ready, now!"

Audrey watched Pete dive forward, and a split second later did her best to imitate him. She initially enjoyed the rush of the wave carrying her, but after a few seconds started coughing when water filled her mouth. Audrey tumbled around in the shallow water, lifting her head up and kneeling down on the ocean floor, continuing to cough.

"You okay?" Pete asked, splashing over and gently touching her arm.

She nodded, feeling embarrassed. "Yeah. I just swallowed some water. Yuck."

"Oh, I forgot to tell you to keep your mouth closed," Pete said, laughing. "I guess there's no polite way to say that to a girl."

Audrey gave him a mischievous smile. "Yes, remember that," she said.

"Do you need a few minutes before we try again?"

"Nah," Audrey said, turning and starting to walk into the deeper water. "Don't take it easy on me just because I'm a surfing virgin."

Out of the corner of her eye she saw Pete blush, and smiled again.

They waited a few minutes before taking a chance on another wave. Audrey kept her mouth sealed this time, and popped up from the surf with an air of confidence.

"You've so got this!" Pete exclaimed.

"You know it," she said.

There was a lull in the waves, and they treaded and floated for a while. Audrey looked at Pete thoughtfully.

"You doing okay? With the whole situation, I mean."

Pete stared out at the horizon. "Yeah. I'm doing ok. You?"

Audrey smiled, noting how Pete suddenly wasn't able to look her in the eye. "Yeah, I guess so. Starting to accept it, I guess."

"Yeah," she said. "Me, too."

"I think I see one coming," Pete mumbled. "Wait for it…wait for it…"

Audrey laughed. "Are you imitating Barney from *How I Met Your Mother?*"

Pete finally looked at her again. "Nothing gets past you."

Audrey nodded. "Except for maybe a decent wave."

Chapter Fifty-Three:

AUG 3

I love this paragraph of Jake's narrative," Emma said, holding her copy of The Sun Also Rises. She read, "'It was like certain dinners I remember from the war. There was much wine, an ignored tension, and a feeling of things coming that you could not prevent happening. Under the wine I lost the disgusted feeling and was happy. It seemed they were all such nice people.'"

Jackie laughed. "Sugar, are you implying that you need to drink wine just to tolerate us?"

"No, but that does make me want a re-fill," Emma said, grabbing the nearby bottle and pouring some into her glass. "I think it speaks to how we can still find joy even when we're in troublesome situations."

"I wish I could," Kari said. "I just dwell on stuff non-stop. Tom used to be more patient with it. Now he just tells to me to get on with things. Even Connor has started telling me to 'stop obsessing.'"

"Fitness gives me that kind of rush," Beth said. "I forget what's going on with the rest of life, and when I've had a great workout I can deal with whatever is happening. Usually."

"I find that in your class," Delphi said. "I get less disgusted with my body, under the influence of sweat."

"Hemingway narrates something similar around that same part of the book," Emma said. "He's talking about the fiesta there in Spain, and he says, 'Everything became quite unreal finally and it seemed as though nothing could have any consequences. It seemed out of place to think of consequences during the fiesta.'"

"But the consequences are always there waiting for you when you get home," Kari said. *"Always, always, always."*

~~~

After Scott Layman's separation from his now-ex-wife Julie, he was fortunate to find a three-bedroom house on foreclosure. It was in the respectable Palm Beach Gardens subdivision and had a newer roof, a decent privacy fence and, as a bonus, a pool. Scott's twin 8-year-old daughters, Hazel and Betsy, enjoyed the house and their time with their father.

He was alone this hot August weekend, the twins with their mother. They were about to go back to school, and were at the Gardens Mall clothes shopping. Scott would get an email later that weekend, most likely, announcing his share of the cost of new clothes, school supplies, and backpacks.

A golf tournament was on television, and Scott had the sound on mute. He sipped from his third glass of iced tea, and waited to see if Curtis Everett would show up as planned. Scott began to mindlessly channel surf, several hundred programs vying for his attention.

~~~

"I trusted you. With everything. With my company. With my reputation."

Mario was eerily calm as he spoke, which made James even more frightened.

"And this is how you repay me. You take advantage of my daughter. A child. Not even 18."

"I'm sorry. I never intended to hurt you. I care for Emma very much."

Mario stared at James, and couldn't doubt the young man's sincerity.

"I'm sure you believe that. But if you fully cared for her, you'd realize that she's too young and naive to know what she's gotten herself involved in. Someday she's going to feel ugly about herself, and she's going to resent you for luring her into a sexual relationship. She might even hate you for it."

James felt defensive, but was mindful enough to take a deep breath. "Emma could never hate me. She's a lot more mature than her years. She knows what she wants."

"James, you might want to stay contrite here."

James nodded. "Okay. Sorry."

"Now," Mario continued, "I'm trying to figure out how we go forward. What do you think I should do?"

James shook his head. "I can't answer that for you, Mario."

Mario stood up and paced.

"I've tapped you as my successor. I didn't realize that meant son-in-law. But tell me: Do you intend to marry my daughter? Because that might make things better. Much better."

James smiled. "I'd marry her in a heartbeat. But she's not ready to get married. She wants to go to college. She wants to date other men, I assume, and see the world a bit."

Mario looked indignant.

"Is that what you want? For her to date other men? What kind of a man are you? I thought you loved her!" He glared down at James.

"I do," James said, trying to remain calm. "But I love her enough to wait for her, if we're meant to be together."

Mario kneeled down, now face-to-face with James. "Life doesn't happen by people waiting around to see if something is 'meant to be.' You go after what you want, and that makes it meant to be. You understand?"

"Yeah, I do."

Mario folded his arms, and sighed. "I'm going to have a talk with my daughter. To truly find out what she wants. In the meantime, get back to work. We'll sort this thing out."

"Okay. Thank you."

Mario stood, and James did as well. The older man gave him an embrace.

"Whatever happens, promise me you'll never hurt her."

"Promise," James said, much more relaxed now.

"Good. Okay, I think Henry's waiting for you. He's got some property he wants you to look at with him."

"Sure enough."

A few minutes later James rode silently in the passenger seat next to Henry Reid. Henry never said a lot, which was fine with James, who enjoyed silence more than most.

"I gotta stop by my house for a minute, I forgot something," Henry said.

"Okay."

They pulled into a modest, older beachside neighborhood.

"Come on in, I'll fix us each a cup of coffee."

"Sure thing."

James followed him inside, then into the kitchen. James believed that Henry lived alone, so was surprised when he heard two male voices. Then a crushing blow to the side of his head made the room spin and explode in color, and James fell to the linoleum. What little he remembered after that consisted of blood and unspeakable pain.

~~~

Curtis arrived about fifteen minutes late, and accepted a glass of iced tea. They sat in the shady area near Scott's backyard pool.

"I'm glad you called," Curtis said. "It had been a while."

"Yeah. I've been wanting to call. Just been so busy, you know."

"I understand."

Scott wiped sweat from his brow. "I'd like to spend more time at your ranch."

Curtis took his time answering. "There's a lot you'd be expected to give up if you came and lived with us. It's a very alternative existence, but a fulfilling one. Are you prepared for that?"

"I need to make some big changes."

"I understand." Curtis leaned closer to him. "Are you prepared to give up your career? Your home here? Your independence over your money and resources?"

Scott hesitated, thinking through those key elements of his life.

"I believe so," he said.

"What about your children?" Curtis asked. "Are you prepared to bring them with you, to become part of our community? Children are certainly welcome. It would be a big adjustment for them, however."

"Their mother would never let me. Not in a million years. So it would just be me."

"Are you prepared to not see them or have communication with them during your time with us?"

Scott was feeling stressed. "I could do that for a while, I think. How long would I be required to stay?"

Curtis shrugged. "You're free to leave anytime you'd like. People usually don't want to, once they get a full taste of life in our community. Like I said, it's very alternative to what everyone is used to.

"All I ask is that you commit to stay for at least six months. It takes that long, sometimes, for people to truly sort through their emotions and make clear, rational choices."

He smiled at Scott.

"Each person has to make their own choice. Our community, and the responsibilities it entails, are not for everyone. For those who embrace life there and thrive, it's a very rewarding journey."

Scott excused himself to refill both of their glasses.

"I'd invite you for a swim, but I doubt you brought your swim trunks," Scott said as he returned.

"It's very hot. Perhaps I should build a swimming pool at our ranch."

"Now, that could seal the deal for me," Scott laughed. "As long as I wouldn't have to be in charge of the chlorine shocking and the pump maintenance."

Curtis asked Scott to tell him a little bit about his daughters. Scott did so, and Curtis listened without interrupting.

"They sound wonderful. It would be very hard for you to not see them."

"Yeah. It would."

Curtis sucked on a piece of ice for a moment, letting it melt inside his mouth.

"Why don't you give this some more thought, Scott? If you want to come live and work with us, simply show up. You don't need to call first. I'll tell the staff to have you on our list of invited guests."

After Curtis left, Scott changed into his bathing suit and jumped into the pool. The water was practically as hot as the temperature outside, but still refreshing. He rubbed some of the chlorine out of his eyes, climbed upon a light-blue raft that still had enough air to support his body, and shielded his eyes from the sun.

Chapter Fifty-Four

AUG 4

It had been raining steadily for an hour when Tom reluctantly got into his car to run errands he'd delayed long enough.

Tom's windshield wipers were on full throttle as he drove well under the speed limit along Williamson Boulevard. There were rows of tall pine trees on either side of the road, with occasional development such as a hospital and a couple of subdivisions.

The intensifying rain made it harder and harder to see. A couple of cars were pulled off to the shoulder with blinking hazard lights. Tom second-guessed venturing out. *Surely Wal Mart could have waited another day.*

As he slowed down to 20 miles per hour, navigating through huge puddles, Tom saw something moving in front of the woods to his right. He slowed more, staring out the passenger side window and trying to discern what he was looking at—and realized it was a dog. He continued driving, slowing to 15 miles per hour, keeping an eye on the road but also glancing over at the dog every couple of seconds.

Maybe I should stop. But, shit, look at the rain.

Tom thought about Connor, who would've insisted on them pulling over had he been along for the ride. He noticed his AA book resting on the passenger seat.

He slowed the car to a halt and pulled over, flicking on the hazard lights. The dog was still there. Tom looked around the inside of the car for an umbrella, but had no such luck. Finally he got out, walking briskly through muddy grass and puddles. The dog stopped and stood in place, watching him. When Tom squatted down and called to the dog, it trotted over to him without hesitation.

The emaciated animal was mostly white but had some tan-looking spots and blotches sprinkled across its coat. It wore a brown collar. Tom didn't know dog breeds very well.

"It's okay," he said, as he gently grabbed a hold of the dog's collar and gave it a slight tug in the direction of his car. He let go of the collar and took a few steps toward the road, hoping the dog would follow. It did.

"Good dog! Come on, let's go!" The dog looked at him with big, brown soulful eyes, and obeyed. Finally they reached the car and Tom opened the rear passenger door and helped the animal inside. He climbed back into the driver's seat, and then turned around to inspect the dog's collar. There was a 321 area code phone number but no name. Tom punched the number into his cell phoned and waited for someone to answer.

After four rings, a man picked up.

"Hello. Did you lose a dog?" Tom asked him

"No. I don't have a dog."

Tom was caught off guard. He'd had no doubt the answer was going to be "yes," and that the person on the other end of the call would be extremely grateful.

"Are you sure? I found a white dog out on Williamson, and his collar has your phone number."

"I don't have a dog. Thanks, anyway." The man stayed on the line a moment longer, and then disconnected the call.

Tom sat confused, staring at his phone. He didn't believe the guy, but there was no point in calling back. Tom wished he had a blanket to throw over the dog. He switched the air conditioning over to heat, hoping to give the animal some relief.

Tom went to the Google search function on his phone and entered *animal shelters, Daytona Beach.* A few popped up, and he called the first one on the list. The line rang nearly a dozen times before going to a voice mailbox. Tom hung up, glanced back at the Google list, and saw a number for a 24-hour animal hospital over on U.S. 1 in Holly Hill. He called, and the receptionist told him he was welcome to bring the dog over.

"You're going to be okay, buddy," Tom said toward the back seat as he drove east. The rain was letting up. The dog was staring at Tom in the rear view mirror, almost smiling at him. It was shivering less and wagging its tail more. *Damn, it was skinny.* Tom saw a McDonalds, went through the drive-through, and ordered two cheeseburgers off of the dollar menu. Before pulling out of the drive-through line, Tom unwrapped one of the cheeseburgers and leaned back to position it at the dog's mouth. The animal's eyes grew sharper, and it opened its mouth and took the burger from Tom's hands, dropping it to the seat and quickly devouring it.

"Wow," Tom said. "You're one hungry guy. You want another one?" He unwrapped the second cheeseburger, handed it back to the dog, and started driving again while his backseat friend made quick work the second burger.

The dog stood up on the seat and leaned its nose toward the front, sniffing for more food.

"I don't have anything else, dude," Tom said. "You'll have to wait until we get there."

The dog remained standing on all fours, looking out the window. The rain was slowing even more, and Tom rolled the back seat windows down a few inches on each side in case his new friend wanted to stick his face out a bit. Several minutes later Tom arrived at the traffic light at Williamson and Mason. Waiting for the green arrow, Tom caught whiff of a horrible smell coming from the back seat.

"Dude!" he said, laughing. He rolled down the driver's side window all the way and stuck his head out to get some air, as the dog's severe flatulence filled the inside of the car. The arrow turned, mercifully, and Tom sped north on U.S. 1. The smell abated for a minute and then kicked in again.

Tom spotted the animal hospital on the left and pulled into the parking lot. He helped the dog out of the back seat, and leaned down to hold its collar as they walked together.

A large, Hispanic woman dressed in a white outfit with pink and yellow flowers greeted him at the front. Her name was Velda. She had Tom fill out some paperwork, and then brought him and the dog to an examination room. Tom asked her to bring a towel, and she returned a moment later and wrapped it around the dog one section at a time, rubbing its fur dry. The dog wagged its tail, and Tom held his breath for a moment to see if any more farts were on their way.

"You poor guy," Velda said, kissing the dog on its forehead.

"Is it a boy or a girl?"

Velda looked underneath the dog, and pointed to a furry encasing of flesh. "Boy. His penis is inside there."

"Good to know."

Velda laughed. "He looks like some kind of hound. Did you call his owner?"

"Yeah. The guy who answered said he didn't have a dog," Tom said, and Velda scowled.

"What a jerk. Happens all the time, people abandoning their pets."

She looked closely at a pink sore on the dog's rear. "It looks like he got hurt somehow. He's been on his own for a while, based on how skinny he is." Velda wiped the dog with the towel some more. "We're gonna take good care of you, my friend."

"So what happens now?"

"Well, you can decide what you want to do," Velda said. "You can leave him with us overnight, and we can make sure he gets fluids and food, and treat him for worms or anything else he might have. That might be a little pricey, so I don't know if you want us to do that. Or you can leave him here, and we'll get him to the shelter when it opens tomorrow."

Tom looked closely at the dog's face. He really did have sweet brown eyes.

"Do you think the shelter will be able to find its owner?"

Velda shrugged. "Probably not. I'm not sure the owner wants to be found."

Tom rubbed the dog's head while it wagged its tail.

"I can print out an estimate of the charges for you if you'd like."

"Sure," Tom said. He pictured Connor, and how ecstatic his son would be if he knew Tom was bringing home a dog. When Velda handed him the estimate of $525, Tom had second thoughts.

"I know, it's pretty expensive," Velda said. "Normally, taking care of a dog doesn't cost that much at one time. But this guy needs some help. I would totally understand if you'd prefer to have us bring him to the shelter."

Tom looked at the soaked little face again. *Rain Dog*, he thought. *That's your name.*

"Can you give me a moment, please? I'm going to go out into the lobby and text my son."

"Sure, take your time," Velda said.

In the lobby, he sent Connor the simple message, *Rescued a dog from the side of the road. Brought him to animal hospital. Think we should adopt him?*

Not quite 30 seconds later Connor replied, *YES!* Then Connor called, excited and full of questions, and Tom quickly summarized the chain of events.

"We HAVE to keep him, Dad! He needs us!" Connor said. "I promise I'll help out a lot. I'll be in charge of all of his walks. And I'll feed him."

"It's a lot of responsibility for us, Connor. Do you think we're up for it?"

"I'm totally up for it, Dad. Please. PLEASE!"

Tom pondered for a moment.

"Dad, what are you going to do?"

"Okay. We'll keep him. His name is Rain Dog."

"Rain Dog. I love it! You're the best dad in the world!"

"I'll remember that next time you're mad at me," Tom said. "I'll be home soon. Rain Dog is staying here overnight."

"Okay! I'm so excited! We'll get the house ready for him. We'll need a bowl for his food and for his water, and a leash, and a collar."

"Sounds like you've given this a lot of thought. I'll be home soon."

Tom walked back to the examination room, and took a long gaze at the newest member of his family. Velda smiled at him as Tom examined every inch of Rain Dog's weather-worn body.

"Let me guess," she said. "Your son wants the dog."

Chapter Fifty-Five:

Maddie was taking an afternoon nap. Ben and Beth settled into their own bed, the stormy weather outside offsetting any ambition for doing anything but grabbing a snooze.

"I never took naps before we had a child," Ben said, fluffing his pillow.

Beth snuggled in close to him, and soon the nap was evolving into much more. Ben saw uncertainty on Beth's face as he reached into the nightstand for a condom.

"Something's wrong," he said.

"Nothing, really."

Ben laughed.

"Something, really."

Beth looked up at him.

"I just wonder if we need to keep using those. It seems silly. Maybe we should just let nature take its course."

"Oh, it'll take its course all right."

"I think it's time, Ben. Maddie is three now."

"We're not on a timetable, though, are we?" he asked, tossing the condom back inside the drawer.

"No. But my clock is ticking, even if yours isn't."

"That sounds like a cliché."

"That sounds like reality," she said, and playfully punched him on the arm.

Ben laid back down and held her.

"We're pretty busy these days," he said.

"Yeah. But the new instructors are working out well. I'm almost to the point where I can be gone for a week and not worry about things."

"Do you still love teaching?"

"I do," Beth said. "But I wouldn't be sad if I could do less of it."

"You'll be doing a lot less once you're pregnant."

Beth peered closely at him.

"You want a son, don't you?"

Ben leaned over and kissed her forehead. "I'm happy with a boy or another girl. You know that."

"A son would be a lot of fun for you."

"Maddie is a lot of fun," he said. "I wish I spent more time playing with her as it is."

"We'll figure it out, Ben. Life is short. We can't take anything for granted."

Beth surprised him by reaching down and stroking his genitals. "We can start trying now," she whispered.

"You're not being fair," he said.

"Who said I have to be?"

"Oh, yeah. I forgot."

Chapter Fifty-Six

The Solomon girls were spending the afternoon with their grandparents. Phil sat on the couch with Amanda in her apartment, watching Alfred Hitchcock's film *North by Northwest.*

They'd been working their way through the director's film library, something Amanda said she'd always wanted to do. She'd previously enjoyed reading all the works of a particular author, or seeing every painting by a specific artist.

"Hitchcock must have been interesting to talk with," Phil said as they watched.

"Yeah. A real character."

Phil kept glancing at Amanda's legs. They were so tan, nicely complemented by the bright orange nail polish on her toes. Her left leg was pressed close against his right leg. *It's now or never,* Phil thought, and he gently rested his hand upon hers. She grasped his in return, and the warmth was jolting and invigorating.

Hitchcock's Jimmy Stewart character was in quite a mess, unable to discern the good guys from the bad. Phil was rapidly losing interest in the plot, however.

"I wonder if we should pause the movie," he suggested, barely above a whisper.

"I wonder," Amanda responded.

"Is that what you want?" Phil asked.

"Is that what *you* want?" she asked back, that mischievous grin on her face that Phil had come to appreciate.

"I believe so."

"Well, I believe so as well."

Amanda reached for the remote, paused Hitchcock, and turned to face Phil. He pulled her close, and everything happened very fast from there. Within moments she was in his lap, kissing him furiously, beginning to straddle him as they started to pull at each other's clothes. At some point during their lovemaking the movie went off of pause, and its overly-dramatic soundtrack filled the apartment.

Chapter Fifty-Seven

Aug 10

Tom sat next to Rain Dog on the couch, stroking the top of his head. Connor was positioned a few feet away, sketching another masterpiece.

"It's cool how he has whiskers shooting out of the top of his head," Connor said.

"Yeah. Lots of details to notice, when you study him closely."

Rain Dog, whom the veterinarian guessed was about two years old, had gained at least 10 pounds since Tom brought him home from the animal hospital. The pink wound was still visible but healing. He was a sweet pet who seldom barked but clearly hadn't been domestically trained. Tom had to clean up a pile of crap at least once per day for the first week, before he figured out the dog's rhythms and managed to get him outside just in time.

Tom and Connor did independent Internet research on Treeing Walker Coon Hounds. They were hunting dogs by nature but also known to be good pets. Rain Dog was definitely a snuggler, sleeping pressed up against either Tom or Connor every night.

"Do you really think that someone might have thrown him from a car?" Connor asked as he sketched.

"I don't know. Sometimes people do things like that."

"Why would someone do that?"

"I don't know. I can't imagine it."

"It's so mean," Connor said, becoming more aggressive in his sketching. "It's so not necessary. If you don't want an animal, just take him to a shelter. Don't throw him out or just leave him somewhere."

"I agree, Connor," Tom said.

"And that person you called, they were totally lying. Why would your phone number be on a dog's collar if it wasn't your dog?"

"Beats me."

Connor set the sketch pad down and hugged Rain Dog tightly. "I'm just glad you found him, and that he's ours now. I finally have a dog like most of my friends. And he's the best dog ever. He's special, because he was lost and we found him."

Despite the adjustment and learning curve he had as a first-time dog owner, Tom found Rain Dog's presence to be comforting and contributing to his deepening peace of mind. A dog had no agenda other than to eat; pee; poop; sleep; walk; and be loved. When Tom came home, Rain Dog stood on his hind legs and wrapped his front paws around Tom's neck, grunting happily and rubbing his face against Tom's. It didn't matter if Tom was gone for a single hour or five hours: the gratitude conveyed in the over-the-top greeting was the same.

Rory visited a few days after Rain Dog's arrival, and was smitten with the new family pet. "It's good to have a dog," he said "It's more love and responsibility to extend to another. Love and responsibility, toward ourselves and others, drive the Twelve Steps."

Tom briefly mentioned Rain Dog during an AA meeting that past week, and several others shared how much their pets meant to them. One woman was about to have to put her dog to sleep, and broke down crying as the other members gathered around to comfort her.

The McBrides also dropped by and Maddie was glued to Rain Dog the entire time, her parents reminding her more than once that he wasn't a "horsie" she could "ride." Tom admired the dog's patience as the little girl hugged on him.

Connor had taken dozens, perhaps even hundreds, of photos of Rain Dog with his cell phone and placed them on Instagram. He printed out some of the photos and plastered them on his bedroom wall, surrounded by a few of his favorite dog drawings and some sketches he'd made from photographs of his mother Kari.

"Do you think Mom would have liked Rain Dog? Would she have let us keep him?" he asked Tom.

Damn good question, Tom thought.

"I'm sure she would have liked him," Tom said. "It's hard not to like him. I can't say whether she would have wanted to keep him or not."

"She never really wanted us to get a pet. Whenever I brought it up she would quickly change the subject," the boy responded.

"Dogs are a lot of work, as you're seeing."

"Yeah. But isn't anything that's worth having a lot of work?"

Tom smiled. *He's a thoughtful soul.* "I agree."

"If she comes home, she'll have to accept Rain Dog," Connor said. "He's part of the family now. He's my little brother."

It was heart-breaking whenever Connor uttered phrases like that. *When she comes home. If she comes home.*

"I asked Grandma and Grandpa Bell if I could bring Rain Dog over sometime. They said yes. They said God had protected him when he was out there in the wild."

"Somebody was definitely looking out for this guy." Tom scratched Rain Dog behind his ears and the hound wagged his tail back and forth, his mouth partly open and forming what looked like a dog's way of smiling.

"They're always talking about God or the Lord or Jesus," Connor said. "They've asked me several times to go to church with them on Sundays."

"Is that something you'd like to do?"

"I don't know. It sounds kind of boring."

Tom laughed. "I'll go with you sometime if you want to check it out."

"Do you want to go?"

"Not really," Tom admitted. "But I would go if you wanted to visit."

"Could Rain Dog come with us?"

"I don't think they allow dogs in church."

"Why not?"

Great question. "It's just not something that churches do. Most places don't let animals come inside."

Connor kissed Rain Dog on the nose. "If there is a God, I think he or she would want dogs to be in church."

"I think you're spot on with that one, Connor."

"I'm going to make a sketch of a church full of dogs," Connor said. "And on top, I'm going to write those words that Grandma Bell is always saying when she talks about God looking out for poor people."

"Which words are those?"

Connor paused for a moment, collecting his thoughts.

"Blessed are the meek, for they shall inherit the earth."

Chapter Fifty-Eight

AUG 15

Det. Rice stood outside the office door for a moment, looking through the small window at Sarosky as he stared trance-like at the white board. She smiled, and opened the door as quietly as possible.

Sarosky glanced back at her, nodded, and then returned to his study of the large mind map he'd been sketching out for months.

"How did you learn how to do that?" she asked him.

Sarosky paused and reflected. "I read a lot of comic books when I was a kid. I'd get so obsessed with the plot lines that I had to diagram them out on big pieces of poster board."

He smiled at her. "I was a nerd."

"No kidding," Rice laughed. "What would you do if the janitor erased it all one night?"

"Kill the janitor," he said dryly, "or myself."

Rice stood next to him, resting a hand on his shoulder. "Your brain really does work in crazy ways."

He pointed to a spot on the white board.

"The gap still remains," Sarosky said. "The missing linkage between disappearance, location, and motive. At this point, I'm just waiting for some clue to drop out of the sky. That's how stuck I feel."

Rice went to the door and glanced through the window for a moment, and when she returned she held Sarosky's face and kissed him full on the mouth.

Sarosky stared at her, stunned and completely speechless.

"How's that for a clue, nerd?" Rice asked.

~~~

Russ was waiting for him in a booth when Cameron arrived at the Mexican restaurant in downtown Orlando. The place was packed with dinner patrons. Cameron saw familiar faces seated at the booth next to theirs, and realized they were members of Russ's security detail.

"Thanks for meeting me here," Russ said. "I wanted to talk somewhere away from Daytona, where I wouldn't run into someone I know."

"No problem," Cameron said.

They ordered margaritas. The waitress brought them a basket of tortilla chips with salsa, and Russ asked her for an order of guacamole and cheese sauce as well.

"You been to this place before?"

"A couple of times. Nelson likes to come here for happy hour."

"Is it more locals than tourists?"

"Yeah, thank God," Cameron said.

Russ was observing the large, open room, as if keeping a lookout for any threats. The Cubists in the next booth were enjoying their food and drinks, but studying the atmosphere as well.

"I want to ask you a favor," Russ said, leaning in closer to Cameron.

"Sure."

"I want you to write another article. But a different kind of article this time. Not that your first one wasn't good. I thought it was really good."

Cameron waited.

"I know that I'm in the minority here, but I'm almost positive that Emma and her friends are still alive," Russ said. "Henry knew something before he was killed. And Mario knows more than he's telling."

"We had that memorial service, and you did a great job; but I think that signaled to the rest of the world that we didn't need their help anymore. That we had given up."

"That must feel frustrating," Cameron said.

"It is. The rest of the world doesn't come home every night to a son who has no idea what happened to his mother."

"So what do you need me to do?" Cameron asked.

"I want you to work on an investigative piece. You've got lots of credibility now, and people will give you some of their time. Follow a few trails that I'll give you, and see where they lead. Be tenacious."

Cameron didn't want to shoot down the idea too quickly. "I've never really been a crime reporter," he said. "I've covered local government, and sometimes do features: light stuff, everyday people kind of fluff. I'm not sure if I'd be the best person."

"You're the best person," Russ said. "Because you earn people's trust. That's the most important thing here."

"I appreciate that. I'd have to sell my editors on the idea, too."

Russ shrugged. "I'd be happy to talk to them with you if you'd like."

Cameron laughed. "I don't think that'll be necessary."

The waitress returned. Russ ordered a plate of chicken quesadillas, and Cameron asked for a veggie burrito with Spanish rice. Russ was almost ready for a second margarita.

"I'll get you started, if you think you'll do it," Russ said.

"Sure."

He glanced over at the Cubists, and made eye contact with one. The man nodded, and Russ nodded back.

"There's a guy named Nick Ferrante, based down in South Florida. He's been making inquiries to Tom Blakely about buying his restaurant."

"He wants to buy Famoso's?"

"Yeah." Russ finished his drink. "He's called the restaurant a couple of times and spoken to Steve, and he's also come into town and chatted briefly with Tom. Julio told me Tom's pretty interested in selling it, and that he wants to take life easy for a while and focus on his son."

Russ studied the restaurant crowd again for a moment.

"Ferrante is an executive with one of those Arena Football League teams, the one that's based down there. I'm not sure why he's interested in buying Famoso's. But Det. Sarosky shared something interesting with Mario last year about Mr. Ferrante."

"What was that?" Cameron asked.

"You remember Delphi Adams, the woman who was part of the book club, who apparently killed herself in her garage last year?"

"Yes."

"Well, Sarosky said he and Det. Rice were tailing Adams for a while around South Florida. He said he saw her having lunch with Ferrante a couple of times."

Cameron waited for more.

"What makes that interesting," Russ said, "is that Adams was having a fling with Mario Lazano before Emma disappeared."

"They were dating?" Cameron asked.

"More like they were fucking."

"Gotcha."

"So, let's put the pieces together," Russ said. "Delphi has a thing for Mario. Delphi befriends Mario's daughter Emma at the gym, and spends a lot of time with her. They form the book club and meet at Delphi's store. Then, Delphi invites the book club ladies to stay at her condo in Boca. She can't join them, because she has to keep the store open all the time, because she's not making any money."

Russ paused, thanking the waitress as she brought him a second margarita. The woman had a piercing in her nose, which he found sexy.

"Emma, Jackie, and Kari vanish," he continued. "Delphi is spending time with Ferrante. Then, Delphi is suddenly dead. Then, two goons show up at the apartment of another one of Mario's squeezes, and claim they have information about our ladies. They insist on giving it to Mario directly. Henry Reid goes up there to investigate, and they kill him and the girl."

Cameron was trying to keep the details straight in his head. "I wish I was writing all of this down," he said.

"It's okay, you can write it down later," Russ said. "Another interesting detail: A few months ago, your friend Julio said there were a couple of creepy guys that were asking questions about Tom and Kari. Henry had photos taken of them. Then he found a way to track them, and started keeping a log of their whereabouts.

"Eventually they must have found the tracker or something, because he stopped getting data. But Mario showed me the full log after Henry died. I'll share it with you."

The waitress stopped by to check on them. Russ gave her a thumbs up.

"One of the more interesting trends Henry noticed," he continued, "was that these two guys spent a lot of time at those Arena Football League events. Not just games, but social gatherings where people from the 'front office' would be present. People like Ferrante. Henry thought the guys might have worked for Ferrante. You ready for the final kicker?"

"Sure," Cameron said.

"After Henry and that girl Heather were murdered, Sarosky and his team did some interviewing with residents at the apartment complex where she lived," Russ said. "There were several people who remembered hanging out with Heather at the poolside that night. Everyone had been drinking, but they could remember enough details to describe the two guys who looked a little out of place. Mario didn't tell Sarosky this, but the descriptions sounded a lot like the two goons that Henry had been tracking."

Cameron had stopped eating, fully focused on Russ's words.

"So," Cameron said, "you think that those two guys worked for Ferrante, and that Ferrante sent them to kill Mario. And that he might have something to do with Emma and the others."

"Bingo."

"Why? What's his motive?"

Russ smiled. "I don't know. That's where you come in. I need you to investigate Ferrante and try to find some answers, because at this point you know more than Sarosky and the police do."

"How's that?" Cameron asked.

"Because Mario won't tell Sarosky that the descriptions of the two goons matches the photographs that Henry had taken. He doesn't want the police in his business any more than they already are," Russ replied.

"Even if it helps the cops to find his missing daughter?"

"Even if it does that. Mario cares more about himself than his own daughter. That's always been the problem with Mario. It's all about him."

"Why don't you give this information to the cops yourself?" Cameron asked.

"I don't think I want to end up in the bottom of the Halifax River."

Cameron was surprised. "You think Mario would have his grandson's father killed?"

"We're talking about a man who's putting his own interests above his daughter's. Who the hell cares about a former son-in-law? But if you take the information I've given you and run with it, and learn things the police might have eventually learned, then Mario doesn't feel betrayed by me—and has to face the good or the bad of whatever you help bring to light. And maybe we get our missing book club mothers back."

The waitress asked if they wanted dessert. *Just you,* Russ thought.

"So what's next?" Cameron asked.

"We'll meet up again, somewhere very private," Russ said. "I'll give you the photographs and the tracking data. I'll provide you with enough cash to cover the expenses you'll have traveling down to South Florida and back. I'll contact you on a regular basis for updates."

"Does anyone else know that we're talking?" Cameron asked. "Besides these guys over here in the next booth?"

"No. And it needs to stay that way. Don't even tell Nelson. Make up something about why you need to go out of town."

That's not going to fly, Cameron thought. But he simply nodded.

Chapter Fifty-Nine

OCT 5

"So you've never done yoga? You should come to one of my classes sometime," Kayla Bane said.

"You should," Amanda agreed, patting Phil's leg as they sat close together at her parents' dinner table.

"I get lots of beginners that come in," Kayla continued. "All you need is an open spirit. It's amazing how good you start to feel after a couple of classes."

Phil was enjoying his first meeting with Amanda's parents. They lived in a historic neighborhood in Tallahassee, where Amanda had grown up before she left on her seven years of travel across the globe. Carl Bane and Kayla Stewart met as undergrads at Florida State University, where he was studying political science and she was an art major. They decided to stay in Tallahassee when Carl got admitted to the law school, and they bought the little house off of College Avenue near the east side of the campus.

Carl's early years after law school were spent at the nearby state capitol building, as an associate in the attorney general's office. It taught him a lot about what was wrong with state government, Carl recalled, and he later joined a non-profit organization that provided legal services to people who otherwise couldn't afford them. He'd done that work ever since, living a much less extravagant life than his attorney friends but one that was fulfilling.

Kayla worked as an art teacher at area middle and high schools while Amanda was growing up, and loved helping children express themselves in creative ways. A year or so after Amanda set off on her globe-trotting adventure, Kayla became certified in yoga instruction and stopped teaching full-time in order to focus on her new calling.

"This is how Amanda kept us informed of her travels," Carl said while giving Phil a tour of the house when he first arrived, pointing to a wall in his home office that was decorated with postcards. Phil glanced through them, and noted that Amanda had been modest in describing the amount of places she'd visited. "Just a few countries," she'd said, and that "few" included cities such as Rome; Paris; Barcelona; Berlin; Amsterdam; Cannes; Dublin; Cyprus; and Sydney, and smaller cities in countries such as Denmark; Switzerland; Austria; and Portugal.

"She's seen a lot more of the world than we have," Carl said. "But we plan to travel more at some point."

"She's a free spirit," Phil said. "One of the most interesting people I've ever met."

Phil wondered if Carl would take the opportunity, while they were briefly alone, to question him about his relationship with his daughter or express any concerns. The two men were close to the same age, in stark contrast to Phil and Amanda. But Carl was friendly and more inquisitive about Phil's academic work than his intentions with his only child.

The majority of the house was tastefully decorated with several of Kayla's paintings. She had a passion for capturing scenes from the Gulf of Mexico, Carl explained, and they drove down to places such as Carrabelle and St. George Island at least twice per month.

"You should bring your girls up here some time," Kayla said as they were finishing dinner. "They would love the Gulf. Are they beachgoers?"

"We go there once in a while. They're more in-doors children. They like to read." Phil paused, thinking of Audrey's blossoming friendship with Pete O'Rourke. "Although, my oldest daughter has started going to the beach regularly with some of her friends."

"Your girls sound wonderful," Carl said.

"I hope I get to meet them soon," Amanda smiled at Phil.

"You will. I know it's time."

"Some things can't be rushed," Kayla said. "They've been through a lot."

"They have," Amanda said. "I just really want to get to know them."

Phil hoped someone would change the subject, and Carl rescued him. "Amanda's insights from travelling have helped me to put my work in a different perspective," he said. "People view the government's responsibility toward its citizens' well-being in an entirely different way in other countries. We're pretty far behind here in the States."

"That's for sure," Kayla said.

"I'm getting so much more out of my studies than I would have if I'd gone straight to college," Amanda said. "When you study art, music, and philosophy after you've had the chance to see their birthplaces, it all makes a lot more sense. And what's fascinating about Phil is how he gets so much of this stuff intuitively. He's got a brilliant, integrative mind."

Phil was embarrassed. "She's just trying to impress you guys."

"Well, you've obviously impressed her," Kayla said. "Why did you decide to go into teaching humanities?"

"The field didn't seem as saturated as psychology or English, which a lot of my friends in undergrad were studying. It was less popular, something that students wouldn't have necessarily had a lot of interface with during their formative years—and so once they got a taste, I figured they'd be inspired."

"He's right," Carl said. "If you randomly stop people on the street and ask them about the humanities, most will just mumble something about art or the Renaissance, or 'that da Vinci guy.'"

"Phil uses a volume of textbooks that first grabbed his heart as a freshman," Amanda said. "I think it's pretty cool that he teaches from his roots."

"Oh? What's the volume called?" Kayla asked.

"*The Search for Personal Freedom,*" Phil said. "It ends in the 1980s, so we have to supplement a little."

Phil recalled numerous dinners in South Carolina with Jackie's extended family. He'd never quite fit in with that group, but felt at home in Carl and Kayla's place—like he was hanging out with peers.

"I really like your paintings," Phil told Kayla. "Do you miss teaching?"

"I still dabble in it a little," she said.

"My mom does a free art camp for kids during the summer," Amanda said. "She gives the children of my dad's clients first dibs at registration, and finds people and businesses to sponsor it."

"That's really neat," Phil said.

Kayla shrugged. "Most of the time no one's nurturing these children's aesthetic side. They're just trying to survive."

Phil and Amanda lay in her old bedroom that night, pressed close.

"My parents really like you," she said. "I knew they would."

"They're pretty cool. Really interesting people, like their daughter."

Amanda began kissing his neck, and Phil felt electricity running along his skin.

"We can't be as noisy as we usually are. It's not polite."

"The walls are pretty thick here," she responded.

"How do you know?" Phil asked.

"Don't ask," Amanda said, and worked her way down Phil's body.

Ben and Beth stepped into the gift shop at Halifax Medical Center and bought a bouquet of flowers. Ben spotted a small teddy bear with a pink apron and purchased that as well. They found their way to the maternity ward, and softly knocked on one of the patient doors.

Julio opened it, and gave them a big smile as they embraced. In the bed was a remarkably chipper Susannah, holding a sleeping baby girl against her chest.

"Oh my God," Beth whispered. "You so did not have a baby just yesterday. You look amazing."

"I feel amazing," Susannah said. "Do you want to hold her?"

"Of course," Beth said, and Ben and Julio exchanged grins.

Beth cradled the tiny girl in her arms, and gave her a soft kiss on the forehead. "Hello, Adriana Rose," she said. "Welcome to our world. We hope you like it here."

"Susannah did amazing," Julio said, sitting on the edge of the bed and taking his girlfriend's hand. "An hour of pushing, and that kid was out. She kept thanking the doctor and nurses over and over. I think they're all in love with Adriana."

"They should be," Ben said. "She's beautiful."

"I wish they'd let us live here," Susannah said. "I'm terrified that we have to take her home and figure out how to take care of her."

Beth laughed. "Everybody feels that way," she said, walking about with Adriana snug in her arms. "You'll be fine. I'll come help you as much as you need. Is your mother coming up?"

"Yeah, she's on her way now. I wouldn't let her come up right away. She stresses me out sometimes," Susannah said. "She gets so over-excited."

"I need a day job," Julio said. "I don't want to miss any bedtimes with this little princess."

"Yeah, you say that now," Beth said. "But you'll be grateful to go to work." Ben looked at her and she stuck out her tongue at him.

"Maddie's going to love her," Ben said. "We'll have to coach her to not pick her up just yet. She might think Adriana is a baby doll."

"Oh, she's a doll all right," Beth said, kissing the baby girl several more times on her head as she gently examined the tiny fingers and toes.

"Someone looks like she's ready for another one," Susannah said, sipping from a cup of water.

"Yeah, keep that bed warm for Beth," Ben said. "I've surrendered to the inevitable."

"Good for you!" Susannah said. "You need more than one."

"That's what they say. Whoever *they* are," Ben said.

Chapter Sixty

OCT 6

Tom whispered *The Serenity Prayer* before he got out of bed. Rain Dog rose from his slumber and stood sniffing around as Tom patted him on the head.

Connor was asleep, and Tom left him a note in the kitchen. He affixed Rain Dog's leash around his neck and steered the hound toward the sidewalk.

"Come on, Rain Dog," Tom said when the dog performed his usual routine of stopping every few inches to sniff the ground. Tom imagined a thousand invisible scent trails pointing in every possible direction, and Rain Dog trying to make a quick decision about which one to pursue. He decided on the hound's behalf, gently yanking the leash rope and picking up his pace so Rain Dog had no choice but to follow along.

Soon they arrived at the scenic road outside of the neighborhood, and Tom led Rain Dog along the shoulder not far from the trees. The dog suddenly picked up an enticing scent and pressed his nose close to the ground, refusing to be scooted away.

Surrender, Rory would say. So Tom simply waited.

Tom felt bad that his first two months of walking Rain Dog were centered on his agenda of going a certain way and reaching a destination. He loosened his grip on the leash, allowing the animal to assume the lead. Rain Dog lived in the moment, taking life as it was presented to him; possessing none of Tom's advantages but nonetheless content with very little. He stopped when Rain Dog stopped. A squirrel darted across their path, and Tom tightened his grip as the hound instinctively lunged toward it and then lost interest when the critter bounced out of sight.

As a few cars passed by, Tom steered Rain Dog closer to the woods. He looked down and saw a plastic Pepsi bottle, and then a crushed Michelob can. A couple of torn candy wrappers were also strewn across the weeds. Every few feet there was garbage, and Tom realized he'd been oblivious to the fact that people steadily littered along the road. Until now, had he truly ever looked down when he was walking; really looked, and *noticed* what was there?

No, Tom, you're always too busy trying to get somewhere or distract yourself from where you are, he thought.

Rain Dog was pacing, and then settled into a squat to take a crap. Tom had forgotten to bring along a bag, but considered this type of property to be "free reign" for whatever creature needed to piss or poop. The dog kicked at the earth behind him for a few seconds after he finished, and then trotted forward.

Tom guided Rain Dog across the street and they started back home. There were a couple more beer cans, a plastic water bottle, and a crushed, empty pack of cigarettes. Tom mused that some of the litterers would probably be furious if a dog shit on their front lawns: a disgusting, smelly, perfectly biodegradable pile of fertilizer-potential shit was what he wanted to deliver to each of their doorsteps, if he could.

Rain Dog continued to take the lead. As they neared their street, Tom gave a few tugs. They passed another man walking his two little yappy dogs of some breed. Rain Dog and the yappers got acquainted, their leashes tangling up amid the necessary protocols of butt sniffing and nose rubbing.

A little while later, Connor and Rain Dog sat on the living room couch as Tom watched the morning news. Tom told Connor about all of the trash, and asked if his son ever noticed it while riding his bike. Connor said he had, and that he sometimes wanted to pick it up but knew his mother wouldn't want him exposed to all the germs.

"You could always wash your hands once you got home," Tom advised.

"Yeah, but what if I touch my eyes or mouth before that?"

"You can decide not to touch."

"Yeah." Connor paused. "I think some of my friends probably litter. I can picture them doing it. They don't care a whole lot about things."

"Point 'em out to me next time you see them, so I can yell at them."

Connor laughed. "You wouldn't really, would you?"

"No. But I think that if I ever catch someone littering, I'll sick Rain Dog here on 'em."

Connor rubbed the dog's tummy, which was considerably larger than when he'd first joined the family. "Aw, Rainy would just lick 'em and love on 'em. They wouldn't be too scared of this guy."

The boy suddenly sat up very rigid, his eyes wide. Connor often did that when he had a new idea.

"Dad, we should grab some trash bags, put on some gloves, and go pick up litter. We could do it like once a week, and the road will always be clean. Haven't you heard of groups doing that, like adopting a highway to keep clean?"

Tom nodded. "I've heard of that. We could do that."

"We could take Rainy with us."

"Yeah. He'd help us sniff out all the trash."

"Maybe people would see us doing it and they'd want to pull over in their cars and offer to help."

"Maybe. Probably won't happen, but I love your optimism, Connor."

"We could get t-shirts made, and wear them each time," Connor said.

"I can see it now: *TRASH PATROL.*"

"I think we should name our company after Rain Dog."

Tom laughed. "We're a company now?"

"Sure. Especially once we have t-shirts."

"Maybe some bigger trash company will buy all of our stock, and then neither of us will ever have to work again."

"I want to have breakfast before we go out with the trash bags," Connor said.

"Oh, we're starting this morning?"

"It's Saturday. Why not?"

Tom couldn't think of a good reason why not.

"Hey," Tom said, "when you walk Rain Dog, try to go a little slower and see what he's interested in. See what direction he goes."

Connor looked at him funny. "I already do that, Dad. Don't you do that?"

"I do now."

"Good for you, Dad."

237

Chapter Sixty-One

OCT 8

"What's the good word?" Russ asked Cameron.

Cameron grabbed his notepad off of his kitchen counter "The good word is *history,*" he said.

Russ frowned. "History?"

"Yep."

"What kind of history?"

"The wonderful thing about history is that it's laden with public records," Cameron said. "One common set of state records involves ownership of businesses. You pick any registered business, and you can track down the owner or history of owners."

"Yeah, I know that," Russ said. "So cut to the chase, please."

Impatient ass, Cameron thought. "Let's take the history of Famoso's: a popular, locally-owned restaurant in a great location, which has hung in there across the decades as many other restaurants have come and gone. Nothing special about the food or atmosphere; just an affordable, convenient place to go out to eat or get a drink."

Russ nodded. "Go on."

"Tom Blakely, as you know, is the current owner," Cameron said. "He bought the restaurant five years ago. The seller was the estate of the late George Patapos, an attorney whose family was in real estate in Daytona, just like your company. I assume you know the Patapos name."

Russ nodded. "Yeah, Mario's mentioned him once or twice, and sometimes I come across an investor who knew the guy. His time was well before I arrived on the scene."

"Indeed it was. The Patapos Group filed for bankruptcy in the early 1990s. They sold a lot of their properties to Mario's company. Somewhere in the mix of all of that, in 1994, they were also deeded ownership of Famoso's from Mario. And Patapos, or his estate upon his death in 2001, owned the restaurant until they sold it to Tom."

Russ frowned. "You're saying that Mario used to own Famoso's?"

"He never mentioned that to you?"

"No. Not that it's any big deal. Mario's bought and sold lots of properties."

"Mario didn't own Famoso's personally," Cameron said. "It was a property of DDC, which purchased it back in 1978 from the family that originally launched the place in the early 1970s. DDC had investments in a few restaurants along the east coast of Florida back in those days.

"The company was registered in 1975, but Mario wasn't listed as one of the owners at that time. Our friend Patapos, whose original career was working as a real estate attorney, was a minority owner and also handled legal business for DDC. The majority owners were a couple of recent transplants from New York named Tommy and Vinnie."

"Sounds like items from an Italian deli."

"Yeah, pretty woppish all the way through," Cameron smiled. "I found plenty of archived articles from the Daytona Beach newspaper about these guys. They were local celebrities: buying up properties, throwing lavish parties. I searched other East Coast papers and found they had a presence in the South Florida market as well."

"I don't think Mario's ever mentioned a 'Tommy and Vinnie' to me. He's not one to really talk about the past, of course. It's always about the next deal we can make."

Cameron sipped from his glass of water. "The most intriguing news article I came across reported their murders in 1979, on the beach."

He glanced at Russ, who raised his eyebrows. Cameron continued, "They were both found shot in the back of the head, in a parked car. Police received an anonymous call from a hysterical woman. There was a ton of media coverage, including articles speculating that police were investigating Patapos for the murder. But no arrests were ever made, at least based on my search of the archives."

"So did Patapos take over the rest of the company after that?"

"That's what I expected to find when I searched the records. Instead, interestingly enough, it looks like our dead boys had named one of their newly-arrived associates as the beneficiary of their DDC ownership and related assets. The beneficiary and new majority owner, as of 1979, was Mario Lazano."

Russ chuckled. "Why would they leave Mario their ownership?"

"I don't know. But Patapos's signature, as the attorney for not just the company but for the men themselves, is all over the paperwork. And it looks like Patapos remained a minority owner for a couple more years, until Mario bought him out and became the sole owner of DDC, whose assets included Famoso's."

Russ stood and paced around. "Can we take a break?" he asked.

"Sure. Let's have a glass of wine."

They sat on the living room couches for a little while, drinking grocery store Merlot. Nelson texted Cameron to see if it was okay to come home yet, and Cameron had a hunch his partner was irritated when he texted back, *Not yet. My subject is still here.*

"My next step," Cameron said as he picked up his glass of wine, "is to find out all I can about Tommy and Vinnie. Their murders seem to have been written off as a random act of violence; maybe an attempted car theft or a mugging gone wrong. But my gut tells me otherwise."

"What's it telling you, specifically?" Russ was tired of his wine already. He was more of a liquor man.

"That something is fishy about the arrangement they had with Mario. Why would they leave their majority ownership to one of their newest junior partners, rather than their wives or kids? They were both married, and they both had young children according to the articles."

"It is strange," Russ admitted. "Mario's charming, but he's not that charming."

"I've managed to get a couple of veteran Daytona journalists to chat briefly with me, over a beer," Cameron said. "They said there's always been speculation that Mario was involved in cocaine distribution, that he has a lot of income that's off the books."

"Yeah, I know," Russ said. "That's nothing new. A rumor gets started and it persists over time. I've grilled Emma about that, and she always swore her father wasn't involved in anything illegitimate."

"Do you think she'd know for certain?"

"Of course she wouldn't. I just don't think Mario strikes me as a guy who has those kinds of ambitions."

"What about Henry Reid?"

"Henry's dead."

"Yeah," Cameron nodded. "He certainly is."

Russ thought of something.

"Hey," he began, "what were those two guys' last names, the Tommy and Vinnie guys? I don't think you told me."

Cameron smiled. "I didn't. Vinnie's last name was Colombo."

Russ smirked. "Like the TV detective?"

"Like the TV detective. And Tommy's first name…well, you might recognize it." Cameron leaned closer to Russ, and whispered, "Ferrante."

Russ stared at the journalist, his eyes widening.

"Shit," he said, and then smiled. "You do good work, my friend."

"Do you mind if I join you, Scott?"

Scott Layman looked up at Sally from his seat at the commissary table. Sally was one of Curtis's key assistants in the business office, and also had a residence in the small cluster of private cabins that was set apart from the others.

"I don't mind at all," Scott said.

He'd been at the ranch for just a month, but the other residents embraced Scott like a long-lost family member. He quickly embraced the required rituals. Before the work day started, everyone gathered in the chapel while Curtis shared a reflection about the nature of authentic community. Sometimes an older man named Dan spoke, and Scott pieced together that Dan was some kind of mentor to Curtis.

From what Scott could tell, everyone on the property revered Curtis, asserting that he'd changed and even saved their lives. Roger, a younger man whom Curtis had asked to spend time with Scott to help him in the transition, was one of those persons who claimed he'd likely be dead if Curtis hadn't given him shelter and purpose.

"Corporate America is polluting the earth, and polluting our minds," Curtis said that morning in chapel. "We're doing something different here. We're stewards of the earth and one another. Our business is on the cutting edge, as is our way of life. For each of us here who has found a better path, there are hundreds more who are longing for change but don't know how to get there."

These thoughts were a sample of what was contained in Curtis's self-published book, *The Universe Spares Its Bright Spots,* which was apparently based on his large collection of journaled observations spanning the past two decades. It was required reading for all community members. Scott's understanding was that Curtis hadn't yet tried to distribute the book beyond the ranch. Curtis was known to spontaneously ask residents open-ended questions related to its contents, and expressed disappointment if they were unable to correctly respond.

Curtis had alluded to a "major marketing campaign" that would happen sometime in the next couple of years. Roger speculated that Curtis was planning to build dozens of additional cabins on the property, and would be sending the residents out to communities across Florida to recruit new people who could bring their talents, resources, and money. At some point, Roger hoped, the community would have enough cash flow to buy out other food companies and radically transform the way they did business.

"You seem like you're fitting in well here," Sally said to Scott, plopping down in the chair next to his. "Curtis thinks highly of you. He says you're the kind of business person we've been waiting for."

"That's good to hear," Scott said.

"He wants you to speak in chapel sometime soon," she continued. "To share your story."

"My story isn't very interesting."

"I doubt that's true." Sally stared intently at him, and Scott looked away.

"Are you scared of me?" she asked.

He laughed. "Should I be?"

"Of course not. But a lot of the other men seem to be."

Sally was attractive in certain ways, but the haircut was a bit extreme and she was too skinny.

"Maybe I'll stop by your cabin later," she said. "Would that be okay?"

Scott shrugged. "Sure. It's not like I have plans or anything. I'll just be reading."

"Let me guess. Curtis's book?"

Scott nodded. "That's the one."

She smiled and patted his arm. "Good for you. It can get boring here at times, for sure. But it's worth it."

Scott watched Sally walk away. It had been a while since a woman had flirted with him. It felt good.

"She's a mess, isn't she?" Roger had quietly approached Scott's table and sat down.

"I don't know," Scott said. "Is she?"

"She's love-starved. I don't know what she's been through, but it must have been rough. When she first showed up, she was kind of zombie-like. Then it was like she flipped this switch, and became this person who never shuts up."

Roger held up his tattered copy of Curtis's book, filled with underlines and highlights. "There's plenty to talk about from what's in here. This is the present and future, and the past is just a painful mirage."

Scott stood. "Speaking of that book, I'm going to go do some reading."

Roger nodded. "I'll see you in the morning."

"Yeah, sounds good."

As promised, Sally showed up at Scott's cabin about an hour later. Scott had high expectations for her prowess in bed by the way they rapidly undressed, but

Sally just lay very still on her back, her legs tense, while Scott penetrated her. She was very quiet afterwards, and soon drifted off to sleep.

Scott picked up the book and continued reading. He didn't know whether he truly liked Sally or not, but it was good to have someone there with him.

Chapter Sixty-Two

Nov 5

Ben walked inside Famoso's during a busy happy hour. He spotted a single empty high-back chair and rushed toward it, maneuvering through the crowd. Julio was attending to other customers, and Ben checked his emails while he waited.

"There he is," Julio said, gripping Ben's hand tightly. "What's going on?"

"You know, the grind," Ben said. "How's the proud papa?"

"Man," Julio said. "Adriana's growing fast. She sleeps all night now, thank God. I thought I was going to lose my freakin' mind during the first few weeks."

Ben smiled. "Yeah, you adjust. It just takes time."

"Susannah texts me about four times a night. Usually it's something cute that Adriana did. A few times it's like, 'I need you here! I can't get her to stop crying or go to sleep.'"

"Those kinds of texts sound familiar."

"I bet. So what can I get you?" Julio asked.

"What's on draught tonight?"

"Michelob Light, Stella, and Shock Top."

Ben considered the choices. "Let's go with a Stella."

"Good call."

Julio went to pour the beer as Ben looked around the crowd. He saw Steve working the room as always, greeting patrons and telling stories. Then he spotted another familiar face. Tom was saying hello to employees and introducing them to a dark-haired, well-dressed gentleman who looked about the same age as Ben. The pair headed in the direction of Tom's office.

Ben's Stella arrived. "I just saw Tom," he said to Julio.

"Yeah, was he back with that smooth-talking dude?"

"He was with a guy in a suit, but I didn't get to hear him speak."

"They've been here together a couple of times recently. Steve says they're working on some kind of deal involving the restaurant."

"Tom told me a while back he was thinking of selling," Ben said.

"Well, it looks like he's doing more than just thinking about it now," Julio said. "I'm a little nervous. I've had enough life change lately."

"I don't think you have anything to worry about."

"It's the unknown," Julio added. "Stability is good for me right now. I'm already wondering whether I can keep doing this for the long haul. It feels like bartending and being a father don't go hand-in-hand very well."

"Give it some more time," Ben said. "But what else would you do, if you didn't tend bar?"

"I'd like to manage a restaurant," Julio said. "But I don't know how to make the leap from the bar to the office. I could do what Steve does, I think. I just don't have any business training or experience."

Ben thought for a moment. "Maybe I can help you in that regard."

"Yeah?"

"Yeah," Ben said. "Would you be willing to give me an hour of your time once every couple of weeks or so?"

Julio shrugged. "Yeah, probably, especially during the daytime."

"We could have lunch, as long as I'm not out of town. We can talk about different business fundamentals, from A to Z. Maybe that would help."

"That would be awesome! Kind of like mentoring?"

"I guess we could call it that. I think we'd learn a lot from each other."

Julio laughed. "Not sure how much you'll learn from me, but okay."

"I learn from everyone I talk to. I'm sure you do that, also. That's a secret ingredient to success."

"Hey, I really appreciate you offering this. I gotta be able to open more doors in the next couple of years."

"It's my pleasure. Who knows, I might end up hiring you some day," Ben smiled.

"Hey, that would be an honor. Even though I don't know anything about the wireless industry."

Ben shrugged, and sipped his beer.

"It's all about the intangibles. You can learn all the technical stuff. I've hired plenty of people from restaurant and hotel backgrounds, because they were so good with people."

Julio saw a couple of new patrons sit down. "I might need to get a part-time job at one of your stores now, just to pay for all the diapers," he said as he went to greet them.

Ben's phone beeped with a text. Beth. *When are you coming home?* He sighed and left some cash for Julio.

∿

In his small Famoso's office, Tom looked through some paperwork with Nick Ferrante.

"I'm glad we could make this work, Tom," Ferrante said. "This place has sentimental value to me, I have to admit. I used to come here when I was a little kid."

"Your family visited Daytona a lot when you were growing up?" Tom asked.

"We sure did. We loved being able to drive on the beach. You can't do that down in South Florida, or really anyplace else."

"I'm glad we could work things out, too. I've enjoyed having this place, but I'm ready to do something else."

"Well, you should have plenty of money to take your time deciding what's next."

The men signed and initialed the appropriate pages, their respective attorneys having already spent time negotiating the deal and leaving the final ceremonies to the buyer and seller alone.

"What do you think you want to do next?" Ferrante asked. "Based on what you've told me, you've got a history of owning a business for several years, then moving on to a new challenge. We're kind of alike in that sense."

"I don't know. I'd like to get more involved in the community in some way. I'm thinking maybe the animal shelter. I've got a dog now."

Ferrante smiled, and nodded. "Good for you. I have a couple of Dobermans. What do you have?"

"A coon hound. Found him on the side of the road a few months ago. He was in bad shape, really emaciated and injured. He needed a good home."

"Well, he's lucky that you came along."

"I'm the lucky one," Tom said. "I also want to spend as much time as possible with my son Connor. I'm a single father now, and fulfilling both roles takes a lot of time and effort."

Ferrante looked at him closely, nodding empathetically. "I'm really sorry about what happened to your wife, Tom. I hope you get some answers before long."

"Thank you. I don't know if I will. But we're trying our best to move forward and make the best out of life."

246

They finished singing and initializing. The men shook hands, but remained seated.

"I don't think I'll make any major changes," Ferrante said. "I love the job Steve has done here, and his management philosophies. You've got a great, motivated team."

"It's a great group. Keep an eye on Julio especially; that kid is going places. He just became a father for the first time."

"You've got it."

They stood to leave. "Would this be a good time for me to make an announcement to the staff?" Tom asked.

"We can do some casual introductions right now," Ferrante said. "I'm going to work with Steve to schedule an all-hands meeting sometime in the next week; just so I can tell them more about myself, get to know them more and see what questions people have. I want everyone to feel relaxed and know that it's business as usual."

"Sounds like a good plan."

From the bar, Julio watched Tom and Ferrante interacting with the servers and bus boys. Steve joined them, and they gradually made their way over to the bar. Julio shook hands with Ferrante, who made an effort to say what great things he'd heard about him.

"I've got a lot of business operations that involve special events," Ferrante said. "There could be some opportunities for you, if you want to expand what you do. We throw some outrageous parties down in South Florida, and are always in need of great bartenders."

"My old stomping grounds," Julio said.

"Even better," Ferrante said.

"Can I get you a drink?"

Ferrante shook his head. "Not tonight. There'll be time for that. We'll talk more soon."

Julio watched Ferrante depart with Tom and Steve. He served customers and waited until a few minutes of down time, and then sent texts to Russ and Cameron informing them that the restaurant deal had been completed. Both responded immediately, thanking him for the information and asking that he continue to keep his eyes and ears open for anything interesting pertaining to Famoso's new owner.

Chapter Sixty-Three

Nov 9

D addy's friend, Amanda."

That was the description Phil used as he prepped his daughters for the big Saturday night dinner he was planning. Amanda would arrive at 5 p.m., and they would have some time to visit together before eating. The girls had lots of questions, especially Natalie, and Phil patiently fielded each of them.

Phil was preparing the main dinner course of chicken cutlets with steamed broccoli, brown rice, and a mixed greens salad. Audrey was making brownies, with Natalie as her helper. Natalie also asked for the responsibility of taking the French mini-baguettes out of the freezer, pre-heating the oven, and setting the oven timer. The youngest Solomon daughter had rehearsed this several times beforehand.

The girls also worked together to set the dining room table. Phil added wine goblets to his and Amanda's place settings, and double-checked everything to make sure it was clean. The napkins were slightly creased in the wrong places. Phil started to fix them, and then left them as they were.

They'd also cleaned the house. Natalie loved to sweep and vacuum, and was put in charge of all things flooring and carpeting. Audrey agreed to wipe down the bathrooms. Phil dusted, picked up general clutter around the house, and trimmed some of the shrubbery. He also cleaned out the refrigerator, wiped away the crud that had built up for who knew how many months, and took out all of the trash.

Amanda arrived a few minutes after five, carrying a large bag that contained a bottle of Cabernet Sauvignon and a present for each girl. The girls seemed happy to receive her greeting hugs. She gave Audrey a copy of John Green's bestseller *The Fault in Our Stars*. Natalie was given a cool journal where she could make lots of different types of creative and reflective entries.

Natalie insisted on giving Amanda a tour of the house. She took her time when they stopped by her bedroom, detailing the stories behind each poster on the wall, certain dolls she owned, and various pieces of jewelry. When they stopped by the master bedroom, Natalie simply said, "H-here's where Daddy sleeps and where Mommy used to sleep."

As the four of them sat in the living room, Phil poured Amanda and himself a glass of Cab and listened as the girls asked Amanda about her tattoos. She wore a sleeveless blouse and a skirt, and the tattoos behind her left shoulder, inside of her left wrist, and exterior of her right ankle were on prominent display.

Natalie pointed to the butterfly behind Amanda's shoulder. "Have you ever been to a b-butterfly garden?"

"I have," Amanda said. "I've been to a couple in Europe, as well as the one that's in Key West. Have you ever been to one?"

"At a zoo once, that M-mommy took us to. Why did you get a butterfly done right there?"

"You know," Amanda said, "butterflies are such free, happy, beautiful creatures. I'd love to feel so free. So a few years ago, the butterfly became my first tattoo."

"It's cool," Audrey said.

"Daddy, do you have any t-tattoos?" Natalie asked Phil.

Phil laughed. "I think you know the answer to that."

"I've been trying to talk him into getting one," Amanda said, patting him on the leg. "I think he should get a tattoo of your names on his big right bicep."

"Yeah, Daddy!" Natalie said. "Then you'll always have us close by."

"That's a sweet idea, but your grandmother would yell at me," Phil said.

Audrey pointed to the inside of Amanda's wrist, where there was a simple outline of a peace symbol. "I like that a lot," Audrey said. "I have a lot of clothes with that on them. So does Natalie."

"Peace is cool," Natalie added.

"Peace is very cool," Amanda said. "I got that one done when I was in South America. The more you travel the world, the sillier it seems that we don't have peace among nations."

"Grandpa says nations have been fighting each other ever since there were human beings around," Audrey said. "He said he really wants to take us to visit Israel, but that it's not safe over there right now."

"That's for sure," Phil said.

"Well, hopefully you'll get to go some day," Amanda said. "I'm sure that Israel is very important to your family."

"Do you celebrate H-hanukah?" Natalie asked her.

"Sometimes," Amanda said. "I like all the holidays. I've celebrated Kwanza with friends before. Do you know what Kwanza is?"

"I do," Audrey said. "It celebrates African heritage. It takes place around the same time as Hanukkah and Christmas."

"That's right," Amanda said.

"D-do you love my dad?" Natalie suddenly asked.

Awkward, Phil thought. Amanda laughed.

"Of course I love him. He's very sweet. I bet you love him a lot too."

"Yep, he's my daddy," Natalie said.

"Natalie's coming out of her shell," Phil said, feeling relieved that Natalie was stuttering a little less each day and giving his youngest daughter a kiss on the top of her head. "She's got a very inquisitive spirit."

"Inquisitive is good," Amanda said. "Life is all about learning. But I'm sure you know that, from your daddy. He's a great teacher."

"It's pretty cool that you're one of his students," Audrey said. "I hope I can be one of his students one day. But I'm afraid he might call on me and embarrass me, and I'll be like, '*Dad!*'"

"You'll be the smartest one in the class. You'll already know all the material from growing up with him," Amanda said.

Natalie pointed to Amanda's right foot, which sported a clean coating of hot pink nail polish. The tattoo on her ankle was a lotus flower. Amanda described the lotus's symbolism of representing awareness and calm, and said she'd gotten this final tattoo when visiting San Francisco.

"Do you think you'll get any more artwork done?" Audrey asked.

Amanda shook her head. "I think I'm done, but who knows? I have a lot of traveling left to do, and a lot of life left to live."

"My dad says I'll have to wait until I'm 18, and then I can decide what I want to do with my body," Audrey said. "But I'm scared of what my Grandma would think, also."

"Let's get Grandma a tattoo for her next birthday," Phil said. "One of each of your faces, right on her shins."

"That would be crazy!" Natalie exclaimed.

"Totally crazy," Amanda said.

Phil excused himself to finalize dinner preparations, and politely declined Amanda's offer to help. The girls talked with their guest about school, friends, and favorite television shows. They also quizzed Amanda about her own parents and where they lived, and thought it was neat that Amanda's mother was an art and yoga teacher. Amanda also explained how her father helped poor people who couldn't afford a lawyer. Audrey said she'd like to have a job like that someday.

They sat down to eat. Natalie described the role that each family member had played in putting the meal together. Amanda said the baguettes were extra delicious, and told Phil she'd no idea he could cook so well.

"It's all a big façade," Phil said. "I'm a one-hit wonder. If you come to dinner again there'll probably be Domino's Pizza on the table."

"Sounds yummy," Audrey said.

"I agree," Amanda said.

"Daddy makes us eat something green every night," Natalie said, poking at her leafy broccoli with her fork. "Sometimes I want to, other nights I don't feel like it."

"I love kale," Amanda said. "Do you ever eat that?"

"I haven't dared try to make that yet," Phil said.

"I put it in my homemade smoothies. I love making a green smoothie," Amanda said.

"I tried a friend's Green Naked drink once," Audrey said. "It was … different."

"We're going to watch a movie after dinner," Natalie said. "Have you ever seen *Parental Guidance?* It's so funny."

"I haven't seen it," Amanda said. "It sounds good."

"Billy Crystal's in it," Phil said. "Know who he is?"

Amanda rolled her eyes. "I know who Billy Crystal is, you dork. I wasn't born yesterday."

"Just the day before yesterday," Phil smiled.

"Dad, you *can* be such a dork s-sometimes," Natalie said, and laughed like it was the funniest thing ever uttered.

"Dads have to be dorky. It's in our job description."

"He's pretty cool, really," Amanda said, letting her foot touch Phil's under the table. "You girls are very lucky to have him."

"Yeah, especially now," Audrey said. "I can't imagine not having Dad."

"I can't imagine not having you guys," Phil said.

Natalie and Audrey volunteered to clear the dishes from the table, while Phil and Amanda relaxed in the living room.

"They're charming little angels," Amanda told him.

"They're on their best behavior. Don't let those cherub faces fool you." He gave her a gentle kiss on the lips, hoping Natalie wasn't spying on them.

"Do you think they've figured out by now that I'm a 'girlfriend' and not just a friend?"

Phil nodded. "Audrey certainly will have, and Natalie is fairly intuitive. Plus, you brought me wine: a very romantic gesture, indeed."

"Do you like the Cab?"

"Very much so. Good choice."

"I was definitely nervous driving over here. I'm not usually that nervous about anything. But I've never dated someone with children before."

"I haven't dated since I had children." They both laughed.

"You're not really 'dating' per say," Amanda said. "You're just tutoring one of your students. Very *private* tutoring."

"Very private indeed," Phil said. "But I think I'm learning just as much from the student, if not more."

Amanda smiled. "Thank you so much for the chance to meet them. They're wonderful. I hope I can see them again soon. Maybe you guys can all come over to my place."

"That sounds great."

Natalie stepped out of the kitchen and dramatically cleared her throat.

"W-who wants a brownie?"

"Who wants a brownie? Who *doesn't* want a brownie?" Amanda responded.

"Would you like vanilla ice cream with yours?" Natalie asked her.

"For sure."

"How about you, Daddy?"

"Just the brownie, sweetie."

Natalie gave them a soldier's salute. "Coming right up," she said, and spun on her heels before heading back into the kitchen.

"She's a trooper. God, she's been through a lot at such a young age," Amanda said.

"She's had a lot of nights crying in my arms," Phil said. "I just let her cry when she needs to."

"Crying is very human."

Amanda leaned against him on the couch. Phil was eager to be alone with her for a few minutes, but knew that would have to wait.

"You knew that I'd love you even more once I met them, didn't you?"

Phil pulled her closer. "I'd hoped there was a good chance of that."

Natalie returned to serve the brownies and ice cream. She asked if they needed a re-fill of their wine glasses, and Amanda cracked up.

"We'll get some more in a minute, sweetie. Thank you, though."

"Okay. Audrey's doing the dishes. She's making a real mess in there."

"Are you going to help her some?" Phil asked.

"Oh, she's doing fine on her own," Natalie said, and plopped down on the couch next to them. "Can I hang out here with you?"

Amanda brushed a few strands of hair out of Natalie's face. "You have very pretty hair. It looks a lot like your mother's, from pictures I've seen."

"Yeah, I've got my mom's hair," Natalie said. "My dad's gotten pretty good at brushing it." Amanda smiled at Phil.

"I've got less and less of my own to brush," he said.

"Natalie!" Audrey called out from the kitchen. "We have a situation in here!"

Natalie stood. "I have to go. There's a s-situation in there."

Phil and Amanda looked at each other and shrugged as Natalie departed. "I think that's Audrey's way of demanding that her sister help her clean up."

"Do you want me to go check on them?" Amanda asked.

"You're the guest."

"You just like being alone with me for a few stolen minutes," Amanda said, and kissed him at length.

Chapter Sixty-Four

DEC 7

On the first Saturday of December, Russ woke up with the intention of getting his Christmas shopping for Pete "out of the way." The kid didn't seem to want anything but iTunes gift cards and cash these days, but Russ was determined to get him something he could actually unwrap on Christmas morning. Mario would probably buy his grandson whatever latest piece of high-end technology Pete asked for; so anything Russ got him would be second-string, anyway.

Around mid-morning, Russ went out to the guard shack to see if any of the detail wanted to take a quick ride with him to the Volusia Mall. No one looked too eager, but his team members informed Russ that it was probably a good idea if he didn't go alone.

"Who's gonna draw the short straw, then?" Russ asked.

Victor, one of the former office Cubists, shrugged and raised his hand. "I don't mind going to the mall for a little while. I might pick up something for my sister's kids while we're there, if there's time."

"Sure. Nothing like a couple of men going shopping together. Very sweet," Russ said, and the group gave an obligatory laugh.

"Boss, we were about to call you anyway," another detail member said. "You just got an overnight delivery. This box."

Russ watched the man, whose name was Bo, hold up a rectangular FedEx box. Russ looked at him before taking a single step toward it.

"We're pretty sure it's not a bomb or anything, Mr. O'Rourke."

"You're 'pretty sure?' That doesn't leave me overflowing with confidence."

"We scanned it," Victor said. "I think someone just sent you a Christmas present."

"Who's it from?" Russ asked.

Victor peered at the label as Bo continued to hold the box up for examination. "It was brought to a FedEx place in Fort Lauderdale at 10:30 last night. They must be staying open later for the holidays."

"It sure got here fast," Russ said warily, still not making a move for the package.

"Do you want one of us to open it for you?" Bo asked.

Russ was starting to feel like a wuss. *Russ the Wuss,* he thought.

"No, let me have it."

Russ took the FedEx box and gave it a small shake. Whatever the contents happened to be, they were very light.

"I'll be back in a few minutes to head to the mall," he said, and walked back to the house with the package.

The evening before was Nick Ferrante's annual holiday party for his staff, friends, and associates, at his lavish beachside home in Boca Raton. The festivities kicked off at 6 p.m. with cocktails and hors-d'oeuvre. A team of valets was busy helping park cars along Ferrante's large semi-circle driveway and across the street at a large lot that Ferrante had rented for the night.

Tom Blakely was included on the guest list along with Steve the general manager. Both had given their thanks but declined; Tom, because he was steering clear of gatherings where alcohol would be a primary focal point, and Steve because he already had another holiday party engagement with his wife's employer.

Two other last minute invitees, however, were able to attend. Cameron and Nelson thanked the valet driver, who politely declined their $10 tip while saying, "Mr. Ferrante is taking good care of us already." As they entered the premises, Nelson remained perplexed by Cameron's explanation of how he'd scored an invitation for them.

A week or so beforehand, Julio was filling in for Steve as the acting manager for a couple of hours. He popped into the back office for a few minutes to call Susannah and check on Adriana. As Julio sat in the swivel chair, a fancy-looking piece of paper on the desk caught his eye. Feeling a little guilty for snooping, Julio read the holiday-themed invitation from Ferrante to Steve and took note of the date.

After he was done talking with Susannah, Julio studied the invitation a bit more and then called Tom. Cameron wanted to do a profile of Ferrante as the restaurant's new owner, Julio told him, to draw additional exposure to the venue. Would Tom be interested in reaching out to Ferrante and seeing if Cameron could get an hour of Ferrante's time?

"Sure, not a problem," Tom said. "I was going to give him a call anyway. I just got an invitation to some big holiday party he's throwing down at his place, but I don't think I'm going to attend."

Julio smiled, and took a deep breath so he wouldn't sound too eager.

"I wonder if Ferrante might want to invite Cameron?" he asked. "He could interview some of the other guests there as well, and really paint an in-depth portrayal of Ferrante. Weren't you saying that he wants to invest money in the beachside revitalization efforts here?"

Tom paused. "Yeah, he said that. I could ask him, I suppose. Do you think Cameron would want to go to something like that?"

"I'm sure he would," Julio said.

"Do you want to go as well? You're one of his employees, after all, and I know that you've already made a good impression," Tom said.

"I'd love to, but Susannah would kill me if I went to Palm Beach County for a party and left her home with Adriana. Maybe next year."

Tom laughed. "Good point. Okay, I'll call him and see what he says."

"Thanks, Tom."

Two days later Nelson found a thin overnight envelope outside of their apartment, addressed to Cameron and containing the invitation from Ferrante.

Now, as they entered Ferrante's house, Cameron and Nelson saw a diverse crowd that looked like a cross-section of South Florida-based reality television shows. There were men in sports coats and women in evening gowns, some of whom looked like business persons and others who could have been actors, models, or athletes. The crowd probably topped 100 people, and the party was spilling into every room of the spacious, open first floor and onto the large deck out back that offered a gorgeous view of the ocean.

Cameron had a thin note pad and pen inside of his jacket, but didn't want to carry it around as he talked to people. It was a party and he wanted to blend in and have people treat him like just another guest. Cameron and Nelson were quickly approached by servers offering hors-d'oeuvre trays and drinks, and both enjoyed a glass of red wine as they walked through the crowd and said hello to anyone who made reasonable eye contact.

"You looking for someone you know?" Nelson asked him as Cameron repeatedly scanned the crowd of faces.

"I'm wondering where Ferrante is," Cameron said. "I might ask someone."

"Take your time. We just got here."

"I know. Relax."

"*I'm* relaxed," Nelson smiled. "I'm going to head over to the bar to see whatever else they have there."

"Okay. I'm going to explore the outside a bit. See you out there?"

"Yep." Nelson left him and Cameron headed out back, where there was another bar. He got the attention of a server, and asked if he knew where he could find Mr. Ferrante. The server pointed across the crowd to a tall, well-dressed brunette, who appeared to be coordinating the serving staff.

Felicia the brunette was warm in her greeting, but Cameron could tell she wasn't up for chit-chatting. He quickly explained who he was and why he'd been invited, and wondered if Felicia could introduce him to Mr. Ferrante. Cameron handed her a business card.

"Would you mind waiting over by the bar?" Felicia asked. "That would probably make it easier for Mr. Ferrante to find you. It's getting really congested out here."

At the bar Cameron ordered a gin and tonic. Dusk was falling along the coastline, and a few seagulls were scampering around for any scraps of food they could find. A handful of people were walking across the shoreline. Although South Florida didn't have much of a winter there was a gentle breeze, and Cameron liked how it felt going through his hair.

Cameron saw Nelson and waved him over. Nelson was drinking a Cape Cod. They people-watched for a couple of minutes before a friendly chap named Rod Bergeron introduced himself as an executive with the Arena Football team. While they were visiting with Rod, Cameron saw Ferrante himself saying hello to people on his way toward the bar. Taking another sip of his cocktail in an effort to soothe his nerves, Cameron took a step toward Ferrante and the two made eye contact.

Ferrante smiled and introduced himself, and thanked Cameron and Nelson for driving all the way down from Orlando. Ferrante spoke kindly of Tom, Steve, and the staff at Famoso's, and said he was looking forward to spending more time in the Daytona area.

"I can chat with you for a few minutes in my office, if that works for you," Ferrante said. "Will your friend be joining us?"

Nelson was still talking with Rod.

"No, I'll let him keeping having fun out here," Cameron said, and waved to Cameron as he walked off with Ferrante.

"Let's go around this other way," Ferrante said. "It'll be less crowded."

They walked to the south side of the back of the property, where a couple of staff members stood outside a door. Ferrante nodded to them as they opened the door, and Ferrante held out his hand for Cameron to go first. They entered what looked like an entirely private section of the house, absent any of the party guests.

Ferrante led him to a fancy spiral stairwell, telling Cameron a quick story of how he came to purchase the house and how much work he did to make it feel like home. He said he loved to spend quiet evenings on the back deck, and would need the remainder of the weekend to recover from the huge throng of people at his home.

"I'm basically an introvert," Ferrante said. "People don't realize that, because they see me hob-knobbing around all of the time. But that's just business. When I'm not working, I'm a home-body. Just ask my wife, Patricia, if you see her downstairs later. She's the social butterfly, not me."

"I get what you're saying. Nelson is more of the life of the party as well, compared to me," Cameron said.

"Well, he'll be fine down there, then. Here's my office, come inside."

Cameron followed Ferrante into a spacious room lined with bookshelves and artwork. A large plate-glass window offered another dreamy view of the ocean. Ferrante invited Cameron to join him at a leather couch sectional.

"I read that piece you wrote earlier this year about Tom's wife and the other missing women," Ferrante said, as Cameron casually pulled out his notepad and left it closed on his lap. "It was very touching. A real tragedy."

"Yeah. Tom has been through a tough time, but he's moving forward," Cameron said.

"Daytona has been the scene of some really heinous crimes, unfortunately," Ferrante said. "I think there hasn't been enough investment in good jobs in the community. They've tried to fix up the Boardwalk area and all of that but there's still way too much crime on the streets, especially drugs."

"Can you tell me more about your trips to the area as a child?" Cameron asked.

"Sure," Ferrante said. "I actually lived there for a while. Not many people know that. I was born in New York, but my parents moved to Daytona Beach when I was a little kid. I moved down here when I was in junior high, after my father died."

"Where did you live in Daytona?" Cameron asked.

"On the beachside, off of Oleander," Ferrante said. "My dad and his business partner owned a lot of real estate, and a few restaurants. They actually were the second owners of Famoso's, so it's really special to me to have brought the restaurant back into my family. Kind of a tribute to my dad, you know, who didn't get to see me grow up and try to make something of myself."

Cameron thought of the murdered Tommy Ferrante and Vinnie Colombo. He felt sweat forming on his forehead.

"After my father's sudden death, my mother moved us down to this area to get away from the bad memories," Ferrante said. "She quickly remarried, to this control freak of a car salesman named Joe Pazziano."

Cameron reached for his pen, but Ferrante shook his head.

"You don't need to write any of that down," Ferrante said. "That's just background for you. We'll get to the story stuff in a minute. You don't mind all that being off the record, do you?"

"Of course not," Cameron said.

"It would be a little embarrassing, everyone knowing my father got whacked on the beach with his business partner," Ferrante said. "My mother worked hard to keep the secret. I've worked pretty hard at it, too."

Cameron sipped what was left of his cocktail.

"We'll get you a refill in a minute," Ferrante said.

"I appreciate your trust in me," Cameron said.

"I know you won't say anything," Ferrante replied. "I can tell."

"Can you tell me more about your father?"

Ferrante walked over to his desk, and came back with a picture frame. Cameron saw a dark-haired, smiling Italian guy arm in arm with a young Nick, who looked to be about nine in the photograph.

"He was a real character," Ferrante said. "Really knew how to make a buck. My mother hardly ever talks about him. I had to piece his history together from people who knew him. His business partner, the guy that was found shot with him—apparently, that guy was bad news. Led my dad down some wrong paths."

"Did the police ever solve the murder?"

"Nope," Ferrante said, putting the picture frame back in place. "The police up there aren't too good at solving anything. In this day and age of technology, they can't even find three book club mothers."

Ferrante sat back down.

"But you know that already, of course," he said.

"That they haven't been able to find the missing women? Yeah. I hope they call me first if they do."

Cameron suddenly realized he'd missed the intent of Ferrante's comment. He felt a bead of sweat run down his forehead and land on his slacks, and wondered if Ferrante noticed.

"You knew my father's murder was unsolved," Ferrante said. "You've done your homework. That's why I can trust you to keep certain things off the record. You're thorough, which means you're a professional."

Cameron attempted a casual smile, but at the same time wiped more sweat off of his face. The door to the office opened, and both men turned to look.

"Do you need anything, Mr. Ferrante?" a man about Cameron's age asked. "Another drink for both of you, perhaps?"

Ferrante looked at Cameron, who was trying not to stare at the guy. He knew his face from photographs Russ had shared with him. "You want another one, Cameron?" Ferrante asked.

"Sure," Cameron said, looking back at Ferrante. "A gin and tonic," he said, glancing back at the visitor.

"You've got it," the man said. "Mr. Ferrante, what would you like?"

"A glass of Pinot Grigio would be great," Ferrante said. "Reminds me of our seafood Christmas dinners when I was growing up."

"Yes, sir," the man said, and departed.

"That was Rex," Ferrante said. "He's a newer member of my team. Very eager, does a good job. But you know all about Rex already."

Cameron frowned. "Pardon me?"

"You know all about Rex. And Frankie, the big guy he's always with. They work closely together. You know both of them, right?"

Ferrante leaned back in his chair, crossing his legs. He smiled.

"Am I right? I don't want to sound presumptuous."

Cameron was thinking fast. "Rex looks familiar. I think he might have come into Famoso's a couple of times when I was hanging out there."

"Yeah, that's probably it," Ferrante said.

Rex returned with the drinks, saying nothing but "My pleasure" when Ferrante and Cameron thanked him, and quickly departed once again. Cameron took a sizable sip of his drink. He wondered what Nelson was up to downstairs, and wished his partner would call to check on him.

The door opened again and this time Frankie, thick-necked and massively built, entered first followed by Rex. Rex shut the door and they simply stood there. Cameron finished his drink and stared at Ferrante, waiting for his host to speak.

"What do you want from me?" he finally asked.

Ferrante shrugged. "It's pretty simple. You're in over your head, and I want to help you. I want you to stay as far away from Daytona Beach as possible. Don't have any more contact with any of your friends there. Not Lazano, or O'Rourke, or employees at my restaurant, or the other families who are in the middle of this unfortunate tragedy. You seem like a nice guy, and I want to keep you out of trouble. Stick to what you know, and don't try to be some famous crime reporter with an impending book deal."

Cameron didn't like having his back turned to Frankie and Rex, but also didn't want to appear scared by glancing back at them.

"Is that fair?" Ferrante asked. "You forget about all this stuff that you're looking into, and everything is fine. It's a fair deal, isn't it?"

"I suppose so."

"Good," Ferrante said, smiling again as he stood. He pumped Cameron's hand. "I don't want you to rush out. I want you and Nelson to enjoy the party. You can tell him that I was too boring to write a feature article about, but at least you guys got to come to a fun party. He'll get that, right?"

"Yeah. He'll get that."

"Excellent. I'm gonna have Frankie and Rex escort you back downstairs. I need to go find my wife before she gets too pissed at me." Ferrante shook Cameron's hand once more, and left him alone in the office with his henchmen.

Frankie smiled, but still looked intimidating even when trying to be pleasant. "What do you say we all get a re-fill?"

<center>~~~</center>

Russ walked into the kitchen of Mario's home, the cardboard box in hand. No one else was around at the moment. He pulled off the perforated edge, revealing shiny red-and-green wrapping paper. He tipped the box on its side and the wrapped, relatively flat package slid out. Russ hesitated, and then ripped off the Christmas paper to reveal a thin steno pad and a ball point pen.

He frowned and picked up the pad, leafing through its several pages of handwriting. Then, what appeared to be a business card popped out of the notebook and landed on the kitchen floor.

Russ picked up the card. It was Cameron Brock's. *What the fuck?*

He flipped through the notebook some more and discovered something else lodged inside of it. Russ fingered the Polaroid photograph, and cursed out loud as he gazed at Cameron's vacant stare, a bullet wound in the center of his forehead.

Chapter Sixty-Five

Dec 8

Nelson, his hands shackled and eyes bloodshot from lack of sleep, wore a jail-issued orange outfit as he stood before Palm Beach County Circuit Judge Esther Walters and plead not guilty to the murder of Cameron Brock. A bespectacled court-appointed public defender, Paul Andresen, stood next to him.

The courtroom was packed with dozens of curious onlookers and numerous members of the press. Nelson kept his head down afterwards, and remained silent as reporters shouted questions at him while he was led into a police car.

A couple of religious right protesters trolled the sidewalk, one holding a large cardboard sign declaring *GOD HATES FAGS*. A police officer noticed the sign and began arguing with the man holding it.

The previous night, as Nick Ferrante and his wife Patricia were saying goodbye to their party guests, Juan Camarala informed his fellow valets that one of the car owners hadn't retrieved their vehicle. They suggested Juan find Felicia the party hostess, which he did, and she rolled her eyes at the news.

"Check the deck area and the immediate beachfront, would you, dear?" Felicia responded. "I'm going to look in the bedrooms. Some people just have no manners."

But Felicia's thorough check of the Ferrante residence didn't turn up any renegade guests in various stages of undress. Juan came back empty-handed as well. Felicia found Ferrante decompressing in his office with a cup of hot tea, and told him about the sole vehicle still parked across the street and the set of unclaimed car keys.

Ferrante asked Patricia to join him while he walked on the beach to see if he could track down the driver of the car, but she was tired and heading to bed. Felicia agreed to accompany him instead, removing her high heels before trudging into the sand. They walked north for about five minutes, seeing no one, and then turned south, walking until they passed the house and continued for another five minutes in that direction.

"There's no one out here," Felicia said, annoyed. "Let's go back."

"We're finally alone," Ferrante said to her, smiling and moving closer.

"Don't make me smack you, Nick. I can see the apple didn't fall far from the tree."

Ferrante laughed and started to walk back toward the house. Something up by the beach dunes caught his eye. He motioned for Felicia to follow him, and seconds later Felicia screamed upon seeing Cameron's body. Ferrante looked around and saw what appeared to be another dead body lying face down, but as he walked closer he saw the person was breathing.

"This guy over here must have passed out," Ferrante said.

"What the hell should we do?" Felicia asked, shaking and unable to keep herself from staring at Cameron's body.

"What do you think? Call the police," Ferrante said.

"Are you sure?"

"Of course I'm sure. There's been a homicide out here."

The slumbering Nelson began to stir before the police arrived, and Felicia told Ferrante she recognized him as the man who'd come to the party with Cameron. Soon the beach was crawling with police. As one team dealt with the body and the crime scene, another escorted Ferrante, Felicia, and Nelson back inside the house to question them. The officials out on the beach found a gun in the sand, about 20 yards from Cameron's body.

The police asked Ferrante if he minded showing them private, separate rooms where they could speak to Felicia and Nelson individually. A couple of cops remained in the kitchen with him while a nervous Patricia made coffee for everyone.

Felicia was the first to be dismissed, and an officer offered to drive her home if she was too distraught to do it herself. Felicia politely declined and headed out.

While Ferrante and Nelson were still being questioned in different parts of the house, detectives ran background checks. They learned that a police report was filed in Orlando a couple of weeks earlier, after Cameron told officers his partner had accused him of seeing another man and threatened to kill both of them. The report stated that Nelson was questioned by police and denied the allegations, and there was no further action taken.

The police also checked the gun found in the sand for fingerprints, and after running the prints through the database a match was found: Nelson.

A few minutes later, Nelson was read his rights, handcuffed, and escorted from the Ferrante home. Police thanked Ferrante for his time, said they'd likely be in touch for further questioning, and left. Ferrante poured he and Patricia each a shot of tequila and they collapsed onto a couch together.

The subsequent news headlines and social media feeds were filled with speculation, regarding the alleged lovers' quarrel that resulted in the murder of the journalist who'd written the touching *#BookClubWidowers* article.

Julio was inconsolable when he heard the news. Susannah alternated between tending to a crying Adriana and her sobbing husband. He went out to the backyard, and Susannah looked out the window and saw Julio literally kicking a tree. Adriana seemed to cry harder with every kick, as if she could feel her mother's tension. Susannah had never seen Julio so upset.

Tom called Rory right away, and Rory sat with him for hours to help Tom fight off the powerful urge to drown his sadness in a bottle. Tom blamed himself for getting Cameron and Nelson invited to Ferrante's party in the first place. Rory reasoned that if Nelson was going to commit a crime of passion against his partner, it could have happened in any setting. Tom wanted to tell Connor about what happened before Connor read about it on the Internet, and Rory helped him think through his approach.

Beth cried until she could barely breathe, and Ben did his best to shelter Maddie from seeing her mother's condition.

"Nelson couldn't have done this," Beth kept saying over and over. Ben responded, "We don't know what their life was like behind closed doors."

He poured her a shot of whiskey. "Drink this. It'll help." Beth stared at the glass for a moment, and then sighed and threw it back.

Phil called Amanda to talk to her about Cameron's death. His life's work in the humanities suddenly felt irrelevant and trivial: "Human creativity and ingenuity can't mitigate the dark impulses that people can unleash without warning," he'd told Amanda, who simply listened and empathized. "In a moment of extreme stress or anger, the best among us can simply snap. No one gets a pass."

Russ stared through a front window of Mario's house. Despite Nelson's arrest and arraignment, he remained certain that the package had come from Nick Ferrante.

Mario thought that sounded ridiculous: "Why would a sports executive and a restaurant owner want to kill a newspaper reporter? He doesn't strike me as the type."

"What does he strike you as?" Russ asked.

"I don't know, Russ. I don't know Nick Ferrante."

When Sarosky and Rice predictably stopped by to question them about yet another dead acquaintance, Russ didn't share his opinion with the detectives.

"Love can make people crazy," Mario said after the detectives left. "I've seen it firsthand. It's a dangerous business. That's why I'm done with it."

Russ smirked. *"You're* done with love?"

Mario nodded. "Have you seen me anywhere near a woman since Heather died? I'm enjoying spending time with my grandson, and doing what I can to run a business in the midst of all these distractions."

Cameron's Winter Park funeral was attended by newspaper colleagues, friends, and relatives, and was officiated by a Catholic priest chosen by the Brock family. Ben; Beth; Sarosky; Rice; and Phil attended, but didn't approach any of the devastated family members. Nelson's family members didn't show up. The ubiquitous members of the press were ignored.

The priest offered a brief homily, and invited a few words from family and friends. Cameron's beloved older brother Josh "The Jock" Brock spoke poignantly of Cameron's character and heart, gripping the podium tightly and fighting back tears.

The O'Rourke, Solomon, and Blakely families prepared for another round of holiday celebrations without their respective mothers. Ben and Beth again invited everyone over for New Year's Eve, and it was Amanda's first opportunity to meet the McBrides and Connor Blakely. Maddie loved Amanda, as expected. Beth talked to Amanda about cross-training while Amanda talked about yoga.

Russ politely declined the invitation and said he, Pete, and Mario were going to enjoy a quiet evening at home. Audrey was disappointed, and she and Pete texted back and forth the entire evening.

The gathering broke up long before midnight. Ben and Beth turned on their bedroom television. Just as the Times Square ball was about to drop in front of the screaming masses, Ben looked over at Beth and saw she'd already fallen asleep while reading. He lowered the volume and watched silently as the minutes bled into 2014 and all of its potential outcomes.

Chapter Sixty-Six

JAN. 6, 2014

The first to present that day, Ben was being grilled by his vice president, Ivan Huerta. He'd not expected this level of questioning about the previous quarter's results. Ben glanced around the room at his peers and saw them shifting uncomfortably.

"You seem tired today, Ben," Ivan said. "Are you okay?"

"Yeah, I was up a little late working on this," Ben said. "I'm fine."

"You just don't seem like yourself," Ivan continued. "I'm hearing you talk about your business, but there's not the usual depth that you bring to the table. It's almost like you took this presentation for granted."

Ben smiled, trying to stay collected. "You've known me long enough, Ivan, to know that's not the case."

"I agree," Ivan said. "But you're throwing excuses at me today. You're saying things that your leaders are going to do, but I'm not hearing about what solutions you're leading with your team right now to make these numbers move in the right direction."

Ben nodded. "I understand."

"Why don't you take a break for now?" Ivan suggested. "Let the others go. It'll give you some time to collect your thoughts, and then after lunch you can come back up. Fair enough?"

"Fair enough," Ben said.

Ben sat down, wiping perspiration from his face. Ivan called for a short break, and the other men and women quickly headed out of the room to check email, return phone calls, and use the restroom.

Fair enough, Ben repeated to himself as he sat there, alone. He dwelled on the word, "enough." *How much was 'enough?'*

Ben's director colleague from Georgia, April Mason, came back into the room and sat down beside him.

"Are you okay?" she asked.

"Yeah. Not my best performance, I guess."

"Happens to each of us sometimes."

Ben looked at the stack of papers in front of him.

"Can I ask you a question, April?"

"Sure," she replied.

"How much do you think is 'enough'? I mean, really enough?"

"Enough what?"

Ben stood, and paced around. "How high is the number supposed to get? We hit our stretch goals, and we celebrate for about five seconds. Then, we find out that some district in California is blowing our number out of the water, so we raise the quotas again. At what point do we say, 'We're doing awesome, let's maintain what we're doing and not lose momentum?'"

April nodded, but didn't say anything.

"Will anyone at the C-suite level ever have the guts to admit that we can't go any further without getting way into the gray?"

"I don't think so," April said. "I don't know if they'd recognize the gray anymore."

Rice was sleeping soundly next to him. Sarosky crept out of bed, and walked wearily across the house to the extra bedroom that served as his office. He studied his personal white board, where he'd duplicated and then expanded his mind-mapping efforts.

Holding a marker in his hand Sarosky slowly scanned each section, taking a couple of deep breaths in an effort to focus. His eyes eventually settled upon one person's name, and Sarosky tapped the marker on the board several times.

Chapter Sixty-Seven

JAN. 11

Tom was pleased to see Rory's name flash across his cell phone screen. His sponsor no longer called every night to check on him, as Rory had done during Tom's early months of sobriety. Rain Dog stirred a bit as Tom sat up in bed.

Rory's voice had none of the cheerful, calm flavor that Tom was used to. "I gotta talk to someone," Rory said. "Can you come over?"

Tom drove, anxious, having no idea what to expect. When he arrived at Rory's small house near Bellaire Plaza, he was greeted by a sponsor who wouldn't make eye contact.

"Come on in," Rory said. "Thanks for coming."

Rory sunk down into a small leather couch in the front room. Tom sat in a recliner, and waited.

"I tried to call my daughter Rosalie tonight," Rory said. "Her husband said she still won't come to the phone. It's been two years since I tried to call her. Two goddamned years. I've been building up my courage, and finally took my chance tonight."

"I'm really sorry, Rory," Tom said.

"I couldn't take it," Rory continued. "I went down to the corner and bought a bottle of Jose. I drank half of it before coming to my senses, and smashing the fucking thing against the kitchen wall."

Ton sat there, stunned, as Rory buried his face in his hands.

"Six goddamned years down the drain," Rory said. "I can't face those guys in the group this week. I can't be anyone's sponsor."

Tom got up and sat next to Rory, wrapping an arm around him. The comfort of Tom's touch unleashed a flow of sobs from the big man.

"I don't need you as a sponsor," Tom said softly. "I need you as a friend."

Rory cried for a long while, unable to say anything else. Tom rubbed his back and waited.

"Can I get you a glass of water from the kitchen?" he finally asked. Rory nodded.

Tom was shaking as he walked. He saw the familiar baby picture of Rosalie that Rory kept on his refrigerator. Tom stared at the baby's face and toothless smile, as the water cascaded into the glass from the dispenser.

He sat next to Rory again, and handed him the water.

"You're not defined by one small setback," Tom said. "You're defined by your journey. And your journey is strong. Nothing in the 12 Steps says we have to be perfect. We admit our powerlessness and surrender anew each day."

Rory was sipping the water and calming down, wiping the tears away. He nodded and reached over to Tom to give him a hug.

"I don't know what to do next," Rory said. "I don't know whether to try calling again, or writing her a letter. Maybe she'll read the letter if I send it to her. Then at least I can express my feelings to her."

"A letter makes sense," Tom said. "Just the act of writing it will be healthy for you."

"Yeah," Rory said. "Even if I never mail it to her."

Rory grabbed his worn AA book from the coffee table.

"Let's read the steps together, okay buddy?" Rory asked, and Tom nodded. Together, they held the book and read through each of the Twelve Steps that had helped alcoholics recover for the past 80 years.

"Let's say the prayer together," Rory said next, and reached out his meaty hands for Tom's.

"God, grant me the serenity to accept the things I cannot change, the power to change the things I can, and the wisdom to know the difference."

Julio had visited people in jail before, but never with this level of security. He sat on the "freedom side" of a thick, glass panel, and watched as a handcuffed Nelson was led in to the other side by a couple of guards. One of them released the cuffs while the other stood two feet away, brandishing a Billy club and ready to strike if Nelson dared make a suspicious move.

Nelson, his face pale, stared through the glass at Julio. Julio picked up his telephone receiver, and motioned for Nelson to do the same.

"You remember me? I'm Julio, the bartender from Famoso's. Cameron was a good friend of mine."

Nelson looked at him for a long moment. "Yeah, I remember you."

Julio tried to keep his composure. "He was a great guy," he said. "Please, please, tell me something that helps me believe you didn't really shoot him in the head."

Nelson's eyes grew watery. "I loved Cameron," he said in a low voice. "I didn't kill him. I don't know what happened, because I passed out and when I woke up I was in custody. I didn't kill him. I could never hurt him, or anybody."

Julio shook his head. "Then why was there a gun with your prints right next to you? If you didn't pull the trigger, who did?"

"I don't know, Julio. I've played the scene over a billion times in my head since I've been here. All I can remember is Cameron going off for a little while to speak with Nick Ferrante, and me chatting with some other people I'd just met. And then Cameron showing back up with these two guys that had fresh drinks for each of us."

"What two guys?" Julio asked.

"I don't know. Two guys I hadn't met before."

"What did they look like?"

The guards remained close to Nelson. Julio wondered how much time they had left.

"I've tried to describe them to my lawyer," Nelson continued. "Their faces are kind of blurry in my memory. One guy was definitely thick and broad-shouldered, and looked like he might have been a linebacker. The other was more my build, kind of thin, and younger."

Julio pondered this. "You said they brought you a drink. What kind of drink?"

"I don't remember," Nelson said.

"Did the police do any kind of blood test on you after you were arrested?"

"No."

Julio smacked the counter in front of him with his palm, and saw the guards pay closer attention to him.

"What is it?" Nelson asked.

"Nothing," Julio said, looking down.

"Do you believe me, Julio? Because I really need someone to believe me. Every day in here I want to die, and part of that is because everyone believes I killed the man I love."

"I believe you," Julio whispered. "I'll do what I can to help."

"I appreciate that," Nelson said. "That will give me enough mileage to make it in here for a few more days."

"Do whatever you can to survive," Julio said. "Hopefully this nightmare will end soon."

The guards came forward and motioned for Nelson to stand. Julio watched as they re-cuffed him, and Nelson smiled for the first and only time during their visit before they escorted him away.

Chapter Sixty-Eight

JAN. 12

Tom and Connor arrived at the Volusia County Animal Shelter about 10 minutes before the new volunteer training was scheduled to begin. Immediately upon entering the lobby they were greeted with a cacophony of cries from caged kittens vying for attention. Innumerable dogs barked loudly from deeper inside the building.

"Let's go see the dogs, Dad," Connor said. "We have time."

"We can't take another one home," Tom warned.

"I know."

They approached the front desk, where three women were juggling phone calls, the finalization of adoptions, and conversations with others who were there for training. Tom checked to make sure it was okay to go back and see the dogs, and they left the lobby to proceed down a hallway.

The barking grew louder and more intense. To their left was an open room full of cages of adult cats.

"These are the cats nobody wants," Connor said. "They want the kittens, so they put those in the lobby. But these guys look more special."

Tom was never fond of cats, but patiently obliged as Connor greeted several of them.

"Ready to see the dogs?" Tom asked.

"Sure. But let's not forget about these cats. They need love and homes, too."

"We won't forget."

They went back into the hallway and found the kennels. The barking concert grew almost deafening. Connor led the way along the first row of cages. The residents were mostly larger, adult dogs, with a couple of smaller breeds here and there. Connor identified three particular dogs he wanted to visit with, but Tom insisted on waiting until after the training class.

"Rain Dog needs a friend," Connor said to each of his favorite three animals. "Do you want to be Rain Dog's friend?"

Connor had been beating the second dog drum since well before the holidays. Tom was running out of reasons to say no, especially since he had lots of time on his hands these days. In addition, Connor had become stellar at feeding and walking Rain Dog.

"People need other people," Connor said, kneeling before a kennel with a large, brown resident. "Just like you need your AA friends, Dad. Dogs need other dogs." He laughed as the dog licked his fingers. "I want to walk this guy for sure. Can we come here a couple of times per week and volunteer to walk the dogs?"

"I don't see why not. But let's get to the class now, so that they'll let us volunteer to begin with."

Connor stood up, reluctant to leave his new friends. "Is the class going to be boring?"

"Yes," Tom admitted. "But it's a necessary hoop we have to jump through."

"Do you think they're going to have food for us?" Connor asked as they left the kennel area and walked back up the hallway toward the lobby. "It's almost dinner time."

"I doubt it. And I'm not sure we'd like the food they have here."

"Are you saying they'd offer us dog or cat food?"

"Well, they're on a budget."

During the class, Tom nudged Connor every few minutes to stop playing on his phone. His son had scant interest in the verbalized list of details the tall, lanky fellow in the front was working his way through: the dog walking schedule, how volunteers signed in and signed out, how many active volunteers they had at the moment and so forth. There were volunteers needed to feed the cats and change their water. Tom asked Connor if he'd heard that last part, but Connor simply looked up from his phone with a blank stare.

We just want to walk your homeless dogs, Tom thought. *Can we cut to the chase?*

Despite paying very little attention during the training class itself, Connor was one of the last of the new volunteers to leave. Tom smiled as his son grilled the instructor, whose name was Walter, with questions about the animals. Tom heard Walter utter the phrase "no-kill shelter."

"We need more teenagers to show up regularly to walk the dogs," Walter told Connor. "Do you think you can do that?"

274

"I can come every day. My dad doesn't work." Connor pointed to Tom, who smiled at Walter and shrugged.

"Well, that's perfect," Walter said. "You'll find lots of different personalities. It'll teach you a lot about dogs, and a lot about life."

Connor gave Walter a quick summary of Rain Dog's rescue story. Walter finally excused himself, and Connor grabbed his father's arm and led him back toward the kennels.

"We probably need to find a staffer or volunteer to open the kennel and let us walk a dog," Tom advised.

"We *are* volunteers now, Dad."

"I don't think we get to start immediately, Connor."

"Well, that's stupid. What more do they have to teach us? We know how to walk dogs."

Tom flagged down a staff member, and a few minutes later they were outside on the fenced-in property, walking a Shepard-Boxer mix named Carlos. Connor asked if the dog was Hispanic, and Tom explained that dogs were dogs and miraculously understood "eat" and "walk" in any language.

"That's pretty cool," Connor said. "Dogs understand what people are saying more than people understand each other a lot of the time."

"That's probably true," Tom said.

Carlos dragged Connor along at a rapid pace, sniffing his way across the property.

"I like this guy a lot," Connor said. "Do you think he's the one?"

"I think we should meet a few more dogs first, to make sure, before adopting the first dog we see."

"You didn't do that with Rain Dog. You didn't keep driving to see if there were any more dogs out there. You found one who needed a loving home, and you made a decision."

"That was different. Let's just give it a few days. Let's walk a few other dogs."

Connor sighed. "Carlos won't understand why he's not coming home with us."

"Carlos will forget about us as soon as he sees someone else or gets some food." Tom looked at his watch. "Besides, I think Rain Dog is ready for his dinner and a walk. We'll come back tomorrow, maybe."

"Okay. Promise?"

"Maybe."

Connor knelt beside Carlos and gave him a kiss on the top of his head. "I can't believe somebody didn't want you, Carlos."

Tom smiled. "That's one of the best things about you, Connor. You have a heart for every person and animal you come across. I learn a lot from you."

～～

Russ and Pete were having a very different conversation. It was a confrontation that Russ had been dreading for the past couple of weeks as he observed his son's behavior, but one he had to follow through on now that he'd searched Pete's room and found a stash of weed.

Pete was immediately pissed off, as Russ knew he would be, and demanded the return of his contraband. Russ refused, saying it was natural for teens his age to "mess around with this stuff," but there was no way Pete was going to keep it at Mario's house.

"Have you told Grandpa about this?" Pete asked, standing just inches away from his father.

"No. He'd be even more pissed than I am."

"Why would he care? He'd probably hire me to work for him. He makes money selling drugs."

Now Russ was annoyed at both Pete and Mario. "Why the hell would you say that?"

"I'm not stupid, Dad."

"Didn't say you were stupid," Russ said. "But don't believe everything you hear about people."

"Mr. Reid was a drug dealer. Wasn't it obvious?"

"No. And you're trying to draw attention away from the issue here. The issue is that you're not going to bring pot into this house."

"I want it back," Pete declared. "I'll take it out of the house. I'll bring it to a friend's house."

Russ smiled. "Ok. Which friend?"

"Don't worry about it."

Pete stepped closer, his nostrils flaring. Russ really wanted to smack him.

"I already got rid of it. I flushed it."

Without warning, Pete shoved his father in the chest as hard as he could. Russ tumbled backward, trying to regain his balance and catching himself just before falling onto Pete's bed. He prepared for Pete to attack again, but the kid got scared and took a few steps away from his father. Russ lunged toward him and grabbed the front of his shirt.

"Don't ever lay a hand on me again. You got that, you little shit?"

Pete made no effort to break free. "Why? Will you send one of your Cubists over to break my legs?"

"If you want to keep living here, you won't bring drugs into the house," Russ

276

said. "And if the cops catch you and your friends with pot, you'll go to jail. This isn't Colorado, you know."

"Well, maybe I'll move there."

"Be my guest," Russ said, and released his grip on Pete's shirt. He stormed out of Pete's room, and heard the boy slam the door.

~~~

Ben replayed the conversation over and over as he drove home from Jacksonville, second-guessing each phrase and word choice. It was the first time he'd had to fire one of his district managers.

"You've got tremendous talent in many areas," Ben had told Stephen, who was a DM for about three years with very inconsistent results. "And lots of experience. You'll be successful in another environment, I'm certain. What Next Gen needs right now is a different skill set than what you bring to the table."

Stephen didn't say a lot during the conversation. The guy knew the decision had already been made, and that getting fired at some point in one's career was simply a reality of the sales business. It was probably just a matter of time until Ben himself was let go, Ben thought. It had happened early in his career, and there was no reason why it couldn't happen again.

Ben felt envious of Phil and Tom as he drove. Phil had a creative, tenured position at a place he could probably work the rest of his life. Tom had taken lots of financial risks across the years that had paid off for him. Ben, on the other hand, would spend the foreseeable future dealing with employee issues and constant pressure to drive a metric higher and higher. During afternoons like today, he wanted to run away from it all.

The work days were growing longer, and Beth was really getting annoyed with him again. Ben had come to dread walking into the house and seeing the look on her face, even when her words were pleasant. He'd go straight to Maddie if she was still awake and try not to interact with Beth right away. Ben was also getting into the habit of staying up later than Beth, unable to wind down his mind.

He was surprised, then, when Beth greeted him with a huge hug and even kissed him on the mouth. She'd made a wonderful dinner of chicken; roasted potatoes; salad; and French bread.

"Mommy's celebrating!" Maddie said as Ben swung her around.

"Celebrating what?" he asked.

"Just life, Daddy. L-I-F!"

Beth smiled and quickly pointed to her stomach. Ben felt his eyes widen and hugged her close. She stayed in his arms for a long time, and Maddie came forward and wrapped her arms around both of her parents' legs.

"Family hug time!"

It was very hard to not tell Maddie about her impending big sisterhood, but Beth insisted they wait a couple of months. She and Ben talked excitedly after Maddie went to sleep, making plans for converting the guest room into a nursery and already debating names of boys and girls.

Everything was great until Beth fell asleep, and Ben started thinking about work again. He lay in the dark for about 20 minutes, then grabbed his tablet and tiptoed into the living room where he settled onto the couch.

Surfing to a familiar porn site, Ben sampled a few different free videos until the found the one that resonated the most and got some needed release and relief.

Chapter Sixty-Nine

FEB. 8

Sarosky drove up to the guard shack outside of the Lazano property and showed his identification. He was familiar enough to the security detail by now, and one of them called Russ to let him know they had company.

Shortly thereafter Sarosky sat in Mario's den, once again being charmed by the real estate millionaire and joined by Russ. He noted that Russ looked several years older than when they'd first met.

"How are your parents getting along?" Mario asked.

"They're okay. Their life revolves around doctor's visits now. It's kind of sad."

"I've been fortunate," Mario said. "I don't have to go more than a few times a year at this point. It's the Sicilian bloodline. My grandparents lived a long time and enjoyed relatively good health."

"I wish I had that bloodline," Sarosky said.

Russ looked impatient. "What can we do for you, Detective?"

Sarosky leaned forward in his chair.

"I got a phone call late last night, from a guy who wouldn't tell me his name," Sarosky said. "Seemed very nervous, and said he 'didn't them want them to find out' that we were talking. He told me he recently left his job at a big farmer's market in South Florida, where he was a customer relations specialist. He worked with the vendors, making sure they had had what they needed.

"One day, the guy said, he was at work at the market, and was walking past a table operated by one of their most successful vendors. And he said he saw a woman working there who looked a lot like Emma O'Rourke, based on his recollection from the news and the Internet."

Russ looked at Mario, and then stared at Sarosky.

"He saw Emma at a produce stand?"

"A farmer's market. Kind of an elaborate produce stand."

"Yeah, I know what a farmer's market is," Russ said. "What the hell would Emma be doing working in a farmer's market?"

"Beats me," Sarosky said. "And, again, the guy wouldn't tell me his name or even the name of the actual farmer's market. And maybe it was just someone who looked like Emma. But I thought it was worth mentioning to you, and maybe worth checking out. I could go down there, visit several of the markets, show her picture and ask if anyone has seen her."

"Did he say if he'd call you again?" Russ asked.

"He didn't. I practically begged him for a way that I could reach him."

Russ was thinking hard. "We could hit several of the markets down there, and show Emma's pictures to all of the vendors. It's a long shot, but it's all we've got."

"'We?'" Mario asked Russ.

"Yeah," Russ said. "Me and Sarosky here. I'll head down there Friday night, to get an early start Saturday on the biggest farmer's markets in the area. I'll do my research ahead of time. You're welcome to go with me, Mario." Russ's sarcastic tone in that final statement was poorly hidden.

"Maybe you should leave this work to me and the other authorities," Sarosky said. "It's our specialty."

"You guys haven't exactly had a lot of success," Russ said. "No offense."

"None taken."

"I'll bring a couple of my guys with me this weekend," Russ said. He turned to Mario. "Will you hang out with Pete up here?"

"Of course," Mario said. "You two don't seem to be talking these days, anyway."

"Long story," Russ said.

"It's always a long story."

Sarosky stood. "Russ, I trust you'll share any leads with me, if you get any? I'll keep doing the same, of course."

"Of course."

Chapter Seventy

MARCH 1

I want to read all of Hemingway's books," Emma said. "Listen to this paragraph here, where he's talking about how graceful and authentic the bull fighter Romero is: 'Romero's bull-fighting gave real emotion, because he kept the absolute purity of line in his movements and always quietly and calmly let the horns pass him close each time. He did not have to emphasize the closeness.'"

Emma paused, giving her friends a moment to soak in the words.

"I'm totally there, inside the bull ring," she continued. "What a lyrical, beautiful way to make an image come alive. I can see Romero. I can see the bull."

"That's a great gift in life, to be able to see the bull," Jackie said as they laughed. "Us southern women are especially gifted at it."

"It's too bad Hemingway was such a jerk in real life," Kari said. "If he could have been as beautiful and gentle as a man, he might not have been married four times."

"People buy books for a great story," Delphi said. "They don't buy them because they believe the authors are great people."

"What's a 'great person,' anyway?" Beth asked.

"Anyone who can help me lose 15 pounds," Kari said. "So that would be you, Beth!"

"Why, thank you," Beth said. "But, seriously: what makes for a great person? What makes anyone greater than someone else? I mean, each of us does good and bad things to a degree."

"Most of us fall into some vast middle ground," Jackie said.

"Some people are just bad people. Just like we talked about with Claude in Edgar Sawtelle. They don't change. I'm not sure they could if they wanted to," Kari said.

"I don't buy into that," Delphi said. "Not trying to pick a fight with you again, Kari, but I think that's such a nihilistic view of life."

"A do-what view?" Jackie asked, spurring more laughter from the ladies.

～～～

Phil and Amanda sat close together on the couch. Vanessa Porter smiled and glanced at her notes.

"It's been a while," Vanessa said. "Obviously a lot's been going on."

"Yeah, it sure has," Phil said. He looked at Amanda, grateful that she was eager to join him in the counseling session. "I thought it might be good to touch base and get your perspective."

"What kind of perspective do you think you need?"

"Well, we've said to hell with ambiguity," Phil said, smiling at Amanda. She rested a hand on his thigh. "For the longest time we were simply good friends while feeling many things inside. Finally, we let the feelings surface—but privately. Now we've pretty much let the world know that we love each other."

"It took a lot of energy to keep it a secret," Amanda said.

"I'm sure," Vanessa said. "How has the world responded?"

Phil thought for a moment. "Pretty well, overall. My girls really like Amanda. She's connecting with them about once a week; not too often, but frequently enough so they get used to her and get to know her. My parents have been very understanding."

"What about your work?" Vanessa asked, and Amanda laughed.

"Yeah, that's the big one," Amanda said. "I'm very proud of Phil. He finally sat down with the dean and just gave it to him straight: that we're all adults here. Everything is cool."

"As far as I know," Phil added, grinning.

"And my parents like Phil a lot," Amanda said. "That was no surprise."

"It sounds like you both have a lot to celebrate," Vanessa said.

"Yeah, we do," Phil said.

"Let's get back to the perspective ask, then."

Phil looked at Amanda, who squeezed his hand and smiled.

"I suppose it's kind of weird to still be married, and to be in this wonderful relationship," he said. "I don't want to overthink it, but it's just a strange status to have. Everyone else gets to say they're divorced or separated or widowed, and I'm just...whatever you call this."

All three of them shared a laugh.

"Not exactly a road well-traveled, is it?" Vanessa asked.

"No," Phil said.

"I'm just encouraging Phil to not dwell on the whole 'status' thing," Amanda said. "Just embrace things as they are, embrace the season for what it is."

"And she's exactly right," Phil said. "But there's all these expectations you have in cookie-cutter western life. These categories that people fit into: everyone needs to find one and be defined by its characteristics. I don't meet any particular expectations anymore. Amanda doesn't either."

"And that's okay," Amanda said.

"Yeah, it needs to be," Phil said.

Vanessa waited, and then asked, "Who's telling you that you have to find a category?"

"No one in particular. The pressure is more like the water in which a fish swims. It's all around us. It's indigenous."

"That's an interesting way to put it," Vanessa said.

"I guess, in the end, I'm the one who's telling me what I'm supposed to be and do," Phil said. "I've found myself researching cases of people who were legally declared dead after so many years. It's a very morbid habit of mine."

"Is that a step you're thinking of taking regarding Jackie?" Vanessa asked.

"I've encouraged him to wait," Amanda said. "It's way too soon."

"I can't imagine having that conversation with Audrey and Natalie," Phil said. "There's no rush. It would be a purely selfish move on my part, a desire to conform to some category like we've been talking about."

"The memorial service was a big step," Amanda said. "That's more than good enough for a while, I think."

～～～

The woman everyone at the ranch called Jane was shivering, her bed covers pulled up to her chin. *I hope he just comes in and goes to sleep*, she thought.

Jane held her breath at the sound of the cabin door opening. She heard Roger's footsteps as he ambled around, heard him in the kitchen getting a glass of water, and kept her eyes shut as Roger used the bathroom. *Breathe like you're asleep*, Jane coached herself.

Roger crawled into bed next to her, and Jane could hear his own breathing. For what felt like hours Roger said and did nothing, and then Jane's insides turned icy as she felt a calloused hand touch her back.

"Naked already," Roger whispered. "Good girl."

Jane knew better than to go to sleep wearing any clothing. Roger made her suffer for this one night, and the bruises were still visible on her body. Jane continued to pretend to be asleep, trying desperately to keep her breathing steady and hoping Roger would give up and stop touching her.

"I know you're awake, baby doll," he whispered into her ear. "We'll see how easily you pretend to sleep through this." Jane felt his fingers sliding along her thighs, making his way toward her pubic area. "You gotta stop pretending you don't like this. I've caught you smiling. I've heard you moan."

Jane kept up the sleep charade for another minute, and could feel Roger growing frustrated. Suddenly he forced her onto her back and spread her legs apart. Instinctively, Jane raised her right knee as forcefully as she could and hit Roger in the face. He yelled and grabbed his nose. Jane then kicked him as hard as she could, and he cursed and hopped out of the bed.

Where the hell is he going? Jane thought as Roger slammed the door of the cabin on his way out. She sat on the edge of the bed, shaking, trying to decide what to do, and then quickly rummaged through some of her clothing in the nearby dresser. Jane pulled on panties and a pair of jeans, and then fastened the first bra she could find and topped that off with a long-sleeve t-shirt.

Jane was looking for a pair of shoes when she heard the cabin door open again. She ran into the bathroom and slammed the lockless door, pressing her body weight against it in what Jane knew was a futile attempt to keep Roger out.

Nothing happened at first. Jane expected to hear Roger's angry voice, but instead it was Sally who called out to her.

"Jane, sweetie, come on out and let's talk about this," Sally said, knocking on the door. "We can work this out. Let's be reasonable."

Jane waited, still pressing against the door.

"Jane? Are you okay in there?" Sally asked.

Jane held her breath. The other side of the bathroom door grew silent. Then, without warning, the door was yanked open and Jane fell to the ground. She looked up and saw Sally standing there in her robe, flanked by Roger as well as Scott Layman. Roger's nose was bleeding.

"Get up, sweetie," Sally said. "Let's talk about this."

Sally helped Jane up and brought her back over to the bed. She sat next to Jane and then looked up at the men. "Guys, maybe give us a few minutes alone, okay?"

Roger just stood there staring with fury at Jane, until Scott nudged him and the two men left the bedroom.

Sally's expression hardened once she and Jane were alone. "Why are you doing this? What do you hope to accomplish?"

Jane glared at her. "I'm trying to accomplish some dignity."

"That's selfish and foolish."

Jane laughed. "How would you know? You're too far gone to have any self-respect left."

Sally slapped her hard across the face. Jane didn't react.

"You came here because you wanted to be here," Sally continued. "There was nothing left for you out there. I came for the same reasons. And now you're being ungrateful. Roger works hard all day long, and you're depriving him of what he deserves."

"You're so fucking brainwashed," Jane said, and Sally slapped her again.

"Listen to me, Jane," Sally said. "Scott and I are going to bring Roger back in here, and you're going to apologize to him. Then, you're going to undress and please him. I'll help out again, since that will soothe his anger. Scott already knows. He's going to supervise, to make sure everything is okay."

"Fuck you."

Sally reached out her hand again, but this time it was to run her fingers through Jane's hair. "It's gonna feel nice," she said. "I'll make sure he's gentle. I'll be gentle with you, too."

Jane started to cry. "There's nothing gentle about him."

"You have to give him a chance. You have to stop resisting. Let yourself love him. Then it will all be better."

"No, it won't," Jane said. "As long as I still have my mind and my heart, it will always be a nightmare."

"You have to surrender. Curtis talks about that all the time in chapel. Surrender. When will you surrender, Jane?"

Jane leaned toward, feeling like she was ready to vomit. Her body was shaking. "The hell with Curtis and his lunatic rants. I'll die before I surrender to this place," she said.

Sally didn't respond right away. Finally, she said, "Is that really what you want, Jane? Do you want to die? Because Scott is authorized now. He can help you with that."

"I don't want to die. I want to leave."

"Don't be ridiculous. The only way to leave here is to die."

Jane looked up at her. "Then fine."

"Then fine? That's it?"

"That's it."

Sally threw her hands up in exasperation. "Wait here," she said, and left the bedroom.

Jane wiped the tears off of her face and blew her nose. She slipped on a pair of sandals and waited. Jane heard the three of them arguing in the kitchen. *This is how it ends,* she thought. *But it's okay.*

The bedroom door opened once again, and Scott led the group back inside. He stood before Jane, smiling.

"Are you sure this is what you want, Jane?" Scott asked.

"Yes," Jane said, refusing to look at Roger. She saw Sally staring at her like a disappointed schoolteacher, and hated her for that. At that moment, she hated Sally even more than she hated Roger.

"Let's take a walk, then," Scott said, reaching for her hand. "Maybe during the walk you'll feel differently. I'll bring you back if you feel differently."

"I'm not going to feel differently," Jane said, and shot a final, defiant look at Roger, who was pressing a cloth against his bloodied nose. Sally attempted to touch Jane on the arm as she walked past, but Jane pulled away from her.

Scott opened the door and escorted Jane out of the cabin. He said nothing at first as they walked across the property. It was dark and no one was around except for the station crews, and they simply nodded or waved at Scott as they walked past.

Jane began to imagine what her execution would entail. She'd heard only rumors, and they varied wildly: *There's a pond where they drown you. There's a cabin where they shoot you. There's poison they make you drink.*

"Are you sure, Jane?" Scott asked again.

"Yes."

They climbed into a golf cart and Scott drove toward the front of the property. *They take you off site, and they shoot you out there; and the world finds you and has no idea who you are and doesn't care, anyway. Not like we care, in here.*

Jane had noticed the small, well-kept cemetery for the few community members who'd already died. Sally told her it was considered a disgrace to die and not be given burial in the cemetery. Those who were taken beyond the property and left out there, dead and rotting, were labeled with the ultimate disgrace of "eternal expulsion."

If you manage to escape, they'll track you down. If you refuse to come back, they'll kill your entire family. If you tell anyone about us, they'll kill whomever you tell.

They were about to pass the final station at the front of the ranch. Scott remained silent. He waved to the men sitting on the folding chairs at the front gate. He stopped the golf cart as they opened the gate without questioning him.

Scott drove onto the side of the two-lane road at the exterior of the ranch. Jane had no idea which direction they were heading.

"Where are we going?" she finally asked him.

"Just a little ways," Scott said. "Relax."

"Relax?"

"Yes."

Jane prayed for a passing car. She would leap out of the golf cart if she had to, and flail her arms and scream to get the driver's attention. Scott would probably start firing his gun at her, if he had a gun, but he might miss and at least she would have a chance.

"It's so peaceful out here," Scott said.

Another couple of minutes passed, and there was no other sign of life on the road. Scott was slowing down. Jane thought about jumping out now and running for it, but didn't know how she would outrun Scott. Maybe she could quickly find a big stick or rock and hurt him before he could do anything. Then, she could get into the golf cart alone and keep driving, until she found something, someone, anything.

Scott stopped the cart. He looked at Jane, and she looked back at him.

"Are you sure this is what you want?" he asked a final time.

"Yes," Jane said. "Do whatever the hell you have to do."

He stared at her. "I can speak to Curtis on your behalf. I can reason with him. I can get you a different cabin, away from Roger."

"You don't have to do that. I don't want to beg Curtis for mercy."

"Okay," Scott said. "Step out of the cart, please."

Jane did so, and waited to see what would happen next.

"Start to walk." Scott pointed in the direction the cart had been heading. "That way, please."

Jane began to walk, expecting at any second to be shot in the back. *It's useless to run,* she thought. *Walk, with dignity. Be in control of your final moment.*

The shot didn't come. Jane refused to look back. With each step she put more distance between herself and Scott. She kept walking into the dark, and the shot still didn't come. Every now and then Jane thought she heard the sound of the golf cart's tires along the gravel on the side of the road, but didn't look back.

When Jane finally paused and glanced behind her, it felt like she had walked at least a mile. She stared into the silent night, and then kept walking.

Chapter Seventy-One

MARCH 9

Dad, did you hear about the airplane?"

Phil was still asleep. It was Sunday morning, and he was used to taking his time getting out of bed on Sundays. Audrey and Natalie rarely came into his bedroom to wake him up unless they really needed something. Audrey was there alone, her cell phone with its ear buds still attached, standing next to his bedside.

"What, sweetie?" he asked, sitting up and stretching.

"Did you hear about the airplane from Malaysia? They can't find it."

"No. What airplane?"

"I was listening to my NPR app," Audrey said, and Phil smiled. He listened to NPR quite a bit, and his oldest daughter had gotten hooked as well. "They said a big jet left Malaysia yesterday, and then disappeared. There were hundreds of people on board. They can't find the plane."

"That's terrible," Phil said.

"I know," Audrey said. "How can you lose an entire airplane full of people? Isn't there, like, way too much technology for that?"

"You would think," Phil said. "That kind of thing rarely happens anymore."

"Do you think they'll find the plane? I worry that it crashed in the water, and they'll never find it."

"I think they'll find it," Phil said. "They always do. Maybe it just went off course and got lost. Maybe they'll all turn up, safe and sound, in a faraway country."

"I hope so," Audrey said, plopping down on Phil's bed. "I want to listen all day. I want to hear any updates."

"It might be on the national news, too," Phil said.

"Do you think it's okay for Natalie to know about this?" Audrey asked. She often tried to shield Natalie from hearing about any kind of crime or tragedy, no matter whom it involved.

"Maybe not," Phil said. "So maybe we shouldn't put on the TV. Just listen to NPR with your ear buds."

"Okay, Dad. I'm sorry that I woke you up."

"It's okay, sweetie. That's a big event."

"What will happen if they never find out anything about the airplane? What will all the family members do? They won't ever know what happened to them."

Phil saw Audrey trying not to cry. He reached out and took her hand.

"They'll do their best to go on," he said.

"I hope they find them soon," Audrey said.

"I do, too."

Jane sipped her coffee slowly. An older black woman sat across from her at the folding table. There were a few other women in the room who hadn't yet gone to bed. It was getting late, but Jane was scared to sleep. Sleep had not been her friend.

"The coffee tastes extra bitter this evening," the woman said.

"Yeah," Jane said, nodding.

"My son is supposed to come get me here this week," the woman continued. "He lives all the way out in California, but he said he's trying to get out of work this week and fly out here. He's supposed to take me to live with him."

"That sounds really good," Jane said.

"What happened to you?" the woman asked her.

Jane looked down at her coffee.

"I'd rather not talk about it. Is that okay?"

"Of course. I'm sorry I intruded."

"It's okay."

"I find it helps me to talk about it some. To tell my story and hear other people's stories. We all got a story worth telling, you know."

Jane hoped the woman would leave soon. "Yeah, I know. I'm just not ready to tell mine yet."

"That's okay, it's okay," the woman assured her. "I once went to a storytelling conference, years ago, when I was involved with the church drama team. Before all of this happened. I remember the fellow up there saying 'a story's got to cook. It's got to cook before it's ready to be served.' I always liked that."

"That makes sense," Jane said.

"So you keep doing that," the woman said, touching Jane's arm. "You let your story cook. And when you're ready, you serve it up to whoever is ready to eat."

"Okay," Jane said.

The woman stood. "I've got to go. I've got to get my stuff packed, in case my son comes. He lives in California, you know. He's trying to get off work. He's got a real important job. He's a vice president."

"That's wonderful," Jane said.

"I'm really proud of him. He moved way out to California, which broke my heart. But I'm really proud of him. You got any children?"

Jane didn't answer. She looked away.

"I'm sorry. There I go, trying to get you to tell your story again when you're not ready to tell it. I'm sorry, miss."

"It's okay," Jane said.

The woman finally left. Jane gripped her coffee mug tightly, and continued to vow to feel nothing. After a few minutes she headed to her room, and prayed for a dreamless rest.

A few more days passed. Martha, the overtly Christian woman who worked at the shelter, gave Jane money to cover her bus fare and a few meals. She escorted Jane to the terminal, and waited around until Jane was safely aboard a Greyhound heading north.

Jane sat alone in a window seat near the rear, staring at the highway as she rode. She was unsure how much time had passed since she walked away from the ranch. Scott had confused her with his mercy, if you could call it that. Martha and the people at the shelter had shown her mercy as well. They'd encouraged her to talk about what happened back at the ranch, but Jane was still too afraid of the possible consequences.

And now, Jane didn't fully understand why she'd suddenly decided to leave the shelter and get on a bus toward home; other than a gnawing instinct that it was time.

The bus made a couple of stops at other terminals and picked up more passengers. Jane observed each of them as they found their seats: an old woman dressed like she was going to a wedding or a funeral. A couple of young women in military service uniforms. A 30-something mother and her young daughter.

The little girl, who had red curls, spotted Jane and smiled. She waved a tiny hand. Jane smiled and waved back. The mother didn't notice the exchange.

Two older women sitting directly in front of her were discussing something they were reading on a tablet. Jane heard enough to piece together that a large group of girls had been kidnapped from their school somewhere in Africa. She realized she had no idea what was happening in the U.S. or the rest of the world.

Jane unzipped the small backpack that Martha had given her. She took out one of the turkey and Swiss sandwiches. There were a couple of bottles of water in the backpack as well.

Each time the bus stopped at a terminal to pick up passengers, Jane's breathing grew more rapid. She was scared that Roger would climb on board, his eyes menacing. Martha and the others at the shelter had assured her that she was safe there, but there was no one on the bus to grant her such assurances.

Jane drifted off to sleep. She dreamt she was walking along a beach, the sun bright and the sand warm. Jane heard the sound of children splashing in the waves. In her dream she felt the cool, salty tide roll across her toes, and gradually woke up with her right hand rubbing her right foot.

The bus finally rolled into the station where Jane was to exit and have the depot workers call her a taxi cab. She felt nervous sitting in the back of the cab, as the driver was a man and didn't speak English very well. Jane watched familiar scenery unfold before her, determined to pay close attention to the taxi's route to make sure the driver wasn't taking her back south toward Roger and the ranch.

Jane alternated between looking out the window for familiar landmarks and stealing glances at the driver's expression. She saw the Mobile station where she often bought gas, the Chick Fil A, and the Walgreens where she bought prescriptions for the family. Her heart was racing; they were almost there. Jane was both thrilled and terrified with the prospect of arriving home.

She saw the Pelican Bay subdivision sign ahead and felt herself stiffen, prepared for the driver to suddenly make a U-turn and take her in the opposite direction. But he proceeded into the neighborhood, passing street signs Jane had long ago memorized and then turning right onto her street.

God, let it still be my street. Jane was panicking, scared that the family had moved and that strangers would be in her house. She debated whether to have the driver wait a minute while she went to the front door, but decided that was foolish. Even if they'd moved surely the *neighbors* wouldn't have moved; at least, not all of them. Someone would know her. Someone would help her.

"Is this it?" the driver asked in broken English. There were two cars parked in the driveway, neither of which Jane recognized; but it was definitely her house. The grass was mowed and the shrubbery she'd once planted looked trimmed and maintained. The mailbox had received a fresh coat of paint since the last time Jane looked at it.

Jane nodded. "Yes."

She grabbed the backpack, and handed the driver enough cash to cover the fare and a small tip.

"Thank you," Jane said, and stepped out onto the driveway. She looked down and saw a couple of small cracks that had gotten larger than she remembered, with a few tiny green weeds peeking through.

Jane wondered if anyone inside had spotted her. She slowly approached the front door, unsure of what to do. It was still her home, as far as she knew, and she was free to simply open the door and walk inside. Jane's keys and anything else she had with her beforehand were long gone, of course, so if the door was locked she would have to ring the doorbell or knock.

For close to a minute Jane stood before the front door, its yellow paint having faded from years of being exposed to the sunlight. Finally she reached for the doorknob and attempted to give it a turn. It didn't budge. Of course it was locked; they had always kept their door locked. *That's just what people did.*

Jane didn't want to ring the doorbell; that felt too impersonal. She saw her hand shaking as formed a partial fist and tapped on the door, so softly that she knew no one would hear. Jane breathed deeply and knocked again, louder this time. She waited, and knocked a couple of more times as she stood trembling.

She jumped when the door suddenly flew open, and Audrey stood there.

Jane started to cry as she saw Audrey's expression go from pleasant anticipation to wide-eyed shock and then tears of her own. Audrey was so much taller, and so beautiful. The girl screamed, "MOM!" and fell against Jane, nearly knocking her over with the force of her embrace.

They stood hugging each other tightly and sobbing with the door wide open, and soon Jane heard other voices and someone called her "Jackie." No one had called her Jackie for a long time, and she'd almost forgotten that was her true name.

Phil Solomon stared at his wife. Before he could say anything else, Natalie rushed past her father and looked up at Jackie and Audrey with a huge smile. Her youngest daughter had several more grown-up teeth since the last time Jackie had seen her. Jackie knelt down, held her arms open wide, and Natalie fell against her as well. Natalie was laughing as much as she was sobbing.

Further inside the house Amanda, along with Tom and Connor, watched the front door scene unfolding from a respectable distance. Whatever the full group had been talking about during their dinner party was long forgotten.

Tom kept shifting his glance between Amanda and Connor. Neither of them had spoken yet; they were simply watching, as Audrey and Natalie gradually led their mother inside the house. Tom watched Phil, saw his ashen face and noticed that Phil had not yet embraced Jackie as his daughters had. Tom looked back at Amanda and saw her forcing a smile through her tears. He glanced at Connor and saw the boy smiling as well while he clutched his sketch pad.

Chapter Seventy-Two

B en sounds like a great guy," Emma said as she and Beth enjoyed their two-for-one margaritas. "Very supportive, helping you launch your business and everything. I couldn't imagine Russ ever doing that. He just wanted me to be a housewife forever, and not go back to practicing law or anything else."

Beth laughed. "Well, Ben didn't have much of a choice. But he has been pretty great about it. Sometimes his workaholism really gets to me, but I'm getting pretty addicted to the studio as well. So I sort of know where he's coming from."

Emma nodded. "How did you guys meet?"

"Believe it or not, at a gym where I worked as a personal trainer."

"Oh," Emma smiled, "was he a client?"

Beth smiled back. "No. that would be unethical, of course."

"Of course."

"How come he never takes your classes at the studio?" Emma asked.

"Well, he's either working or watching Maddie for me. Maybe he'll surprise me and show up one day on a weekday morning in his stretch pants."

Emma sipped her drink. "Oh, I'd love to see that." Beth gave her a quizzical look, and then laughed when she realized Emma was only joking.

~~~

Russ hadn't been home for several weekends in a row. He'd visited every multi-vendor farmer's market he could find in South Florida, spanning from West Palm Beach in the north to Homestead in the south and out west to communities such as Wellington and Pahokee. Russ was sure he was overlooking a few venues, but it was a massive population area to cover.

At each market, Russ patiently trekked from vendor to vendor to show Emma's photograph. At each place, he learned nothing. After the first weekend Russ threw caution to the wind and stopped traveling with his security detail. He wanted to be alone and not have to worry about other people's needs.

He sat in a Starbucks in Deerfield Beach, feeling resigned and exhausted. Russ flipped aimlessly through a notepad he was using to chronicle each market visit. The pages included scribbling, diagrams, and questions. The notebook had become his life, and the search for his ex-wife his part-time job.

He stared at Emma's picture and wondered why he was looking so hard for a woman who couldn't stand him—in order to return her to a son who felt the same way. Russ was tempted to toss the notebook into the trash and move on with his life. Phil was certainly moving on, as was Tom; and those guys were *still married* to their missing wives.

Russ talked himself back into staying the course, reminding himself that Pete would eventually outgrow his teenage sullenness and one day be grateful if his mother were found alive. It was a long-term strategy that drove Russ's efforts, and thinking long-term was good for work and life these days since the present moment sucked.

He closed the notebook and leaned back in his chair, taking a look around the crowded café. South Florida was full of good-looking women. He needed to start dating again, to get some semblance of a life. Maybe he could find a younger woman who was both hot and smart, like Phil had found with that tatted little squeeze Amanda.

A man who looked a few years older than Russ glanced in his direction a couple of times. The guy was standing in line, waiting to order his over-priced coffee or whatever the hell he was getting.

Russ flipped open the notebook again, and found a blank page. On the top, he wrote *PLANS FOR MY FUTURE*. He jotted down several brief statements: *Leave DDC. Move out of Daytona. Find a quiet place.*

He continued to brainstorm, and then had the feeling someone was hovering nearby. Russ looked up, and saw the man from the coffee line holding his cup and smiling.

"Mr. O'Rourke? I'm Scott Layman," the man said, extending his hand. "Mind if I join you?"

Russ stared up at Scott, suspicious of the stranger who knew his name, and then segued into marketing professional mode.

"Sure," he said. "Take a load off."

Scott thanked him and sat down.

"Scott, have we met?" Russ asked. "Forgive me for not remembering. I'm usually pretty good with names and faces."

Scott shook his head. "We haven't met. I've been looking forward to chatting with you, though."

Russ waited.

"You've been working pretty hard at this," Scott said, pointing to the notebook. "But nothing has come of it yet. Am I right?"

"I'm not sure that I follow you."

"Your exhaustive interactions with every farmer's market vendor on the Southeast coast of Florida," Scott said. "All it's given you is a somewhat healthier diet on the weekends. It's good that you're buying some of the fruits and vegetables along the way, although I do notice that you have an appetite for the free bread and chocolate samples as well."

Russ folded his arms. "You seem to know a lot about how I spend my time."

"I network with a lot of these markets," Scott said. "It's my job to know what's going on. They all seem to know you. It wasn't hard to learn who you were and what you were up to."

"Am I doing something illegal? Am I trespassing?"

"Not at all," Scott replied.

"Am I harassing people?"

"Nope. Although I'm sure you have the potential in you." Scott laughed at this own joke, but Russ was impassive.

"Then what can I do for you, Mr. Layman?"

Scott reached into his shirt pocket and handed Russ a card, which simply bore Scott's name and the title *ORGANIC PRODUCE* as well as a phone number.

"What is it you want?" Russ asked. "Do you want me to go like your Facebook page or something?"

"What is it that *you* want?"

"Don't play games. You know what I want." Russ was growing irritated. "If you have a lead for me, then say it. If not, I'm going to be on my way."

Scott glanced at his watch. "We have to get going. You're going to have to trust me. The rest of this journey you're on today is about show and not tell."

"Why the hell would I trust you?"

"Do you have any other options right now? Is anyone else coming over to the table to help you try to find her?"

Russ watched Scott stand up. He stayed in his chair.

"You'll leave your car here," Scott said. "Lock all of your personal belongings inside of it. You don't ask any questions until we're on our way together, in my car."

"On our way where?"

"That was a question, Russ."

"You're trying my patience, Scott."

Scott smiled. "I'll be out in the parking lot. You'll see me sitting in my car. Waiting."

Russ watched him go, utterly bewildered. The more he thought about Scott's name, the more familiar it sounded. But he had no context. Through the windows, Russ saw Scott get into a silver KIA.

He thought about Henry, Heather, and Cameron, and still wondered about Delphi. All dead. Russ knew very well that he could be the next to succumb to a mysterious fate. If they wanted to kill him badly enough, he would die whether or not he tagged along with Scott Layman

Russ wondered who else in the busy Starbucks knew his name, and felt a grip of paranoia as he glanced around. He finally got up and went out to his car, glancing at Scott as he passed the KIA.

Ben had fallen asleep on the couch. He never did that; he was always careful about shutting off the tablet and quietly easing his way back into the bed next to Beth.

He felt fingers gently tapping his arm, and gradually opened his eyes. Beth was sitting next to him on the couch, holding his tablet, looking unsettled and like she might have been crying.

"I thought you might want to come back to bed," she said. "Or would you prefer to stay here?"

Ben stretched, smiling and trying not to overreact. "I fell asleep. Let's get back to bed."

He stood, but Beth stayed put, absent-mindedly rubbing her pregnant belly.

"You must have been really tired," she said.

"Yeah, I guess so."

"You look pretty tired all the time these days," Beth added. She still hadn't made any effort to get up.

"The job is pretty relentless. I'm starting to hate it. That's never happened before."

Ben plopped back down. He looked at the tablet in her hands, and then back up at his wife.

"You know that I'm not freaked out by this kind of stuff," Beth said. "We dabbled in it some together when we were first going out. It can give a couple a bit of a sexy edge. The fantasizing can be fun."

"Yeah," Ben said.

"I just need to know if there's anything happening besides fantasy," she continued. "Because you haven't exactly been proactive in the bedroom, and I'm having a hard time believing you're fully satisfied with strangers on a small flat screen."

Beth handed the tablet back to him, and waited.

"No, there's nothing happening, Beth," he said, moving closer to her. "You know I wouldn't do that."

"I don't think you would," Beth said. "But I can't go so far as to say I 'know' you wouldn't do it. I don't think any wife can say that about any husband. No one can predict the future."

Ben laughed. "Well, I guess any person, male or female, could say the same thing about their partner."

Beth nodded. "Yes, they could. And I would never ask you if you were having an affair just for the sake of asking. But when you're kissing me a lot less and screwing me hardly ever, it makes me curious. And you can't blame the pregnancy, because we were like rabbits when I was pregnant with Maddie."

Ben smiled. "I understand."

He reached for her hand. She took it, but without a lot of warmth.

"I love you, Beth. More than ever."

"I love you, too. I don't doubt your love."

"Good. You shouldn't."

"I have another question," she said. "Have you ever been tempted? I mean, really tempted? You travel a lot. You're in hotels a lot. I would never know."

Ben immediately thought back to Chicago and the conference where he'd met Allison the previous year. He had to make a quick decision. Stating that he'd never been tempted would sound like a stretch, and it was untrue. Ben's decision was to gamble with the truth.

"I had an opportunity to sleep with a woman I met at a conference last year, in Chicago," Ben said, looking Beth straight in the eyes. "She was being very assertive. She asked me to join her in her hotel room. I declined. I called you, instead."

Beth waited to see if Ben had more to say, and then nodded. "Is that it?"

"That's it."

"You didn't talk to or see her again?" she asked.

"I didn't."

"Did you wish you had?"

Ben wasn't expecting that type of follow-up question.

"No. It would have made me feel horrible."

Beth nodded, and pointed to Ben's tablet. "But you wish you could have sex with those women in the videos that you watch every night after I fall asleep."

"I don't know. I don't think I want them in particular. It just feels good to be mindless for a few minutes, and to blow off some stress."

Beth nodded. "I get that." She pointed to her belly. "Please try to understand that I'm a little more vulnerable in my emotions these days. You know what I mean?"

"Yeah, I know."

"Some women feel extra hot and attractive during pregnancy. I did with Maddie. That hasn't kicked in yet with Baby No. 2."

"I understand," Ben said, then added with a smile, "I think you look hotter than ever, though."

She leaned forward and kissed him. "Thank you, you're sweet. What I'm saying, Ben, is that even if I'm actually not the hottest thing in the world right now, I'd like to be your first choice when you need to blow off stress."

Ben smiled. "Okay. You will be. You are." He kissed her back.

"And you know that as your best friend, I'd like to be your first and main choice when you need to talk about that stress in detail. I could probably handle you having a one-night stand, although I'd be pissed and upset for quite a while. I'd get over it. I don't think I could handle you giving your heart and mind away to someone else."

Ben pulled her closer, and touched her belly himself. "That's not going to happen," he said. "I don't need and want anyone else but you. It took a long time for me to meet the person I wanted to marry, and I'm not going to let her go. Ever."

They held each other tightly for a long moment, saying nothing. Ben wondered if she'd fallen asleep in his arms.

"I want out of this job," he whispered, not sure if Beth could hear him. "I don't know how to get out. There's too much to lose."

Beth kissed his neck and pulled back slightly so she could see him. "You know that I'd never ask you to stay in a job you hate. You have other options. You've got an incredible resume and an incredible network."

"Yeah, I know," Ben said. "I'm just worried that it's the same everywhere else. That it's never enough, and that's the universe in which we live and work. Everyone has hopped onto the same treadmill that's operating out of control, and no one knows how to jump off."

"Maybe you don't have to jump. Maybe you can just slow it down."

"Maybe," he said. "But someone is going to have to show me how to do that. Because I'm out of answers."

"Forget looking for answers anymore tonight. Let's go back to bed," Beth said, standing and reaching for his hand. They walked arm in arm back to the bedroom. The tablet remained on the couch.

Beth lay on her back. Ben leaned over and gently rested the right side of his face on her stomach, listening for the life within her. She smiled and rubbed his hair a bit with her fingers. After a couple of minutes he moved his face up to her breasts, and kissed her flesh several times.

"They've gotten bigger," she said. "Do you like that?"

"I sure do," he said.

"That part makes me feel hotter, at least."

He kissed her shoulder and neck. "How does that make you feel?"

"Even hotter."

"Good."

"But you're exhausted," she said. "We should get to sleep."

"Yeah, I know," he said.

"Spoon me and put your hand on the baby. I want to fall asleep like that. It helps me feel secure."

Ben adjusted and did as she requested. Before long he heard the familiar cadence of Beth's breathing, and soon he also was asleep at last.

A few minutes later, a phone call from Phil Solomon woke both of them.

Chapter Seventy-Three

MARCH 10

Beth peeked inside of Maddie's room to make sure she was asleep. She smiled at the sound of the little girl's gentle breathing. Beth shut the door all the way, and went back to the living room where Ben and their guests awaited her.

Phil and Jackie sat together on the love seat, resembling a couple in the awkward getting-to-know-you stage. Tom sat on the couch next to Ben, and Beth plopped down on the other side of her husband.

"How are the girls doing?" Beth asked.

"We're having fun catching up," Jackie said. "All day long they think of new things to tell me. They've grown so much. I'm grateful for all the selfies and other pictures they took. And Natalie's letters left me bawling."

"There's no shortage of tears right now," Phil said.

"Is Mario coming over?" Tom asked Ben.

"No, we invited him. He appreciated being asked, but prefers that we fill him in later."

There was a soft knock at the front door, and Ben checked the peep hole to see who it was. The group greeted Sarosky and Rice as they came in and sat down in an adjacent chair.

"Mrs. Solomon, it's wonderful to meet you at last," Sarosky said. "I really appreciate you calling me and inviting me here tonight."

"Thanks for coming," Jackie said, as Rice gave her a hug.

Jackie took a deep breath. Phil patted her on the leg, and she forced a smile.

"Detectives, I'm scared as hell. I'm scared for my family and for these people here. I don't know what you're going to do with the information I'm about to share, but I'm begging for your discretion."

Rice nodded. "I understand. You've got it."

"I don't want the press to know about this. These people down there on that ranch might think I'm dead, and I want them to keep thinking that until you catch them by surprise."

"Understood again," Rice responded.

Jackie looked at Beth. "I'm not sure where to begin," she said.

"Just begin at the beginning," Beth said.

Sarosky presented a notepad. "I'm going to take some notes for my own benefit, Jackie. That will help me to retain key details as well as ask you clarifying questions. Is that okay?"

"That's fine," Jackie said.

Sarosky looked at the others in the room. "Is Mr. O'Rourke not able to join us?"

"We don't know where he is," Ben said. "We've tried to get in touch with him for weeks now."

"Mr. Lazano doesn't know of his whereabouts?" Sarosky asked.

"If he does, he's not talking," Tom said.

"Gotcha. Mrs. Solomon, I'm sorry to delay you. Please begin."

"No worries," Jackie said.

She looked at Tom.

"Tom, Kari was there with me, at this big ranch. I have no idea whether she's still there."

Tom stared at her, his mouth open, feeling his eyes moisten. It was several seconds before he could form any words in response.

"That's great to hear! Was she okay last time you saw her?"

Jackie looked away from Tom. "She was fine, physically. Mentally, emotionally …I have no idea who she is anymore."

Tom waited for more.

"She's become this whole other person. They've indoctrinated her. I don't think she would leave even if she could."

"Seriously?" Tom asked. "Even if she could come back to her family? To Connor?"

"I don't know," Jackie said. "I didn't see her for a long time. For the first year, maybe; it was hard to know exactly how much time had passed. But when I did see her, and tried to speak to her, all she wanted to talk about was how she'd finally 'found her path and her place.' When I'd talk about you or Connor, she'd just look at me blankly and go off on some other tangent."

Tom thought through his history with Kari. In general, she was an unhappy person. She was anxious most of the time. But she'd never seemed susceptible to having her complete value and belief system turned on its head. The Kari he knew would never abandon her family. *But,* he thought, *how completely can you know someone, know what someone is capable of becoming or not becoming? How completely can you know yourself, and what choices you might make down the road?*

"She was calling herself 'Sally,'" Jackie added. "I'm not sure how that started. And she cut her hair really short; practically shaved herself bald."

"Sally," Tom repeated. "What the hell?"

"I wonder if you wouldn't mind backing up a bit," Sarosky asked after the group grew silent. "Perhaps tell us what you remember about that night, the night when you arrived at Delphi Adams's condo."

"We had a great trip," Jackie said. "I remember texting Phil and telling him we'd arrived. We had some fun girl talk before falling asleep.

"After falling asleep, I don't remember a whole lot."

"What details can you recall?" Rice asked. "Anything specific will be helpful, even the smallest thing."

"I remember coming in and out of consciousness a lot," Jackie said. "I was in some kind of room. Occasionally I would see faces, and hear voices, but it never felt like anyone was talking directly to me. About me, maybe, but never directly to me."

Phil looked at each of the others, and wondered if they fully believed Jackie's story. He was convincing himself to believe it, unsure if he had any other choice.

"Like I said, I don't know how much time passed by," Jackie continued. "I don't know how long I was out of it, or kept out of it. But one day I was fully awake, and a man who called himself Roger was sitting near where I'd been sleeping. He said he was there to look after me, to help me find my way."

She glanced nervously at Phil.

"Roger took me on a tour of the property, but several other men walked with us. I'd been kept in a small cabin. It was one of many. The property is massive, with a huge garden that apparently is used to grow produce they sell to various places.

"I quickly learned that my 'way' was Roger's way. Or rather, the way of the person who was in charge of the community, whom everyone called Curtis. There were mandatory chapel services each day, during which Curtis would speak about different ideas."

"What kind of ideas?" Sarosky asked.

Jackie reflected. "Economics; the environment; the evils of all the world's religions and governments; that kind of stuff," she said. "Some of it made sense, but a lot of it was just really out there. I didn't really care a whole lot what he had to say. I just wanted to get out of there, but I had no idea regarding where 'there' was. I didn't even know for sure what state I was in, although the weather still felt like Florida and the trees still looked like Florida."

Jackie glanced at Phil again.

"This next part is hard to talk about," she said.

"It's okay," Phil assured her.

"It soon became obvious that Curtis had given me to Roger as his romantic partner." She glanced at Beth, whose face was streaming with tears. "I was forced to live with him in that cabin. Forced to do things. He told me that bad things would happen to me if I resisted, that my family would be hurt if I tried to escape."

Phil put his arm around Jackie.

"Do you need a minute?" Rice asked.

She shook her head. "No, I'll keep going." She looked back at Tom. "I finally saw Kari. She seemed to have a lot more freedom than I did. I was never alone, I was always escorted by Roger or some of the other men, or I was always in their line of sight. Kari didn't greet me like an old friend. She was more like a hostess who was excited that I had come to some big party, and kept rambling on about how glad she was that I'd decided to come to live in their community."

"It's so weird," Beth said.

"Yeah," Jackie nodded. "At some point, a new guy named Scott came on the scene. He seemed to be rather important there from the start. From what I could tell, he and Sally were involved."

Jackie glanced at Tom again but he was staring down.

"I put up with Roger's control and abuse for months and months," she said. "I had no role in the community other than to support Roger, who was a gardener. They sometimes let me work near him in the garden, which I did because I was just glad to have something to do to pass the time.

"I would sometimes ask Roger when I could leave, and he always said for me to be patient, to open myself up to the community, that eventually I wouldn't want to leave. If I persisted, he would grow angry and begin to make threats."

Sarosky looked through his notes. "How did you manage to leave?"

"One night, Kari and Scott came to my cabin at Roger's request, after I'd hurt him," Jackie said. "Scott took me off alone, in a golf cart, across the property. I was terrified. I'd heard rumors that people sometimes simply disappeared. I thought I was either going to be punished or killed. I was scared for my family, that no matter what I did or didn't do they would somehow find the girls and hurt them; that they would hurt Phil, or hurt my parents or his parents."

Jackie continued to visualize her final night at the ranch.

"Scott drove me off of the property, and starting going down some dark road. And then he had me get out, and I thought again that he was going to kill me; and he told me to walk, and I walked. And I kept going, expecting to get shot in the back, but he never followed me. I walked until I couldn't anymore, and eventually I came to a gas station and figured out that I was in Okeechobee County."

Sarosky looked excited. "So you were able to get your bearings," he said. "Where did you go next?"

"I was too scared to go to the police, to tell anyone anything. I had nothing with me but the clothes on my body. I stopped at the first church I could find, and waited outside until someone came around. I told them I was homeless, and woman who worked there drove me to a shelter. And that's where I was until I came home."

"Did you tell anyone in the shelter what had happened?" Phil asked her.

Jackie shook her head. "No. I was still too scared to tell anybody anything. They tried to get me to talk. They tried all kinds of things: to get me into rehab if I needed it, to go to church, to call family or friends. Finally, they helped me get to the Greyhound Bus depot."

"You haven't said anything about Emma," Beth interjected.

"I know," Jackie said. "I don't know for certain whether Emma was there. I'd heard that Curtis had a wife, or some kind of romantic partner of his own. There was a woman who would come into the chapel with him, but she was always wearing sunglasses and some kind of scarf on her head. I never got a close enough look at her to know for sure.

"I asked Roger about her a couple of times, but he told me not to worry about that woman—that she wouldn't harm me, whatever that meant. I never saw her anywhere else except for on the other side of the chapel."

"Do you think," Sarosky asked, "that you could describe the location in Okeechobee County? Do you remember the name of the road you were walking on when you got to the gas station?"

"It was a county road with a number; 714 or something like that," Jackie said. "I was walking east, toward I-95. But I couldn't tell you how many miles I'd walked in the dark during the night. The place where I was kept was somewhere off of that road, I guess. Somewhere west of 95."

Sarosky smiled. "Jackie, this is huge. We're not looking for a needle in a haystack, necessarily. There's only so many ranches that will fit your description. We'll find this place, and find who's there."

"They're dangerous," Jackie said. "They have guns. I don't know what else they have there. I don't know who else they brought there against their will. No one else seemed upset with being there. I'd never felt so alone in my life."

Beth got up and hugged her. Jackie smiled and gently patted Beth's pregnant belly when they broke the embrace.

"Why don't you take a break for a while?" Beth asked. "I'll make you another cup of tea."

"That would be great," Jackie said.

She looked at Tom. "Tom, I'm sorry. I'm so sorry I don't have better news for you and Connor."

"We can help her," Tom said. "We just need to get her out of there. Once she's out of there, she'll come to her senses."

Ben looked at Sarosky and Rice. "Detectives, what's your plan?" he asked.

"When she's ready in a few minutes, I'm going to ask Jackie to give me more detailed descriptions of Curtis, Roger, and Scott, and any other people that seemed particularly significant," Sarosky said. "Then, after we leave here tonight, we're going to have some very secure conversations with our superiors and agencies in Okeechobee who can partner with us. We'll work on getting a search warrant so we can enter the property.

"In the meantime, before we leave, we're going to have some people assigned to escort the Solomons home and guard their house."

Sarosky looked at the others.

"What about the rest of you?" he asked. "Do you feel you need some police protection? Mr. Blakely?"

Tom shrugged. "I don't think so. It sounds like Kari is doing whatever they want her to do, so her family probably isn't in any danger. I have no idea, to be honest, but I'd rather not have people around the house. My son would freak out."

"Mr. and Mrs. McBride? What about you?" Sarosky asked.

Ben looked at Beth, waiting for her to take the lead. "It's okay," she said. "Just focus on protecting Jackie and her family. That's the most important thing right now."

Chapter Seventy-Four

APRIL 5

The man with the long, gray hair and beard seemed to know everyone who was there, both volunteer and visitor. James watched him for a while as the man proceeded across the large room with its long tables. He intuited that it was just a matter of time until they made eye contact and the man initiated a conversation.

James had spoken to no one for the past few days that he'd been staying at the shelter, except for muttering an occasional "thank you" when it was appropriate. So far the volunteers had left him to himself, which he appreciated.

The long-haired man plopped down next to him, and smiled. He extended his hand. "Dan."

James hesitated, and then shook Dan's hand. He thought for a moment before simply responding with, "Curtis."

"Nice to meet you, Curtis," Dan said, sipping from a cup of coffee. He gestured to James's plate and bowl. "Can I get you some more soup or bread? Maybe a sandwich?"

James shook his head. "I'm good, thanks."

"You're kinda young to be here, aren't you?"

James shrugged. "I don't know."

Dan continued, "Not that homelessness has any demographic. I'm just not used to seeing men who barely look 30."

"Well, I didn't expect to be here, either," James said, forcing a smile. The older man seemed genuine.

Dan chuckled. "I bet."

They were silent for a moment.

"Curtis, what happened, if you don't mind me asking?"

James looked closely at Dan, and was tempted to tell him the full, horrible story. Instead, he just shrugged. "Some bad fortune. And one big mistake."

The man nodded. "Well, Curtis, bad fortune and mistakes are going to happen. But you're young enough to grow away from them. More than young enough."

"I hope so," James said. "I'm just trying to catch my breath here and get some perspective. I need some clarity about the path going forward."

Dan stood up. "Stick around at the table for a little while if you don't mind. I'd like to come chat with you some more after I'm done checking on everybody else. You're different from the rest of these guys. Your mind isn't saddled by drugs or alcohol. I can tell."

James nodded. A few minutes later, Dan returned.

"Curtis, I want you to have this," he said, handing James a thin booklet. "You might find it interesting."

James looked at the booklet as Dan wandered off again. He had to read the title twice to get a full sense of it.

The Universe Spares Its Bright Spots.

~~~

Russ sat near the back of the chapel, half-listening to Curtis pontificate about the dangers of mass production. He was more intrigued by studying the expressions of the other people who filled the large room.

Russ's eyes were once again drawn to the woman who sat at the far end of the front pew, not far from where Curtis was speaking. She wore large, dark sunglasses and had her hair up in a scarf, as usual. Russ only saw the woman during chapel, and always from a distance.

Nearly a month had passed since Russ left his car at the Deerfield Starbucks and gone with Scott to the ranch. Scott introduced him to everyone as "Ron," and then brought Russ to a private room to meet with Curtis. Russ hadn't seen Scott since then, which surprised and annoyed him.

During their first and only private meeting, Curtis posed a few questions. He asked Russ "what he was looking for from life," and "what the concept of community meant to him." Curtis briefly described the nature of their organic farming business, how they generated revenue, and how everyone shared everything with everyone else.

"No one here cares where anyone else is from, or what their life was like beforehand," Curtis had said. "We leave our pasts at the door. All that matters here is what we're creating together."

Curtis also asked Russ what kind of work he wanted to do. Everyone had to have some kind of job, Curtis advised, in addition to the required daily journaling. Russ said he preferred to do something with his hands; that he'd always done white collar types of work and was "ready for something more tangible." Curtis asked if he wanted to start off mowing the property, noting that it was a big job and would take up most of his time, and Russ agreed.

Russ couldn't decide whether Curtis was a brilliant visionary or a whack job. He read Curtis's book the first couple of nights he was there. During his hours on the large green riding mower, Russ thought through what he was hearing from his new boss. The guy definitely had a marketing mind. It was easy to become captivated by Curtis's charisma, and Russ had to keep reminding himself why he'd come to the ranch in the first place.

Curtis set Russ up with a fully furnished cabin. Other residents had the job of ensuring that everyone's cabins were stocked with toiletries, linens, and other necessities. The front doors didn't have locks. People were respectful about not barging in on one another, but Curtis said there was no need to lock each other out since they were all family and shared everything.

Russ noticed a small cluster of cabins that were farther away than the others, and closely guarded. He wondered if Curtis and the mysterious woman lived back there.

"I don't think we've met," a younger man said to Russ as he followed the group out of the chapel. "I'm Roger."

"Ron," Russ said.

"I've seen you mowing the property," Roger said. "You do a nice job."

"Thanks," Russ said.

"What did you think of what Curtis said during the service today?"

They were walking in the direction of the cabins. Russ needed to change and get to his riding mower. He doubted he'd retained enough of what Curtis had babbled about to form a sensible response to Roger's question.

"Profound as usual," Russ replied.

"Yeah," Roger said. "He's given me a new life here. I hope you find the same thing."

"Me, too," Russ said. He was close to his cabin.

"Roger, can I ask you a question, please?"

"Sure, Ron."

"There's a woman who always comes into the chapel with Curtis and sits near him. Do you know her name?"

"She goes by 'Lenore,'" Roger said. "They say she's his wife, but no one ever sees or talks to her. Supposedly no one is allowed to speak to her if they do see her."

"Curtis never talks about her during his messages?"

Roger shook his head. "No." He frowned, and lowered his voice to a whisper. "Probably best not to ask more questions about Lenore. People here get suspicious when too many questions are asked."

"I'll remember that," Russ said, smiling.

A short while later Russ steered the riding mower along the property, a baseball cap on his head to avoid sunburn. He cut a section of the land that was quite a distance from any of the buildings. It included a walking trail that led to a small maze-looking area that Curtis had referred to as a prayer labyrinth.

Russ saw a figure moving in his direction along the walking trail. He kept the mower going, occasionally glancing over at the walker. The woman might have been heading to the labyrinth for some alone time, and Russ steered the machine farther away in order to not be a nuisance.

The woman, however, started walking toward him and waving. Russ turned the mower and drove across the grass toward the path, and then came to a stop and killed the ignition. He waited while the woman approached. She was skinny with very short hair. Russ had seen her before in chapel and in the commissary, but didn't know her name.

"I'm Sally," she said, reaching out her hand and taking Russ's sweaty palm in hers.

Chapter Seventy-Five

Beth was focused on the next move in the routine, trying to ignore the weird shakiness. She assumed she hadn't had enough protein, and after getting through the class would eat some Greek yogurt.

She caught herself stretching the water breaks to give herself additional time to rest. There were still 20 minutes left in the class. Beth led the group through the final routine before the cool down. They pedaled the bikes for a minute, dropped to the floor for push-ups, and then ran over to the bags to do alternating kicks.

Suddenly, the class appeared to transition into slow-motion and the room grew darker. Beth felt herself go down to one knee, and had enough cognizance to lay down on a nearby mat before everything went completely black.

When the room became bright again, Beth was sitting up on the mat and two of the women, Arlene and Wendy, were close by asking her if she was okay. The others stood at a respectable distance, and everyone looked worried. Beth was embarrassed as Wendy handed her a water bottle.

She tried to stand, but the dizziness was still there and her legs felt useless.

"Just rest," Arlene said. "Honey, you're pregnant. Should we call an ambulance?"

Beth shook her head. "No, just give me a minute."

A minute turned into five, and Beth finally asked the group if they minded if the class ended early that day. Arlene and Wendy stayed at her side as the others gradually made their exit.

"Maybe you should call your husband," Arlene said. "You should at least go to the doctor."

"Thank you both," Beth said. "I just need to sit here for a little while longer and see if I feel better. I think I'm doing better already."

Beth started to get up, and the room spun back into darkness.

~~~

When Beth awakened she was in a hospital bed and Ben was at her side, his features handsome and concerned. He smiled at her.

"Is the baby okay?"

"Yes," he said. "We're just trying to make sure that you're okay."

"Has Dr. Martin been here already?"

"She'll be back soon. I talked with her. She suspects that your blood sugar is a little messed up. She's hinting about you being on bed rest for a little while until things balance out."

Beth sighed. "I wasn't ready for something like this yet. I stayed active during my entire pregnancy with Maddie. I wanted this one to be like that, too."

"Me too, but sometimes life has other plans for us." Ben squeezed her hand. "The most important thing is you being okay, and this little person growing inside of you being okay."

"I know. What about Maddie? Where is she?"

"Don't worry about that," Ben said. "She's with Kerry."

"Okay."

"I've been thinking," Ben said, "that while you're on bed rest, it'll be pretty difficult for you to take care of Maddie. At first I thought about getting some recommendations on a full-time nanny. But then I had an even better idea."

"Which is?"

"I'm going to take a short leave of absence," Ben said.

Beth stared at him. "Seriously?"

"Yeah, seriously."

She was excited. "Can you do that? Would you even want to do it?"

"I want to do it, and I don't give a damn whether I can or not," Ben replied. "I've given this company my blood and if they can't do without me for a few weeks that's their problem."

Beth smiled. "I really appreciate that, sweetie. But it's probably not necessary. It sounds like a lot of trouble for you."

"It's not. I'm actually pretty excited about it. I need a break, as you know."

"Yeah, I know," she said.

'I'm going to call Ivan and tell him of my intentions," he said.

"Okay. Do you know if I have to stay here overnight?"

"I don't think so. Dr. Martin should be back by shortly."

Beth closed her eyes for a moment.

"I hope I get to see Jackie again soon," she said.

Across town, Phil and Jackie sat with Vanessa Porter in the therapist's office. Phil was reluctant to bring Jackie there, but felt the situation was well beyond his expertise.

Vanessa asked Phil to let them visit alone for a little while, to give Jackie a chance to open up to her. As he sat in the waiting room, holding a book but not able to focus on reading, Phil reflected on the last several weeks of events. He'd only spoken to Amanda once, although they'd texted several times. Each word of their last conversation felt fresh in Phil's mind.

"You haven't done anything wrong," Amanda kept telling him. "You don't owe me an apology or explanation. I knew the risk. I thought it was a very small risk, but I knew it."

Phil longed to take her into his arms. "I can't just shut this off," he'd told her. Amanda had responded, "I don't think I have any other choice. You're not going to break apart your family. The girls just got their mother back."

"They've asked about you a couple of times," Phil had said. "They ask if they're still going to see you."

"What do you tell them?" she'd asked.

"I tell them I don't know."

Amanda had waited a long moment before saying, "You know that I love you. But I'm a realist, Phil. You've given me a great adventure, and I'll always treasure it. But there's not a place for me in your life anymore."

Chapter Seventy-Six

Pete O'Rourke was bored out of his mind. He texted friend after friend, trying to find someone he could hang out with for the afternoon. Everyone was either busy with family stuff or had to get homework done. He'd started with Audrey, as usual, but she didn't respond. She'd been blowing him off for weeks now, and Pete didn't understand why.

He surfed Instagram and Twitter for a few minutes, taking a look at the most popular hashtags and noticing that a lot of people were re-tweeting *#BringBackOurGirls*.

As he scrolled through his texts, Pete re-read the last one he'd sent his father a week ago. Once again, Russ hadn't responded. Pete hated his father more than ever.

He really wanted to get high, which helped him feel less angry and afraid. Bodysurfing provided a similar rush.

Pete looked in his phone contacts and found the number for a guy named Evan, whom he'd met at the boardwalk last week. Evan was older, in his mid-twenties, and said to text if Pete ever wanted a fix. He could meet Pete at the boardwalk, and all Pete needed to do was get there and bring $50.

Mario was pretty cooperative about having his men drive Pete places he needed to go, without asking a lot of questions. His grandfather was also generous about giving Pete cash when he needed it. He texted Evan, and waited.

Sure thing, Evan responded a few minutes later.

Fifteen minutes later Pete walked out the front door, cash in hand, and waited at the top of the circular driveway as two of the Cubists pulled a car up to get him. He opened the rear passenger's side door, and plopped inside.

Right next to Mario, who looked sterner than Pete had ever seen him.

"Drive," Mario said, and the car proceeded down the driveway. Pete stared at his grandfather, nervous, waiting for Mario to say something else or ask him questions. But Mario just sat there, staring out the window.

Maybe Mario had to go out anyway, Pete hoped, and was just tagging along while they dropped him off. His grandfather never went anywhere alone anymore, so it made perfect sense.

"When do you want us to pick you up?" Mario finally asked, without looking at Pete.

Pete shrugged. "I don't know. A couple of hours, I guess."

"You know to call me if you have any problems, right?"

"Right."

The car neared the beachside and pulled onto A1A. Pete had told Evan he would meet him in the small Ocean Deck parking lot. The car scooted up the small side street that led to Ocean Avenue and parked. Pete saw Evan waiting for him and started to get out of the car.

Mario touched his arm. "Wait a second," his grandfather said.

"Yeah?"

"How well do you know this guy?"

Pete hesitated. "I don't know. Pretty well, I guess."

"You met him down here?"

"Yeah."

"Stay in the car for a minute." Mario motioned to the Cubist in the passenger seat. "Bring him over here." Pete watched in surprise as the Cubist got out, and walked over to where Evan was standing. They spoke to each other for a moment, and then Evan followed him back to the car.

"Scoot over to the middle here," Mario said to his grandson, and a bewildered Pete did so as Evan climbed into the back seat.

"Let's go," Mario said, and the driver took them back toward A1A.

Pete looked at Evan, whose face was impassive. "What's going on?" he whispered, but Evan said nothing.

"Just relax," Mario said. "We're going on a quick field trip. Sorry to interrupt your plans, but this is important."

Pete glanced at Evan and then back at his grandfather.

"You guys know each other?"

"Just relax," Mario repeated.

They drove through one of the older beachside neighborhoods until they reached a run-down looking apartment complex. The driver stopped, and Mario motioned for the Cubist in the passenger seat to get out. The man did so, and then opened the passenger rear door and held it open for Evan to exit.

"Go with them," Mario instructed Pete.

Pete was scared. "Why?"

"Just go."

"What is this place?"

"It's the field trip location. Just go. You'll only be gone for a few minutes."

"Are you coming, too?" Pete asked.

"I'm going to wait here," Mario replied.

"Come on, dude," Evan said.

Pete hesitated and then got out. He walked a few feet behind the other two men as they approached an outside stairwell, and headed up the creaky metal stairs to the second floor. Evan took the lead as they walked down the exterior hallway, passing a stray cat along the way that hissed at them.

They reached unit #205, and Evan rapped on the door. He waited a few seconds and then repeated.

There was no response. Evan looked at the Cubist, and stepped aside to allow the man to kick in the door with efficient force. Pete gasped, and lingered behind as the Cubist and Evan charged inside and disappeared into a back bedroom. Pete wanted to run back down to the car, but was too scared to move.

Evan and the Cubist re-emerged, dragging a skinny, Hispanic-looking man out of the bedroom. The Cubist had his arm around the guy's head and was muffling his mouth so he couldn't scream. Pete wanted to run more than ever.

"Stay put!" Evan yelled at Pete.

They threw the guy down onto a couch, and the Cubist held him by the hair as Evan pulled out a pistol and inserted it into the man's mouth.

"I gave you lots of chances," Evan told the man. "More than most people get. Today, we say goodbye."

Pete screamed as Evan pulled the trigger and the Hispanic man's head exploded, blood covering the wall behind him. Pete finally ran, stumbling down the creaky hallway to the steps and nearly tripping as he scrambled into the back seat of Mario's car.

"Grandpa, get me away from here! Evan just killed somebody."

Mario put his arm around him, pulling him close.

"I know," his grandfather said. "It's a dirty business, isn't it?"

Pete stared at Mario. Evan and the Cubist came back down and got into the car, and the driver slowly pulled away.

"Grandpa, what's going on?"

315

"That was the field trip," Mario said. "Consider it a gift: the chance to see the inevitable end of the path you were going down, without having to actually keep going."

Pete was scared to hell of Evan, and sat as close to his grandfather as possible. Evan looked at him and smiled.

"Why'd you shoot that guy?" Pete asked.

"He'd been ripping us off," Evan said. "It was time."

Pete looked back at Mario. "Grandpa, you know Evan?"

Mario nodded. "Yeah, he works for my men. He does a good job. We're going to take him home, now."

Evan touched Pete's arm. "I don't want to see you out on the boardwalk area ever again. Is that clear?"

Pete nodded. "Yeah."

Evan continued, "You're going to make some new friends, understood? You're gonna blow off most of your old friends. They're not really friends. Got it?"

Pete simply nodded again.

No one in the car spoke again until they pulled into a neighborhood that Pete didn't recognize. Mario thanked Evan as he got out of the car. Pete was relieved; he never wanted to see that guy again.

Mario looked over at his grandson.

"You wanna get some good pizza for dinner tonight?"

Pete shrugged.

"You hungry yet?"

The thought of food made Pete sick. "Not really."

"Okay, we'll wait a couple of hours. You'll get hungry again."

At that moment Pete no longer hated his father. He desperately wanted Russ to come home.

Chapter Seventy-Seven

The dog park was empty when Tom and Rain Dog arrived. It was on the same property as the animal shelter. He sat down on a bench as Rain Dog ran around, stopping to pee a couple of times in between chasing scents.

Connor had been invited to a friend's house. Tom needed a break from his son, who was constantly asking if "Mrs. Solomon knew where Mom was." Each time, Tom tried to explain that Jackie wasn't ready to talk about what had happened to her.

Tom's sponsor Rory was back up to speed, which was helpful because Tom really needed him. The guilt of his ambivalence had returned: wanting Kari to return but not eager for her to live with him once again.

Rain Dog got excited, running up to the south side of the fence and wagging his tail. Tom looked and saw a red-haired woman walking a dog that looked like a beagle. They were heading toward the dog park, and the beagle grew excited as well upon spotting Rain Dog. The red-head opened the gate, and her dog ran straight to Rain Dog. The two of them hustled off together to explore and play.

The woman looked to be in her late 30s. She was casually dressed in jeans and a tank top, and her hair fell carelessly across her shoulders. Tom gave her a friendly wave, and she smiled and sat down on the bench.

"Those two are fast friends," she said, watching the dogs play.

"Yep. They didn't even do the obligatory butt-sniff," Tom said.

She laughed. "So much for the formalities. What kind of dog is yours?"

"He's a hound dog, I believe. I rescued him last year."

"Oh, nice. From the shelter here?" she asked.

"Nope, from the side of the road. He was in bad shape."

"Good for you. Violet there is a rescue from here. I couldn't believe someone turned her in, she's so sweet."

"She looks sweet. Do you have other dogs?" Tom asked.

"I just had one pass away. Had him for 13 years, a bull dog. Raymond was his name. I still miss him a lot."

"I'm sorry," Tom said. "He's my first dog, so I've never had to go through something like that."

The woman looked surprised. "Wow. First dog. It's not very often I meet a virgin."

"Good to know you're staying away from high school boys," Tom said, and she smiled.

They watched the dogs play. "I'm Tom, by the way," he said. "Do you mind if we just shake hands?"

"Sara," she said. "And yes, I'm not up for a butt-sniffing today. Thank you for your manners."

"It's one of my better qualities."

"Good to know. Manners can be rare these days, sadly."

"I even hold doors open," Tom said.

"Your stock keeps rising. If I see you scoop poop, you'll definitely be getting my phone number."

Tom was starting to feel wired. A flood of emotion surged inside of him.

"What if I scoop your dog's poop as well as my dog's poop? Does that definitely get me a dinner date?"

Sara thought for a moment. "Yes, I think so. But only if you wash your hands."

"I'm a washer."

"I thought you probably were. Just making sure."

"No worries."

"So, Tom," Sara said, "is this your gig? Instead of meeting women at bars, you meet them at dog parks? Very cutting edge."

Tom shrugged. "The poop scoop offer doesn't play very well in the bars. And I don't drink."

"I gotcha."

"Plus, I had this bench first. I think you're the one picking me up. Just saying."

Sara laughed. "Just saying? You must have a teenager."

"Good guess. Same for you?"

"Nope. Divorced, but no kids. I work with teens, though. I teach history at Ormond Middle."

"I'm so sorry."

"Don't be," she smiled. "I get most of the summer off."

"I have all of the summer off. I sold my business, so now all I do is hang out at the dog park and pick up school teachers."

"Hmm," Sara said. "I'm expecting a really nice restaurant now."

"I was trying to decide between Wendy's and Arby's."

"You had me at Wendy's. Some people say I look like that girl in those stupid commercials."

Tom studied Sara up and down. "She doesn't do you justice. And she's way too into those hamburgers."

"I agree," Sara said.

"Velvet is peeing," Tom noted, pointing across the park.

"Good girl. It's Violet, by the way, not Velvet. I'll still go to dinner with you. So, I take it you're divorced as well?"

Tom sighed. "Would you still have dinner with me if I told you it was complicated?"

"If you told me dinner was complicated?"

"Funny. No, my situation."

"That depends on how complicated it is. Fair enough?" Sara asked.

"Fair enough."

"Let's just say that my wife left two years ago and never returned. Can we discuss the details over dinner?"

"Sure. Is there something scary about you I should know?"

"I used to have a really strong body odor. I've taken care of it since she left." Tom smiled.

"She's a fool, then."

"Maybe so."

Shit. I've got to talk to Rory, Tom thought, his body almost trembling with adrenaline.

Chapter Seventy-Eight

APRIL 6

The reconstructed ranch chapel, now positioned so it was parallel to the eastern seaboard and facing due north, was teeming with anticipation. Dan stood up before the community, its members gathered around him in a large semi-circle in the chapel. James—known to everyone as Curtis Everett—was sitting the closest.

"Curtis has been with us for three years now," Dan said, "which is really hard to believe. I knew from my first conversation with him that there was something special: the depth, the clarity of his thinking. And then, once he joined us here and the months passed and I realized his understanding of business and people…I knew that I'd finally found my successor."

Dan glanced about at the faces before him. They hung on his every word. He'd loved them each as a father figure for many years, having found most of them when they were estranged from their families, jobless, and homeless. He'd given them purpose, direction, and shelter.

"Curtis can do for this community things that I cannot," Dan continued. "He can take our organic gardening and farming efforts to another level commercially. That will enable us to continue to enhance our quality of life, while making room for newcomers. He can help us to build relationships with sister communities across the country and the world. There's no telling what we can become…what each of you can become, under Curtis's leadership."

James, a bit embarrassed by all of the laudatory attention, took a brief glance at his friends. The ones he made eye contact with smiled in a reassuring manner.

Dan paused and cleared his throat. "I'm not going anywhere," he chuckled. "I'm going to live out my final years, however many there are, here among my friends. But *at this moment, I pass all leadership and decision-making authority to Curtis." He looked at James and beamed. "My friend, come forward and let us bless you and your leadership."*

James stood and walked over to Dan, kneeling before him. The other members of the ranch community gathered around, laying hands on James and upon each other's shoulders if they couldn't reach James himself.

"Curtis, the universe brought you to us as one of its brightest spots, and we accept and embrace the wisdom that exceeds any one of us alone," Dan said, his eyes closed. "We grant you our loyalty. We grant you our service. We pray that you would be filled with light, and that your words and actions would continue to inspire us and increase our vision."

Dan paused, and allowed silence to fill the chapel for a while.

~~~

Curtis was sinking into the past as he took Lenore into his arms. Her hair smelled just as he'd remembered.

He tried not to think about his scar as he kissed her along the neck, feeling her nails gently exploring his back. Lenore might notice the scar and she might not, Curtis thought. If she did, they'd talk about it. There was nothing to worry about. He might even point it out before she noticed it.

For several months after Lenore's arrival at the ranch, Curtis had given her a lot of space. He wanted to capture her heart the way he did many years ago.

Once she realized who he was she called him James, but only in private. He'd told her he preferred Curtis, emphasizing that "James is dead," but eased up on that when he saw the tears in her eyes.

Curtis alternated between kissing her upper body and her lips, and felt her hands moving from his back to his rear and then back up to play with his hair. He tried his best to stay fully present, to be in this love-making moment and not a moment from the past: to not rob himself of the current joy, by dwelling on how painfully things had ended the first time.

"Are you okay?" Curtis asked her.

"Yes," Lenore said. "Are you?"

"Yes."

Curtis kissed his way down to her stomach, loving the way she was starting to pull his hair a bit. He reached his arms up so his hands could massage her breasts, and felt her nipples grow harder. Soon Curtis was kissing the inside of her thighs, and then pleasuring her with his tongue. After a couple of minutes

Lenore placed him inside of her, and Curtis loved the strength of her body as she responded to his thrusts.

He wanted to last; he wanted the experience to go all night and never end. They belonged together; that much had always been certain, and the way their bodies formed such natural rhythms was a tangible representation of that reality.

"I love you," Curtis whispered.

"I love you, too," Lenore said.

"I never stopped."

"I never did either."

Without warning she put her hand on his chest and rolled him over, straddling him. Running her fingers through her hair, Lenore slowly rotated her hips, leaning forward at times to rub along his chest, neck, and face. Curtis closed his eyes, breathed deeply, and let her take full control.

After they'd both climaxed, Lenore rested her head on his stomach. He rubbed her back and they were quiet for a while. Then Curtis felt her gently run a finger along his testicles, and she looked up at him.

"Do you mind if I look at it?" she asked.

"No, I don't mind, but just this one time," Curtis said, and breathed deeply. He tried to relax as Lenore leaned down and examined his scar, the spot where the knife had cut him just deep enough to send a lasting message. The men who did it were clear about their orders: to scar him but not destroy him. They'd also bloodied his face and broken a couple of his ribs.

"Are you glad you're here?" he asked her.

"I am," Lenore said.

They lay together for a while.

"By the way, I'm really sorry about Dan," Lenore said. "I know he was like a father to you."

Curtis closed his eyes. "He sure was."

"How old was he?"

Curtis smiled. "You know, I'm really not sure. He would never tell anyone."

"That's funny," Lenore smiled.

"Yeah, it is. Crazy guy."

"I can't believe he just collapsed in the garden like that," she said. "No warning."

Curtis pulled her in more tightly. He found he wasn't able to look Lenore in the eyes at the moment.

"Life doesn't always warn," he whispered.

In the less-secured section of the community's cabins, Russ heard a knock at his door. He'd fallen asleep, and the knocking was incorporated into a dream he was having about walking along the streets of his boyhood neighborhood in New York. He was knocking on the door of his own house, trying to get in, but his parents weren't answering.

Russ sat up in the dark, and realized the knocking was real. He crawled out of bed and went to see who it was.

Sally was there, wearing a long t-shirt, smiling.

"I'm sorry if I woke you. Do you mind if I come in?"

"Sure," he said, and held the door open for her. Sally headed straight for his bedroom and sat on the edge of the bed, staring at him.

"You're pretty straight-forward about things, aren't you?" Russ asked, sitting beside her.

Sally smiled. "I guess so. I was thinking about what you said earlier today."

"About how it's time for you to get over Scott?"

"Yes," she said. "He's obviously not coming back. He's not who I thought he was. Anyone who would abandon me, who would abandon this place, isn't worth worrying about."

Sally kissed him aggressively.

"Ron, I want you to be rough with me. Is that okay? You seem like you would be rough, like an alpha male."

"I'll be however you want me to be," Russ said, and pulled the long shirt off of her.

The sex was rough indeed, and rather brief. "I want to go at it again," Sally said. "As soon as I can get you hard." She caressed him, and kissed his neck while doing so.

"You're a beast," he said.

"You bring out the beast in me."

"Oh, I'm pretty sure the beast was already there."

"No one else has been rough enough with me. Finally, you came along." He was getting harder in her hand. "I want to know everything about you," she said.

Russ laughed. "Isn't that against community etiquette? I thought we were supposed to not worry about people's past, and focus on who we're all becoming."

"Yes," Sally admitted, "but a woman can't help but wonder. I think that works for people in general here; but when two people become intimate, as we have, it's very natural to want to know more. To want to know everything."

She climbed on top of Russ and kissed him, rubbing herself against him.

"Tell me about you," he said. "You go first. Ladies, first."

"Oh, that's not fair," Sally said. "You're taking advantage of me, Mr. Ron."

"You wanted an alpha male. This is what we do."

"Will you still like me if I tell you everything?"

Russ grabbed her buttocks and pushed himself inside of her once again.

"Does that answer your question?"

"It certainly does," she said, and they made love again, this time for a bit longer but with the same intensity. They finished up with Sally flat on her back, Russ pressing her down, and lay there together for a while.

"I had a family," Sally said after a while. "I left them to come here. They didn't understand me. I was ready to kill myself. This place saved me."

"You have a husband?" Russ asked her.

"Yes," she said.

"Does he know where you went?"

"I have no idea," she said. "I don't think so."

"What about your children? Don't you miss them?"

"They caused me a lot of suffering," she said, and Russ felt her grow tense under him. "I try to forget about them. I try to forget everything."

"It's okay," Russ said, kissing her neck. "You don't have to talk about any of them."

"Thank you," she said. "Tell me about you, now. Do you have a family?"

"I was married, but not anymore," Russ said. "I have a son. I had an important, high-pressured job. I like cutting grass a lot better."

Sally smiled. "You're very good at it. You look very sexy out there on the mower. You look like a warrior on your big machine."

"I didn't realize it was so macho."

"You're very humble," she said. "Why did you decide to come here?"

"I needed to get away from all the stress and pain, just like you," Russ said.

"Yeah," Sally said. "I guess that's why all of us are here. To find something better, more peaceful. You won't leave me, will you, the way Scott left?"

"Forget about Scott. I won't leave you."

"Good," she said." I promise I won't keep talking about him after tonight."

Sally slowly lifted herself, and Russ adjusted so she could lay on her side. He faced her, their legs entwined.

"What do you think about Curtis?" he asked.

"Curtis is amazing. He's changed my life. Have you gotten to talk with him yet?"

"A little."

"He helped me a lot when I first got here," Sally said. "He's also coached me at times when I've gotten 'too intense,' as he puts it."

"I see him enter and leave chapel with a woman each time," Russ said. "Who is she?"

Russ saw Sally's expression darken a bit. She frowned, and then smiled again. "Why do you want to know? Do you want to sleep with her, too?"

"No," he laughed. "I'm just curious."

"Her name is Lenore. No one knows much about her," Sally said. "She's never seen anywhere else. I guess he brings her food to their cabin."

"Have you ever been inside his cabin?"

"No one ever goes to Curtis's cabin. He's a very private person, when it comes to his personal space. We respect that."

Sally gave him a long kiss.

"Don't ask any more questions about Lenore," she said, still smiling but with a glint in her eyes that made Russ uneasy. "Focus on me. On us. I'm more than enough woman for you, Ron."

Chapter Seventy-Nine

APRIL 7

"You've got to let us finish doing our job, Mr. Lazano," Sarosky said, sipping from a cup of coffee as he sat with Mario in his den. "After weeks of careful surveillance, getting their ducks in a row, my peers in Okeechobee believe they've located the exact property. They're meeting with the state attorney later today to attempt to get a warrant. That way, if there are charges to be filed, we've done our due process."

"Would you like something to eat, Detective? A pastry, perhaps, or some fruit?" Mario asked him.

"No, thank you."

"You look a little hungry."

"I'm good, but thanks," Sarosky said.

Mario helped himself to a pastry, which he popped into the microwave for 20 seconds. He grabbed a paper towel and sat down, running his finger along the flaky crust.

"I appreciate you coming here and telling me ahead of time," Mario said. "I know that you've been personally committed to this case. None of us expected any of these women to be seen again. We'd given up hope. I'm sure Mr. Solomon and his daughters are beyond grateful."

"They're very grateful. Mrs. Solomon still has a lot of healing to do, as you can imagine."

"Of course." Mario took a bite of pastry, and wiped his mouth. "So she couldn't say for certain whether my daughter was on the property?"

"No," Sarosky said. "But she positively identified Mrs. Blakely. Let's just say we're going with the odds that Emma is there. We want to enter the property in a peaceful, due process manner, to be able to thoroughly search and avoid any incidents. If these people really are armed and dangerous, as Mrs. Solomon indicates, then sending in the SWAT team will put a lot of lives at risk."

"I understand," Mario said. "We don't need another Waco."

Sarosky nodded. "So, do I have your commitment that you won't take matters into your own hands?"

Mario laughed, finishing off the pastry. "You overestimate me, Detective. If I could have taken this matter into my own hands, I would have done so by now. It's been nearly two years since I've seen my daughter. If I had any lead whatsoever, any indication of where she was, I'd have moved heaven and earth."

Sarosky finished his coffee, and stood. "I'll be in touch by the end of the day, even if I don't have any real news," he said, exchanging a firm handshake with Mario. "Again, please don't say anything to your grandson yet."

"Of course."

Sarosky paused. "And you still haven't heard from Mr. O'Rourke?"

Mario shook his head. "It's a tough time for Peter, being without both of his parents. But he and I are bonding. His father needs to sort things out, to re-think his life and what he wants to be and do. I've given him leave from his position with my company so he can 'go find himself,' as the cliché goes. I'm sure that he'll return if there's good news with Emma."

"Well, please give my regards to Pete," Sarosky said. "And remember, if there's some way I can help get him some extra support, please let me know."

"I'll do that, Detective. Thank you so much."

Sarosky left, and Mario sat down in his favorite recliner. He picked up that morning's edition of *The Wall Street Journal*, which was delivered to the guard shack each morning, and glanced at the front page headlines.

A couple of minutes later, there was a soft knock at the study door.

"Come on in."

Scott Layman entered, and Mario offered him coffee and pastry as well. Scott shook his head.

"I've just had breakfast," Scott said. "How are you feeling this morning?"

"Better," Mario said. "But I don't like growing older. I don't recommend it."

Scott laughed. "I'm not sure I'd prefer the alternative."

"Both have their pros and cons."

Scott said down.

"Thanks for waiting until Sarosky left," Mario said. "Your presence here would just complicate things with him."

"Not a problem," Scott said. "Do you think he's taking things seriously?"

"He's at least pretending to," Mario said. "But he's small time, in over his head. Even if a backwoods judge down there signs a warrant and they enter the property, James Thorne will have found a way to hide Emma and that whack job Kari."

"So what's your next move?"

Mario shrugged. "It's best that you not get further involved. Just know that I've made my plans, and this matter will be resolved before daylight tomorrow."

"Those people are ready to die for their precious community and their leader," Scott said.

"I know. Weak-minded fools. It's very sad."

"People need to believe in something, I suppose. Or someone."

"More people need to believe in themselves," Mario said. "That's the problem with this world. Too many people caught up in expectations of what others can do for them or help them become, instead of taking their own risks to succeed."

Mario had a coughing fit. Scott offered to get him a glass of water, but Mario waved him off.

"You've done well," Mario said. "You played your part to perfection. It took a lot of courage."

"I appreciate your confidence in me," Scott said. "And your generosity. I can take of my kids for a long time now."

"Good. It's not easy being a single father. I've been fortunate to have plenty of resources for the last few decades, but the emotional strain is independent of money."

"Yeah, it sure is," Scott said.

"Stay here with me for a few more days, if you don't mind," Mario said. "I could use you as a sounding board. I might have something permanent for you, if you're interested. I don't know what Russ's plans will be when he comes back, but you'd be a good counter balance to him. You're a lot more level-headed, a lot less emotional."

"We've really kept him in the dark," Scott said. "Do you think he'll come out of this alive?"

"I'm trusting his instincts to lead him to respond in the moment," Mario said. "My men know him well, obviously. If Russ is smart, he'll stay out of the way long enough for them to do their job."

Audrey and Natalie were watching a movie in the den. Phil and Jackie sat at their kitchen table, drinking coffee.

"I know you're conflicted," Jackie said. "I promise that I'm trying to work on forgiving you. And I understand if part of you is angry at me."

"You haven't done anything wrong," Phil said. "You were forced to do what you did."

"That doesn't take away the sense of guilt," she said. "The sense of shame and weakness."

"I understand. Just know that I don't think any less of you. If anything I'm extremely proud of your courage and resiliency. Not many women could have gotten out of there the way you did, and then been so discreet afterwards. It's remarkable, really."

"I appreciate that."

Jackie looked at him with sad resignation.

"Do you love her? I really need you to be honest with me. We can't spend any energy being afraid of the truth."

Phil looked down, and then back at his wife.

"Yes. I do."

She nodded, making an effort to stop herself from crying.

"I understand. You're only human. I guess you've got a decision to make, though."

"Jackie, there's no need for me to rush any decision. Feelings can fade over time. I need to give all of this time. Let's focus right now on helping you and helping the girls."

"Well, I appreciate that," she said, "but what if your feelings don't change? I don't want you to spend the rest of your life full of regret, wondering what might have been with Amanda."

"I don't think Amanda wants to break up our marriage. She's given me my space. She's trying to move on."

"Even if she does, you might not be able to," Jackie said. "Just know that I'm working on getting past whatever anger and resentment I have. I'll work through it. I want you to be happy."

"I am happy. I'm so grateful you're back, that you're safe. Can we just take life a day at a time right now?"

Jackie nodded. She stood. "I'm going to go check on the girls, to see if they need anything."

"Okay." Phil remained in the kitchen, alone, suppressing the desire to text Amanda and see how she was doing.

~~~

"It's nice to just sit here and eat, and not have any other responsibility," Tom said as he and Ben looked through the Famoso's menu.

"I'm sure," Ben said. "I can't look at a cell phone without thinking about work."

"But you're enjoying your time off, I hope?" Tom asked.

"Yeah. Beth is doing much better. I'll probably go back to work soon. I don't want to. I'm jealous of you."

Tom laughed. "Don't be too jealous. You wouldn't want to switch places with me."

Ben pointed in the direction of the bar, where Julio was serving a group of ladies. "Do you think we should tell him? He's pretty good at keeping confidences."

Tom nodded. "Yeah, when he gets a quiet moment we can call him over here. He's been a great support to me. He hasn't been the same since Cameron was killed, though. He's much more withdrawn, and on edge. I've encouraged him to get some help."

"I imagine you're going through a lot of emotions right now yourself," Ben said.

Tom waited while the server took their dinner orders.

"I had a long visit with Rory last night, after I got home from your place," Tom said. "He helped me explore all the different angles of how to deal with this; to honestly embrace what I want and don't want, to examine what excites me and scares me. And how to respond."

"That sounds pretty helpful."

"He's a great guy," Tom reflected. "Don't know where I'd be without him. Or with you, for that matter."

Ben shrugged. "I haven't done a whole lot."

"You've done a ton. You got me to go to meetings. That's made all the difference."

Tom glanced back over at Julio.

"I'm worried about Connor no matter what happens," he continued. "If Kari doesn't decide to come home, if she wants to stay with those freaks down there, then Connor continues to have life without his mother. Eventually, he'll find out that she abandoned him. And if she does come home and she's a lunatic, then he has to deal with that, too."

"And you'll have to deal with it."

"I've got to deal with it either way," Tom said. "Either path is tough." He smiled. "I met someone, you know. A woman at the dog park. Her name is Sara."

Ben smiled. "Good for you. You've been a monk for a long time."

"It's not easy for someone in my situation to fill out the Match.com profile," Tom grinned.

"I think Phil can relate. He's a bit farther down the road than you are, though."

"Yeah. That poor guy. I guess he wins either way, though. At least Jackie still seems to be Jackie."

"Maybe Kari can come back to her senses," Ben said. "People have survived cults before. Anything is possible."

"Anything is possible," Tom agreed. "I just don't know if I want her back. The marriage was crumbling before she disappeared, remember? This situation doesn't exactly improve odds that were already pretty bad. And I've managed to build a fairly content life without her. Does that sound cold and heartless?"

Ben shook his head. "That sounds honest and makes sense. You needed to grow as a person, and embrace some new tools to help you. You've been doing all of that. Kari will have to make some tough choices as well. I think you're focused on the most important things, which are your emotional well-being and nurturing Connor; and if you keep doing those things the situation with Kari will take care of itself."

"I'm having a tough time not saying anything to Connor yet," Tom said.

"Be patient for a few more days."

~~~

"I'll do anything for you, Ron," Sally whispered to him. It was close to midnight. "Anything. You name it."

Russ reflected on this as she stroked and kissed him.

"I want you to take me to Curtis's cabin," Russ said. "I want to talk to him further, and meet Lenore."

Sally chuckled, but continued to work her way up and down his body. "I told you no one goes in there, silly. And forget about her."

"How well do you know her?" he asked.

Sally looked up at him.

"Not at all. How well do you know *me*, darling?"

She sat fully on top of his abdominals, running her nails along his chest.

"Not as well as I could," Russ said.

"Well, tell me what you'd like to know," Sally said, leaning forward and kissing his left ear. "I'll whisper it to you."

"Tell me where you lived before you lived here," Russ said.

She ran her tongue along his ear. "That's such a boring part of my life. I lived in such a boring place. You'd think less of me."

"I promise that I won't," he said.

"Let's stop talking for a while," Sally said. "I don't even want to whisper. I just want to feel."

"What would you like to feel?"

Before Sally could answer, they were jolted by the sound of gun fire somewhere across the ranch.

Chapter Eighty

So," Emma said, "I guess we need to pick our next book. I've heard good things about *And the Mountains Echoed*."

"That book sounds too sad," Jackie said. "*Edgar Sawtelle* was sad. And *Sun Also Rises* was sad as well. Jake and Brett are the ones who truly love each other, but they can't really be together because of Jake's injury. He can't make love."

"'Oh, Jake, we could have had such a damned good time together,'" Delphi quoted. "And he says, 'Yes, isn't it pretty to think so?'"

"That's a weird term to use," Kari said. "'Pretty.' You wouldn't hear a man say that today."

"Yeah, but the message there is timeless," Jackie said. "They're reflecting on what they could have been together, if circumstances were different. If only. It's tragic, really."

"I'm a realist," Emma said. "Things are what they are, and you have to embrace them. It certainly sucked for Jake, though."

Kevlin held her goblet out and Lisa—the closest one to the wine bottle—gave her a refill. "It sure did suck to be him," Kevlin said.

"What would each of you do if the man you loved suddenly couldn't have sex?" Kari asked. "Would you leave him?"

"That's why I left Russ," Emma quipped, and they laughed.

"I can't imagine it," Jackie said. "But I guess you don't know what you'd do until you're in a situation."

~~~

Four carloads full of armed men pulled up to the outside of the ranch, expecting to be greeted by Curtis's guards. The group's leader, a Chilean named Felix, stepped out of the front passenger seat of the first car, semi-automatic weapon in hand, and carefully approached the guard shack. He stared down at the bodies of three men who'd been cut down with bullets, at least one of whom was still breathing as he bled to death.

"We aren't the first ones here," Felix said when he returned to the car. He looked at the two men in the back seat. "Go open the gate, so we can drive through." Felix sent a quick text to the other drivers, updating them on the situation.

Moments later the four cars sped through the entrance of the ranch, splitting their course into separate directions. Felix had his driver move toward the cabins. Another car sped toward the large multi-purpose building, while another drove toward the garden and the final car proceeded to the chapel.

Felix pointed ahead toward an empty golf cart, parked near the first set of cabins. "There," he said. "Park there."

The four men grabbed their weapons and sprinted out into the night. Felix and Martin, one of the men from the back seat, began flinging open cabin doors. Other doors opened for them as community residents heard the noises. "Stay out of the way!" Felix yelled at each person who got too close, as he and Martin searched cabin after cabin.

"We need to keep working our way toward the rear," Felix said to Martin.

At that moment more gunfire rang out, coming from deeper into the ranch. Felix and Martin ran toward a second, much smaller set of cabins, leaping over a couple more bodies of community guards along the way.

"There they are," Felix said, pointing toward a group of three men who were scaling an eight-foot concrete wall, with another set of dead guards at their feet.

"They still don't know we're here. They've been too busy gunning down all of Everett's people." Felix heard more gunshots from other parts of the property.

The three men had fully disappeared on the other side of the wall. Felix paused to collect his thoughts.

"I don't care if they kill Everett," Felix said. "But we can't let them hurt or take Mrs. O'Rourke."

Inside Curtis's spacious cabin, Lenore watched him pace around with his cell phone. He'd tried guard after guard, but was getting no responses.

"Who do you think is out there?" she asked.

"I'm not certain," he said. "But I knew this day would come. You've heard me predict in chapel, haven't you, that one day people would rise against us?"

"Do you really think that's what this is all about?"

Curtis went over to a safe in the bedroom and punched in a code. It sprang open, and he pulled two small pistols out of the safe.

"Do you know how to use one of these?" he asked Lenore, handing her one.

She frowned. "Are you kidding me?"

Someone started pounding at the locked cabin door. Curtis motioned for Lenore to run into the back bedroom and stood pointing his gun at the door, his arm shaking more than he wanted it to.

There was a loud burst of gunfire outside, and the pounding stopped.

Outside, Felix examined the bodies. "I've seen them before."

He and Martin pointed their weapons at the cabin door.

"Your guards are dead, Curtis," Felix called out. "We're not here to harm you. We just need Emma. Send her out peacefully, and we'll leave you alone."

Curtis's arm continued to shake as his pointed his pistol toward the locked door. He looked back at the bedroom, and motioned for Lenore to stay put.

Russ and Sally had gotten dressed and run outside, like most of their neighbors. Sally screamed as she tripped over Roger's dead body, and ran in the direction of Curtis's cabin.

"Where are you going?" Russ yelled, trying to keep up with her.

"They're going after Curtis!" Sally said, panicked. "We've got to protect him."

"Be reasonable, Curtis," Felix said loudly. "You know she doesn't belong here. You know she doesn't really love you. Set her free, if you really love her."

Inside the cabin, Curtis glanced back at Lenore. She shook her head.

"Don't believe them, sweetheart. These people have always tried to keep us apart."

"You are trespassing!" Curtis yelled through the door. "I will call the authorities if I have to, and have you removed."

Outside, Martin laughed. Felix yelled back, "Curtis, you have almost as much to fear from the authorities as you do from us."

"Get away from there!" a woman's voice shouted from the darkness. Felix and Martin whipped around and saw Sally running toward them, with Russ in tow.

"Get back!" Felix yelled at Sally, as he and Russ made eye contact. "Mrs. Blakely, go back to your cabin and take cover!"

Russ's eyes widened as he stared at Sally.

"I'm a member of this community, and you have no right to be here!" Sally screamed. "You've killed people tonight! Curtis told us you'd come one day and try to destroy us, just like the Nazis did with the people of Europe."

Sally attempted to hit Felix and Martin, who were exercising considerable restraint not to bash her over the head with their guns. Russ grabbed her arms and attempted to drag her away. She kicked backwards and nailed him straight in the groin.

Curtis opened the front door as Sally lunged at the two men once again. Their backs were to the cabin, and Curtis fired sloppily until his gun was empty. He injured both Felix and Martin, but in the process inadvertently lodged a bullet into the chest of the man he knew as Ron.

Sally screamed as Russ fell to his knees. Russ watched Curtis lower his gun, and then saw a very familiar woman quietly exit the cabin with a pistol of her own. He managed to smile as Curtis turned to face the woman whom everyone had been calling Lenore. She shot Curtis several times in the chest. He crumbled to the ground, dead.

Lenore rushed over to Russ as he sunk further to the ground, starting to cry.

"You stupid sonofabitch," she whispered to him. "You were always a stubborn, stupid sonofabitch. But I loved you."

"I loved you, too" Russ mumbled, before the last bit of life left his body. Lenore gently kissed his forehead.

"Lenore, how could you kill Curtis, you fucking bitch!" Sally screamed at her. "This place is my whole life! What's going to happen to me now?"

Lenore slowly stood to face Sally.

"We're both going to get our real lives back," she said softly, extending her hand toward Sally. "Come with me. We've got to run."

Sally slapped her hand away.

"I'm not going anywhere! I'm staying here with Curtis!"

"James—I mean, Curtis—is dead! Come on!" Lenore yelled. She stared at Sally. "Sally! *Kari!* Please."

"Don't call me that!" Sally said. "That's not who I am anymore."

"You have no idea who you are, Kari," Lenore said. "You never really did. But I can help you, and your family can help you, if you'll let me take you out of here."

Sally was sobbing, kneeling next to Curtis's body, a pool of blood beneath him.

"It's too late to help me, Emma," she said, staring down at the gun still clasped in Curtis's lifeless right hand. Sally freed the gun before her friend could stop her, pointed it at her own temple, and pulled the trigger.

Chapter Eighty-One

Curtis's men offered to come inside the chapel with Curtis and his three visitors, but their boss shook his head.

"Just wait outside, please." The men did as they were told.

"You sound like you really need to talk," Curtis said to the man who'd introduced himself as Nick Ferrante.

Ferrante nodded, but instead of speaking he reached into his jacket and pulled out a small photograph. He handed it to Curtis, who studied it for a long time before glancing back at Ferrante and his companions.

"Where did you get this?" he asked softly.

Ferrante shrugged. "It took a little work. Not too much effort."

"No one had a copy of this picture except for me. And I destroyed my copy long ago."

Curtis stared at the photo of himself and the teenaged Emma a moment longer, and then looked back at Ferrante.

"Why did you bring this to me? What do you want?"

Ferrante folded his arms and smiled. "We have mutual interests."

Curtis glanced over at Henry Reid, who was keeping his distance. "I'd hoped I would never see you again," Curtis said, and Henry nodded.

"I get that. It was nothing personal, though."

Curtis then pointed at the other man who'd accompanied Ferrante but had yet to speak.

"And what about you?"

The man cleared his throat.

"I'll help facilitate the subterfuge back home," Ben McBride replied. "I don't want Emma O'Rourke to ever set foot anywhere near Daytona Beach again."

Frankie and Rex pulled up to Ferrante's Boca Raton house and approached the front door.

"You have an update?" Ferrante asked as they came inside.

Frankie shook his head. "We can't reach them."

"Well, hopefully they're busy."

"Yeah. They'll call me as soon as they're done."

Ferrante frowned. "They know to take Everett alive, correct?"

"Correct."

Ferrante motioned for the two of them to follow him toward his den. "Come on, let's have a drink."

"I left my phone in the car," Rex said. "Is it okay if I go get it?"

"Go ahead, be quick," Frankie said, annoyed.

Rex departed. "What are you drinking, Frankie?" Ferrante asked him, pouring a shot of Patron.

"Captain Morgan. Straight, no ice," Frankie said.

"You've got it, my friend." Ferrante poured Frankie's drink, and raised his own for a toast. "You've done nice work. Here's to you."

"Thanks," Frankie said, and clanked his glass against Ferrante's.

Ferrante heard the front door open again. "What you want to drink, Rex?" he called out, not bothering to turn and look.

"I'm not real thirsty," Julio Ramos said as he entered the den. "And if I was, I'd fix the drink myself."

Ferrante smiled with surprise. "Julio, what's happening, mi amigo?" he asked, walking over and giving Julio a quick embrace. "I didn't realize you were with these guys tonight."

"They're teaching me the ropes," Julio said. "I've been spending a little bit of time with them lately."

"Good. I've always thought you had more talent than just standing behind a bar," Ferrante said.

"He's got more talent than you realize," another voice said, and Ferrante almost dropped his glass as Mario Lazano entered his den, accompanied by Rex.

"Well done, gentlemen," Ferrante said to Frankie and Rex. "This is a welcome surprise."

Mario calmly approached Ferrante, who took a step closer to Frankie. "Aren't you going to be hospitable, and offer me a drink as well?"

Ferrante looked from Frankie to Rex to Julio, and then back at Mario. "What are you having?"

"How about a simple glass of red wine? Preferably, from Tuscany."

"I'll take care of it," Julio said, stepping past Ferrante and finding a corkscrew. As he did so, Mario motioned for the rest of them to take a seat.

"I'm glad you're making yourself at home," Ferrante said.

"Well, I know this is a little awkward for you, Nick," Mario said. "I thought it would be good if we just tried to speak like businessmen to each other."

"Yeah. Whatever you say."

"Without the emotion," Mario added.

"All right. Start talking," Ferrante said.

Julio brought Mario his wine, and Mario nodded his thanks.

"How did you get Henry to betray me?" Mario asked. "He was with me a long time. He knew my daughter when she was young. What incentive could you have possibly offered him?"

"He was with you a long time, all right," Ferrante said. "And he was getting old, and he was tired. He kept waiting for you to give him what you'd promised him, that larger slice of the pie. He was only human."

"You shouldn't have killed the two women, also," Mario said, looking from Ferrante to Frankie and Rex. "That wasn't necessary."

"I'm sure they were both a great piece of ass," Ferrante said.

Mario nodded. "They were. But they were also human beings."

Ferrante shook his head. "I was foolish not to realize that Everett would have no intention of letting Emma leave, no matter how much money we were promising to get from you."

"Ah, finally," Mario said, "We have evidence of at least one man too principled to be bought off. His actual name is James Thorne, by the way."

"I don't care about what kind of a man he is or his real goddamned name," Ferrante said, "but his luck has run out tonight. As we sit here, my people have stormed that ranch and taken Emma. She'll be reunited with your grandson; all you have to do is help me log into your bank account. You're not going to walk out of here alive, but you can rest in peace knowing that you've done the right thing to secure her release."

"You seem pretty confident that things are working out for you tonight," Mario replied.

"I should have done it months ago," Ferrante said. "Maybe even a year ago. I kept waiting for Everett to come to his senses."

"It's too bad you had to involve the other women and their families," Mario said. "Why not just take my daughter? Why ruin three families when you could just ruin one?"

"It wasn't my preference," Ferrante said. "Henry thought it would look less suspicious, less obvious that Emma was targeted."

Mario swirled his wine glass. "Henry always had a bright strategic mind." He studied Ferrante. "You remind me quite a bit of your father, you know."

"Yeah? In what way?" Ferrante asked.

"Oh, it's hard to narrow it down. Confident, to the point of arrogance. Stubborn. Careless, even?"

"Careless, huh?"

"Yes, sir."

"It took a lot of careful planning to bring about tonight's events," Ferrante said. "Years of patient, careful planning. Studying each of your moves. All with the goal of someday having you in this very type of situation: letting you reflect a final time on what a coward you were when you walked up to my father's car on the beach, and shot him in the back of the head."

Mario laughed, and Ferrante tried to control his anger. Julio remained behind the bar, watching the entire exchange unfold with a detached amusement.

"I'm amazed that anyone still believes that urban legend," Mario said. "I'd heard that old man Patapos met with you before he died. I suppose he convinced you that I was the trigger man rather than himself, huh?"

Ferrante shrugged. "It didn't take a whole lot of convincing. You were holding a grudge because you weren't making as much money as you'd supposedly been led to believe. Then my dad and his partner are murdered, and suddenly you're running the company. It just made sense that you made your bones on the beach 35 years ago, when I was just a kid whose father didn't come home one night."

"Patapos sure had the last laugh," Mario said. "Literally."

"It's a little late for you to try to convince me that someone else killed my father," Ferrante said. "Everything points to you."

"You believe what you want to believe," Mario said. "But don't pretend that what you're doing is just about a son mourning his father. You want my real estate, and you want my distribution channels. So you can drop the hypocrisy, and just get on with it. Have your boys here take me out onto the beach, like they did that young newspaper guy, and get it over with."

Mario glanced over at Julio.

"Well, there's no point in delaying things, then," Ferrante said. "Shall we go over to my laptop and make a little transaction?"

"I'm not giving you a cent, Ferrante. You'll have to find someone else to give you money in order to let her go. Maybe you can ask my grandson to liquidate some of his trust fund."

"It's amazing that money is so important to you, even now, when you've run out of the ability to spend it," Ferrante said. He stood, and motioned for Mario to walk with him across the house toward the sliding glass doors that faced the ocean. Frankie and Rex were close behind, followed by Julio.

The five of them walked across Ferrante's deck, which had been filled with holiday revelers the night Cameron Brock was murdered, and stepped onto the sand.

"You're making me get my best pair of shoes dirty," Mario said.

"You won't have to walk very far," Ferrante replied.

"You know, your neighbors are going to complain that this is gonna hurt property values. Every time you kill someone back here, it makes the neighborhood just a little bit trashier."

They walked for a couple more minutes, until arriving at a spot that sufficed for Ferrante.

"Mario, turn your back to me and look out at the ocean," Ferrante said. "Think about your life, and what could have been if you hadn't been so self-absorbed."

"It's a beautiful night," Mario admitted. "There's a full moon. Look at its reflection glistening along the water."

Frankie took a step forward, and pulled out his pistol. He cocked the hammer, and took aim at the back of Mario's head.

"Wait a second," Ferrante said, motioning for Frankie to lower the gun. "Why don't we let our new pledge here do the honors? Make him a real man?"

Everyone except for Mario looked at Julio.

"You want me to shoot him? Seriously?" Julio asked.

"This is how you get street cred, kid," Ferrante said. "Until you take a life, no one's truly afraid of you."

Frankie extended the gun toward Julio, with the barrel facing down. Julio stepped forward, nervous, acting as if he was afraid to squeeze the handle too tightly.

"I've never shot a gun before," he said. "My mother wouldn't let us have guns."

"Your mother's gonna be proud of you after tonight," Ferrante said.

"I'm not so sure about that. And what am I going to tell my little girl someday? That her daddy killed a gangster?"

"I prefer the term entrepreneur," Mario said, still staring at the water.

"Okay, kid, stop whining," Ferrante said. "This is a milestone moment for you. I don't have all night."

"Go ahead, Julio," Mario said, turning slightly to face the bartender. "No hard feelings on my part. Everybody's gotta go sometime, anyway."

Julio raised the gun and pressed the barrel against the back of Mario's head. He took a deep breath and squeezed his eyelids shut.

"Yeah, shut your eyes, kid, good idea," Ferrante said. "That helps improve accuracy."

Julio opened his eyes and then rotated his posture so he was facing Ferrante, pointing the gun at him instead. He smiled at Ferrante's bewildered reaction, and squeezed the trigger three times.

Mario kept looking at the ocean. Julio stared down at Ferrante's body, stunned at what he'd done, and then handed the gun back to Frankie.

"You guys did nice work the past couple of years," Mario said, turning at last and shaking Frankie and Rex's hands. "I don't know if I could have pulled off what you did. But in the end, we all benefited from the fact that this guy laying here really was as arrogant and stupid as his old man."

"I only did this for Cameron," Julio said. "I didn't do it for you. I don't want this life, this life that all of you guys lead. Can I just go in peace, please? I have a fiancée and a baby girl waiting for me."

Mario looked at Frankie and Rex, who simply shrugged.

"Yeah, go in peace," Mario said. "You need anything, ever, you call me. Don't get careless. Don't screw around on your woman. Play it straight, and you'll be happier. You understand?"

"I understand," Julio said.

"Good," Mario said. "Now, let's go find out whether my other guys got Emma, Kari, and Russ the hell out of that place tonight."

"Do you think the cops are there, too?" Julio asked, and Mario simply shrugged.

"You won't forget your promise to help spring Nelson, right?"

"Don't worry," Mario told Julio. "He'll be a free man soon."

As Mario and Julio walked back toward Ferrante's house, Frankie and Rex stayed behind to take care of the body.

Chapter Eighty-Two

Emma had wandered away from the others, and approached Ben as he was grilling burgers and chicken on the backyard deck.

"Do you need some help?" she asked.

He looked up and smiled.

"No, I'm good, thanks. Glad you could make it today, Emma."

"Yeah, well it's kind of fun to finally meet the husbands," she said, and then added, "and see if they match the descriptions I hear about during book club."

Ben grinned. "Uh oh, I hope I measure up to expectations."

"Oh, you're fine. And besides, Beth doesn't gossip much, unlike a few of the others. I won't say who I'm referring to, but her name rhymes with 'scary.'"

Ben laughed. "Sounds like I'm missing out on some fun meetings."

"Nah," Emma said, looking at the grilling meat. "You need a clean plate or something to put those on once they're done? I can go into the kitchen and get one for you if you'd like."

"Aww, you don't have to do that."

"Well, I'm relieved knowing I don't have to." Emma smiled, and Ben found his mind scrambling for any possibilities of getting her alone for a few minutes. It was crazy to even consider, yet so hot at the same time.

"You're very sweet. That would be great," he said.

"Be right back."

Emma smiled and turned. Ben watched her walk away. She was wearing a strapless dress that gave stark evidence to how hard she was working out at Beth's studio. Her shoulders were muscular and her calves were thin and tight. Ben's mind *was flooded with distraction as he attempted to turn the pieces of meat over to see if they were almost done.*

A little while later, Emma stood nearby chatting with Lisa Grayton and her husband. When Ben was certain no one was watching, he snapped a picture of Emma with his phone and made a mental note to delete it later.

～～

"What the hell!" Ben yelled, half-asleep as the persistent knocking at the front door finally stirred him.

Maddie was calling them from her room. Beth, clutching her belly, did her best to rush off and check on her. Ben stumbled out of the bedroom toward the front door, looking through a window and seeing Sarosky and Rice standing outside.

He opened the door.

"Detectives—what's the problem?"

"May we come in?" Sarosky was glaring at him.

"I guess so," Ben said, stepping aside so they could enter. "It's the middle of the night."

"How much did you know about Mario Lazano's people raiding the ranch last night?" Sarosky asked angrily, standing close to Ben. Rice leaned in close to Sarosky, taking his arm in an effort to calm him down.

"I don't know what you're talking about," Ben said, seeing Beth carrying a sleepy Maddie out of the corner of his eye. He wished his wife would take their daughter back into her room, but Beth seemed intent on watching the scene unfold.

"That's bullshit," Sarosky said, lowering his voice only a little as Rice touched his arm. "I think you've always known more than you're letting on. You've had an extraordinary level of interest in this case, especially regarding Emma O'Rourke."

Ben glanced over at Beth, who was slowly rocking Maddie back to sleep. Beth scowled at Sarosky.

"She's my close friend," Beth said. "Of course we have a high level of interest."

"Bob," Rice whispered, "come on. You've got to dial this back."

Sarosky glared at Ben.

"Mr. Lazano has a lot to answer for," he grumbled, and flung open the front door and headed back out into the night.

Rice looked at the McBride family.

"It's been a stressful couple of years," she said. "Sorry about this. He's also not looking forward to his meeting with the mayor and police chief first thing in the morning."

344

Ben nodded. "I take it something big has happened."

"Yeah," Rice said, "I'm sure you'll learn all about it soon enough."

Rice left, and Ben walked over to Beth. Maddie looked up at him sleepily, and reached for him. He scooped the little girl into his arms and carried her off to bed, feeling Beth's eyes following him.

Chapter Eighty-Three

JUNE 20, 2014

f I can get away from the other ladies for a couple of hours, you could come meet me," Emma said to Ben, both of them naked and face to face in his hotel room in Tampa. "Couldn't you make an excuse to be in West Palm Beach that Friday for work?"

"I don't know," Ben said, "stroking her cheek. Seems a little risky."

"This whole thing is risky. That's what we love about it."

"Yeah."

They kissed, and Ben gently pulled Emma on top of him again, her dark hair falling into his face and along his chest.

Later that night, Ben woke up and found Emma sitting in a nearby chair.

"Are you okay?"

"Yeah, I'm all right. Just having trouble sleeping. Sometimes it helps me to get out of bed, instead of just tossing and turning. Go back to sleep, and don't worry about me."

Ben had a meeting that started at 8 a.m. the next day, so he rolled back over and drifted off once again.

When his alarm woke him at 6:45 a.m., Emma was gone. Ben noticed a piece of paper on the nightstand with some writing on it, and read it several times. He crumbled up the note and laid his face in his hands.

～～～

Emma and Pete walked through Greenwich Village. Her son hadn't spoken much during the flight up from Florida. She observed him taking in the sights and sounds, and felt positive about the possibilities of their relationship.

Her house in Daytona was up for sale, and they were staying with one of her law school friends in Manhattan while Emma looked for an apartment to rent. Her mother Carmen had begged them to stay with her, but Emma politely declined.

For many weeks after the bloody rescue at the ranch, Emma lay awake in the middle of the night. Her feelings would alternate between rage at James and deep, swallowing sorrow for killing him. She'd blame herself for Russ dying, and even for Kari dying. She'd feel anger toward Mario for forcing James out of her life when she was young. Things might have turned out very differently, she'd surmise.

And Emma still dwelled heavily on Ben and Beth, and hoped her guilt would heal with the passage of time. Ben had texted her a couple of times to see how she was doing, and she'd responded the first time only with a short message: *I'm fine, thanks.*

Mario had begged Emma to stay in town, noting that he wanted to retire and turn DDC over to her. She declined, encouraging her father to sell the company and "go live on an island somewhere where young women can wait on you all day long."

Emma wanted to ask Mario how much Pete had seen of his business dealings, but was afraid to know.

"I used to go into that little bakery all the time, when I was a student here," Emma said, pointing across the street. "I drank a lot of coffee and ate a lot of crepes there."

"I like it up here," Pete said. "There's a lot more to do."

"That's for sure," Emma said. "There's no place like New York."

They went into the café, and Emma talked her son into eating a blueberry crepe. They sat in silence for a while, people watching. Finally, Emma decided to take a chance.

"You haven't said much about your dad."

Pete simply looked at her.

"Do you have questions about what he was doing before he died? Or questions about other parts of his life?" Emma paused. "Or just anything that you want to express?"

Pete shrugged. "I don't know," he said. "I didn't see a whole lot of him during the final months. In general, we didn't get along very well during the time you were gone. He got mad at me a lot."

"I'm sorry about that," Emma said.

"It's okay. It's not your fault."

"Your dad and I definitely had our differences," Emma said. "But I'll never forget that his last act in life was to try to rescue me from that place. He sacrificed himself. I didn't want him to do that, but I'll always appreciate it."

"Yeah. That was pretty cool of him, I guess." Pete stared down at the table.

"I'm sorry, Pete. I feel like I took your father away from you."

"You didn't."

Emma looked at her son. She worried about his future. There were three men who'd been significant in her life above all others: her father, Russ, and James. They each had their positive qualities, but their horrible dark sides as well. She didn't want Pete to become like any of them, and yet she saw that he possessed some attributes of all three.

They left the café and wandered through Washington Square Park. A hipster with a full, scraggly beard was strumming a guitar. Passers-by occasionally dropped coins or dollar bills into the large can the musician had set out in front of him. Pete pulled out his own wallet and gave the guy a five dollar bill.

"I want to learn how to play guitar," Pete said a few minutes later.

Emma nodded. "That sounds pretty cool. I'm sure there's a lot of good teachers around here."

"Acoustic, though. I'm not interested in electric."

"I won't argue with you there."

"Do you think we can look around in some guitar shops today?" he asked her.

"Yes. We can do whatever we want."

"Cool," Pete said. He offered his mother a rare smile, and then texted Audrey. *Wish you were here.*

Me too, the girl texted back.

Phil, Jackie, and the girls each had their own backpack as they hiked a trail in Great Smoky National Park in eastern Tennessee. Natalie griped the first half-mile or so, but then got into the scenery and started chattering about every bird and squirrel they passed.

"It's really beautiful," Audrey said as they approached a clearing with a magnificent view of the mountains. She snapped several photos with her iPhone and quickly uploaded them to Instagram.

"It sure is," Jackie said. "Florida's so flat. You don't realize it until you go somewhere else."

Phil was silent during most of the hike, unable to prevent himself from dwelling on what he and Amanda might be talking about if she were with him instead. Jackie had begun, in recent weeks, to drop hints that they might consider a separation. *We've been separated for two years,* Phil thought, but didn't say that to her. Jackie began sleeping in the guest room, and they hadn't made love since she returned home. There was one evening when they'd tried, but as soon as Jackie got naked she felt a pit in her stomach and told Phil she simply wasn't ready.

There was an awkward moment a few weeks back when, during dinner, Natalie had asked Phil if he still loved Amanda. Jackie broke the tension by laughing. Phil stumbled through a statement along the lines of, "I love her as my friend," and then Audrey jumped in and changed the subject to fashion.

Phil had moments of rage when he wanted to kill the men who had done this to his wife, but others had already taken care of that. Then he'd feel grateful for the time with Amanda that he would've never experienced otherwise, which naturally led to his innate Jewish guilt. Phil was seeing Vanessa once a week, with no end in sight to the therapy sessions.

He saw another family hiking nearby, a couple with two young girls and a boy. They waved, and as he waved back Phil wondered what their lives were like. *Did they know how easy they had things?*

Phil took a swig from his water bottle, and smiled as Audrey asked if they could take a hiking trip every year.

"That sounds wonderful," Phil said. "Let's make that a goal."

"Can it just be you and I sometimes?" she whispered back to him.

"Of course."

"I mean, Natalie can have her own hiking trip with you, too. I'm not going to be selfish."

Phil laughed and gave her a hug. "There's nothing selfish about you. I can't tell you how lucky I am to be your dad." Phil kissed her on the forehead, and Audrey kissed him back on the cheek.

Natalie asked her mother to pose for a picture with the mountain scenery in the background, and then they squeezed in close together for a selfie.

Phil unzipped his back pack and saw the worn copy of Frankl's *Man's Search for Meaning*. He paused to flip to the last page he was reading, and noticed a familiar quote from the concentration camp survivor.

"In some ways, suffering ceases to be suffering at the moment it finds a meaning, such as the meaning of a sacrifice."

The Blakely house was packed with Tom's friends from AA, along with their spouses, partners, and children—as well as Sara, Tom's new girlfriend he'd met at the dog park. Rain Dog was the hit of the gathering, wagging his tail and eagerly awaiting a treat—dog or human food—from whomever would give him one. Connor proudly showed off his hundreds of sketches to anyone who took an interest.

Rory had been a gem to Tom since Kari's death, answering the phone immediately whenever Tom called. And Tom was grateful that Sara had given him space, while also not shutting him out of her life.

"Kari made those choices," Rory kept reassuring him. "Kari was who she was, long before you came into her life. Forgive Kari, and forgive yourself."

Tom told Rory he wanted to do research about men and women whose spouses or children had gotten caught up in cults. He wondered if there was a support group. Rory said Tom should feel free to learn whatever he needed to, but reminded him that he already had a support group.

The smell of burgers, dogs, and chicken filled the backyard. Ben, Beth, and Maddie were there, and Ben insisted on manning the grill so Tom could enjoy his company. Beth was really showing now, and Maddie held her mother's hand and told everyone she was going to be a big sister.

Before they started eating, Rory called everyone together and asked them to form a circle and hold hands. Sara gripped Tom's hand tightly, smiling at him as Rory led the group in the Serenity Prayer.

Maddie asked Beth what the prayer meant, and Beth tried her best to explain.

"It's kind of like being happy with what you have," Beth said to her daughter. "Like when you get Christmas or birthday presents. You might not get everything you wanted, but you're thankful for what you did get."

"But what's 'the wisdom to know the difference?'" the little girl asked.

"What do you think it means?" Beth asked.

Maddie considered her mother's question for a moment, and then asked, "Hey, can I get another American Girl doll for Christmas?"

Beth laughed. "We'll ask Santa."

"I'll share it with the baby. I *promise*," Maddie said, patting her mother's tummy.

Beth leaned down and kissed her on the top of her head.

"You're going to be an incredible big sister."

Tom joined Ben at the grill. "You really know how to burn a hot dog beyond recognition," he said.

"That's my specialty," Ben replied. "Makes me really popular at the company picnics."

"I'm sure," Tom said. "How's it been since you went back?"

"A little tense," Ben said. "My boss isn't used to me turning off my phone at times. He'll probably fire me before long. But it's all good."

"That would be a foolish mistake on his part," Tom said. "What would you do then?"

"I have no idea," Ben said. "Something different, maybe. Something totally different."

"Maybe we can go into business together," Tom said. "I'm starting to get bored with all of this free time. I can only walk dogs so many hours each day."

"Maybe we could," Ben said, rescuing one of the chicken breasts before it became too charred. "What do you think we would do?"

"Whatever we love, and whatever the world needs the most."

"That's really narrowing it down," Ben said.

"We'll figure it out," Tom added. He spotted Connor mingling with the crowd, and smiled.

"As horrible as this ordeal has been," Tom said, "I think it's helped all of us to grow and become better people. The adults and the kids."

Ben nodded, and then glanced across the yard and saw Det. Bob Sarosky staring at him, puffing away on a cigarette.

"Yeah," Ben said, studying the food he was grilling. "I guess it has."

About the Author

John Michael De Marco is an author and executive coach based in Franklin, Tenn. He enjoys time with family, friends, and pets, along with writing; reading; fitness; traveling; music; wine; dark chocolate; movies; and college football.

To learn more, please visit www.johnmichaeldemarco.com

A Request, Please

If you've enjoyed this book, would you please consider writing and publishing a review on sites such as Amazon, Facebook, Instagram, Goodreads, and so forth?

This helps other potential readers to decide whether to download a sample or purchase a copy. I read all of my reviews, and learn a great deal from each one of them. Thank you very much in advance.

Very Truly Yours,
John Michael De Marco
Franklin, Tennessee

56016759R00197

Made in the USA
Charleston, SC
11 May 2016